Readers adore Tasmina Perry's gripping novels:

'Gripping from the off and with all the sexy, scandalous brilliance that we've come to expect from this author, this book is a genuine must *****' *Heat*

'A book to cancel plans for – we were completely gripped' *Closer*

'You'll love this suspenseful thriller' *Best*

'Tasmina Perry's mix of glamour, social insight and psychological tension makes for a slick page-turner and the suspense ratchets up towards the end' *Sunday Express*

'An enjoyable and suspenseful read' *Woman's Own*

'Enjoyable and suspenseful' *Woman's Weekly*

'Tense, escapist fun' *Red*

'A psychological thriller to race through' *The People*

Tasmina Perry is the *Sunday Times* Top Ten bestselling author of thirteen novels. She left a career in law to enter the world of women's magazine publishing, and went on to become an award-winning writer and contributor to titles such as *Elle*, *Glamour* and *Marie Claire*. In 2004 she launched her own travel and fashion magazine, *Jaunt*, and was editing *InStyle* magazine when she left the industry to write books full time. Her novels have been published in seventeen countries. Tasmina lives with her husband and son in London, where she is at work on her next novel.

By Tasmina Perry

Daddy's Girls
Gold Diggers
Guilty Pleasures
Original Sin
Kiss Heaven Goodbye
Private Lives
Perfect Strangers
Deep Blue Sea
The Proposal
The Last Kiss Goodbye
The House on Sunset Lake
The Pool House
Friend of the Family

FRIEND
of the
FAMILY

TASMINA PERRY

REVIEW

First published in 2018 by HEADLINE REVIEW
An imprint of HEADLINE PUBLISHING GROUP

First published in paperback in 2019 by HEADLINE REVIEW
An imprint of HEADLINE PUBLISHING GROUP

1

Cataloguing in Publication Data is available from the British Library

ISBN 978 1 4722 0857 6

Typeset in Sabon by Avon DataSet Ltd, Bidford-on-Avon, Warwickshire

Printed and bound in Great Britain by Clays Ltd, Elcograf S.p.A.

Headline's policy is to use papers that are natural, renewable and
recyclable products and made from wood grown in well-managed
forests and other controlled sources. The logging and manufacturing
processes are expected to conform to the environmental regulations
of the country of origin.

HEADLINE PUBLISHING GROUP
An Hachette UK Company
Carmelite House
50 Victoria Embankment
London EC4Y 0DZ

www.headline.co.uk
www.hachette.co.uk

To Fin

Prologue

The photo album felt heavy in her hands. She paused, running her fingers over the grain of the leather, feeling its weight. No wonder nobody used these any more: chunky, unwieldy things, stuck under beds or in the loft, shoved to the back of a wardrobe, which was exactly where she had found this one, hidden behind a shoebox full of ticket stubs and half-empty notebooks. And the very idea of photographs! Going into an *actual shop* on the high street to get them printed, as if they were precious artefacts to be kept for evermore. Whoever had the time for that these days? So self-indulgent. So *arrogant*. So twentieth century.

A fixed smile on her lips, she flipped open the cover to the first sheet of vellum, worn and lined like an old woman's skin, the neatly inked title reading: *Oxford 1995*.

She turned the page, and there they were in their glossy glory, a swirl of primary colours and monochrome, all energy and poses and cheesy grins only slightly dimmed by time. How young and good-looking everyone was! Dated clothes and hair, sure, but the smiles were genuine; a little self-conscious, perhaps, but carefree. Yes, that was the word. Like they had nothing to apologise for. Every one of them making eye contact with the camera, looking straight down the barrel, daring you to judge them, daring you to say that they weren't anything but the young and the beautiful, the nation's elite, their futures just sitting there waiting to be plucked like a perfect rose.

Her eye was drawn to one photo in particular. It was innocuous really. A group shot at a party. Hundreds, thousands of people had taken snapshots just like this. Young people in some bar, all raising their glasses – champagne bowls, naturally – winking and laughing, mugging for the camera, shouting, 'Cheese!', celebrating what? Glorious endings or thrilling beginnings? She supposed the picture represented both.

As her finger traced the face in the middle of the shot, she wondered what Amy had been thinking as she sipped her champagne and grinned for the camera. Had everything been mapped out in her head, her clever post-college plan to scramble to the top already carefully thought out and engineered? Or had it really been a matter of good timing, the right friends and luck?

No one could be that lucky.

She felt her fingers curling, nails scraping across the paper. How could she have looked so happy? she thought, pulling the photo from the page, crushing it in her fist and flinging it away from her, skin crawling from its touch. She tore at the next picture and the next, ripping them from the book, grinding them between her hands, mashing and tearing, a guttural groan coming from deep in her throat. 'How dare she?' she hissed, again and again, wrenching out whole pages in twos and threes, dropping them like confetti until there was nothing left to tear. She grasped the thick cover and tried to destroy that too, but it was too thick, too heavy, the leather doing its work, holding its shape. Instead, she flung it across the room with a scream and watched it spin into the corner.

'Look what you made me do,' she whispered, her hands

twisting in her hair, trying to steady them. 'Look what you made me do.' And finally, she began to cry.

Chapter 1

To the untrained eye, it was an amazing cover. Glossy and glamorous, it featured a hot new Hollywood actress and was crammed with tempting cover lines: 'Online dating guide', 'Orgasms 100% guaranteed', 'Autumn style must-haves'. All the buttons were pressed, everything the young and fashionable urban woman could possibly desire. And yet editor Amy Shepherd knew it was a disaster.

'Does she look so miserable in all of her photos?' she said to the woman hunched over the computer screen. 'Come on, Gem, there has to be something.' Gemma Carling was the best art director in magazines – that was why Amy had poached her from Condé Nast six months previously – but even she couldn't work miracles.

'Photoshop only goes so far, Amy,' she said. 'I can shave off a few pounds, get rid of spots, but I can't make the bitch any less gloomy. You remember what her agent said.'

Amy nodded. 'Carly doesn't do smiling.'

Landing Carly Zima for a cover shoot had been a major coup for *Verve* – a boost the magazine badly needed. Back in its 1990s heyday, *Verve* had been a byword for kick-ass feminism, a style bible for self-assured young women who knew what they wanted: sex, career and fashion – all three, all the time. Amy could remember the days when stars would come into the office personally, courting the staff, taking them out to dinner, desperate to feature in its pages. But that was a long time ago, and it was becoming harder and harder to get an exclusive on anything.

'No chance we could do a reshoot?' Gemma's voice was hopeful, but they both knew the answer. Part of the reason for her moody face was that Carly had done the photo shoot under duress; she had been forced to participate by her sponsors. So yes, she had turned up. Six hours late, sure, but she had come. Clearly she had believed that was the end of her part in the matter. No amount of coaxing from top fashion photographer Emile Noir could get her to show any amount of *Verve*'s trademark sassy confidence.

'She looks like her dog's just died,' said Gemma.

Gallows humour. It was a big thing in magazines these days. If they didn't laugh, they'd cry.

'Amy?'

She looked up to see her PA, Chrissie. She was holding up a phone, jiggling it slightly. 'Sorry to interrupt, but you asked me to remind you about your twelve thirty meeting?'

'Oh crap.'

Amy stood up and grabbed her ever-present desk book. 'Look, I know we're flogging a dead horse here, Gem,' she said. 'But see what you can do about giving it CPR?'

Gemma gave her a grim smile. 'Sweet talker.'

Amy glanced at her watch and broke into a run, her heels clacking, Chrissie trotting along beside her. 'Conference room, twenty-third floor,' the PA said, handing her a sheaf of printouts. 'And don't forget you have a lunch at Tanjerin, one o'clock.'

'Thanks, Chrissie, you're a life-saver, as ever.'

The lift to the executive floor of Genesis Media was empty, giving Amy time to check her make-up in the mirrored walls. There were faint lilac semicircles under her eyes, but it was no surprise that she looked exhausted. She had been in the office particularly early that day, leaving home before Tilly, her livewire five-year-old, had even stirred, making sure her husband David would hold the fort until their nanny Claudia arrived at seven o'clock.

The rest of the day had been spent reading through dozens of pages of editorial, crossing out and rewriting in the margin like an angry teacher, liaising with HR about her junior fashion editor, who had been caught bunking off work when she was supposed to be on appointments, and dealing with dozens of irritating emails relating to everything from paper stock to Tilly's new school uniform. Amy knew that there were tougher jobs out there – she wasn't going down a mine or flying off to a war zone – but still, she felt physically and emotionally fried.

The lift bobbed and stopped. As the doors stuttered open, Amy was out and down the corridor, pushing through the double doors of the boardroom with the barest glance at her watch. Only three minutes late: acceptable. Douglas Proctor was a stickler for timekeeping and cut no slack for creative types. In fact, he clearly thought they were a hindrance to the smooth running of the organisation, but he tolerated Amy. Or had so far.

The incoming MD of Genesis Media was standing at the window, back to the room. He was currently the company's chief operating officer, but was being promoted due to the imminent retirement of Genesis chief William Bentley.

'Ah, Amy,' he said, turning. 'Sit down. I thought I'd ask Denton to join us this morning.'

She smiled at the slim, suited man at the table, even thought she couldn't bear the sight of him. Denton Scoles, finance director, chief bean-counter at Genesis Media and arch-enemy of creativity, represented everything that was wrong with magazines right now. Ever since his arrival twelve months earlier, he had overseen two huge rounds of editorial redundancies, claiming that an overworked hub of a dozen subeditors and designers could work across Genesis's twenty titles, and had famously nixed the annual *Verve* Christmas party for being 'unproductive'.

'Is William not joining us today?' Amy said, immediately regretting her remark. Douglas's cool gaze told her that the new order had already been established and that their genial boss had not been invited.

'How's the October cover looking?' he asked, not bothering to reply to her question.

Amy didn't dare tell him they might have to reshoot.

'Just making the final tweaks, but we're very excited. I think it's going to sell well.'

'Good,' said Douglas, sipping some water. 'Because I hardly need tell you the figures are on a downward trend.'

She was taken aback by his bluntness. 'Perhaps,' she said, slowly. 'But as we know, the entire sector has taken a hit and we've been affected less than other titles.'

As if on cue, Denton turned his laptop to face her.

'The new circulation figures are out next week, but here's where we are at the moment,' he said, touching his pen against a graph on the screen. 'The red line is *Verve*, the blue *Vogue*, the green *Elle*, et cetera, et cetera. Almost every title down from where they were ten years ago.' He paused for a moment to let the fact sink in. 'Now,' he said, tapping a key and flipping to another graph. 'Here the trend is reversed: all lines bending upwards. Blogs, Instagram, Twitter, all trending through the roof.'

'But how many of them are making money?' said Amy crisply.

Yet again, Douglas ignored her comment. 'Magazines have limitations. We just can't compete on time-sensitive subjects. Even the daily papers are starting to look pointless:

8

going to print before an election result is announced, missing a terrorist attack that happens in the middle of the day. And monthlies? You're recommending trends that are already over.'

'We know the challenges,' said Amy, wondering if they were about to hold her responsible for the decline of an entire industry.

'We have to start thinking of ways to make more money. Events, sponsorship, courses, digital innovation . . .'

Amy nodded. She and William had had an almost identical conversation six months earlier, admittedly in different circumstances: a long boozy lunch at which they had wistfully reminisced about the golden age of magazines, when there was an orchid on every desk and afternoons were spent flitting from press launch to film screening. But despite their nostalgia for times past, they had both been determined to inject some excitement back into publishing, and had come up with the idea of creating a new marquee event for *Verve*.

'I totally agree with you, Douglas, which is why we're throwing the Fashion 500 party,' she said, wishing that William were there to back her up. 'The fashion brands have money. If we can create a London equivalent to New York's Met Gala, we'd strengthen the brand, position ourselves as a mainstream luxury and generate buzz.'

'That's what we wanted to discuss,' said Douglas, not looking impressed. 'Denton is worried that costs are spiralling . . .'

'I was asked to sign off a twenty-thousand-pound order for flowers,' said Denton over the top of his glasses. 'Fifteen thousand for laser-cut invitations, the same amount again for a vodka luge. This is not the court of Louis XIV, Amy.'

'Just the last days of Rome,' she muttered.

'You are one of the most experienced editors in the

group,' said Douglas with more grace. 'We need you at the heart of our team that strategises new revenue streams for the companies. But right now, a fashion party that's going to cost a million pounds sounds like part of the problem rather than a solution.'

Amy was determined to hold her ground. She knew she was a golden girl at Genesis Media. Three editors at the company had been fired in the past eighteen months, but she wasn't worried about her position just yet. She was confident that in the new round of ABCs – the industry's much-watched circulation figures – *Verve* would demonstrate steady numbers, and in the current climate that was the best you could hope for.

'Douglas, the gala is about positioning and perception. As you know, that's everything in the fashion world. We want to look confident. We want to send a message to the world that we are investing in *Verve*. That's how we shore up the ad dollars, that's how we get seven-figure sponsorship deals. Already we've got the CEOs of three banks, and almost every major fashion house confirmed to attend.'

'Some people will do anything for a free lunch,' said Denton.

'Do you think something tangible will come out of it?' asked Douglas in quiet challenge.

'If we don't see an immediate uplift in advertising volume and yield, I'll eat my Prada hat,' she said, trying to lighten the tone.

Douglas had the courtesy to smile. 'Very well. Keep me in the loop, all right? This has got to work.' He glanced at his watch, indicating that the meeting was over.

Amy scooped up her notebook and said her goodbyes. She looked down and noticed that her hands were trembling a little. As she approached the lift, the door pinged open and Juliet James, editor of *Living Style* magazine, stepped out.

'Next up?' said Amy, attempting a smile.

Her best friend rolled her grey eyes. The two women had known each other for over twenty years and could communicate without even speaking. Juliet was generally unflappable, but Amy could tell that she was dreading her meeting too.

'How is he?' she asked in her refined husky drawl.

'Denton Scoles is in there. And he has spreadsheets.'

'Oh God,' Juliet replied, closing her eyes in mock horror. 'Tell me you're up for a liquid lunch as soon as I'm out.'

'Can't,' said Amy. 'Not today.'

'You blew me out last Friday, you callous bitch,' Juliet said theatrically.

'I'm meeting an old friend from school. I haven't seen her in about fifteen years and she's hardly ever in London, so I've got to go. In fact, you know her. My friend Karen from home? Karen Price. She used to come and stay at the house in Holywell Street sometimes.'

Something passed over Juliet's face.

Amy had forgotten that Juliet disapproved of Karen. Juliet was from a hunt-ball public-school background and would be the first to admit that she had been an outrageous snob at uni. Karen hadn't been the 'right sort'; but then neither had Amy.

'Of course: Karen,' said Juliet. 'What's she doing now?'

Amy shrugged. 'It's been so long since we caught up, I've got no idea. But I'll fill you in on Sunday.'

'Give her my love.'

Amy left the building and went out onto the street. Sometimes she felt like a shark; that she had to keep moving or else she would cease to exist. She had completely forgotten about her lunch date with her old school friend until her assistant had reminded her earlier, and it was very tempting just to cancel it. But although she had no ties to her home town any more, she and Karen had once been close – as close as sisters – and nostalgia and a pinch of curiosity made her keep it.

The tower was on the South Bank, wedged between Tate Modern and the London Eye, once an abandoned wasteland of wharves and warehouses, now transformed into a buzzing media enclave. A newspaper, a TV studio and a theatre were all within a stone's throw of each other, which of course attracted a rash of restaurants – Mexican, Lebanese, Thai street food – plus the kind of bars that flattered editors and producers into feeling young and edgy. People milled about; the media set in suits with open-necked shirts, or summer dresses and ballet flats, mingling with well-informed tourists, students, cycle couriers and buskers. Amy wove between them towards Tanjerin, a Japanese restaurant, pushing inside.

Of all the restaurants in London, Tanjerin was still her favourite. She had been eating here regularly ever since it opened, partly for their melt-in-the-mouth California rolls, but also because it was rare to see anyone from the magazine world in here. It was dark and cramped; not the sort of place to be seen, which was anathema to the media set. It was the sort of place she could come alone and not be noticed.

'Your friend is already here,' said Charlie, the maître d'. Amy looked around expectantly, her smile of anticipation slowly turning to a frown. Where? Where was her friend? A couple leaned across a table for two, hands touching, amongst groups of Japanese businessmen and an assortment of hipsters. And then she saw her.

'Karen,' she said, trying not to let it sound like a question. She hadn't seen her at first because, stupidly, she had expected her to look exactly the same as she had in 1995. The woman stood; *of course* it was Karen. Older, heavier obviously; it had been over a decade – but Amy recognised the way she held herself, the shape of her neck, the slightly puzzled smile. 'So good to see you,' she said, stepping forward and embracing her. 'It's been, what?'

'Fifteen years,' said Karen. 'You're looking good, Ames.'

Ames. No one had called her that since she had stepped onto the train at Bristol Temple Meads station heading for university. It sounded odd, alien. But also somehow reassuring.

'You're looking great too,' she said. It was the polite thing to say, a very English reflex. But in truth Karen looked old. Of course no amount of wheatgerm or Pilates could stop the march of time, but her skin was pale and lined, sagging under the eyes, and she had put on weight, the fat pooling around her neck.

'So what are you doing in London?' asked Amy, taking a menu from the waitress.

'Here to see a show. Wicked.' Karen grinned.

Amy didn't know if she meant the musical or if it was an expression of excitement.

'One of the girls at work won tickets in a competition, so we thought we'd make a weekend of it,' Karen continued. 'Four of us have come down. We're staying in the Royal Hotel, right near Oxford Street.' She said it like she was describing the Taj Mahal. 'That's where the others are now, emptying out Topshop I shouldn't wonder.'

The waitress was hovering with her order pad. They liked a quick turnaround at Tanjerin – another reason why Amy had chosen it.

'Bloody hell, this might as well be in Greek,' said Karen, looking up from her menu. 'What's *unagi*?'

'Freshwater eel. It's good.'

'Eel? *Urgh*,' said Karen, wincing.

Amy searched the menu for something her friend might

like. She came so often to Tanjerin, she hadn't stopped to think that its food was a little too directional for many people's tastes.

She ordered a selection of rolls for both of them, and a bottle of San Pellegrino. Then, seeing the disappointment on Karen's face, she held up a hand. 'What the hell, why not? One glass of wine can't hurt, can it?'

'Never remember having to talk you into drinking before, Ames,' said Karen. 'You were always the one ordering the shots in the Dragon. Do you remember that night we did all that tequila, then went skinny-dipping in the canal?'

Amy burst out laughing. 'God, yes! Wasn't Jenny there too?'

'And Cookie, that lad she was seeing. Getting a right eyeful he was, thought his luck was in until you stole his shoes.'

'Did I?'

Karen laughed too, and for a moment she looked exactly as Amy remembered her: the lopsided smile, the sparkle in her eyes. Back when they'd both had their lives in front of them.

'Don't you remember? You called him a pervert and threw his trainers over a fence so he couldn't follow us, then we ran back to Jen's.'

Amy shook her head. She genuinely hadn't thought of those times for years. It felt like someone was recalling a movie she'd watched and dimly recalled, instead of her own life.

'So come on,' she said. 'Tell me everything. Are you still living on the estate?'

'God, no, I moved out to Potts Field about ten years ago.'

'Nice,' said Amy honestly. Potts Field was definitely a step up from Westmead, the tough pocket of the city where they had grown up.

Karen shrugged. 'It's okay, I suppose.'

'And you're working at a . . . shop?'

'A florists to you.'

'Not Mr Jones still?'

Karen gave a half-smile. 'Same place, but Mr Jones moved back to Wales years ago. It's called the Rose Yard now, it's like a chain? There are loads of them all around.'

The waitress returned with two glasses of Chardonnay, and Amy held up her glass in a toast. 'Here's to . . . the Dragon.' She smiled.

'Although it's a carpet shop now,' Karen replied, clinking her glass against her friend's.

A silence rippled between them.

'How's Tilly?'

Amy was surprised that Karen had remembered her daughter's name.

'I can't believe she's almost finished her first year at school. She starts Year One in September.'

'It goes quickly,' said Karen with a smile. 'Remember, children are just lent to you.'

'And how's Josie?' asked Amy finally. She said it brightly, as if it was just another idle query, but this was the thing she had been dreading. Josie was Karen's daughter, but she was also the elephant in the room, the real reason Karen and Amy hadn't seen each other for years.

In Amy's first year at Oxford Brookes, Karen had come to visit and things had been just as they had always been. They had gone drinking, clubbing, having a scream: best friends for ever, as the kids said nowadays. By her second year, they were starting to lose touch. Karen had a boyfriend, Lee, and she came less often; the letters arrived only sporadically. They both promised nothing would change, but it did, of course it did. Amy was experimenting with new friends, new ideas, trying on different clothes and skins. In hindsight, she supposed Karen was struggling to cope.

Money, family, the isolation, it was all there between the lines, but Amy had her own concerns. She had essays to write, study groups, a string of exciting new boyfriends. The summer she had graduated, Karen had fallen pregnant with Josie and everything changed for ever. Amy moved to London, and Karen just got on with it, she supposed, and although they had seen each other a couple of times in those first few years, soon Amy found herself slipping in and out of Bristol on her flying visits to see her parents, without even telling Karen she was coming. Perhaps they would have drifted apart anyway, but they had both seen Josie as the deal-breaker, the not-so-invisible barrier that came between them, an excuse to cut the ties that had seemed so tight back on the estate.

'She's doing okay.' Karen shrugged.

Amy frowned. 'Is there . . . is she all right?'

'She's fine. Just struggling to get off the ground since uni.'

'She went to uni? I didn't know that. Where did she go?'

'Brighton. English and media studies, got a 2:1.'

'Bright girl.'

'I'm so proud of her, but you know what it's like these days. They end up with a zillion pounds of debt, then can't get a job. And there's nothing happening in Potts Field.'

'What does she want to do?'

'She wants to be you, of course.'

Amy was taken aback. 'Me?'

Karen laughed. 'You should see your face, like it's a crazy idea. Look at your life: brilliant job, going to parties, flying all over the world. Honestly, Ames, you've done amazing. And there's me at the florists.'

'You've done fine, Karen. And you've obviously raised a pretty special girl.'

'I just hope university hasn't gone to waste. She must have sent out two hundred CVs, but she just can't get a foot in the door. Still, I'm sure it was the same when you started.'

Amy didn't meet her gaze. It hadn't been like that for her at all. An evening job in an Oxford student pub, The Bear, had changed everything for her. Although she was studying at Oxford Brookes, working at the Bear put her in the orbit of students from the older, grander Oxford University. Her friend behind the bar, Pog, was studying at Lincoln College, and when a room came up in his city-centre house share, he asked her if she wanted it. At once, a world of connection and privilege opened up to her. Getting her foot in the door at one of London's magazine houses wasn't difficult at all when you knew who to call.

'Why doesn't she come and do some work at *Verve*?' she said without even thinking.

Karen's face lit up. 'Are you serious?'

'We're not recruiting at the moment, so it would only be work experience. She'd basically be there to get coffee and, if she's lucky, do some photocopying, but she'll get a sense of the way it all works and it'll look good on her CV.'

Karen's mouth was open. 'That would be amazing, Ames! Josie will be over the moon.'

'We can't pay her or anything, and it'll only be a week.'

'Anything, anything at all. It will mean the world to her.'

It was a moment before Amy realised her old friend was crying.

'Karen, what's the matter?'

'Sorry, sorry. It's just . . . it's been so hard. Josie's the light of my life, but it's been tough. God, you have no idea. And being on my own, money being tight, I've . . . But if I can just get her started, get her standing on her own two feet, I'll feel it's been worth it.'

Amy leaned over the table towards her. 'I should have been a better friend.'

'You had your own life to live.'

'I could have done more. I should have paid more attention – to both of you.'

Karen shook her head. 'Do you remember that summer we went to north Wales? Hitched to Anglesey?'

Amy smiled. 'How could I forget? We drank half the booze in Wales.'

'Well, do you remember sitting on that clifftop?'

Amy nodded. It was one of the few clear memories she had of those times, one of those perfect days that only happen when you're a teenager. Cider, friendship, boys, open spaces, possibility.

'We were staring out to sea, watching the gulls, and you said, "One day I'm going to open my arms and fly across that bloody sea. I'm going to go to America and Japan and Australia and I'm going to have everything we've ever dreamed of."'

'Did I say that?'

Karen nodded. 'And that's what I want for Josie. I want her to spread her wings. I want her to see the world, do all the things and have all the opportunities that you've had. I guess what I'm saying is that it's not just Josie who wants to be Amy Shepherd when she grows up. I want my daughter to be just like you too.'

Chapter 2

Marion's Brasserie had only been open three months, but it was about as hot as it was possible for a restaurant to get. Even before the chic Notting Hill diner had opened, people were talking about Marion's as 'the new River Café'. There had been a feature in *Vogue*, mentions in the society pages, whispers about the ultra-secret booking line only open to insiders. It didn't hurt that owner-chef Pierre Hubert was already a celebrity in his own right, having made his name in the notoriously picky gastro scene of the French south; hence his much-heralded debut in the Smoke had seen the paps camped outside Marion's like shoppers anticipating the Boxing Day sales.

Amy, David and their daughter Tilly walked straight past a group of anxious would-be diners hovering at the front door hoping for a cancellation, and were shown to a long table at the far end of the restaurant.

'Better late than never,' said an attractive brunette, getting to her feet.

'Sorry, sorry. Tilly couldn't decide which tutu to wear.'

'Blue,' said Claire Quinn thoughtfully. 'Very Elsa. Very *Frozen*,' she said as Tilly squealed with delight.

Juliet James and her husband Peter were already sitting nursing bloody Marys.

'Where's Max?' asked David, sitting down next to Juliet.

'Table-hopping,' said Juliet, skewering an olive.

'Lucky lady of the moment, Kate Kennedy,' smiled Peter, gesturing over to their friend.

'The MP?'

Peter nodded.

Peter James was nice enough, but he was what they used to call a stiff: boring, conventional. He even looked the part: tall and thin and very upright. Amy always thought of him as 'the Grey Man'. He was yin to Juliet's yang. While Juliet was acerbic, knowing, switched on, Peter seemed to live in a bygone age of clubs and dinner parties and country houses. There was no doubt the two of them shared common ground in that they both thrived in the upper echelons, though Juliet liked to mix with the new elite – Old Etonian actors and entrepreneurs – while Peter preferred the fox hunters and art collectors, people who spoke about their great-great-grandfathers as if they were still running India. Amy doubted he had done anything unusual or unexpected in his life.

'Minister, I think you'll find,' said Juliet, tossing back her red hair. 'Trade and industry. Max will have schmoozed her into some sort of complicated tax break before she's finished her starter.'

Everyone laughed, and Amy was reminded how much she loved her Sunday lunches.

'Where are Hettie and Alex?' she said, looking around for Claire and Max's seven-year-old twins.

'Nev has taken them to play in the garden. Tilly, why don't you go and join them,' said Claire, motioning towards an enclosed courtyard at the back of the restaurant.

Tilly squealed and ran off.

'I'll go and check she's okay,' said Amy, getting to her feet.

David stopped her with a gentle touch on the arm. 'Tilly's

fine,' he said. 'She's five now. She's not going to swallow the soap. Besides, she's with Hettie.'

Amy looked down at him, biting her tongue. It was one of those niggling snag points that parenthood threw up. David had been sent to boarding school at the age of seven and believed that children should be given independence as soon as possible, whereas Amy was a modern mother who wanted to wrap her daughter in cotton wool until she was thirty. They disagreed on just about everything in between, too: schools, diet, bedtime; about the only thing they did agree on was the fact that Max and Claire's daughter Hettie was like a big sister to Tilly and, against all genetic precedent, a good influence.

'Nev's such a star. I can't believe she's going back to Spain,' said Amy.

'Neither can I,' replied Claire, raising an eyebrow. 'Before the bloody Provence trip as well.'

'Amy, David,' said Max Quinn, throwing his arms out in an extravagant gesture as he returned to the table. 'Where's my darling god-daughter?'

'Playing with *my* darling god-daughter outside,' grinned David.

Amy couldn't resist a smile. The two men were so different in many ways. At university, Max Quinn had been a poster boy for the Hooray Henry set: floppy hair, flinty eyes, cufflinks and sports cars, looking down on everyone else and scrabbling for places in the City, where they'd make even bigger pots of money. And he hadn't changed a bit since. He was still obsessed with money, still loud, brash, braying. Sometimes Amy had to stop and ask herself why he was one of her closest friends – at Oxford she'd barely tolerated his pompous antics – but somehow he had a way of growing on you.

Her husband was a much more restrained character.

When Amy had first met David in Oxford, she had mistaken his quiet pragmatism for stand-offishness, but had soon come to admire his loyalty and kindness, even before they had become a couple many years later.

But the two men shared one thing – twelve-hour working days and hugely successful careers, David in finance, Max's as CEO and founder of the yummy mummy's favourite fashion label Quinn – and they were bonded by a steadfast friendship that Amy envied, even though she sometimes worried, on their raucous boys' away-weekends to Beaujolais or Vegas, that Max was a bad influence.

Max sat down and summoned the waitress to bring them some drinks. 'No need for menus,' he said, ordering the chef's special for everyone.

'So,' he said, swilling his red wine around his glass. 'Are we sorted for Provence? Tell me all plane tickets are booked and paid for.'

This would be Amy's first visit to Claire and Max's Provence bolthole, a villa in the dusty hills just outside the pretty village of Lourmarin. She and David had spent a few days in Lourmarin six years previously; the honeymoon period, as Amy thought of it, wedged between the romance of their wedding and the drama of childbirth. In her mind, it had all been sunlit and rose-tinted, a whirl of EasyJet and packing like Grace Kelly in *Rear Window*: just a ball gown and a hairbrush. Presumably there had been real-life problems back then too – cover shoots and dull meetings about budgets – but she didn't remember anything but four-poster beds and roaring fires. She blushed at the memory.

'Claudia's still all right to come?' asked Claire quickly. After Nev had announced that she was returning to Madrid, Amy's own nanny, a cheerful Dutch girl, had been drafted in.

'She thinks it's the most exciting thing that has ever

happened to her,' smiled Amy, happy that they could bring her. 'And we're glad we'll be able to go for a few adult dinners. Do I sound terrible saying that?'

'Maybe I can get us a table at Bastide Moules,' said Juliet, checking her messages.

Juliet's magazine, *Living Style*, was an upmarket interiors magazine with a few pages devoted to food and travel. Its circulation was a fraction of *Verve*'s but Juliet seemed to have every PR and society shaker on speed-dial and had even managed to get a table at mythical foodie haunt El Bulli for David's birthday a few years earlier, with only a week's notice. The Bastide had the reputation of being the new El Bulli. It was rumoured that it had already received a million reservation requests for the five thousand covers it did in a season. Amy had no doubt that Juliet could get them in.

'I can't wait for three weeks in the sun,' she said with a sigh, already thinking about the warm, dappled French countryside.

'Have you told Douglas you're out of the office for that long?' said Juliet, sipping her wine.

'William signed it off.'

'You should still tell Douglas. You know what he's like.'

'I've not taken longer than a week's holiday in five years. If I don't have a decent break this summer, I think I might go mad.'

'Has she told you we've got a pact?' said David, eaves-dropping. 'We're going to switch off our phones and not even take our iPads.'

'Maybe you could persuade Max to do the same,' said Claire, rolling her eyes.

'Bollocks to that,' Max declared. 'Empires are not built without hard work.' He downed his wine in one.

'Max, when did you become such a workaholic?' asked Amy.

'When I bought my first helicopter.'

'I'll book us some spa treatments,' Claire said. 'There's an amazing woman in Lourmarin who does reflexology.'

'I need more than a foot rub,' said Amy with a sigh.

Max raised an eyebrow. 'That's what Monty Young said when he twisted his ankle skiing. His missus found him the best physiotherapist in London. The next thing you know, he's left his wife and three kids for her.'

'Monty's left Suzie?'

Monty was one of their old friends from Oxford. They didn't see him much, but Amy sporadically bumped into his wife at charity fund-raisers. The last event had been a January lunch, when Suzie had talked excitedly about the chalet they had just bought in Meribel. Things obviously hadn't panned out as she'd hoped.

'Darling, it's the season for it,' said Max. 'Four mates from school – all divorced in the last six months.' He made a slicing motion across his neck. 'A lot of lawyers making a lot of money right there.'

For a long time, Amy had been unable to understand the statistic that over 40 per cent of marriages ended in divorce. Although the days when every other summer weekend seemed to be spent going to a wedding were past, she hadn't heard of many separations – until recently. Just one or two at first: the couple who'd been clearly unsuited from the start, another who had eloped to Vegas a week after meeting in New York. But lately there were more unexpected ones: a lovely mum and dad she knew from the school gate; the marketing manager at work who had found out her husband was having an affair.

'Is everything all right?' Claire put her hand on Amy's shoulder.

Amy blinked hard and put down her glass. 'What do you mean?' she said, realising that she did feel a bit spaced out.

She loved seeing her friends, but it always meant being switched on, especially when Max was in such high spirits. Truth was, after such a stressful week at work, the only thing she wanted to switch on was her TV in the company of a bottle of wine and a box of salted caramel truffles.

'You just seem a bit run-down.'

Amy tried to laugh it off. 'The pressure's on at work.'

'Did you get the chat about digital innovation?' asked Juliet, rolling her eyes. 'Denton seriously asked me if *Living Style* had potential as an estate agent.'

'If it's any consolation, he wants to turn *Verve* into the new Tinder.'

The three women laughed.

'You know who you should also see,' said Juliet, leaning forward. 'Dr Al Saraf.'

'Who's he?' asked Amy.

'You've not heard of him? Dermatologist. Genius behind BlissVit.'

'BlissVit?' said Amy, feeling a little stupid. She did, after all, edit one of the top women's glossies: if there was a hot new beauty treatment out there, she should have heard of it.

'His own patented vitamin complex. It's supposed to be amazing. It takes ten years off. You *glow*.'

Amy knew she was looking tired. She felt tired. If a doctor could really make her look younger – or even a little more perky – how could that be a bad thing?

'I'll give you his mobile number,' Juliet said.

'You really need to write your own little black book.'

'Then the special secret numbers wouldn't be secret any more.'

'Amy,' Max cut in. 'David was just telling me he got you a Tracey Emin for your birthday.'

Amy felt herself blush. It was an extravagant gift, but

David had got a huge bonus from the bank a few months earlier.

'It's an investment,' she said, smiling. 'You should approve.'

'I'll be the judge of that. How about we come round and take a look? I don't know about you, but I don't want to go home yet, and apparently we only get this table for two hours.'

'Even you?' said Amy, mocking him.

'Everyone's welcome to come back for a drink,' said David, raising his hand in surrender. Max was already asking for the bill.

Amy flashed her husband a look.

'What's up?' he asked.

'She's coming at four.'

'Who's coming?' said Max, throwing down his Amex.

'Is that today?' said David with a frown.

'What's happening?' said Max, now curious.

'We've got a house guest this week,' Amy said.

'Anyone interesting?'

'The daughter of a friend. She's doing work experience at Genesis, so she's staying with us for a week. We're going to welcome her with open arms, aren't we, David?'

A sly look crossed Max's face as he got up from the table.

'How old is she? I don't think you want to be encouraging David to open his arms too much.'

Amy laughed along, but realised she hadn't actually considered that. She was inviting a young woman into their home without even having met her – well, not since she was a toddler, anyway.

'That's good of you,' said Claire encouragingly. 'I know how hard it was for me when I came down to London.'

'The world would be a better place if we were all kinder to people,' Amy said.

'I can be kind.' Max looked at Claire with a mock-innocent smile. 'Can we have a hot girl come and stay at our house too?'

'What's a hot girl, Mummy?' chimed Tilly.

'No one says she's hot,' hissed Amy at Max, as Tilly skipped out of the restaurant, lost in another world, dancing her finger puppets through the air, using parked cars as handy stages for her play.

'Whose daughter is it?' said Juliet as the three women started walking ahead.

'My old school friend, Karen.'

'And she's staying with you all week?'

'David's a bit nervous because we've never met her. But what could I say? I can't offer work experience and not help with accommodation. You know how expensive hotels are in London.'

The men caught up with them as they neared Amy and David's house.

'By the way, there's a concert at the castle in Lourmarin every Thursday. I'll get tickets if anyone is interested,' said Claire.

'Who's playing?' asked David, hooking an arm around his wife's waist.

'Classical music.'

'Count me out,' said David.

'Philistine,' laughed Juliet.

'At least he's honest,' said Claire. 'Max insists on going to anything that's on at Cadogan Hall, then puts his sunglasses on and falls asleep.'

Amy enjoyed the gentle banter that rippled between them. Their tight group was not the family she'd imagined twenty years earlier. All of them were from a different world to her; even Claire, who pretended to hail from more down-to-earth stock, was actually the daughter of Yorkshire landowners and had a trust fund. But after Amy's parents had both passed away in the past three years, that was what they had become. Family.

They took a left and turned off the busy main drag into an elegant side street. The sight of Amy's home was something that still caught her by surprise. It was not one of the biggest terraces in Notting Hill, but the slim white Georgian house was one of the prettiest, with a huge pink magnolia bush in the tiny square of front garden and black-and-white chessboard steps that reminded her of *Alice Through the Looking-Glass*.

She stopped at the gate as she noticed someone sitting at the top of the steps. She had once found a homeless man in her porch when she had arrived home late at night, and for a second her heart started to pound hard.

But when she took another glance, she noticed it was a young woman, long bare legs stretched out in front of her. Amy was taken aback. Despite her simple clothes – shorts, T-shirt and trainers – there was no escaping how pretty she was. Long honey-coloured hair fell down her back, and her striking eyebrows reminded Amy of a popular supermodel.

'Damn, she's early,' she said. 'I wanted to tidy up first.'

'That's the work experience girl?' said Max over the top of his sunglasses.

'I'm Josie,' she said, standing up and trotting down the steps. Amy was surprised by her easy confidence.

'Well, hello,' said Max, stepping forward to introduce himself.

'Never let women in your house with longer legs than you,' said Juliet under her breath.

'It's only for a week,' said Amy, pasting on her best smile and going over to say hello.

Chapter 3

'Coffee, I need coffee.' Amy rushed through the kitchen still buttoning her blouse, tote bag swinging from the crook of one arm.

Claudia handed her a silver flask. 'Already done. And there's a hot water and lemon for now,' she added, pointing to a mug on the table.

Amy grinned. She knew that busy middle-class parents always said this about their nannies, but she didn't know what she'd do without Claudia. She arrived at the crack of dawn, taking Tilly to and from school in term-time and looking after her full-time during the holidays, while efficiently fielding all the other time-consuming day-to-day admin niggles such as paying the milkman, letting the gardener in and managing the cleaners who came three times a week to tidy the house and do the laundry and ironing. She was genuinely part of the family, about the only steady, reliable part of their chaotic household. A household that had grown suddenly with the arrival of Josie earlier that week.

Not that the addition of Josie was anything that Amy could complain about. Over the past three days she had been polite, charming and quiet – barely a sound coming from the granny flat in the basement where she had been billeted. More importantly, she had been brilliant with Tilly, who adored her; something to do with Josie being closer to Tilly's age, Amy supposed. Or perhaps it was the way she was happy to get down on her hands and knees and join in Tilly's flights of fancy, which was exactly what a creative child like Tilly needed. Amy had to admit that neither she nor David had the time, and Claudia was far too blunt and authoritarian to indulge a five-year-old.

'Morning, Tilly,' said Amy, dipping to kiss her daughter on the head. 'Can Mummy have a piece of your toast?'

Tilly spread her fingers over her plate, frowning. 'Why?'

'Because Mummy is running really late for work but I am very, very hungry.'

David came up behind her and handed her his bowl of granola. 'You like this stuff more than me,' he said, pulling on his jacket.

Amy kissed him on the cheek. 'Shouldn't you have left?'

'Waiting for a call from Hong Kong. Thought it was better to take it in my study than on the mobile.'

'Where are my bloody car keys?' she said, only half listening to him. She'd planned on driving to today's shoot, had now left it too late to get the train, but although she had tried every coat pocket, every bag, she couldn't find them anywhere.

'Mummy's lost her keys again,' squealed Tilly between big slurps of smoothie.

'Why don't we help Mummy look,' said Josie, giving Tilly's tummy a tickle.

The little girl giggled hard, and Amy felt herself melt as she watched Josie take Tilly on a treasure hunt around every pot and drawer in the kitchen.

'What about the spare set?' said David.

She puffed out her cheeks and glanced at the clock above the kitchen door. 'They *were* the spare set.'

'I'm sure they'll turn up. In the meantime, get Geoff to take you.'

'What about you?'

'I'll get the Tube,' he said, and Amy blew him a kiss across the room.

'I love your bag,' said Josie, eyeing Amy's clutch when they were in the hall. 'Claudia's got one just like it.'

Amy smiled. It was one of the perks of the job: in the run-up to Christmas, fashion PRs would shower editors with gifts, and handbags were the most prized.

'You're right,' she said, opening the front door. 'I was lucky enough to get given two of the same.'

'So you gave it to Claudia,' Josie said, her eyes wide.

Amy made a mental note to see if she could rustle up something nice for Josie. Today she was wearing a plain white shirt and navy skirt, the sort of thing they sold in supermarkets as 'back-to-work fashion': it should have looked bland, but Josie was slim and pretty enough to pull it off. It was that old Marilyn Monroe thing about looking good in a potato sack; some people, annoyingly, just had it. Amy remembered that Karen had had a little of that too. She wasn't the most striking beauty in the world, but she just had the 'X factor': somehow clothes, however ordinary, fitted her better and colours flattered her more.

Geoff, David's driver, was sitting in the car and leapt out when he saw Amy and Josie come down the steps.

'So he's a driver, not a taxi,' said Josie, lowering her voice as they approached him.

'David has a driver. I don't. But as we have to go to Berkshire today and I have lost my car keys, David has made the noble sacrifice of letting Geoff take us.'

'Wow,' said Josie, clearly impressed.

'We're heading for Cliveden in Taplow. Geoff, you have the address?'

* * *

Geoff snaked around the back streets of Ladbroke Grove until they hit the Westway heading out of town. At least most of the traffic was moving the other way. Today was the shoot for next month's cover, and Amy was dreading it, including as it did the many variables of a white-hot actress, a diva photographer and being on location rather than in a studio.

'So why is the shoot happening out here?' asked Josie when they were on the A4.

Amy was glad to have a little time in the car with Josie. This was the third day of her internship, and Amy had been so busy with meetings, she had barely seen her. She had heard good things about her from the staff, however: she was bright, friendly and eager to help, which was a relief. Given the 'switch-off' pact with David for Provence, Amy had to make sure everything for the next two issues of the magazine was perfect and iron-clad, which meant she didn't have the time to supervise Josie.

'Number one, because Cliveden is beautiful. Number two, because it's not far from Heathrow and Miranda, the cover star, and the photographer both have flights straight afterwards. It's taken six months to make this shoot happen and it's a tight squeeze now that it is.'

'This is so glamorous,' said Josie with a grin.

'I warn you, it's a lot of hanging around.'

'So why are you going? Are you doing the interview?'

Amy laughed. She'd loved interviewing celebrities at the start of her career, because their lives were so different from her own. But she'd quickly realised that although she was a good writer, she wasn't a great one, so had moved into editing copy rather than generating it in order to move up the ladder.

'I always try to pop in to the cover shoot. The cover is everything. A great one can add fifty thousand to our sales.

A bad one and we can lose twenty per cent.'

'This is a million times better than I thought it was going to be.'

'Really? You should have been an intern twenty years ago. I opened a lot of envelopes, but there was so much fun too.'

'Are you trying to put me off?'

'I'm saying it's harder,' replied Amy. 'Smaller staff, tighter budgets. But it's still the best job in the world.'

'I know. I've seen the beauty cupboard.'

Amy smiled back. 'I could happily live in the beauty cupboard. One day I think I might just move a bed and a camping stove in there.'

'No you wouldn't. Your house is lush.'

'I suppose it is.'

It made her stop and think. Her life seemed normal to her now. She was always careful to make sure Tilly understood the value of money. To realise how lucky she was. She encouraged her daughter to give coins to every busker they enjoyed hearing play at Portobello Market, and to collect pennies from the back of the sofa, as she herself had done as a child, to save up in a jar. But there were so many other things that they took for granted – the private school education, the fancy holidays, the cars, and the ability to go to Pret after ballet class and spend twenty pounds on hot chocolate and cake without even blinking.

Until Josie came. Seeing her past up close made her remember that her life wasn't normal. It reminded her of where she came from. Over the past few days, the sound of Josie's Bristolian vowels and casual slang had occasionally made Amy bristle, because she knew it still lurked in her own lexicon. Her smart Home Counties accent almost never slipped these days; people who met her for the first time assumed from her polish and confidence that she had been educated at the finest schools and colleges. But this week, when she had been talking to Josie, she had found herself remembering who she used to be.

'So what are you going to do after this week? Back to Bristol or Brighton?'

Josie wrinkled her nose. 'Landlord's flogged our house to someone else. He hiked the rent up anyway, so I couldn't afford it. So I'm going back home.'

'Your mum will be pleased.'

'I guess. She always says that she's glad my dad has gone, but I'm not sure she means it. She gets lonely.'

Amy nodded, wondering if Karen had had a partner since Lee. Their lives had become so distant from one another, she was ashamed she didn't know.

'Did you ever meet him?' Josie asked.

'Who?'

'My dad.'

'A couple of times. But we didn't really know each other.'

'She deserved better,' said Josie. 'We both did.'

'Do you still see him?'

Josie shook her head. 'Don't want to. He beat her up. Did you know that?'

'No,' Amy said, feeling sad and angry. She couldn't tell the young woman that she'd never liked the cocky mechanic. Yes, he was handsome, even charming. But she had always felt uneasy at the way Karen either gushed about him or sidestepped his name. Amy knew she should have done more to warn her friend.

'Did you always want to leave?' said Josie after a minute.

'Leave where?'

'Westmead.'

'I guess. But not because I was unhappy. I just wanted to see what else was out there. I applied to a bunch of colleges randomly. Got into Oxford Brookes and that was what really changed my outlook on the world.'

'Is that where you met David?'

'Yes, but it was really my friend Pog who changed everything. I worked with him behind the bar in a student pub in Oxford. He was frightfully posh – so posh it was almost as if he was from another planet. But we got on really well, and when I used to tell him what I dreamed of doing – going to Paris, moving to London, falling in love with someone rich and handsome – he told me to go for it. I wasn't convinced at first. I thought it was easy for him to say with his trust fund and his connections, but he used to reply, "Why not you?"'

'Why not me?' repeated Josie as if to herself.

'Your mum doesn't doubt you can do it,' said Amy with a maternal smile. 'And neither do I.'

Cliveden was a photographer's dream, with fountains, pathways and a stunning honey-coloured facade.

'I don't like the look of those clouds,' said Amy, peering out of the window. She knew that they had some shots planned for outdoors.

Josie craned her long neck and pulled a face. 'Wouldn't it be better to reschedule?'

Amy sighed. 'I'd love to, but we're lucky to get Miranda at all. Plus we don't have the time. This issue has to go to the printer's in three days and we have nothing else to put on the cover.'

Janice Evans, the magazine's fashion director, met them in the reception. She was tall, blonde and Welsh, and refreshingly no-nonsense for someone in the notoriously flouncy fashion world.

'Are they here?' said Amy, following her through the house towards the stable block.

'Got here half an hour ago. Miranda's in hair and make-up already. Liz Stewart is in there doing the interview.'

Amy felt her shoulders fall. It was good news that the talent was here on time, but she was never convinced that interviewees distracted by stylists and publicists made for the best copy.

'Her manager insisted. Apparently they've got to be out of here by lunchtime.'

Miranda's American manager, Karrie, was sipping at a cup of coffee impatiently, frowning with every sip as if it were toxic.

'I hope this isn't going to take long,' she snapped, putting her drink down on the windowsill. 'Miranda's just bouncing back from tonsillitis.'

Amy had her platitudes at the ready. She was used to dealing with celebrity entourages, who tended, as a breed, to be sullen and negative, perpetually whining about their client being on the verge of succumbing to Asian flu or whatever jet-setting disease was in the news that week.

'It helps that we have a really strong idea. When the concept is good, we can usually nail it quickly,' she said.

'About that,' said Karrie. 'I was just talking to your art director, and she told me about the bubble bath . . .'

'That's right,' said Amy. 'The image we had in mind for the cover is Miranda in a big bath full of bubbles. It will be fun, glamorous. Very *Rolling Stone* meets *Vanity Fair*.'

'Miranda is a serious actress,' said Karrie pointedly. '*Persuasion* is out in November and there's Oscars talk already. We can't let anyone be distracted by photographs that are not on brand.'

Amy didn't like to point out that until twelve months ago, Miranda Pilley was best known for an ABC sitcom.

'Elise von Keist is one of the best photographers in the world,' she said. 'Almost every set of pictures she takes becomes iconic. Miranda's publicist seemed very keen on the idea when we signed off on it two weeks ago.'

'We do want to make this work,' said Karrie, her threat not even thinly veiled. 'But a bath. Bubbles. You're going to have to rethink.'

'Shit,' muttered Amy after she'd gone. She was aware that Josie was standing awkwardly behind her. 'Can you go and find some coffee, and then Janice, can you show Josie the clothes we've brought along to the shoot.' It wasn't the most exciting job she could give her, but she was sure Josie wanted to feel useful.

'Nice girl,' said Janice, watching Josie trot towards reception. 'I had her in the fashion cupboard yesterday, sending shoes back to the PRs. No one likes doing returns, but she did it all in half the time my assistants usually take, and she didn't bother me once. If she needed an address, she just picked up the phone.'

'She's keen, I'll say that much,' said Amy, still thinking about what they were going to put on the cover.

Liz Stewart, the journalist commissioned to write the cover interview, emerged from the dressing room.

'That was quick,' frowned Amy.

'I was shooed away.'

'How was it?' she asked hopefully. Liz was one of the best celebrity interviewers in the business and had once won a writer-of-the-year award on the back of a ten-minute interview she'd done with Catherine Zeta-Jones in a bathroom in New York. If anyone could get good copy from a twenty-minute tête-à-tête, she could.

'About as responsive as a week-old corpse,' Liz said tartly. 'Apparently she's ill.'

'So we've been told. Did you get anything?'

'I tried. She was difficult. Every time I veered onto the personal stuff, they just shut me down.'

'Isn't she dating Leif Tappen?' said Janice with interest.

Tappen was still one of the bad boys of Hollywood, even though he was in his fifties.

'She won't sit in a bubble bath for a cover shoot. She isn't going to admit to dating Hollywood's baddest bad boy,' replied Amy.

'I heard he was on heroin.'

'In the nineties. But all is forgiven when your movies have made three billion dollars at the box office. Liz, I need something, anything for a cover line.'

'It will be a great piece,' said Liz, returning to her usual bluster. Somehow Amy didn't believe her.

Liz left and Janice went to show Josie the dressing room. The art director, Gemma, emerged from one of the suites looking frazzled.

'Will you remind me in my next life never to have any dealings with celebrities?'

'Did it always used to be this hard?' said Amy, sipping her coffee.

'I bet *Mode* don't have to put up with this shit.' Gemma smiled.

The two women looked at each other and laughed. It was true. Certain magazines could still call the shots. *Vanity Fair* had legendary power. *Vogue* and *Mode* still seemed to be able to get the ungettable.

'You've heard about Ros Kimber?' said Gemma.

'What about her?'

'She's leaving.'

'You're kidding!'

Gemma shook her head. 'My friend at *Mode* just texted me. Apparently there will be an announcement this afternoon.'

'God,' whispered Amy. This was big news, huge. Ros Kimber was the editor of British *Mode*, Genesis Media's flagship title and fashion magazine powerhouse. Ros was a formidable woman, grey-haired and elegant, and although she was now in her mid-fifties, after two decades in the role she'd never shown any sign of slowing down.

'Is it a case of her jumping, or was she pushed?' asked Amy.

'Jumped, I should think. *Mode*'s still packed with ads, so she's been making money. My guess is someone's made her an offer she can't refuse, probably one of the big houses in France.'

Amy nodded. The truth was, it didn't really matter what Ros Kimber's plans for the future were; all anyone was thinking right now was who was going to step into her shoes.

'You've got to be a front-runner,' said Gemma, knowing exactly what her boss was thinking.

Amy looked straight ahead of her. 'I'm not sure it's the right move,' she said, almost automatically. Like politicians who bashfully denied they'd ever entertained ambitions to be prime minister hours before announcing their candidacy, glossy magazine editors always claimed they were uninterested in vacant positions. There was a certain truth to it: there were so few editors in the women's market, it was a high-risk strategy to apply for another job. It was fine if you were successful, but what if you weren't? Your current employers would believe – correctly – that you were dissatisfied, and even worse, that you were planning on jumping ship armed with valuable insider information about budgets, staffing and profit-and-loss. On the other hand, not applying for such a dream role looked callow and unambitious.

'Of course it's the right move,' said Gemma. 'What, you *like* shooting in England waiting for the rain to come? If we were shooting for *Mode*, we'd be in Namibia or Sri Lanka with a two hundred K budget. And note I said "we" there. I would of course expect you to take me with you.'

Amy gave a throaty laugh. 'Of *course* I'll take you,' she said. But Gemma was right: at *Mode*, she'd have power.

There would be no feet-dragging or tantrums from the likes of Miranda and Karrie.

For a moment, Amy allowed herself to dream. She wouldn't just be sitting on the front row for the collections; she would be given an exclusive preview. Designers would be desperate to know her verdict, like some Roman emperor giving a thumbs-up or -down denoting whether people around the world would wear blue or green, leather or silk next season. Collections might even be hastily changed according to her suggestions.

She would have access to the very best photographers, celebrities and writers, prize-winners and literary heroes. The editor of *Mode*. She felt dizzy even thinking about it.

The industry gossip distracted her from the fact that Miranda was taking ages in hair and make-up. Despite gentle prodding, it was gone noon by the time she emerged.

'Let's look at the clothes,' said Janice, waving her into an adjoining suite.

Amy watched Miranda listlessly slide the gowns along the rail. 'Is this all you have? They're a bit too sexy. I mean, don't you have any Purfoy or Taormina? Something beautiful like that?'

Amy tapped a finger against her lips, as if she were considering it. Purfoy and Taormina were the hottest new boutique labels. They barely produced a dozen pieces a year, most of them so cutting-edge they wouldn't look out of place in an art installation.

'Is everything okay here?' said Elise, standing at the door, hands on hips.

'Karrie and Miranda think the clothes are too sexy.'

'But sexy is good,' said Elise with a little shrug.

'There's nothing suitable here.' Miranda was pouting.

Elise shrugged again. 'Well, I have to leave for Dusseldorf at two o'clock.'

This was why Amy hated coming on shoots. They were hotbeds of ego and jostling for power and position. She smiled thinly and made her excuses, asking Janice to follow her.

'Tell me you can get something biked over here within the next hour,' she said.

Janice blanched. 'We're in Berkshire. It will take a couple of hours at least.'

'Does Cliveden have a shop?' suggested Josie, who was hovering nearby.

'Actually, I've got some things in the car,' said Janice. 'I'm doing a freelance shoot tonight.'

'Great. Let's see them,' Amy said.

'Do you need another coffee?' asked Josie.

'Thanks. And make sure Miranda and Karrie have got everything they want. In fact, let's have an early lunch break so we can sort this and start shooting.'

Janice disappeared, returning a few minutes later with five billowing gowns. All were beautiful and intricately tailored, but they lacked the *Verve* sass.

'It's modest fashion,' she explained, running her hand down the lace arm of a long yellow dress. 'The shoot tonight is for a magazine based in the Middle East.'

'There's nothing else?'

Janice shook her head. 'This is the best I've got.'

Amy glanced at her watch. 'The yellow dress is too bridesmaidey. Let's go with that red one for the cover and shoot against a white backdrop,' she said, clapping her hands together.

Miranda tottered out of the dressing room in the red dress. It looked hot and heavy, with a high, tight neckline, and already she was sweating, her grim expression indicating her displeasure.

'She wanted serious,' whispered Gemma, trying to raise a smile.

'Let's just do this,' said Amy, folding her arms across her chest.

She felt a flutter of anxiety in her belly as she watched Elise get to work. She knew she could not afford another duff cover. Under normal circumstances, Miranda's miserable appearance could always be construed as street. But two sober covers on the trot looked like a repositioning. Which would be fine if Amy wanted to make *Verve* more serious and achingly fashionable. But she did not.

She glanced at her watch: 1.45. In another half an hour Elise would be gone. Liz Stewart had already left, but Amy wondered if she could speak to Karrie and maybe squeeze out a phone interview.

She went into the dressing room, but there was no one there except Josie, who was clearing up the coffee cups and food leftovers.

'Thanks for doing that,' said Amy.

Josie threw the rubbish in the bin. 'Are shoots always like this?' she asked.

'Creative egos can be delicate.' Amy smiled.

'Do you like that dress? The red one.'

Amy looked at her in surprise. 'The craftsmanship is incredible . . .' she began, then stopped herself. 'But she looks like a lobster, doesn't she?'

Josie laughed, and then fell silent for a moment.

'Do you know why I buy *Verve*?' she said eventually.

'Tell me,' challenged Amy.

'You make other-worldly people seem more ordinary.'

'Is that a compliment?'

'Absolutely.' Josie nodded. 'The other fashion magazines . . . sometimes they make celebrities seem scary. They put them on a pedestal in clothes that cost more than a car, and if they think that makes them aspirational, they're wrong. It makes them irrelevant.'

Amy had never really considered this before and had to concede the younger woman had a point.

Josie took a step towards her, coming up so close that Amy thought she was going to whisper in her ear.

'I heard something before,' she said, in a voice so low Amy could hardly hear it. 'Miranda was talking to her manager. She told her she's getting married. To Leif Tappen.'

Amy looked at the younger woman wide-eyed.

'When did you hear this?'

'Ten minutes ago. When everyone was having lunch. Apparently he proposed at the weekend. She's not wearing a ring, but he's given her one.'

'You're sure about this?'

Josie looked at her without blinking. 'I'm sure.'

Amy had noticed Josie's quiet self-assurance the very first night they had met in Notting Hill. But now it was clear that it was coupled with the smarts to get on.

'That's the story I want to read,' Josie added. 'I want to read about Miranda Pilley the bride-to-be. I want to see her happy and in love. I want her to tell me that's it's possible to tame the bad boy . . .'

Amy put a grateful hand on her shoulder. 'Great work,' she said, her mind fizzing with ideas. 'So good I think you have to stay at *Verve* another week. If you want to, that is.'

'Totally.' Josie grinned eagerly.

Amy returned to the shoot and went straight over to the rack of clothes, pulling out the yellow dress. Yes, it looked like a meringue, but now that was exactly the look she was after. She beckoned to Janice, who came running with grips between her teeth.

'Hmm?'

'Get Miranda out of the red dress and into this,' she said, aware that the shoot would soon be winding to a close.

'I thought you said it was too bridal'

'Change of mind.'

Elise came over with her hands in her pockets. 'I think we are done here.'

'I need another set-up. The yellow dress. I want the shot to look clean, white.'

Elise let out a soft sigh to register her disapproval at being asked to do one more thing. Janice took the dress to Miranda, who agreed to put it on.

'Then we're finished, right?' she asked.

Amy instructed the hair stylist to unpin the actress's severe bun, then switched some music on. She took a stem of hydrangea from a vase and handed it to Miranda, who took it with surprise.

'Smile,' said Amy, throwing her hands in the air as Miranda's mouth curled upwards.

Elise fired off some frames and showed Karrie and Amy on her laptop. 'Looks like the homecoming queen, yes?' She shrugged, pleased with her work.

Amy nodded with excitement.

The yellow was still more primrose than ivory, though that could be sorted with Photoshop. But most of all, the image made her smile, made her swoon, made her want to celebrate what it was to be young, successful and happy. It wasn't inaccessible or lofty, as Josie had pointed out about so many other fashion shoots. Instead it was an image that simply celebrated what is was to be in love.

'The love issue,' she said, smiling to herself, imagining the photo of Miranda surrounded by joyful, upbeat cover lines.

And the timing would be perfect. When pap photos and engagement rumours began to trickle out to the tabloids,

Verve would have the glossy, glamorous exclusive that everyone wanted. The readers were going to love it. Douglas Scoles was going to love it. And what was more, as Douglas Proctor and the decision-makers at *Mode* magazine were going to love it.

Chapter 4

Amy glanced at the time on her screen. It was gone six. The day had slipped through her fingers like sand, but at least most of the next issue was finished. Elise's shots of Miranda had worked perfectly as spreads inside the magazine. The art team had added inset photos of balloons and confetti, while Liz Stewart's bland interview had been cut to just a couple of columns and beefed up with a quick 'Things I love' sidebar that Amy had extracted out of Miranda as the shoot had wound to a close. Not that anyone would really be looking at the words. They rarely did these days, and although that fact was heartbreaking for someone like Amy who had grown up believing in the power of the written word to entertain and illuminate, she had to admit that it was perfect editorial: punchy, visual, exclusive.

'Are you ready to go? Everyone's left already,' said Chrissie, poking her head around the door.

After nearly forty years in charge, their boss, William Bentley, was stepping down from the top job to retire and indulge in a spot of quality time at his estate in rural Gloucestershire. Although his last day at Genesis was tomorrow, his retirement party had been arranged for tonight, with all senior editorial staff being invited to attend.

'What time does it start?' said Amy, printing off the

Miranda Pilley shoot. She folded it up and put it in her handbag, knowing that William would love to see it even if he had one foot out of the door.

'Seven o'clock sharp. Speeches at eight thirty. Then no doubt on to a strip club.'

Amy laughed. Chrissie had been at Genesis longer than she had, and they both had affection for their outgoing boss.

William was a lovely man, happily married in the proper sense. His idea of a good time was a fine cigar or a brisk walk across the fields with Gina, his wife, and Winston and Nelson, his two grey lurchers. Amy had always rather hoped that she and David would end up in a similar place.

'Right, I'm on my way. Can you just send Josie in if she's still here?'

Her lipstick was in her pocket, and she used her reflection in the window that overlooked the South Bank as a mirror as she swiped a slick of colour across her lips.

'You wanted to see me?'

Amy sat back in her swivel chair. 'I'm at an event tonight and in meetings out of the office most of tomorrow, so I'm hardly going to see you. But I just wanted to tell you how great you've been over the past couple of weeks. The Miranda Pilley feature looks incredible, features say you've submitted some fantastic ideas, and the fashion team say you've been so helpful with the returns and the coffee runs.'

Josie beamed a broad smile back. 'I'm just glad to be given such an amazing opportunity. Thank you for letting me stay for two weeks. You didn't have to do that.'

'Thank David and Tilly. I had ulterior motives to keep you. They were just happy to have you.'

'Really?' Josie said, wide-eyed.

'Really.' Amy wondered if she sounded a terrible liar.

She paused. She knew she had to let the young girl down gently.

'Look, I know you want a job, and I'll be honest, there isn't anything just at the moment. But I'll give a reference to anyone you want me to and keep my ear to the ground for any position that comes up. There's always something for the right sort of person, even if you have to wait a few months.'

'It's fine. I wasn't expecting a job. But anything you can do to help when I'm back in Bristol would be appreciated.'

Amy opened a drawer in her desk and pulled out a paper bag, handing it across.

'I think you love the beauty cupboard as much as I do, so I've sorted out a few bits and bobs I thought you might like. Just some make-up, couple of body creams. I don't get sent as much as the beauty girls, but it's nice stuff, and you can never have enough products, can you?'

She was aware that she was babbling. The truth was, she was finding this a little awkward, playing the boss at work, then seeing Josie coming out of the guest bathroom at home. She knew it mostly stemmed from the guilt she was feeling about having effectively abandoned Karen and her daughter all these years. Yes, she had given Josie some valuable media experience, but a fortnight's unpaid skivvy work and a little bag of beauty products seemed pretty inadequate for ignoring her supposed best friend for almost two decades.

'Are you going out with David?' said Josie, loitering by her desk.

'No. William, our MD, is retiring. He's having a big party.'

'Will there be any celebrities?'

'It will be lots of advertisers and suits. But William knows everyone, so you never know. Why don't you come?' she added rashly. 'A few people from the office will be there, and you've met Juliet. I can introduce you to our HR director too, so you're on her radar.'

* * *

48

The moment they walked into the Bankside Café, Amy knew she had made a mistake. The idea had, of course, been to show Josie that the media wasn't all queuing for lattes and licking stamps, to show her the glamour of the board-room and management level: high-powered media moguls sipping champagne and discussing the Cannes Lions. And already, at first glance, it was full of the great and the good. Bigwigs from the luxury goods companies, and a smattering of showbiz faces: theatre directors and well-known models.

Juliet was standing with a group of young men in sharp suits who Amy guessed were her advertising team. Designers dressed like teenagers, editorial wore whatever they could cadge from the fashion department, and ad people looked like salesmen from a Park Lane car showroom.

But she had hoped that more of the *Verve* team would be here for Josie to chat to. Certainly all the department heads had been invited, but with no one in sight, she knew she had to stay with the girl until she could leave her talking to somebody else.

She saw William through the crowds and gave him a cheerful wave.

'What a turn-out,' she said, giving him a quick peck on the cheek.

William lowered his voice. 'Loved today, ignored tomorrow.' He smiled. 'The moment your byline slips off the masthead is the moment half these people won't even smile at you on the street.'

Amy laughed and knew he had a point. She'd heard rumours that the Printroom, the pub across the road from the Genesis building, had been booked for tonight's shindig and had only been upgraded to a finger buffet at the smart South Bank restaurant when the group's New York-based CEO Marv Schultz had said he would be flying in to wave William off.

'William, this is Josie Price. She's been interning at *Verve*. She's also an old family friend.'

'I know people disapprove of nepotism, but I've always rather been in favour of knowing what you're getting,' he chuckled.

'Don't let HR catch you saying that,' said Amy, taking a glass from a passing waiter.

'Don't be too hard on me. If it wasn't for a little word in my ear many years ago, the world of journalism might have lost you to teaching or PR. Speaking of which, here's Juliet.'

'You know it's not too late to change your mind. Genesis needs you.'

'I think we both know that Douglas has already had my security pass deactivated,' he quipped.

'Really?' said Juliet in surprise.

'No. But I have a round of golf at Wentworth pencilled in with your father on Monday. I aim to start my retirement as I mean to go on.'

'Jules, you remember Josie,' Amy said.

Juliet extended a pale, slim hand.

'I love the new issue of *Living Style*,' gushed Josie.

'Why, thank you.'

'I know it's not really aimed at me, but I love looking at the interiors and the gardens. The party pages too: it makes me feel as if I'm at the Oscars or something.'

Juliet raised her eyebrows at Amy. 'The girl has taste,' she said.

'And talent,' added Amy.

Josie blushed a deep red and looked down into her glass. William excused himself to talk to Marv Schultz just as Douglas pushed through the crowd.

'You two. A word,' he said in a low voice, steering Amy away from the crowds into the foyer of the restaurant. Juliet followed them and Josie disappeared to the bar.

'We have a problem,' said Douglas, his face serious. It was only then that Amy noticed that Grace, Douglas's PA, was trailing behind him.

'What's up?'

'What's up,' he said through tight lips, 'is that we have lost William's leaving gift.'

'Oh shit,' said Juliet, putting down her drink.

'"Oh shit" is exactly right,' said Douglas, glaring at Grace. 'Apparently it has been delivered to the Genesis building, but no one can locate it.'

'What is it?' asked Amy.

'A humidor, hand-made at Purdey's with exquisite marquetry in the shape of his bloody house. Not to mention two grand's worth of cigars inside.'

'Stolen? Lost?'

'No, no,' said Grace, looking visibly shaken. 'I'm assured it was delivered and signed for.'

'So where is it?'

'I don't know,' she said, shamefaced.

Douglas waved a hand to silence her. Amy had never seen him so angry. 'She thinks it's in the post room,' he said. 'Only the bloody post boys have all gone home, which means someone's going to have to run out to the newsagent and see if they can get William a box of Milk Tray and a couple of packets of Hamlet.'

Grace began to speak, but Douglas shook his head. 'I was being ironic, Grace. Any ideas?' he said, looking from Amy to Juliet. 'You get on with William. What would he like? Preferably something we can get biked over within the next forty-five minutes, before he's scheduled to make his speech.'

'Forty-five minutes?' said Amy glancing at her watch. Half past seven: it was very unlikely any fashion PRs would still be at their desks, so no favours could be called in.

'Anything,' said Douglas, a note of pleading in his voice. 'A suitcase, a cigar cutter, even a silk tie, just as long as we've got something to present him with.'

'I can send our fashion director to Selfridges. She has excellent taste,' said Juliet quickly.

Douglas shook his head. 'She'll never get there and back in time.'

'Then we can put back the speeches,' suggested Amy, her mind searching for a solution.

'Can't. Marv has to leave for Paris at nine.'

Amy looked back at the party, where William was deep in conversation with Marv Schultz. She pulled out her mobile and nodded to Douglas. 'I'll see what I can do.'

Juliet disappeared to find Carlo, her luxury editor, to see if he could rustle something up within the hour. Amy stood in the foyer and hit her address book, mostly coming up against annoyingly breezy recorded messages or numbers that just rang out into the void. A call to Berry Bros, the exclusive vintner's in St James's, was more promising. They were closing soon but could bike over a case of good Bordeaux immediately and arrange for William to spend an afternoon with the fine wine team at a date of his convenience. He would love that, she felt sure. It was job done, unless Juliet could come up with something even better.

Catching Douglas's eye, she gave a discreet thumbs-up and flashed her hands open and closed to signify twenty minutes. She doubted if it was possible to get from Pall Mall to South Bank that quickly in rush-hour traffic, but Douglas was close to having a coronary and she wanted to calm him down.

She felt a tap on the shoulder and spun round, wondering if Berry Bros had worked miracles, but it was only Josie.

'I think I'll be off now. Unless you need me to do anything.'

'Actually, I do need something,' she said, filling her in on

William's missing present. 'I've got a replacement gift on its way. It will probably come gift-wrapped, but just in case, I need you to go to the office, pick up ribbon, tissue paper, anything you can find. Quickly,' she added as Josie ran obediently out of the restaurant.

Amy returned to the party and was swept into a gaggle of advertisers whom she greeted with a broad and welcoming smile, instantly indulging in easy small talk that belied the behind-the-scenes panic that was going on. She was not a naturally gregarious person; didn't know the precise moment she had learnt to switch on the charm, although it had struck her recently, when she had met Karen, that it was probably not the countless hours at fashion dinners and product launches that had done it. At Oxford, when she'd worked at the Bear, she'd mixed with some of the grandest students from Christ Church, Oriel and Magdalen, students who thought nothing of coming for a drink in white tie, tweed or subfusc, students who seemed a world away from her friends down the road at Oxford Brookes.

She felt a presence at her shoulder. 'Any luck?' whispered a voice.

She peeled away from the group to talk to Juliet.

'A case of fine wine to present him now and a tasting experience in the cellars of Berry Bros. And you?'

'A set of luggage. Maybe,' Juliet said. 'Or whatever Carlo can rustle up from the office.'

'Why do I suddenly feel as if I'm on an episode of *The Generation Game*?'

'Grace needs sacking for this,' said Juliet with a faint flare of her nostrils.

'It wasn't her fault.'

'Really? The present was her responsibility. How she could have let it get to seven p.m. until she started panicking is beyond me.'

'So when's the luggage coming?' asked Amy, looking around for another drink.

'I don't know,' said Juliet with an irritation that said she was anxious not to fail her boss. 'And the wine?'

Amy gave a soft, resigned chuckle. 'You know, maybe William will see the funny side of it if we come clean.'

'Maybe. But Marv Schultz isn't known for his sense of humour.'

'Miss Shepherd?'

Amy turned to face the voice.

'I've got a delivery for you.'

She'd been expecting a courier in bike leathers rather than a fifty-something crook-backed man in a green fleece, but she was just glad to see that he was holding a large cardboard box.

'That was quick. Thank you so much. Berry Bros are a total lifesaver.'

'Who's Berry Bros?'

Amy frowned. 'You're not from the vintner's?'

'No, miss. I'm Gerald, from the post room. Josie came and got me at the pub. Said you needed a parcel that was down there. Sorry if it's caused any bother, only we tend to knock off at six.'

'No, that's fine, Gerald,' said Amy, too happy to see the package to care about the whys and wherefores. 'Can you help me to get it open?'

Gerald instantly produced a Stanley knife and expertly slit the cardboard. Amy pushed aside the packing material and pulled out a polished wooden box.

Gosh, that's lovely, she thought. You didn't need to know anything about woodwork to appreciate that it was a thing of exquisite beauty, the walnut panels positively glowing, the inlaid country scene – she recognised William's house from the one occasion she and David had been invited to a party there – elegant and stylish. Amy had never smoked a cigar in her life, but she thought she might consider taking it up if it meant you got to own heirlooms like this.

When she looked up, Gerald had already disappeared, taking the cardboard with him. Clearly Douglas had guessed what had happened, because he was already tapping a pen against the side of his glass and shushing the room to silence. 'I think it was Gandhi who once said . . .'

Douglas's speech was mercifully short, William's heartfelt and funny. The presentation of the humidor brought tears to the old man's eyes, which he covered by generously announcing that champagne was on him, causing an unseemly rush to the bar. Until that point it had only been free wine and soft drinks, thanks to a decree from Denton Scoles.

'How on earth did you do it?' asked Amy, clapping as William stepped off the makeshift podium.

Josie shrugged modestly. 'Well, I've spent a *lot* of time in the post room the past week, dropping things off for Janice or picking them up for the beauty department, and the post boys are pretty friendly. Anyway, one of them told me they don't mix with the writers in the Printroom; instead they drink in the Wellington on Cole Street, so I ran around there and grabbed Gerald.' She smiled to herself.

'What's so funny?'

'Oh, he didn't want to come. He said . . .' She paused, then looked at Amy. 'Well, he said some rude things about Genesis management.'

'So how did you get him to do it?'

'I think I told him that you'd crush his nuts, then stuff his pension down the toilet.'

Amy burst out laughing. 'Now that's initiative.'

Josie smiled shyly for a moment, then looked over Amy's shoulder, mouthing, 'Wow!' Amy smiled: Carlo, it had to be.

'Miss Shepherd,' said the tall Italian, walking towards her carrying a wicker basket. 'I cannot find Juliet, but I know this matter is urgent.'

Amy put a reassuring hand on his shoulder. 'The crisis has been averted, Carlo. My assistant helped locate William's original present.'

'That is good news,' he said, looking crestfallen.

'But I'd love to see what treasures you have brought us,' she added.

Carlo laughed, placed the basket on a table and opened it with a flourish, pleased that his efforts were at least about to be recognised.

'For your consideration,' he said, picking out the items one by one. 'For the wine and spirits connoisseur, a Pol Roger Cuvée Sir Winston Churchill and this bottle of twenty-five-year-old malt. For the recent retiree, I have a cashmere blanket in a soft putty shade, perfect for lounging around the house on winter days. And finally – and my favourite, I will admit – a wristwatch. Swiss-made. One of the standout pieces at the Baselworld jewellery fair . . .'

He shut the basket and his face fell in disappointment.

'What a shame none of it will be finding a good home tonight.'

'You have excelled yourself, Carlo, and I know William would have loved everything here,' Amy said, smiling. 'However, you are wrong about none of it finding a good home. I'd love to take the champagne.'

Carlo looked delighted as he handed over the bottle, which Amy insisted on paying for.

'This is for you,' she said, giving it to Josie as the Italian disappeared into the crowd. 'Thank you for being such a star.'

Chapter 5

Note to self, thought Amy, gripping the white leather arm rests. Injections hurt.

'Just relax,' said Dr Al Saraf soothingly.

'That's fine for you to say,' she said, unscrewing one eye enough to see that the syringe was still half full, 'you're not the one being pumped full of gloop.'

The doctor laughed. 'Remember that the gloop is good for you.'

She'd already had a two-hour consultation on the benefits of today's session. How the cocktail of B12 and various other secret ingredients would promote muscle growth and balance her hormones, as well as boosting her energy and keeping her alert.

He pulled out the needle and pressed a ball of cotton wool into the crook of her arm. 'There, all done. Wasn't so bad, was it?'

Depends on whether you're used to getting jabbed, thought Amy. She gave a non-committal grunt.

'The good news is that once your system becomes accustomed to these vitamin shots, you can start doing it yourself.'

'Injecting myself?'

The doctor nodded. 'It's a far superior method to taking supplements orally. It takes a bit of practice, but I can provide you with everything you need. Saves you coming all the way across London once a fortnight, hmm?'

It made sense, but Amy could barely stomach the sight of needles when Dr Al Saraf was handling them. The idea of injecting herself at home made her feel queasy. Then again, she needed something. With the rush to get the new issue finished, and the next two issues after that planned and commissioned in preparation for her three-week holiday, she felt more run-down than ever. Despite telling herself that she just needed a rest and some sunshine, Dr Al Saraf's tests had shown that she had a yeast infection, a micro-nutrient deficiency and high cortisol levels, which warranted a more comprehensive plan than the simple injections that Juliet had recommended.

Once Dr Al Saraf had demonstrated how to safely self-administer her shots, he came with her to reception. Within a few minutes, Amy had paid a four-figure bill and collected two boxes of BlissVit vials and syringes.

Out on Harley Street, she looked back at the Georgian terrace, feeling a little kick of . . . something. Did she feel more clear-headed? More energised? She was sure that getting a treatment – any treatment – in a place so synony-mous with medical excellence had a placebo effect on its own. But she definitely did feel more positive, which had to be a good thing, right?

There was no denying that David's relaxation pact couldn't come soon enough as far as Amy was concerned. She was running on empty, down to the last fumes before the engines coughed their last and the jet nose-dived into the tarmac. She hadn't wanted to admit it to David; hadn't wanted to admit it to herself, but the stress of the changing workplace was taking its toll.

She had once read a pop-psychology book – those happy, happy days when she had had the leisure to actually *read* –

that had offered the idea that all humans needed to feel progress. Workers needed to feel valued, getting promotions or bonuses, seeing projects completed. Parents needed to see their kids grow and bloom and yes, even fly the nest. If you didn't have progress, if you didn't feel you were moving forward, that was when the problems began. Lack of motivation, lack of energy, dissatisfaction in relationships, putting on weight.

Unconsciously, Amy touched her stomach. She was fine in that department, at least. Well, as long as she stuck to her no-carbs, no-red-meat regime. One burger and she'd be the Michelin Man. But in every other danger area, she knew she was struggling. With William gone, she could feel the screws tightening at Genesis Media. Even her efforts to escape and refresh her career were another source of stress.

She still hadn't heard from *Mode*. The day after the company had announced that Ros Kimber was stepping down, she had sent a carefully worded email, expressing an interest in the position, to the HR director and Douglas Proctor, but had received nothing beyond a one-line holding message saying that they'd be in touch. That had been over a week ago, and the intervening silence had suggested to Amy that maybe her stock in the industry wasn't as high as she'd thought.

At least central London was bathed in sunshine: not the kind that made workmen strip off their shirts and office girls wear sandals and little shorts, but enough to make everything look bright and vibrant. Standing on the stone steps of Dr Al Saraf's clinic, Amy took off her jacket and tucked it under her arm, feeling the sun warm her skin.

'Amy Shepherd? Is that you?'

Amy's stomach sank. Suzanne Black was also an editor, her equivalent at *Silk* magazine. *Silk* had pretensions to be an edgy fashion title, using waif-thin models and dressing them in unknown-but-out-there designers, but in reality it was just another conventional women's glossy with advice features, get-the-look spreads and beauty tips. Amy took some satisfaction from the fact that it had a tenth of *Verve*'s circulation, but was constantly irritated that advertisers seemed to hold the magazine – and its editor – in such high regard.

'Hello, Suzanne.' She was about to ask what the other woman was doing in this part of town, but on any given day you might see anyone from London's fashion fraternity popping into one of the many clinics for a shot of discreet Botox or filler.

'So what do you think about Ros leaving?' said Suzanne. 'I hear she was kicked out for demanding too much money.'

'Really?'

'Well, some have been saying she wanted a million per year; others that she wanted a new job title. Personally, I think it was a grudge between her and one of the management. That's the inside track, anyway.'

'Don't you think she, well, just wanted to move on?'

Suzanne frowned. 'Move on? From the best job in media?' She barked out a laugh.

'Maybe she's looking for a new challenge.'

'There is no bigger challenge than *Mode*, sweetie. I mean, we both know that, right?'

Amy didn't entirely agree with her. She had spent so long absorbed in the world of magazines that she had barely stopped to consider the world outside. But when she did, she had started to notice that many of her old colleagues were forging big careers in new sectors: retail, advertising, PR. Suzanne had probably recognised that too, but Amy didn't want to debate the relative merits of the *Mode* editorship compared to other careers. The other woman was making a direct challenge. *Are you applying for the job?*

'I should go,' said Amy, glancing at her watch. Suzanne gave her a thin smile of disappointment, her attempts to extract Amy's precise intentions unsuccessful.

It was almost three by the time she got back to the office, where Josie was sitting at Chrissie's desk sorting through the post. Amy felt a pang of guilt at her little sigh of relief that it was Josie's last day. Of course, she was glad the internship had gone well, glad that Josie had done well; she had certainly got more media experience in a fortnight than most interns got in a whole summer. And Amy had been grateful for all her help. But she knew she would also be glad to have the house back, just the three of them, herself, David and Tilly, their little gang back together. Was that selfish? Maybe, but she needed to completely relax, and although Josie had been no trouble at all, there was still the feeling at the back of her mind that you had to be 'on', checking the guest had towels, was comfortable, hadn't left curling tongs burning a hole in the carpet.

'Where's Chrissie?' she asked, balancing her bag on her PA's desk as she flicked through the mountain of invitations and press releases waiting to be taken through to her office.

'Errands. She asked me to man the phones while she's gone.'

Amy slipped off her coat. 'You can leave early if you like. I know you've got a train first thing in the morning, so if you want to go home and pack, just say the word.'

'I don't mind staying till six,' Josie said cheerfully. 'In fact I'm going out tonight with some of the girls. One of the PAs upstairs is off on maternity leave. Having drinks down at the Printroom.'

'That'll be fun,' smiled Amy, aware that she sounded about seventy, although her own days of drinks followed by crawling around London searching out cocktails and boys and late-night drinking dens didn't seem so far away. 'Tilly and I were going to take you out for some supper, but a party with the girls sounds a much better offer.'

'So long as you don't mind . . .' replied Josie, more anxiously.

'Of course I don't. I'll be here myself for a while anyway. When it's your last day in the office for three weeks, it feels like there's a never-ending list of things to do.'

Chrissie's phone rang and Josie picked it up. 'I'll just put you through,' she said, looking at Amy. 'It's Bethan Charles from HR.'

The HR director could have been ringing about any number of things, but the call caught Amy off guard. Anxious that others in the office had overheard, she spun round to head to her office, her jacket nestled in the crook of her arm, knocking over the pile of post and the handbag, spilling its contents all over the floor.

'Shit,' she muttered.

'I'll deal with that,' said Josie, springing out of her chair and starting to scoop up the mess.

In her office, Amy sat down on her swivel chair and exhaled deeply to compose herself.

'Obviously we want to talk to you about the *Mode* job,' began Bethan.

Obviously. Amy's relief was palpable. 'We know your work, but we're getting all the shortlist candidates to prepare a presentation.'

'Of course,' said Amy quickly. So far it was fairly standard. Occasionally an editor would be anointed without presenting a brand vision, but boards were more cautious than ever. After all, *Mode* wasn't immune to the downturn in the industry. 'When do you want it for?'

'Realistically we won't be seeing anyone until the last week of August, first week of September. But if you could get your presentation to us within the next couple of weeks, that should get the ball rolling.'

Tilly was fast asleep when Amy got home, her Peppa Pig duvet half kicked off, her beloved stuffed elephant clutched under one arm.

'She had a big day,' whispered Claudia as Amy closed the door and tiptoed back down to the kitchen.

'How was Kew Gardens?' School had finished two weeks before, and Claudia had planned a packed schedule of fun activities for Tilly before the Provence trip.

'She loved it. She bought a notebook and a sachet of seeds. We've planted them over there already,' said Claudia, pointing to a corner of the back garden.

Amy smiled, but her heart wasn't in it. She'd have loved to help Tilly plant her seeds and had lost count of the number of times she had felt sad and envious that her nanny got to spend so much quality time with her daughter.

'And we packed. The case is open in the guest bedroom. Tilly couldn't decide which swimming costume to take, so I'm afraid we've put the lot in.'

'Have *you* packed?'

'I've been packed since last Monday.' Claudia grinned, and Amy could only imagine her excitement about going to work in a luxury villa for the next three weeks.

'Thanks for everything, Claudia,' she said, grateful that there was one less job to do that night. 'I think Geoff is picking us up at nine o'clock tomorrow.'

'Is it still all right if I stay here tonight?'

'Of course,' said Amy. Claudia often stayed in the guest bedroom on evenings when she babysat, or when the family had a particularly early start.

'I've brought my case. You don't mind if I go out tonight though, do you?'

Amy had noticed that Claudia was wearing a pretty print dress and heels, her long hair, which was usually scraped back into a bun, brushed and loose.

'Course not,' she smiled. 'Are you going anywhere nice?'

'Just for a drink and something to eat.' Claudia blushed, and Amy sensed gossip.

'Ah, a date.'

'Not really. Well, maybe.'

'You make me nervous every time you say that. Our beloved Claudia is going to go off and meet someone fabulous and have lots of babies and leave us for ever.'

'I only met him on Saturday. I wouldn't be too worried yet.'

'You deserve someone amazing,' Amy said, settling a maternal arm across her nanny's shoulders.

'Here's hoping,' Claudia said, and picked up her handbag.

In the few seconds after the front door had closed behind her, the place was silent except for the quiet rise and fall of Amy's breath. She went to the fridge and retrieved a bottle of rosé, opened a couple of evenings before and still cold and crisp.

Pouring a large measure into a wine glass, she went and sat on one of the big sofas in the living room, not bothering to turn on a light, enjoying the peace and stillness and the soft grey light that slanted through the glass onto the walnut floor. Even, so, it was hard to settle, hard to ignore the sensation that she should be doing something. The *Mode* application wasn't going to write itself, and if it was going to be done in the next two weeks, she'd have to work on it in Provence, which meant sorting out old copies of the magazine to take, and loading her laptop with images and ideas she kept in all sorts of places – in her study, her desktop, in notebooks scattered around the house . . .

◃ ◃ ◃

'Hello?'

A voice woke her up. She opened her eyes and peered through the dim light.

'David? You scared me.'

'Why are you in the dark?'

'I must have dozed off. What time is it?'

'Almost nine thirty.'

She stood up and gave him a lazy kiss on the lips. 'Hard day?' she asked.

'There were lots of odds and ends to tie up. But if working late means I don't get hassled all holiday, it will be worth it.' He stroked a curl of hair behind her ear. 'What about you?'

'I couldn't get out of the office quick enough,' she whispered, kissing the curve of his neck.

'Why don't I get this homecoming every night?' David asked.

'House guests for a start,' she said playfully.

'Has she gone?'

'She's out. Claudia's staying here tonight but she's gone to meet a friend, and Tilly's asleep.'

'Which makes just the two of us . . .'

'At last,' she said, undoing his tie. She pulled the length of silk from around his collar, and as it fell to the floor, they started to kiss. His hands came around her back and he unzipped her dress, practised fingers unhooking her bra in one easy movement.

For a moment she was reminded of the days before Tilly, before their big house in Notting Hill, when they had both worked hard and played harder. Between client dinners and corporate networking they had had fun together. Parties, clubs, restaurants, and sex. Lots of it.

Sometimes it was hard to believe that they had once checked into hotels in the City because they'd wanted each other so urgently, or that they had woken up in the night three, four times, just to make love. These days, the only time Amy got up mid-slumber was for a pee, and hotel stays were at family-friendly resorts with kids' clubs and artificial lagoons rather than rain showers for two and room service that brought you breakfast in bed.

Her dress slid to the floor and David fumbled with his belt. His lips crushed her mouth and she held his face in her hands, hungry to drink him in. Desire had taken her by surprise, but as she closed her eyes and groaned softly, she knew she wanted nothing more than to feel her husband inside her.

'Now,' she panted, falling back on the sofa, pushing down the thin lace of her panties and kicking them off onto the floor. David, naked now except for his unbuttoned white shirt, positioned himself on top of her, easing her thighs apart to enter her. She kissed his nipples and pulled him close as their bodies moved in rhythm, slowly at first, then faster and faster until she felt the fire collect in her belly. Sweet, tight longing.

'Still got it,' he smiled. 'Why don't we do that more often?'

'Apparently Max's villa has a guest cottage.'

'Want to be out of earshot, do you?'

'Well, if you're going to insist on being naughty . . .'

'We'd better get dressed,' he said reluctantly.

'But I'm enjoying myself.'

'And then before we know it, there'll be a jangle of keys in the lock and Josie will walk in.' He said it light-heartedly, but the thought of Josie finding them like this – naked, postcoital – the thought of her seeing David's cock, made Amy feel cold.

'Come on, let's go to bed,' said David. As he stood up, she could hear her phone vibrating in her bag.

'It might be—'

'It won't be work,' he said firmly. 'Not at this time.

Besides, we're on holiday. They can get used to doing without you. You're never going to go off grid in Provence if you can't resist them now.'

She forced herself to let it ring out. 'See,' she smiled. 'I can do it.'

Her husband looked magnificent in the dark. Biannual triathlons kept him muscular and fit, and his handsome, regular features gave him an impressive silhouette.

'I love you, Amy Parker,' he whispered, and she smiled into his shoulder. She didn't hear her married name spoken out loud very often. She'd loved David for so long, years before they had reconnected after university and started dating, and sometimes she still had to pinch herself that he loved her back.

'I love you too, David Parker.'

This time it was his phone that started to ring.

'Do you think someone wants to reach us?' she said.

'I'd better answer it . . .' David frowned as he fished his mobile out of his jacket pocket. 'It's Claudia.'

'It had better not be FaceTime,' Amy mouthed, glancing at his cock.

He put the phone to his ear, and his frown deepened.

'Get dressed,' he said, ending the call. 'See if Josie's on her way home, or else we'll have to get Tilly up.'

'What's wrong?' asked Amy, sensing trouble.

'Claudia's been mugged. She's on her way to hospital.'

The hospital was surprisingly quiet for a Friday night. Perhaps it was too early for the booze-fuelled casualties, thought Amy, wondering how long it would be before she could get home. Josie had returned ten minutes after they had got the call from Claudia, but Amy knew that if Tilly woke up and discovered that her parents weren't at home, she would get fretful.

'So what do you think happened, Sergeant?' asked David.

'From what we've been able to gather so far, it seems Miss Smit was walking along a back street from the Tube when someone came up on a moped and grabbed her handbag. It happened fast and she's understandably pretty shaken and can't really remember anything more specific. A passer-by spotted her and called an ambulance.'

'Weren't there witnesses? The streets are pretty busy on a Friday night.'

The policeman shook his head. 'It was a secluded area: Garden Terrace, which I believe is about five minutes from your home address. It's pretty typical, I'm afraid. The muggers loiter around affluent areas – rich pickings, but quiet and out-of-the-way. In some ways, she's lucky.'

'Lucky?'

'There's been a spate of acid attacks lately. They can be really nasty.'

'Can we see her?'

Claudia was sitting grey-faced and groggy in a hospital bay, her arm already set in a cast. Her flatmate Maria, a Spanish nanny, was sitting with her, holding her good hand. Amy sat down on her other side.

'My handbag's gone,' said Claudia, still visibly shaken.

'We can get you another one,' said Amy, touching her shoulder. 'All that matters is that you're okay.'

'I can't come to Provence,' Claudia said, stifling a sob.

Amy didn't know what to say. 'Maybe we can change your flight.'

'I've got a cast . . .'

'I'm sure you can fly after a couple of days.'

'How can I work like this? How can I drive? Look after the kids?'

Amy didn't want to seem insensitive and agree with her, but she was right. She wasn't going for a holiday; she was

68

going to work, and she couldn't do that with a cast on her arm.

A doctor came through with a clipboard and stood at the end of the bed. David introduced himself and asked him to explain Claudia's injuries.

'Well, the fracture of the wrist is fairly minor. But I've looked at the X-rays of the ankle, and the break is on the fibula, which may mean surgery in the next few days if we want it to heal properly.'

Claudia started to cry.

'There's nothing to worry about. You'll need a cast boot for five to six weeks afterwards, and a few sessions of physio, but there's no reason why you shouldn't be back to normal by mid-October.'

Amy felt her heart start to thump in panic. She couldn't afford Claudia to be out of action for so long. The Provence trip would keep them away for three weeks, but September was busy: four fashion weeks and the gala dinner, as well as the *Mode* application.

She felt dizzy under the hot lights.

'Are you absolutely sure she needs surgery?'

'I'll have to speak to my colleague and get his view. If we can reset the bone through a procedure called closed reduction, then surgery isn't required and recovery time could be quicker.'

David and Amy walked away from the bay to get a coffee from the drinks machine. Amy knew what they were both thinking, so she thought she might as well speak up first.

'We can't go to Provence and leave her like this,' she said, almost downing the hot liquid in one.

'We can't miss the trip because she's broken her ankle,' David replied. 'We'll all just be sitting around miserably. Besides, before Max and Claire's nanny decided she was going back to Spain, Claudia wasn't even coming.'

Amy looked at him sharply. 'Of course, it's much more important that Claudia gets plenty of rest,' she said.

'Wouldn't be much use picking Tilly up either,' said David.

'Maria said her mum is going to come over from Amsterdam.'

'Let's make sure we pay for that,' said David, as if it was letting them off the hook.

It was 5 a.m. by the time they got home. It felt too late to sleep, as if they should push on through. They sat down at the kitchen table and Amy poured them glasses of cold juice from the fridge.

'It's just horrible.' She put her hands to her face. They were cold and smelled of disinfectant, so she cupped them round her glass.

Claudia's ankle had been reset manually, but the hospital wanted to see her again within the week to make sure it was healing properly. Which made the situation better than they had first thought, but still, it had been an upsetting and unsettling evening, not least for Claudia herself.

'I wonder if Max is up,' said David, looking at his watch. However much concern they felt for Claudia, this was an awkward situation in that Max had been insistent that a nanny come with them to Provence.

'What's the point of having the best wine cellar in Lourmarin if we've got to spend the whole bloody time babysitting?' he'd said when the idea of the trip had first been suggested.

Amy hadn't wanted to say that being on holiday with your own children wasn't exactly babysitting, but she had to admit, the thought of spending a lazy three weeks some-where beautiful, with great rosé, a stunning pool and the company of good friends, did sound better with the prospect of childcare.

'Claire said he's been worried about a paunch and is out running at six every morning, but I'd still leave it half an hour,' she said, making herself a Nespresso.

'Maybe there's a local hotel with a kids' club that can ship someone out to the villa for a few hours every day.'

'We don't want strangers looking after the kids, David.'

'You're right,' said David, rubbing his cheeks. In the cool light of the early morning, Amy noticed how weary he was looking. Two big back-to-back M&A deals had meant ninety-hour working weeks, and the stress was beginning to catch up with him. He'd never been much of a drinker, but lately she'd noticed that he'd gone from the odd drink in the evening to two or three glasses of whisky as he sat in his study watching Bloomberg, keeping track of the markets.

'It would have been nice, though. Someone to just whisk the kids off for a while.'

Amy nodded in quiet agreement. It wasn't that they didn't want to swim in the pool with Tilly, or play hide-and-seek among the cypress trees, but Claudia being at the villa would have given them both a break. In Amy's case, it wasn't even to spend a couple of hours chilling on the terrace. She had the *Mode* application to do, and if she was going to do it justice; if she was going to give herself a real shot at the job, she was going to have to spend much of her free time working.

She heard footsteps in the hall and a figure appeared at the kitchen door. Josie was wearing white cotton pyjama shorts and a little vest, her long hair falling over one shoulder. Amy wondered how it was possible to look so pretty when you had just got out of bed.

'How's Claudia?' she asked.

'Broken wrist and ankle, and very shaken up.'

'Poor thing,' she said with a grimace. 'Did they catch who did it?'

Amy shook her head. 'No. It was a moped attack. They just disappeared into the night. But the police are involved, so with a bit of luck they'll track the little bastard down with CCTV or something.'

'Thanks for looking after Tilly,' said David. Amy noticed that he didn't look at her.

Josie smiled and twisted her hair. 'No worries. She didn't even wake up.'

She turned as a small sleepy-eyed face appeared behind her.

'I want some breakfast,' said Tilly, her voice muffled by the soft toy rabbit she held close to her mouth.

Josie scooped her up so she sat on her hip. 'I was just telling Mummy and Daddy you were asleep. It's still the middle of the night,' she said, giving her a squeeze.

'But everyone is up. And it's light.'

'Come on, sweetheart, I'll take you back to bed,' said Amy, standing up.

'No. We're going on holiday. I want some juice and then I have to put Mr Rabbit in my bag.'

'Is Mr Rabbit going on holiday too?' smiled Josie, pushing the toy's head up and down in a nod.

'Of course he's coming,' said Tilly in surprise.

'In which case,' whispered Josie, 'maybe we should go back to your room and pack his case too.'

David waited until the footsteps had disappeared upstairs.

'Are you thinking what I'm thinking?' he said.

'What?'

'Josie, of course. Why don't we take her instead?'

Amy hesitated. 'I don't know . . .'

'Why not?'

'David, we've had her here for two weeks already. I was looking forward to it being just the three of us again.'

'But it won't be anyway, will it? Not at Max and Claire's villa.'

Amy didn't say anything, trying to rationalise why she felt herself resisting, why her husband was persistent, but she could come up with no decent explanation.

'She's not some random stranger; she's your best friend's daughter. She's been great at the office, she's great with Tilly . . . and God knows we need the break. Why don't we just ask?' said David.

Amy thought of the amount of work she had to do in Provence. The features ideas, the mood boards, the due diligence. She was going to be busy, and knew they needed some help if David was going to get the relaxation he needed.

She sighed and flapped her arms against her sides. 'Sure, why not?'

David went to the bottom of the stairs and called for Josie to come back down. She returned to the kitchen holding Mr Rabbit, and stood there until Amy spoke.

'Obviously Claudia can't come to Provence any more, so we were wondering if you'd like to come instead.'

She watched the younger woman's reaction. Surprise, confusion, delight.

'You really want me to come? To *Provence*?'

Amy felt her jaw clench but told herself this was the right thing to do. The right thing for everyone.

'It's not a holiday,' chimed in David. 'You'll be looking after the kids. Tilly and our friends' two children. But the house is great, the people are nice. Of course, if you've got something else you have to get back for – a job, a boyfriend – then we totally understand.'

'No way! This is the best opportunity ever. I can cook and clean and I even have my driving licence if you need me to run errands. The only thing is, my passport's in Bristol and I thought you were getting a lunchtime flight.'

David put up a hand. 'Let me see if I can switch us onto

a later flight and we can get the passport couriered over. I'll ask if we can transfer Claudia's ticket into your name as well. Saves us buying a new one.'

Tilly scampered into the room and grabbed David's legs.

'Tilly, Josie's coming to Provence with us. What do you think about that?'

'Hooray,' squealed the little girl, peeling herself off her father and transferring her affections to her new friend.

'Are you sure?' said Amy. 'It's all incredibly last-minute, so I just wanted to make sure you're fine with it.' For a moment, as she looked at Josie, all she could see was Karen's face as she'd arrived in Oxford, her eyes full of awe and wonder and excitement.

'Fine with it? Are you kidding? I'd love to come with you.'

'There we go. The perfect solution,' said David, turning to the coffee machine.

Amy nodded, hoping that her husband was right.

Chapter 6

Oxford, 1995

Karen reached out and slammed her hand onto the clock, cutting off the DJ mid-gush.

Nine o'clock. *Jesus*. She couldn't remember the last time she had slept in so late. She snuggled down under the duvet and smiled to herself. God, she could *so* handle being a student. Cheap booze, fit boys and lying about all day; and they paid you for it too. She considered trying to slip back into the dream she'd been having before the alarm woke her. For once, it had been a good one. She couldn't quite remember the details: something about a big boat like a cruise liner, and there had been music. She frowned. Had she been singing? Maybe she'd been auditioning for one of those talent shows her mum used to like when she was a kid. No, it was drifting away from her, the images plinking out like soap bubbles, but the feeling of warmth and well-being stayed with her.

She opened one eye, then the other. The Artex ceiling, the paper ball lightshade: they were unfamiliar, but that was definitely her dress draped over the chair. A smile spread across her face as the sight of the sequins brought the night back. The pub, all that wine – fancy wine, mind you – and that boy, the one who'd said he liked the shape of her neck. The one who'd tried to kiss her in the doorway.

'Hey,' she murmured, turning over and stretching a foot to her left. The other side of the mattress was unoccupied. She frowned, smoothing her hand across the sheet. Wasn't even warm. She sat up, trying to ignore the sudden flare in her temple. 'Amy?' she said. Or rather, that was the intention; what came out was more of a croak. 'Amy?' she tried again, feeling foolish the second time around. She glanced around the tiny room. Bed, wardrobe, desk piled high with scary-looking textbooks, but no one else was in it.

Reluctantly, she swung her legs out of bed and stood up. She remembered Amy's dressing gown being hooked on the back of the door, but it was no longer there, which meant she'd either have to venture out of the room in her Snoopy nightie, or go to the bathroom, have a shower and get dressed.

She opened the door, crept out onto the landing and peered over the banister. Music was coming from below, and the tempting smell of frying bacon. She padded downstairs feeling slightly awkward. This was a shared house and she barely knew any of the others; she didn't want to bump into them half dressed, but her hangover was so bad that only a bacon sandwich could get rid of it.

'Morning, sleepyhead.' Amy was sitting at the kitchen table reading a newspaper, hands curled around a cup of tea. 'Did the alarm wake you? Sorry, forgot to turn it off.'

''S'all right. Needed my beauty sleep,' said Karen, yawning.

'James didn't seem to think so last night,' said Amy. 'He kept saying you were perfect.'

'James? Was that his name? All right if I make a cuppa?'

'If you can find a cup. And we've only got Earl Grey.'

Karen pulled a pained face and bent down to open the

fridge, looking for milk. 'No way. Has someone really labelled his sausages?'

Amy raised her eyebrows. 'Shared houses, it can get very political.'

'Yeah, I saw the washing-up rota.' It had been neatly drawn up in felt-tip pen – multiple colours, so Karen knew it wasn't the boys' work – and Blu-tacked to the kitchen cupboard, right above the overflowing sink.

'So when are you coming back to Westmead?' she added. Amy had mentioned it was the last week of term and Karen couldn't wait to have her best mate back in Bristol.

'I'm not.'

'It's not so bad, you know.' Karen switched on the kettle so she didn't have to look her friend in the eye.

'No, I don't mean that. It's just that now I'm out, I want to keep going, you know? There's a big wide world out there and I want to see it. David and Max are going to Goa for two weeks and they've asked me to join them, so maybe I'll do that if I can get a bit more money together. But I'll probably just head to London. You know you can earn six quid an hour doing corporate waitressing shifts. And Juliet reckons she can get me some work experience at the magazine house that publishes *Mode*.'

'Sounds amazing,' Karen said wistfully.

'Got to play catch-up with you, haven't I?' Amy said. 'You've got your own money and your own place, a car . . .'

'You mean a shitty flat and a rusty Fiat Panda. It's not exactly glam, Ames.'

Amy grinned back and Karen wondered if she was just being kind. She wasn't stupid; she knew that her friend's life was on a different path. She had noticed it immediately that first term when Amy had started at Oxford Brookes and she had come up from Bristol to gatecrash the freshers' bop. She had never seen or heard anything like it: she'd met people dressed in wetsuits drinking yards of ale, spoken to girls who'd taken their ponies to boarding school, and learned about alien things like seminars and wine societies. But over the past few months, since Amy had moved in with a group of students from Oxford University, she had orbited in an even more remote parallel universe. Her new friends didn't just sound posh; they were practically royal. As for the student house, it might have woodchip on the ceiling, but perched in the town centre, surrounded by the colleges' golden domes and secret doorways, it was like something out of a fairy tale.

Karen made herself a tea, although she didn't like the floral smell rising from her mug.

'So how's Lee?' said Amy.

Karen sat down at the table, sighing.

'That good, huh?'

'Ah, he's . . . I dunno, Ames. He's all right, I suppose. There are plenty of girls who'd give their right arm to be going out with him, but he's . . .'

What? What was he? Karen thought. Violent? Sometimes, after he'd had eight or ten pints, but then who wasn't after a skinful? And it wasn't even that anyway. He was disappointing. That was it. He was good-looking, he had a Golf GTI and Patrick Cox shoes. But that was all. And she had the sense that this was all he'd ever have, because it was all he wanted. Westmead suited Lee; it was his world. Karen had always thought it would be enough for her too. She dropped her hands helplessly onto the table.

'I dunno, I just thought he'd be something. And he isn't.'

Amy looked at her, nodding, and Karen could tell she understood. Like, actually, really understood. She didn't have to tell her the details: that Lee had once threatened to push her out of a taxi for talking to the driver, or that he would go into a rage if she wore heels that he said made her look like a slag. She didn't need to tell Amy anything because she just knew. That was best friends for you. When you'd grown up together, sharing crushes and dramas, you didn't need to explain.

For a moment, Karen felt like they were sixteen again, sitting in McDonald's sharing a milkshake, bitching about teachers and boys, talking about their dreams. They were going to hitch down to London and go to one of those clubs they'd read about in Amy's magazines, *i-D* or *The Face*. They'd meet a rich bloke and he'd offer them modelling contracts. Or they'd go to America and open a shop selling jewellery or perfume. But Amy had done something about those dreams: got a place at Oxford Brookes, worked for the student paper, met all these interesting and exciting people. Karen had done nothing.

'When do you have to get back?' asked Amy, glancing up at the clock above the fridge.

'Trying to get rid of me?' Karen smiled.

Amy blushed guiltily. 'Not at all. It's just that it's the ball tonight and Juliet's got me in with the caterers. I've got to be there at three.'

'Can't I stay?'

She looked doubtful. 'I'll be working till gone midnight and everyone else has got tickets.'

'Maybe I could get one.'

'Kaz, they sold out weeks ago, and it might be a bit weird seeing as you don't really know anyone . . .'

Karen felt her heart sink, realising for the first time how much she wanted to stay. Or rather, how little she wanted to go back. To what? A job that started at five in the bloody morning? Her mum, always putting her down? Lee?

'Hey, hey, hey!'

The door burst open and a tall, dark man struggled inside, his arms full of rustling plastic. David. Karen felt

79

herself flushing and tugged her nightdress down.

'Oh, hi, Karen,' said David, and she was pleased to see his own cheeks redden a little at the sight of her.

'Where've you been?' said Amy, standing up to help him.

'Picking up our suits for tonight.'

There was more rustling behind him as Juliet pushed inside. 'Bloody men and their stupid white tie,' she huffed, dropping two large bags next to the fridge. 'All the way to Walters and back. Why do their clumping shoes have to weigh so much? My arms must be three feet longer.'

David gave her the benefit of his hundred-watt smile. 'If your arms were three feet longer, you'd be an orang-utan,' he said. 'Max and I are very grateful.' He bent and grabbed her hand, kissing the back of it like a lovelorn knight. Juliet slapped him away, giggling.

'I don't know what possessed me to agree to help you losers. A lot of thanks I get.'

'I'll get Max to buy you a drink tonight.'

'Well, let's have a look then,' said Amy, nodding towards the bags.

'Later,' said David. 'I shall appear like Aphrodite emerging from the shell.'

'Wasn't she naked?' said Amy.

'Hmm. Maybe I'll just wear the bow tie then. If it's good enough for the Chippendales . . .'

Karen's heart fluttered a little as she imagined David in just cuffs and shiny briefs. He was gorgeous, after all – and he had gone to Harrow, which meant he was rich. A proper Prince Charming, not that she would ever get anywhere with him; he seemed too much of a gentleman, unlike the lads in Westmead.

'I'll leave Max's here,' said David, hooking a bag over the kitchen door. 'If he ever comes home, tell him I want the money before he even touches it.'

'You can also remind him he owes me a bottle of Bolly,' added Juliet.

They left, heading off to their respective rooms. Karen had never really understood the co-habiting thing, never having done it herself, unless you counted the endless men her mother would allow to sleep over, padding about in the dark hours. It seemed weird, girls and boys just sharing a space as friends. Maybe it was because she had never had any male friends who hadn't wanted to shag her.

She took another sip of her tea – did people really *like* this stuff? – and watched, amused, as Amy started reading her paper again. The *Telegraph*. The Amy from Westmead would never have read the *Telegraph*. Neither would she have drunk Earl Grey or eaten olives. But then that Amy was gone, wasn't she? thought Karen with a sharp stab of bitterness. That was the truth. When Amy had first come to Oxford, stuck in halls on the outskirts of town, it had been easy to pretend that nothing had changed. They'd gone drinking in the Oxford Brookes Union still dressed like twins; the letters had kept coming every few days, even when Amy had made friends on her English course. But then she'd got her job at the pub in the town centre and fallen in with this posh crowd.

And now? Karen reflected on her friend's bobbed hair, her white shirt, the jazz on the CD player. Amy might think of Karen as a grown-up with all the trappings of adulthood, but it was she who looked grown up. She wasn't the same Amy who'd bunked off school and giggled over a milkshake.

She looked up at a series of thumps from the direction of the stairs, followed by a crash and a blur of arms and hair.

'Pog!' cried Amy, jumping up. 'I didn't know you were back.'

'Sorry, been in my room. Got in about three this morning. Do I look awful?'

He was a giant of a man, and as he shook his red curly hair, something – dust, dirt, twigs? – cascaded to the floor. 'Shower's out again. Been hitting it with a spanner, but not sure I'm not making it worse.'

'Pog, this is Karen, my oldest, dearest friend from back home. Karen, this is my housemate Pog. Where is it you've been?' she asked, turning to him. 'Egypt?'

'Scotland, last-minute change. Was supposed to be diving in the Red Sea, but Charlie's parents have split and his ma's in the villa, so we went up to Skye, spot of cragging. Much rather be in a bothy than some marble-encrusted monument to Mammon anyway.'

Karen smiled weakly, having no idea what he was talking about.

'Right, who wants a bacon sandwich?' he said, opening the fridge and having a ferret around inside.

'If you're making, I'll have one for the road,' said Karen, hearing her stomach rumble.

'One for the road?' said Pog, brandishing a rasher. 'Not leaving yet, are you? It's the big night tonight. The ball.'

Karen shrugged, looking across at Amy.

'I have to work,' said Amy.

Pog frowned. 'But don't you get to join in the fun when you've finished? I thought that was the deal?'

'Apparently I don't get off until about midnight. And anyway, Karen hasn't got a ticket.'

Pog's face lit up and he clicked his fingers. 'I think Max has a spare. He was taking Belinda Grey, but . . . well, I think there was an incident at the boat club.'

Karen's heart jumped. Last night, when all the housemates had gone to the pub, all anyone could talk about was the Commem Ball at New College, which apparently was going to be the biggest and craziest night out in history. She had felt like she always did in Oxford: the gatecrashing pleb.

82

Everyone was cleverer, wittier, wearing more expensive clothes. God, they even *smelled* better than her, all the girls wafting around in a cloud of fifty-quid perfume. Scent. She had to remember to call it scent; 'perfume' was a dead giveaway. Still, after Posh James had tried to stick his tongue down her throat and his hand up her top, she had felt accepted enough then. And she knew she wanted a bit of that again.

'I'll bet Max has already found some busty blonde from Teddy Hall to take,' said Amy.

Karen narrowed her eyes. Last night, she had felt that old solidarity with Amy again, thinking that neither of them was going to the stupid ball. But Amy had lied about that, hadn't she? And now it was obvious that her so-called friend was trying to get rid of her. She turned to Pog.

'We can at least ask him,' she said, giving him her sweetest smile.

Pog laughed. 'Oh, I know exactly where he is.' He beckoned with one crooked finger. Amy and Karen exchanged bemused glances before Karen followed him down the corridor. He stopped at the door of the small downstairs bathroom. 'I should warn you, it's not pretty in there.'

He pushed the door inwards with one finger and it creaked open, revealing the bath, a mildewed curtain half pulled across. Karen gasped. A leg was sticking out.

'Is . . . is that him?'

Pog strode in and whipped back the curtain. Max was sprawled in the bath, fully dressed, one arm hooked lovingly around a green bottle.

'I can only apologise,' said Pog. He leaned forward and twisted the shower tap, sending a torrent of cold water cascading down on Max. The reaction was immediate and extreme.

'Shit!' He leapt upwards, his legs pedalling in the air,

hands scrabbling at the tiles, then twisted sideways and landed with a clatter on the floor, causing both Pog and Karen to jump back.

'Pog, you bloody sadist!' he yelled, trying to get to his feet and slipping back to his knees. 'You cretin, I'm wringing!'

'Language, Maximilian,' scolded Pog. 'Ladies present.'

Max looked up through his dripping fringe. 'Hello, Karen,' he said, pulling uselessly at his sodden collar. 'Didn't, ah, see you there.'

Pog threw him a towel. 'Pull yourself together. Bacon sandwich?'

By the time Max ambled into the kitchen, he had dried his hair and clearly recovered a little of his customary swagger.

'Sorry about that,' he said, pouring the dregs of the champagne bottle into a dirty glass and raising it in a toast. 'Got back late after the Oriel shindig. Didn't seem much point in tackling the stairs at that point.'

Pog nodded as if that was a perfectly reasonable explanation.

Max sat down opposite Karen, who tried not to look at his bare chest.

'On to more pressing business. I hear Lindy Grey has chucked you,' said Pog, handing him a bacon roll.

Max frowned as he bit into it, ketchup dripping down his chin. 'I chucked *her*, mate. She's a liar for starters. Been making out that her old man's landed when he's actually some sort of shopkeeper.'

'He's on the board of Waitrose,' said Amy, without looking up from her paper. 'She's always down the Bear on a Friday night. She's really nice. And pretty, too.'

Max waved his glass dismissively. 'Point is, she deceived me over her prospects.'

'Isn't her grandad like the fiftieth richest man in England or something?'

'Exactly,' said Max, pointing an accusatory finger. 'Fiftieth. I mean, I have to think about my future, don't I?'

Karen gaped at him. Max was clearly serious. Amy had already filled her in on his background: he too had been to Harrow, and his father was a lawyer, but by Oxford standards, where every second student seemed to be a European princess or a viscount with a family seat, he wasn't exactly a huge catch. Dripping wet, his dark eyes just a little too close together, he had a weaselly look about him, but one thing he didn't lack was self-esteem.

'Anyway, the point is,' said Pog impatiently, 'I presume you now have a spare ticket for the ball tonight?'

'Possibly . . .' said Max uncertainly. 'Why?'

'A man of your high social standing can't be seen to arrive at the biggest ball of the decade alone, can he?'

'I suppose not.' Max's eyes had retreated into suspicious slits.

'Well, good news. Karen here has been gracious enough to agree to accompany you.'

A lecherous smile came over Max's face. 'Have you now?'

Karen suddenly felt very exposed as she became aware of his eyes running over her, her old nightie barely hiding her curves.

'Oi!' said Pog, throwing a tea bag at him. 'She has agreed to *accompany* you, nothing more. And I'd say she's being more than generous, given that she'll have to be seen with you in public.'

'Steady on, old man,' said Max, a kicked-puppy look on his face. 'As it happens, I was going to ask her myself.'

He went down on one knee and clasped his hands together. 'Karen . . .' He paused and looked across to Amy.

'Price,' she said.

'Karen Price, could you find it in your heart to join me tonight?'

Karen had only met Max twice before, on the night she'd arrived two days earlier, and the previous evening in the pub, and she hadn't liked him on either occasion. But this morning he was funny, and although she didn't want to boost his ego any more by laughing, she couldn't hold it in any longer.

'You twat,' she grinned. 'Okay, you may take me to the ball.'

He jumped to his feet, scooping up the suit bag from the door. 'Righto,' he said. 'Be ready at seven.'

Karen locked eyes with Amy. For a split second, she saw something – annoyance, envy? – pass over her friend's face. But then she shrieked with laughter.

'It's like the world's worst Disney movie. You have my sympathy, darling.'

Yeah, maybe, thought Karen, but I'm going to the ball with an actual ticket, and you'll be bringing me my champagne, won't you?

'Why don't you come too, Amy?' said Pog. 'I know a few people at New College. I bet I can get you a ticket.'

Amy shook her head. 'I need the money, Pog. Moving to London won't be cheap. The bank's already on my back about my overdraft, and anyway, I can't let the caterers down on the day of the ball.'

'You can always stay with me over the summer if you want to save a bit of cash. It's a bit draughty, and if I'm honest, a bit dull. But we've got plenty of room. Like, about forty.'

'It's sweet of you, but I'd still be in the same position in the autumn.' She looked over at Karen. 'No, I'll just come and find you lot when I've finished. It goes on until dawn, doesn't it? I'll be the one in the waitress outfit.'

Karen's eyes opened wide, feeling her triumph draining away. 'Oh shit,' she said.

'What?'

She looked down at the Snoopy nightdress.

'What the hell am *I* going to wear?'

Chapter 7

Juliet's wardrobe was a sea of taffeta.

'Where do you wear all this stuff?' said Karen, tracing one hand across acres of vibrant-coloured fabric.

'Darling, this is my sixth ball already this term. I had to beg Mummy to take me shopping to Peter Jones last week because I'm sick to death of looking at some of these rags, I've worn them so often.'

Amy smiled from her position on the edge of Juliet's bed.

'Asking an Oxford Uni student why they've got a wardrobe full of gowns is like asking why they have a library card. Balls are part of the learning experience. It's like they haven't quite realised that it's not 1906 any more.'

Juliet sighed and looked Karen up and down. 'Look, I'm just not sure anything's going to fit you. I'm flat as a pancake and you've got . . . bosoms.'

'Come on, Jules,' said Amy, glancing at her watch. 'You're got to have *something* in your dressing-up box.'

Juliet plunged her hands into the back of the closet and pulled out a bottle-green dress from its dusty depths. Made from stretchy nylon, it was long and simply cut; at first glance, it was the most unremarkable piece of clothing she owned, and maybe that was the point, thought Karen, detecting the other girl's reticence to lend her anything.

'That might fit,' said Juliet, holding it up.

'Let me try it on,' Karen grinned, pulling off her nightie and slipping the dress over her head. She smoothed her hands over her hips, adjusted the neckline, then turned and looked in the mirror.

'Wow, I don't recognise myself,' she said in surprise.

'Kaz, you look amazing,' said Amy, jumping to her feet. 'I've got some earrings you could borrow, and if you twist your hair up like this,' she scooped up a handful and fixed it into a loose bun, 'you'll look like a fifties movie star.'

Karen didn't have a big ego. It was hard to feel confident about herself when she always had Lee telling her that she was fat and frumpy, that she needed to go on a diet and dye her hair and wear more make-up, but she had to admit that Amy had a point. The dress clung to her curves in all the right places, her creamy boobs spilled seductively over the low neckline, and with a slash of red lipstick, a splash of diamante, and her blond hair piled high in the way Amy was suggesting, she knew there was more than a passing resemblance to a young Marilyn Monroe.

'What do you think?' she said, flashing a look at Juliet.

'I think you might want to take a restraining order out on Max, because that old dog won't be able to keep his hands off you,' said Juliet, closing her wardrobe door.

'I wish you were coming tonight,' said Karen, sticking a fork into her baked potato and taking a long swig of her Diet Coke.

They'd come out for lunch in a café on the high street popular with students. Amy had filled her in on the history of the Commemoration Ball, explaining that colleges took it in turns to host the formal white-tie bashes. It was apparently the last big night out of the academic year; lectures had finished for most people weeks ago, and many students had left already, or, like Pog, returned simply to attend the biggest ball of the year. Even though Karen was excited about attending, she still couldn't help but think it was a swansong, with Amy about to graduate and head to London and not back home to Westmead.

'I will be there, remember,' smiled her old friend.

'Give me a wave whenever you can for moral support.'

'Max is fine.'

'I didn't mean that. I meant people looking down their noses at me.'

Amy's face softened.

'Most people are okay, Kaz. I'd be lying if I said I hadn't felt people sneering at me when they found out I was at Oxford Brookes. But you have to ignore them. Just stick with David, Pog and Juliet. They're lovely.'

Amy seemed so confident in her new surroundings, Karen thought. She had noticed all the 'darling's and 'super's that had crept into her friend's vocabulary, and she supposed that Amy had worked hard to fit in seamlessly. Karen didn't blame her; in fact she almost felt proud of the way Amy had shed her roots in the last three years. Why wouldn't you want to get as far away from the estate as possible? What was so great back there? And what was the point in coming to Oxford if you weren't going to make the most of it, educate yourself, better yourself, make contacts, learn about the world outside?

But even Amy's polish would sometimes get caught out. Karen didn't understand the subtleties of class, but she knew they were there; imagined what it would be like for Pog or David or Max to come down to the estate for the evening, and how people would respond to their plummy accents: with disdain and just a little bit of fear.

'I notice you didn't put Max in the lovely category,' she said.

'I can think of many words to describe Max, but "lovely" isn't one of them.' She said it with some affection and it put Karen at ease. But then her expression darkened. 'Look, it's none of my business, but . . .'

'What?'

'You going to the ball with Max . . . Have you told Lee? I mean, if he knew you were going out with another guy, he might be jealous.'

'We're not joined at the bloody hip, you know.' It came out more harshly than she'd meant. 'Besides, it's not a date. Max is just giving me the ticket.'

Amy didn't say anything; just looked thoughtful.

'You're right about David though. He is lovely.'

'I suppose,' Amy said. 'David and Pog are both great. Like brothers.'

Karen watched her blush. Amy had never admitted she fancied her handsome housemate, but it was obvious. Her long, breezy letters that arrived regularly on Karen's doormat in Bristol were full of references to her friend: David this and David that.

'Who's David going to the ball with?' Karen asked.

'His girlfriend.'

'I didn't know he had one.'

'Well, he does.'

'More's the pity, hey?'

Amy sipped her tea. 'What's all this about David all of a sudden?'

'He's gorgeous, and you seem to get on well . . .'

'He's my mate, Kaz. Yes, he's good-looking, but after three years in Oxford, I'm not sure I really want a posh boy. And I think after a night out with Max Quinn, you might agree with me.'

Amy glanced at her watch. It was almost two o'clock. The high street was clotted with tourists and the breeze through the open window smelled of blossom and promise.

'I'd better be off,' she said, summoning the waitress for the bill.

Karen wanted the lunch to drag out longer and felt a sudden surge of panic that this was it. The moment when Amy grew up and they went their separate ways.

'I'm really going to miss you,' she said, feeling a thickness in her throat. 'You know, when you move to London.'

'Kaz, I left Westmead a long time ago and we're still friends.'

'University isn't real life, though, is it? It's life on hold.'

'London's not far from Bristol. We've just got to make sure we make the effort.'

'Speak for yourself. You haven't been home in ages.'

'I was home at Easter. But it's hard. I work at the pub every weekend.'

'We should make a pact,' Karen said. 'You come back home every month, and I'll come to London every month. That way, we can see each other every couple of weeks.'

She waited for Amy to say something, but she didn't.

'Even better,' she said, another thought forming in her head, 'I could move to London.'

'Move to London?' Amy didn't say it unkindly, but there was a note of surprise.

'Why not?' said Karen, feeling more excited as the idea took hold.

'Your job, for a start. And what about Lee?'

'I could get a new job,' she said, reaching out over the table. 'Something fun, like the things you're thinking about. You know I've always liked hair and make-up. I could be a make-up artist. Maybe work in film or television.'

'I don't think it's that easy,' said Amy cautiously.

'Don't you want me to come?' said Karen, her eyes narrowing instinctively.

'Don't be like that. I'd love you to come to London. I just think you've got to think it through.'

She knew what Amy was really saying. That she belonged in Westmead. That pitching for the bright lights of London was too ambitious for the likes of little Karen Price. Well, Amy herself wasn't settling for anything normal, like being a barmaid or a receptionist, and she was no better than Karen; if anything, at school, Karen was always seen as the prettiest, the most popular, so why shouldn't she dream big too?

The waitress brought the bill over and Karen reached for her purse.

'My treat,' she said. 'For putting up with me.'

Amy didn't move her gaze away. 'Kaz, you know if it's not right with Lee, you can just finish with him. You don't need to move to London to get out of a relationship you don't want to be in any more.'

'I want to move to London for me. Not for him,' Karen said quietly.

'Or maybe you'll want to move to London for Max.' Amy's face broke into a playful grin, lightening the mood.

'Stop it,' said Karen, swatting the air with her hand. 'I know he's a lech. But this Cinderella wants to go to the ball.'

'Well, if he gets too lechy, you have our permission to kick him in the nuts.'

'I thought he was your friend.'

'He is. I just know what he's like. What they're all like.'

'Posh people?'

Amy nodded.

'But I thought you liked them,' said Karen slowly. 'Joining an Oxford Uni house share, I thought you might even want to be one.' She said it lightly, but her words had a barb that she meant to hit home.

Amy didn't flinch. 'I don't want to *be* one. But I want their contacts, I want their opportunities and I want their money. I'd only been in the house a month and Juliet was talking about her godfather getting me a job at his magazine firm. I'll never get those sort of openings without knowing the right people.'

'If you can't beat 'em, join 'em. Right?'

'Something like that,' Amy smiled.

Chapter 8

'How bloody long are they going to make us wait?' Max looked down the line, scowling. They had been standing in the queue snaking towards New College for fifteen minutes.

'Don't get so het up, Max,' said Karen. 'It's only early.'

Truth was, Karen was enjoying it out here in the last of the evening sunshine, shoulder to shoulder with elegant floppy-haired men and primped girls, their eyes bright and shiny. The fact that the queue passed under the picturesque Bridge of Sighs only added to the excitement. Twice in the past few minutes Japanese tourists with huge cameras had taken their picture. Karen felt special standing out here. To passers-by, she was one of the students, the elite of Oxford. For one night, she fitted in.

It was all an illusion, of course. Max had insisted on stopping at a friend's flat for pre-ball cocktails, and there, Karen had been Karen, the common girl with the funny accent. And what was worse, no one questioned why she was there; she could tell from the glares of the girls and the pinched smiles of the men that they all assumed she was Max's entertainment, a bit of rough to underline his roguish manliness. So to cover her embarrassment, she had drunk too many cocktails – no doubt confirming everyone's prejudices and making her feel a little woozy right now.

'Bollocks to this,' said Max, grabbing her hand. 'I'm not standing around here with everyone staring.'

He pushed out of the queue and strode down the street, pulling Karen, tottering on unfamiliar heels, in his wake. The line ended at a gate, where two girls in cocktail dresses were checking tickets off on clipboards before allowing revellers through the velvet rope.

'Max, we can't just barge up . . .'

But Max wasn't listening. 'Sorry, ladies, would you mind awfully if we slipped in? Just got a call from Jonno on the lights crew; he's got a prob with the par cans tripping out.'

Karen glanced at him. His face was the perfect balance of charm, apology and annoyance: just a partygoer who wanted to enjoy the ball but had reluctantly agreed to help out the incompetent Jonno. Whatever else Max was, he was a brilliant actor. If Karen hadn't known he was completely full of shit, she would totally have swallowed his story.

The clipboard girls didn't even blink. 'Sure,' said the first, lifting the rope. 'Backstage entrance is to the left. Good luck!'

Karen pressed her lips together to stop herself from giggling as they quickly walked past the gate and into the courtyard of New College, heading towards the festival-style stage that had been assembled at the back of the quad.

'Par cans?' she whispered.

'No idea,' said Max. 'Some sort of big light, I think. My stepbrother's into the theatre; must have picked it up from him. Now, let's get you a drink.' There was a table to their left, champagne flutes lined up like soldiers. 'Two each, I think,' said Max, scooping them up.

Karen sipped her drink and took a moment to look around. She had heard that the Commem Ball was the grandest one of the year, but the size, scale and beauty of everything around her made her catch her breath. Behind her, a huge magnolia shimmered pink and ivory in the soft lighting. The honey stone walls glowed, and the castellations and leaded windows made her feel like a princess in a medieval fairy tale.

There were already at least two hundred guests milling about on the grassy quad, which rose to a mound.

'What's that?' she asked.

'Legend has it it's a plague pit, and no one dares touch it,' said Max, swallowing his first drink and dropping the glass onto the ground with a thunk. 'Personally, I think it's just the dirt left from digging the master's wine cellar that no one could be bothered to cart away. Easier to make up some story than to pay the peasants to get rid of it.'

Karen was about to point out that she was one of those peasants, but Max had turned away to greet a group of rowdy posh boys already looking red in the cheeks.

'Canapé, madam?'

She turned to see a waitress holding a silver tray. 'No, I'm fine . . .' she began before recognising the laugh. 'Ames! God, sorry, I didn't expect . . .'

'It's fine,' smiled Amy, dropping into a small curtsey. 'I'm just here to serve my betters. We're not supposed to fraternise. Sure I can't tempt you?'

Karen shook her head. 'I'm only just fitting into Juliet's dress as it is. If I eat anything, I'm worried I might blow a seam.'

Amy looked at her watch. 'I'll see you in four hours. Got a break then. Meet at those giant swing things, okay?' She nodded at the small funfair on the lawns beyond a fabulously ornate gate.

Karen sipped her champagne, trying to soak up the moment.

'What are you doing talking to the staff?'

She turned and saw Max.

'That was Amy, you numbskull.'

'I know it was Amy,' said Max. 'I'd know that arse anywhere. I was making a joke. Come on, I see David by the bar.'

Wow, thought Karen. No wonder David had refused to give them a preview of his dinner suit now it had full impact. Tall and broad, he filled it like James Bond, with a louche air like the Rat Pack. 'Hey, David,' she said, air-kissing him. 'Like the tux.'

'Actually it's a tail coat, ' said the girl next to him. Annabel. Or to be precise, Annabel Cary-Hunt. Apparently the name carried some sort of weight in the upper echelons, or so Max had suggested. Perhaps it did, but she seemed like a rude little cow to Karen.

'Haven't I seen that dress before?' said Annabel.

'Probably, it's Juliet's. It's lovely, don't you think?'

Annabel nodded, although her face said quite the opposite. She herself was wearing a sheath of cream silk and carrying a black padded Chanel clutch. Yes, she was pretty, but beyond that, Karen couldn't understand why David would want to spend more than about three minutes in her company.

'Where's Amy tonight?' she asked.

'She's working,' said David. 'Which is what we should all be doing really, rather than messing about pretending to be Anthony Andrews in *Brideshead*.'

'Screw that,' said Max, waving his flute in the air. 'I'm going to keep clinging to this as long as I can. They're going to have to prise the gown out of my fingers.' He saw David's expression and shook his head. 'Seriously, you really want to get to work so soon? We're going to be chained to those bloody desks for the next forty, fifty years.'

'Speak for yourself, Maxie. My plan is to do my deals from my private jet as it comes in to land on my private airstrip in some tropical tax haven. And the sooner I can get *there*, the better.'

Annabel reached out and squeezed his hand. 'And that's why Daddy loves you,' she said.

'Do you think your old man will give me a plum job too, Bels?' said Max. 'I'm prepared to start at the bottom. Well, maybe somewhere nearer the middle.'

Annabel laughed. 'I don't think so, Max. You crashed his car, remember?'

'Oh crap,' he said. 'I'd forgotten about that. Then maybe I'll stay here and do a doctorate or something.'

'The coward's way out, mate,' said David, clapping him on the shoulder. 'A man gets out there and makes his own destiny.'

'My destiny is on the dance floor.'

The crowds were much thicker now, as they made their way towards the raised dance floor. There were bands due on later, but in the meantime, some DJ was spinning cheesy pop.

'I love this one,' shouted Karen over the boom of the bass.

Max was a surprisingly good dancer, shaking his hips and twirling her with ironic glee. She found herself chuckling, then laughing out loud at his antics.

'I'm the king of the swingers,' he sang into her ear, 'the jungle VIP.' For an uptight snob, he could be a real laugh.

After three songs, she waved her hands in surrender.

'I'm exhausted,' she laughed. 'Let's go get a drink.'

Max linked his arm with hers and pushed out of the heaving throng. 'The queue at the bar's crazy. I know where we can get one more easily.'

He led her down a series of cloisters, then pushed open a wooden door. 'In here,' he whispered. Karen paused, but he opened his jacket and produced a silver flask. 'I keep a very good cellar,' he said. Shrugging, Karen followed him inside and he shut the door.

She swigged from the flask, wincing at the sickly sharp taste.

'Napoleon 1894,' said Max with a wink. 'Stole a case from my father's stash last Christmas, not that the old duffer will notice the difference.'

He moved in close, pushing her into the corner.

'Max,' she began, but he smothered her protests with a kiss. His hands were everywhere, but primarily on her breasts and arse. Karen felt fleetingly grateful for Juliet's long gown, which at least meant he couldn't easily get his hands up her skirt.

'Max, no!' she said, wrestling her way out of the corner and pushing firmly against his chest, but he just bounced back like an eager puppy.

'No what?' he mumbled into her shoulder. 'No, wait until I unzip this dress, or no, let's find a room to do this?'

It was like trying to fight a randy octopus.

'No, as in get the fuck off me, Max!'

He finally stepped back, a frown on his face. 'No?' he said incredulously. 'You're joking, right?'

'Deadly serious,' said Karen.

'You're turning me down? Christ!'

If it hadn't all been so creepy, Karen might actually have laughed. 'Just because we came here together doesn't mean I'm going to shag you, Max.'

'Oh no? And what did you think the deal was exactly? You're quite happy to take the free entry and the free drinks and the golden ticket to the high life, but you're not prepared to give anything in return, is that it?'

'I'm not a piece of meat you can just buy, you arrogant shit.'

He stepped forward, backing her into the corner again.

'Oh no? And is what's in here so very precious?' he snarled, pushing his hand between her legs. 'Don't make me laugh, you fucking whore.'

Karen had just enough room to swing her elbow out, jabbing Max in the solar plexus; he let out a surprised 'Oof' and bent in two, slipping down the wall. She didn't wait to see if he was still breathing; she rather hoped he wasn't. Wrenching the door open, she ran out, instinctively moving away from the noise of the main party, wanting to put as much space between herself and that little shit as possible. How could he? Did he really think she would just offer herself up to him as payment for his stupid ticket? Was that honestly how he thought people behaved?

She turned a corner, then another, going deeper into the college grounds. It was quiet here, just the throb of bass from the disco and the odd peal of high-pitched laughter. She leaned against a wall, pressing her hands hard against her lips, trying to stop herself from shaking. Was that all they thought she was: a slag? A *whore*? She closed her eyes and remembered the way the girls at the cocktail party had looked at her. Like she was unclean.

Christ. She sucked in air through her nose and blew it out, trying to calm herself. It was barely nine o'clock and already she wanted to go home, but Amy would be tied up for hours yet. She thought of all those braying pissed-up bitches judging her, all those red-cheeked public school boys drooling, expecting her to play her role, to *know her place*. She couldn't stay here, no way. Maybe she could find a quiet café, sit it out for a few hours, then come back to meet Amy.

She made her way back towards the entrance, the velvet rope abandoned now, only a solitary security guard manning the gate, who assured her that he'd let her back in later. Feeling sordid and slightly cowardly, trying not to increase her pace, she walked away, back under the Bridge of Sighs.

She didn't really have anywhere to go, but was heading vaguely in the direction of Amy's student house. She hadn't seen Pog at the ball; maybe he'd still be there?

She had almost reached the corner when a dark figure appeared out of a doorway. Heart jumping, Karen stepped into the road to avoid him, but he moved to block her.

'Going somewhere?' he said.

Karen looked up, her mouth open.

Lee.

Chapter 9

'Lee, what the hell are you doing here?'

'I could ask you the same thing. Nice dress. Bet that cost an arm and a leg.'

'What? It's Amy's friend's.' She shook her head. 'No, I mean why have you come here, to Oxford?'

'I came to get my girlfriend – at least that's what I thought I was doing. Looks like I was wrong.'

'Wrong about what?'

'That you're my bloody girlfriend!' he shouted.

Karen flinched and stepped back, stumbling in the gutter, and Lee's hand shot out and gripped her arm. 'You're not, are you? All that shit about wanting to move in together was just bollocks, wasn't it?'

'What the hell, Lee? Where's this coming from?'

He dropped her arm, shaking his head. 'Nah, screw it. I'm gone.' He turned and stalked off.

Utterly bewildered now, Karen followed, but he was walking too fast. He crossed a road without looking, causing a car to brake and blare its horn. She hurried across, catching up with him as he passed beneath the forbidding stone carvings surrounding the Sheldonian. 'Lee, where are you going?'

He turned, opening his arms wide. 'Back to bloody

Bristol,' he said. 'Why not? There's nothing to keep me here, is there?'

When Karen didn't respond, he swore under his breath and turned away.

'Stop,' she said, catching his hand. 'At least talk to me.'

He resisted, but she dragged him up the stone steps into the courtyard surrounding the theatre. At least it was a little more private.

'How long have you been here?'

'I went to see you at the florists and they said you'd booked a couple of days off and had gone to Oxford. So . . .' He looked away, embarrassed.

'So what?'

'So I was worried, wasn't I? Wondered what you were doing here, so I came to find you, and now you've made me look such a prick.'

'And what about how you treat me, Lee? Have you forgotten what happened last week?'

'I came here to tell you that I missed you! That I . . . I bloody loved you. And what do I see the moment I get here? Saw you in the queue with some posh twat, his hands all over you. I tried to follow you but the bastards wouldn't let me into the party.'

Oh crap.

'Lee, it's not like it seems, honestly. I just went with Max because he had a tick—'

'Of course he's called Max,' he sneered. 'Rich wankers are always called Max.'

Karen bristled. Her first instinct was to defend Max, then she remembered leaving him on the floor and bit her tongue.

'Look, I just wanted to go to the ball and that guy had a ticket, that's all it was. And it's not like you're in any position to be lecturing me on how to behave, is it?'

'So you were using him? Like you use everyone.'

'What the hell is *that* supposed to mean?'

'You don't even like Amy any more and yet you're here living her life, borrowing her friends. You hate that bitch.'

'Don't speak about her like that.'

'Why not? You do. You're always going on about how she's run off with her fancy new friends and left us behind, how she's got above her station.'

'That's not what I meant.'

Or was it? Karen didn't know any more. It was true she would slag off Amy after a few drinks, but that didn't mean she hated her.

'Amy's my friend.'

Lee gave a cruel laugh. 'She wasn't all that good a friend when she was rubbing my cock under the table at Christmas.'

'Bullshit.'

'Is it? Every time you went to the loo, she was trying to get me to go back to hers. I said no because . . . well, because of you.'

She glared at him, unsure whether to believe him.

'Look, Lee, it's nice you came to check on me, but what's this all about really?'

'What? You think I'm playing some sort of game?'

'Yes, I fucking do!' She stepped back and pulled up her skirt to show him her thigh. Flowering across the left-hand side was a purple and yellow bruise the size of an orange. 'Look at that. You think that's in my bloody head?' She drew back her hair. 'And there? Can you see the scratches? The ones where your fingernails sank into my neck? Is that all just a fantasy?'

Lee pressed his lips together and looked away.

'Oh, right, so you didn't throw me down the stairs? You didn't try to strangle me?'

'I was pissed, I got angry. If you hadn't been looking at Tony Dean like that, I'd never have done anything.'

She nodded, snatching at the tears now running down her face. 'Yes, it's all my fault. Of course, that must be it.'

'No, I mean, it was all just a . . . It didn't mean anything. I still love you. Look, I'm here, aren't I? I wouldn't have come if I didn't care about you.'

'Lee. It's over.'

His eyes locked with hers and Karen immediately knew she had made a mistake.

'Over?' he said, stepping towards her. '*I'll* tell you when it's over. I'll decide.'

She backed away, immediately bumping into the railings.

'You think I'm going to let you go back to the Dragon and spread shit about me?' he said, his voice low, menacing. Lee was four paces away now, his hands opening and closing, that familiar look on his face: frowning, slightly bemused, as if he couldn't believe she'd forced him to hurt her again. 'You think I'm going to allow that?'

Karen's hands found cold stone: the gate. She threw herself sideways, half stumbling down the steps onto the pavement.

'Hey, hey!' cried a voice, and she felt hands on her, holding her up. She whirled around to see the alarmed face of a middle-aged woman with greying hair and the all-weather anorak of a tourist. 'Are you okay, love? Do you need help?'

Karen turned to look up at the gate, but the courtyard beyond the railings was dark and empty. Lee was gone.

'No, no, I'm fine,' she said. 'Thank you, though.'

'Are you sure?' The woman looked dubious, and Karen wondered what she had seen, what she saw when she looked at her. Some young girl in trouble, or an impostor, someone who didn't fit into the picture of Oxford?

'Yes, I'm just . . . I'll be fine.' She backed away, smoothing down her dress. 'Maybe shouldn't have had that last drink.'

She forced a weak smile, then turned away from the woman and tottered across the road, back towards New College. Amy would still be working, she knew, but she wanted to talk to her. *Needed* to talk to her. Right now.

Chapter 10

Present day

'Wow!'

Amy and David looked at each other open-mouthed as their car rolled through the gates of the villa. It was enormous, like a movie-set palazzo. Max and Claire were standing on the drive as they clambered out of the powder-blue Range Rover that Max had sent to collect them from the airport. Juliet and Peter, who had been on the same flight as them, pulled up right behind in another 4x4.

'Max, it's a bloody monster,' called Juliet as she stepped down onto the gravel.

'That's what all the ladies say.'

Amy walked over to embrace their hosts, her eyes still wide. 'I never thought I'd say this, Max,' she said, sliding her sunglasses onto the top of her head. 'But you've actually outdone yourself.'

The property was spectacular, built from pale stone with ivory blocks around the doors and windows, the gently sloping roof dimpled with pink and white undulating tiles. The details – the pastel shutters, the whitewashed steps – all said 'traditional French farmhouse', but the scale, and the elaborate sculptured fountain in the middle of the drive, spoke of unmistakable wealth.

'I have to say, I'm impressed, Max,' said Peter.

'Not bad, is it?' said Max, putting an arm around Claire, his garish Hawaiian shirt riding up. 'And *mi casa es su casa*, or whatever it is.'

'We're glad you could all make it,' smiled Claire. Amy could see she had made a special effort for their arrival, with blow-dried hair falling in waves over a Tom Ford pale linen dress. Or perhaps she always looked perfect when she was relaxing at home.

Max waved regally towards the Range Rovers. 'Alain will bring your bags; come in and have a drink.'

Just then, Tilly came sprinting up and threw her arms around Max's legs. 'Uncle Max! Uncle Max!' she squealed. 'We brought Josie with us! Isn't that good?'

Max patted her head and looked up, shading his eyes against the sinking sun as he watched Josie climb out of the second car, one long leg at a time.

'How's Claudia?' asked Claire quickly.

'Shaken up, broken ankle and wrist. But it could have been worse.'

'All's well that ends well, eh?' said Max, who still hadn't taken his eyes off Josie. Shaking off Tilly, he stepped forward, offering her his hand. 'We met briefly in London,' he said smoothly. 'Max Quinn. This is my place. You're *very* welcome, Josie.'

'Don't mind him, Josie,' said Claire.

Amy had no idea how Claire put up with Max's behaviour. She liked to think her old housemate had never cheated on his wife, but she never paused on the thought too long, knowing deep down it was probably a question not of if, but how often.

'Come on through, I think we could all do with cooling

off,' he said, touching her shoulder and leading her into the house.

The interior of the villa was as impressive as the outside, the double entrance doors giving way to a high hallway sparsely furnished with angular modern pieces. Max was right, it was cooler in here, shutters and long voile curtains keeping out the heat of the fading day.

'Your rooms are all in the east wing,' said Claire, indicating a staircase to the left. 'They have the best views over the valley and they all have access to the pool.'

'There's a pool?' said Tilly, doing a little celebration dance.

Max boomed out a laugh. 'Of course there is,' he said, opening a pair of French windows and ushering them through. 'Where do you think Hettie spends all day every day?'

'Tilly, don't run!' called Amy as her daughter scurried off in search of her playmate.

'Too late,' smiled David. 'But don't worry, I gave her the talk of doom at the airport. No pool time without an adult, armbands at all times. Hopefully it sank in.'

Amy watched as Tilly ran around the edge of the pool, wishing David hadn't used the word 'sank'. Tilly had been having swimming lessons, but this was not just a pool; it was more like a series of landscaped grottos with an ornamental bridge crossing the middle and diving boards at either end.

'I'll keep an eye on them,' said Josie with a reassuring smile, disappearing down the steps. Amy watched her go, wondering if she was thinking the same thing as her: this was all a long way from Westmead.

The adults settled down on the terrace on a series of chic outdoor sofas and Claire brought out a tray of drinks. David took his and offered a toast: 'To Provence, sunshine and' – he looked meaningfully at Amy – 'relaxation with friends.'

Amy tried not to think about her *Mode* application and raised her glass.

'No one had better even think about working,' said Max. downing his drink. 'Crappy phone signal, only internet's via the satellite, and the post only comes about twice a week. Can't even get the TV to work, not that you'd want to watch it.'

'It's okay, I've brought a book,' said Amy. 'I can't actually remember the last time I read one all the way through.'

'Same here,' said Juliet. 'I've brought an Agatha Christie, and this time I'm determined to finish it.'

'I read all the time,' said Max.

David laughed. 'Yeah, right. I seem to remember at Oxford that you once *paid* a second year to read a book for you.'

'In my defence, it was a deathly dull thing on jurisprudence about a foot thick. But nowadays I've got more time and I'll read anything: thrillers, biography, science stuff, you name it.'

'We have a library,' said Claire proudly. 'You'll see it next to the dining room.'

'This place is like a living game of Cluedo,' said David. 'You've done well, Maxie. Considering what an idiot you are, of course.'

Max raised his glass. 'Duly noted.'

'So how often have you managed to get here since you bought it?' asked Amy.

Claire pulled a face. 'The twins and I are here most of the summer, but Max flies in and out when he can.'

'Busy busy,' said Max.

'Isn't it a little, well, big for just the four of you?' asked Juliet.

'I'll be honest, I was as surprised as you,' he said.

'What do you mean?'

'What he means is that he hadn't actually seen it before he bought it,' said Claire, raising an eyebrow.

Amy and David gaped at him.

'Funny story,' said Max, wiping his mouth with the back of his hand. 'Met this guy in Monaco, Jean-Claude. Belgian he was, but loaded, private jet, all that. Says he's got this place in Provence but never gets to go there, some sort of tax wrinkle. Asks if I want to buy it.'

Claire leaned forward. 'Just to add, Max was pissed.'

Max waggled his hand. 'A little refreshed, I will admit. Anyway, I said I'd take it off his hands. So I wrote him a cheque—'

'A blank cheque,' interrupted Claire.

Max nodded. 'Luckily Jean-Claude had been on the pop too, so I think he missed off a few zeros. Total bargain.'

Claire shook her head ruefully. 'Even so, you're right, Juliet, it *is* a little too large.'

'Well, we're certainly happy to help you out by filling up a few rooms,' said Peter, raising his glass again.

'So, how about we go out to dinner?' Max suggested.

'I don't know,' said Amy. 'Tilly will be knackered after the journey.'

'Which is why you brought Supernanny, right?'

'She's not the nanny, Max,' she said in a hushed voice that urged him to do the same. 'She's a friend of the family who's doing us a favour, so don't treat her as an employee, okay?'

Max held up his hand. 'Whatever you say. We can go to La Petite Table another day.'

'La Petite Table is supposed to be fantastic,' said Juliet.

'Had to pull a few favours. Saturday night in August. People have had their names down for a table there since birth.'

'Well I don't know about you, but the cocktails have perked me up,' said David, patting Amy's leg encouragingly.

'I can watch the children if you want to go.'

Amy looked up to see Josie standing awkwardly at the top of the steps. 'They're in bed already anyway.'

'How on earth did you pull that off so quickly?' said Max.

'I bought this at the airport,' said Josie, holding up a book with hand-drawn animals on the cover. 'I used to love it as a kid. Always made me drop off dreaming of mice and the moon within five minutes.'

'Where are Hettie and Alex?' asked Claire warily.

'In their rooms. They came into Tilly's room for the story, then I told them to go to bed. So they did.'

'Can you come and live with us, please?' said Claire, shooting Amy an impressed look.

'So what are we waiting for?' said Max, rubbing his hands together. 'Let's go and see whether this French wine is all it's cracked up to be.'

It was a twenty-minute walk into the village. Max led them through the gates and down a series of winding lanes, the waning sun slanting through the poplars, casting giant shadows across the parched fields. Amy was glad of a chance to stretch her legs. The air was warm and smelled delicious, and the grand chateau on the edge of the village glowed against the peach sunset. The soft buzz of summer seemed to be all around them. She linked her arm through Juliet's as the others walked ahead.

'Isn't it perfect?' she said.

'Exactly. So stop worrying,' said Juliet.

'I'm not worrying.'

Her friend raised her eyebrows. 'Of course you're not,' she said with a knowing smirk. 'But I'm sure Josie is perfectly capable of looking after three children, especially when they are all already in bed.'

'How do we know she isn't smoking weed and inviting the locals round for a party?'

'Not sure she'd have switched to drug smuggling so soon, not on her first day in the job anyway. And if she knows anyone in Lourmarin to invite to a party then she's a better networker than Max.'

Amy nodded. Juliet was right, of course. It was silly to fret over every little detail – but then that was what she did, wasn't it? She had made a career out of making the trains all run on time.

'So what's really bothering you?' said Juliet finally. Amy glanced at her friend, then sighed. Juliet knew her too well.

'I just hate leaving the office, you know that. And it's such a bad time, too. Apparently Douglas is taking three days off, but he's spending it at the Edinburgh Festival schmoozing advertisers. And here I am lying about in the sun. I'm worried he'll think I'm a slacker.'

'Unlikely. You've hardly taken a single day off since he came to the company. And I'm in the same boat, remember?'

Amy nodded, not entirely reassured. Of course she couldn't say so, but Juliet's magazine did not have the same weight of expectation heaped on it. *Living Style* was well loved, of course, but it didn't attract the revenue or the headlines like *Verve*, and consequently she didn't feel the pressure as much.

'So are you applying for the *Mode* job?' asked Juliet.

Amy glanced at her, knowing from the sly smile on her friend's face that she wouldn't be put off with a shrug.

'You do know the sweepstakes have already started,' pressed Juliet. 'The *Evening Standard* has you down as a five-to-one shot, the dark horse coming up on the rails.'

Amy didn't know whether to laugh at that or feel insulted. Five to one?

'So who's the favourite?'

'There's a lot of speculation that it's going to go to an outsider. People are even saying Kate Moss might be interested.'

'Kate Moss? Well, if Douglas can persuade her to come in for interview, we might as well give up now and go home.'

Juliet clearly wasn't going to be deflected. 'Come on, you know as well as I do that you'd be fantastic,' she said.

Amy didn't want to tell her friend how much she wanted the job. Apart from anything, there was some truth in those wild rumours: a brand as strong as *Mode* didn't need an experienced editor. They could, if they so chose, appoint someone from the world of high fashion. A respected figure-head like that would still attract the all-important advertising money, and might, Amy had to admit, actually make the title look more edgy and ambitious. All of which made her application even more difficult.

'It's a huge job, Jules,' she sighed. 'And it's even more ginormous when you have a five-year-old.'

Juliet snorted. 'Don't tell me it's not what you've always wanted.'

'Of course, but seriously, I'm not sure I'm what they're looking for.'

'I thought you'd left that behind,' she said more sharply.

'Left what behind?'

'That reverse snobbery, that "everyone else is better qualified, better connected" nonsense. You're as good as any of them, Amy. Better, because you haven't been handed it on a plate.'

'Well, what about you?'

Her friend gave a soft snort. 'I'm the editor of *Living Style*, not *Silk* or *Major* or *Underground* or any of those super-fashion titles.'

'I know,' said Amy. 'But plenty of people have landed the top job on a big fashion title without ever having been on a single front row. Besides, no one has more class than you.'

'Precisely. I'm too posh. Too English, too twentieth century. Besides,' Juliet smiled, 'I like my life. I like that my job isn't too demanding, that I can do it standing on my head. It means I can be gone by four o'clock on Friday to the house in Hampshire and not come back until Monday morning. I'm not sure life would be like that as editor of *Mode*.'

Amy wasn't sure if her friend was trying to make a point after David's announcement that they had come here to relax, but she saw the wisdom in her words anyway. David made no secret of the fact that he hated her disappearing to fashion weeks in Paris and Milan twice a year; as editor of *Mode*, she'd be practically living in the shadow of the Duomo. No one ever said more work and more pressure made for a better lifestyle, did they? David kept talking about moving away from London altogether, about how it was a poor environment to bring up a child, and Amy couldn't really disagree with him on that. Like any working mother, she was constantly whipping herself with the thought that she wasn't spending enough quality time with her daughter, that she was being selfish, perhaps even setting her up for insecurities in later life. What if Tilly only remembered the time she'd spent with Claudia? What if she only remembered the fun holiday with Josie, who'd always had time for her? Christ. It was a minefield being a modern parent.

'Anyway, I've already made my decision,' said Juliet. 'I'm backing you.'

Amy looked at her in surprise, and Juliet laughed.

'It's like the contest to be leader of the Tories or something, isn't it? I don't think I'll get the nod from the party, so I'm putting my weight behind whoever I think *is* going to win. Maybe that way I can get a job in cabinet.'

'You wouldn't want to work for me, would you?' said Amy, half wondering if Juliet was serious. Juliet stared at her, then burst out laughing.

'No, you're right. I couldn't bear it if you got given better handbags than me.'

Amy grinned. 'Well, if I do get the job, I'll split them with you, fifty-fifty.'

'It's a deal,' laughed Juliet. 'Now let's catch up with Max before he's drunk the village dry. We *are* on holiday, remember?'

Lourmarin was near perfect, like a Disney version of a cute Provençal town. Surrounded by fields and vineyards and nestled in the shadow of the medieval chateau, the streets were cobbled and winding, lined by shuttered houses draped in wisteria and shops selling pretty *objets d'art* that spilled out onto the dusty streets: terracotta pots bursting with long stems of lavender, artfully distressed picnic tables, stylish straw totes, muslin scarves in every colour.

'I could buy up most of the things in there,' said Juliet, emerging from one of the most chic-looking stores.

The tempting alleyways finally converged on a narrow square where half a dozen bistros and cafés had set out tables and umbrellas, jostling for candlelit perfection under a bruising purple sky.

'*Monsieur Max! Mon ami!*' The rotund patron of La Petite Table stepped forward and embraced Max, gesturing to a long table set back from the main drag. 'You see? I save the best table in the village for you and your friends.'

Max shrugged. 'Then how can we refuse?'

The six friends sat down and ordered drinks, and charmed by the ambience, Amy finally felt her shoulders relax. She looked over at David, laughing with Peter, and smiled indulgently. He was handsome and funny and he'd always supported her ambitions, but wouldn't it be nice to spend more evenings like this, drinking red wine under a warm purple sky with people she loved? Maybe David was right: maybe they should move to the countryside, enjoy each other's company and watch Tilly grow up. What was the point of chasing another pot of gold, then another and another? Eventually the rainbows stopped for everyone.

'Max Quinn, is that you?'

A tall grey-haired man in a white shirt approached their table to a cry of recognition from Max.

'Charles, you old bugger! What are you doing here?'

'Got a place over in Vaugines,' replied the man, as Max rose to clasp his hand and air-kiss his wife.

'Come and join us,' he said, waving his hand extravagantly towards the table. 'We have wine, olives and the very best company. Everyone, this is Charles, my old boss at McKinsey.'

'Well, I don't think anyone can ever claim to be Max's boss, but yes, I tried.'

Amy smiled, but felt her heart sink. It wasn't that she didn't want to meet this friend of Max's, but she spent half of her working life glad-handing strangers, making small talk with advertisers, agents and management, and sometimes she just wanted to switch off. She scolded herself for being so uncharitable as Charles introduced his wife, Pandora, and Daniel, *le patron*, brought over two more chairs.

'So was he really that bad?' asked David. 'I've always wondered.'

'Rotten!' shouted Max.

Charles laughed. 'Well, I will say our loss is retail's gain. I do read the business pages and feel proud.'

'Proud that you fired him?' asked Juliet with an almost straight face.

'I wasn't technically fired,' said Max. 'It was more that I stopped going into the office.'

'Yes, I've been meaning to talk to you about that . . .' smiled Charles.

Max leaned across to clap the older man on the shoulder. 'Seriously, Charles, if you hadn't thought I was complete crap, I'd still be stuck in middle management.'

'I never thought you were crap, Max. Far from it. I just always knew you were destined to be your own man rather than a company one.'

Ice broken, Max poured more wine and began to regale them all with tales of his rank incompetence in the world of work: missed meetings, and, on more than one occasion, theft of office stationery. Amy laughed along, every now and then catching David's eye and exchanging a secret shy smile. No, she could definitely get used to this kind of life, she thought.

'So how did you all meet?' asked Pandora, after Daniel had brought out a superb crème brûlée to round off their meal.

'University, would you believe,' said Juliet, looking meaningfully at Max.

'Oxford, wasn't it?' said Charles.

Juliet nodded. 'Class of 1995. Feels like two minutes ago, but it was over twenty years.'

Pandora nudged David and nodded at Amy. 'So come on, were you two college sweethearts?'

Max put his arm around David's shoulder. 'True love never dies,' he said, batting his eyelids.

'We were housemates,' said Juliet, taking charge. 'Max and David were at Lincoln; I was at St Hilda's, desperate for some male company.'

'I assume you found it,' said Charles, nodding genially in Peter's direction.

'No, I'm a Cambridge man,' said Peter. 'Horses brought us together.'

'This sounds like a romantic story,' said Pandora, clapping her hands.

'Didn't start that romantically, actually,' said David. 'It was a weekend party at an estate near Oxford and I'd taken Jules as my date.'

'Platonic,' said Juliet quickly. 'Very platonic.'

'Peter was a friend of the host,' continued David. 'Anyway, we'd all arranged to go for a hack at the crack of dawn, but I had a hangover, couldn't face it, so Juliet and Peter were the only two who turned up. And then Peter saved her life.'

'You saved her?' gasped Pandora. 'How?'

Peter waved his glass modestly, so Juliet sat forward.

'My horse was skittish. We were crossing a field and disturbed a grouse; it flew up and frightened the horse, which then bolted, galloping through a gate out onto a road.'

'I looked up and she was gone, like a bullet,' said Peter. 'Didn't catch her for about three miles.'

Juliet smiled softly and touched his hand. 'But you did.'

'And then you lived happily ever after,' cooed Pandora.

'My wife likes romantic movies,' smiled Charles. 'And you two, Amy? Did you have a similarly dramatic beginning?'

Amy shook her head. 'We first met in the pub. I worked behind the bar. David liked his beer. He didn't even ask me out once.'

'But my friend Pog asked you to move in.'

'So you dated his friend first?' said Pandora eagerly.

Amy laughed. 'No, it was a house share.'

'I was thrilled,' said Juliet. 'Finally, someone else in the house who understood the concept of deodorant.'

'So did love blossom over the kitchen table?'

'Actually, David was dating someone else . . .' said Amy.

'Pippa!' said Max, banging the table. 'She was fit! And rich!'

Amy turned to Pandora, who looked utterly confused now. 'Her name was actually Annabel,' she said. 'And she *was* pretty, although a bit of a cow.'

'I don't think you're allowed to say that about partners' exes even if it's completely true,' smiled Juliet.

'So, nothing happened,' continued Amy. 'Jules and I moved to London together and Max and David shacked up in Chelsea doing whatever they were doing.'

'Shagging!' shouted Max, drawing disapproving glares from half the square.

'*Anyway*, we lost touch,' said Amy, raising her eyebrows at David.

'I was working every hour in the City,' he said.

'And I was off my nut in Ibiza most of the time,' said Max, keen to remain the centre of attention.

'Then I met him again in the street. It was London Fashion Week and the houses always try to outdo each other with imaginative venues for their catwalk shows. That year Simone did their show in an old bank off Threadneedle Street – it's a hotel now, I think – and I had just left.'

David leaned in to continue the story. 'I was walking up Fenchurch Street, on my way to a meeting, and boom! I saw this beautiful girl on the other side of the road. Wearing, I should add, a ridiculous red dress.'

'It was McQueen,' corrected Amy. 'Very chic, very directional.'

'Caught the eye, I'll give you that,' smiled David. 'Anyway, I ran across and we stood on the corner chatting. In the rain. For an hour.'

Amy didn't say so, but it was one of her favourite moments. David had looked handsome and accomplished in his dark chalk-stripe suit; he'd been funny and complimentary and he'd insisted on holding his umbrella over her until the shoulders of his suit were sodden. The truth was, neither of them had wanted to leave, fearing that the other would disappear like a dream.

'*So* romantic,' said Claire dreamily.

'You'd think, wouldn't you? But then she ignored me for about a fortnight,' said David with a hurt expression.

'A girl has to play hard to get,' smirked Amy. 'You have to let the man know who's boss.'

'Like there's ever been any doubt about that,' smiled David, touching her hand.

Amy didn't add that she had finally called David and taken him to an event in Soho, some art gallery she had thought would impress him, but they'd both been bored within ten minutes and bunked off giggling to a crappy basement salsa bar, where they'd done tequila shots, danced close and stumbled back up the stairs, snogging all the way to David's place. She'd spent the entire weekend wrapped in his sheets – and in him – and she had never really left.

'A whirlwind romance,' said Juliet. 'You were married about six months later, weren't you?'

'Nine,' said Amy. 'Didn't seem much point in waiting. Especially since we'd wasted so much time.'

'That's just like me and Max,' said Claire. 'We were less than a year.'

Max nodded, shrugged. 'That's because I was on the shelf, though, and starting to go bald. I didn't think I'd get anyone else to put up with me. Thought I'd better snap her up.'

'You old romantic,' said David, punching him on the arm.

'Ow!' he said, rubbing the spot. 'That hurt!'

'It was meant to.'

Conversation turned to children and schools and celebrity gossip among the women, and business among the men. Max revealed that his firm were toying with the idea of expanding into America, reasoning that 'The Yanks can't get enough of anything British.'

Charles took a more sober view. 'I can get some of our analysts to look at the market out there for you if you'd like.'

Max snorted. 'With respect, Charles, I'm not wasting any money on management consultancy bollocks – I'd much rather spend it on boots on the ground, get a top-notch team in the States. Just need to find someone I can trust.'

'Why don't you do it yourself?' said Peter.

'I would, but Claire's having none of it, are you, darling?'

She shrugged. 'The twins are happy at school.'

'Well, what about you, David?' said Peter. 'You're always saying you need a change. The finance side would be a cakewalk for you, and you know Max's business inside out, don't you?'

'I ought to, he's been bothering me with every last bloody detail for the past twenty years,' said David ruefully.

'I think it's a brilliant idea!' said Claire, flapping her hands with excitement. 'Amy, you could get a snazzy New York editorship and we could all spend our summers in the Hamptons.'

'Amy doesn't need a job in New York. She's going to be the next editor of *Mode*,' said Juliet, her words slurring slightly.

'Has the job come up?' said Claire in surprise.

'Ros Kimber announced she was leaving last week,' said Juliet.

'Really? How did I miss that?' she asked. Claire's background was in the fashion industry and even though she only did the odd bit of consultancy work these days, she always enjoyed being up to date with the gossip.

'You've been in Provence with patchy Wi-Fi,' said Max.

Amy shot Juliet a look and avoided David's gaze. 'I'm not sure I'm even going to apply,' she said, playing with her napkin.

'Not sure?' laughed Max. 'Sweetheart, cocks are being blown for that job as we speak.'

Charles and Pandora coloured in the evening heat and Amy glared at Juliet, who just shrugged and reached for the wine. She never had been able to hold her drink.

'Shall we have another bottle?' she said.

'Not for me,' said Amy, putting her hand over her glass. 'I think I'm getting a headache.'

The taxi could only fit five.

'Don't worry, we'll walk,' said David, taking Amy's arm as the others climbed into the car.

'Are you sure?' asked Claire. 'It's pretty dark on those lanes.'

'It's a beautiful night and the stars are out,' he said, and Amy felt her heart sink. She knew David had an ulterior motive, but he didn't say anything as the taxi pulled away and they strolled arm-in-arm back between the honey-coloured houses and out into the country lanes with their low hedges, crickets chirping around them. Finally Amy could stand the silent treatment no longer.

'I suppose you want to know why I didn't tell you about the *Mode* job,' she said, glancing towards David. He shrugged non-committally, but she knew him well enough. 'I didn't say anything because it's only just been announced.'

'Juliet said it was last week.'

'We've been so busy in the run-up to the holidays, and with Josie around, there's not been much opportunity to talk.'

David nodded, but he didn't look convinced. 'And?'

'And what?'

'And are you going to go for it?'

She took a deep breath. He wasn't going to like it. 'I think I have to, really,' she said. 'I've got to show ambition or give up. I'll need to submit a presentation before the end of the month.'

'*This* month?'

She nodded. 'I'll have to write it while we're away.'

'Can't it wait?'

'No, it can't.'

'Why?'

'Because I can't choose the timetable, David. If Ros bloody Kimber decides to jump ship, I can't exactly ask her to wait six months while I have a holiday.'

He was quiet for a moment, and Amy knew he was trying to control his temper.

'Listen, I understand that jobs like this only rarely come up, but this is the first day of a break that's supposed to be total relaxation.'

'I know, David, but—'

'Aren't you sick of it?' he said, turning to face her. 'Don't you look around at all this . . .' he gestured towards the dark countryside, so still and quiet around them, 'and want more of it? Juliet's an editor, Peter's in the City; I don't notice them working as hard as we do. They're always at their cottage in the country or in Paris or Rome – and not on business.'

'Juliet's editor of *Living Style*,' said Amy defensively. 'It's a small job. I've never worked out what Peter does, but from what I can gather, it's a lot of long lunches in Coq d'Argent.'

'So what? Don't you think we have enough? Enough money, enough work to do, enough everything? Where does it stop? When do we stop and draw a line and say we're content?'

Amy's instinct was to push back, tell him how important it was to her, ask him to support her just one last time, but she knew what this was about. George Moore, one of David's best friends, had died of a heart attack six months earlier. He had started at the bank in the same band of bright-eyed, bushy-tailed graduate recruits as David, and they'd risen through the ranks together, hopping between the big financial giants, earning money, fat bonuses and industry praise. They'd played squash once a week, and gone on a boys' shooting trip to Scotland every autumn, until George dropped dead during a triathlon, leaving three kids under ten and a grieving wife.

'I know you want to slow down,' said Amy. 'But what about seizing the day? What about taking an opportunity when it presents itself? David, this chance won't come again.'

'And is that so terrible?'

'So now you're saying I should give up my career?' said Amy, annoyed that he seemed to be pouring cold water on her ambitions.

'No, I'm saying you don't *have* to go for this particular job.'

'And then what? *Verve* isn't going to last for ever, you know, and I don't want to end up as an ex-editor, freelancing for day rates that haven't gone up in fifteen years. And yes, I know you make a great living. But I need something for me. I couldn't sit at home like Claire ironing socks.'

To her surprise, David laughed. He stopped and turned, looking into her eyes.

'Okay, okay, I hear you,' he said. 'But just get the application done as quickly as you can. The pact remains. A couple of days on this, then relax: is that a deal?'

'It's a deal,' she smiled, leaning in to kiss him. But behind his back, out in the dark, Amy was crossing her fingers.

Chapter 11

'Couldn't she have worn a smaller bikini?' said Juliet, peering over the top of her sunglasses.

Amy looked up from her sunlounger. She had spent the morning working on her application and she was practically buried under a pile of magazines; luckily Claire had every issue of *Mode* from the last year. It had been a quiet morning: Amy, Juliet and Claire sitting on the terrace reading, while Josie played with the children in the pool. Amy had been vaguely aware of splashing and laughter, but hadn't paid much attention. Now she followed Juliet's gaze down to where Josie was just leaping into the water, to the squealing delight of the girls.

'Ah, it is pretty dinky, isn't it?' she said. She couldn't help but admire how good Josie looked in the tiny bikini. Her figure was long and lean, her stomach flat and toned, and after just a few days in Provence her skin was soft and golden, making her cat-like blue eyes even more striking than usual. Amy wondered if she knew how attractive she was, or whether she took her perfect youthful figure for granted. 'We didn't have much choice, unfortunately,' she said. 'Josie had packed for a week in an office in London, so we had to do a smash-and-grab at Monsoon at the airport.'

Claire put a tray of cocktails on the table between the sunloungers.

'Iced tea on the right. Boozy version on the left.'

Amy went to the left, taking a glass that smelled of rum and left a pleasant burning sensation on her lips. She *was* on holiday, after all.

'So are you staying all summer?' she asked, settling back in her lounger.

'I might as well.' Claire shrugged, slipping off her kaftan. 'Although I have been asked to do some consultancy work for Hunter wellies in the last week of August.'

Amy nodded encouragingly. Claire had been a successful fashion stylist before she met Max, appropriately enough on a shoot for her future husband's fledgling fashion brand. She had stopped work as soon as they had married, devoting all her energy to renovating their houses and bringing up the twins. But Alex and Hettie were now seven, at school for a big chunk of the day, and Claire had confided to Amy that she wanted to get back into the workplace, beyond the odd days' freelancing.

'Stop myself from getting boring,' she'd quipped. 'Don't want Max running off with someone with something more to say than a run-down of school-gate gossip.'

'It's good that people haven't quite forgotten about me yet,' she said now. 'But still, it's hard to tear myself away from this place.' She tilted her head towards Amy. 'Listen, I feel a bit cheeky asking, but if we don't come back to London at the same time as you, I wondered if maybe Josie could stay another week here and help out with the kids.'

'Why cheeky?'

'Well, if Claudia's still off her feet, won't you want Josie stepping in back in London?'

Amy had to admit that she hadn't given much thought to

childcare beyond their three weeks in Provence, but Claire's question had concentrated her mind. If Claudia was unable to come back to work at the end of August, perhaps she'd have to ask Josie to help out.

Juliet dipped her sunglasses again. 'Aren't you worried about having such a pretty young thing around the house with Max in residence?'

Claire smiled ruefully and shook her head. 'I was actually thinking of that as a positive. Max has been talking about getting back to the office, but if Josie hangs around, so might he.'

'Now why would he look at anyone but you?' said Juliet admonishingly.

Amy shook her head. 'Max is too busy looking at his own reflection to pay any serious attention to attractive young women, however tiny their bikinis.'

Claire looked as if she was about to respond when Amy was distracted by Tilly running over, showering water everywhere.

'Mummy, Mummy!' she cried, beaming with excitement. 'Watch me! Josie is going to teach us how to cannonball into the pool.' Off she dashed, leaving little wet footprints in her wake.

'Not sure you'd get that with a Norland nanny,' said Juliet archly, turning back to her book.

Amy smiled, which turned into a soft laugh. Here she was working herself into a frenzy about the *Mode* application when the sun was out and her daughter was getting the purest pleasure from simply jumping into the pool. Besides, she thought, looking down at the magazines spread out in front of her, she knew this stuff inside out. She didn't need to study for this particular test because she'd been cramming for it for ten years. Every time the latest issue landed on her desk, she'd think about the tweaks and changes she'd make:

who she would have used for the cover, how the features could have been improved, which fashion and beauty photographers were bold and innovative. The perfect issue of *Mode* had been in her head for the last decade.

'Darling, is that your phone that keeps buzzing?' said Juliet, sipping her iced tea. 'If you don't bloody turn it off, I'm going to have to throw it in the pool.'

'Sorry,' winced Amy, reaching for her handbag. She had put it on silent, but the vibrate mode was rattling the glass table. Strictly speaking, the terms of the pact with David said that they had to turn their phones off completely, but you never knew when someone might need to get in touch with you.

Call me, said the message on her screen. *Pretty urgent*. It was from Tracey Jones, her deputy.

Amy got off her lounger and walked to a quiet spot under a cypress tree, a bad feeling in her stomach. Tracey was usually very capable, but this was exactly why Amy couldn't relax when she was out of the office.

She tapped in the number and Tracey picked up on the first ring.

'Hi, boss,' she said. 'Hate to disturb you on holiday, but I thought you should know right away. We have a major date clash with the Fashion 500 gala.'

'Another event?'

'Exactly. We've just got wind that E-Squared are throwing a dinner on the same night.'

'The tech people?' Amy covered her mouth. It couldn't have been much worse. E-Squared were major players in the digital world and in recent months had been moving into media and fashion. They had money and they were hot; a deadly combination. 'We always knew that there was going to be some overlap,' she said hopefully. 'It's Fashion Week after all.'

'Yeah, but it sounds like they're throwing the kitchen sink at it. They've invited half our guest list already. They haven't announced a venue yet – apparently it's a *pop-up* – but it's going to be big and it's going to be in London.'

'Oh shit,' whispered Amy. It wouldn't matter if *Verve* was the hottest magazine on the planet; if it was a choice between Soho and a two-hour drive into the country, celebrities were going to choose close to home every time. She rang off and went back to her sunlounger.

'Everything okay?' said Juliet.

'That was work,' said Amy distractedly.

'Don't let David hear you say that,' said Claire, her smile fading as she saw the serious look on Amy's face.

'What's up?' asked Juliet, sitting up and placing her book on her lap.

'E-Squared are throwing a dinner on the same night as the Fashion 500 gala. And it's in London.'

'Ah,' said Juliet, immediately grasping the gravity of the problem. 'Do we know what they're doing? Is it just a dinner or a big party?'

'Doesn't really matter, does it? They're inviting the same fashion people, and fashion people are fickle.'

'But your party's going to be enormous, isn't it?' said Claire. 'Surely people won't miss out on that.'

Juliet shook her head. 'It's the distance, darling. It could be a visit to the Hanging Gardens of Babylon, people get jumpy when they have to leave Zone Two.'

'Can't you fly them there in helicopters?'

Amy smiled. 'I think you've spent too long in Max's orbit, honey. And no, it's too expensive and too intrusive for that many people.'

'Well you can't cancel now,' said Juliet. 'We're just going to have to find some way of getting them all there.'

'What about a cruise?' said Claire.

Amy groaned. 'Serious ideas, please. We can't move Blenheim to the coast.'

'No, I meant like a river cruise. Max and I went on one on the Nile a few years ago. It was gorgeous, all ball gowns and silver service, so chic.'

Juliet pouted thoughtfully. 'Blenheim's just north of Oxford, isn't it? Could you cruise up the Thames?'

But Amy wasn't listening. She'd swung her legs off the sunlounger and reached across to Juliet, picking up the Agatha Christie novel she'd been reading. 'What about this?' she said, holding up the cover. 'Not *Death on the Nile*, like Claire's cruise, but *Murder on the Orient Express*!'

'Murder?' said Claire dubiously.

'We get one of those old steam trains and ask everyone to dress up in 1920s glam. Butlers with white gloves, and beaded dresses and fur coats and . . .' She looked up, her eyes sparkling. 'Don't you think that'd be amazing?'

Juliet stared at her for a moment, then a smile drifted across her face. 'It's perfect,' she said. 'Absolutely perfect.'

Chapter 12

Max groaned as he dropped a cardboard box on the table. 'Christ, this is the hardest I've worked in ten years,' he puffed, using the tail of his garish shirt – bright blue parrots today – to mop his brow.

Amy looked up from her lounger. She had spent the hour since lunch furiously making notes about the Blenheim Express, as she was now thinking of it, and felt more energised than she had in ages.

'What are you doing, Max?' she called.

'Oh, haven't you heard?' Max tore open the box and held up a dress. 'We're doing a photo shoot.'

That piqued Amy's interest, and she put down her notebook and walked down the steps from the terrace. To her surprise, she found a young man in shorts crouching at the far end of the pool fitting a long lens to a camera on a tripod.

'That's Willem, he's the snapper. Does a lot of our catalogue shoots,' said Max, still sorting through the box of clothes. 'Don't know why I haven't thought of it before, really. I'm sick of paying corporate rates for all those location houses. Some of them charge twenty grand a day. I reckon this place could pay for itself within five years.'

Claire walked over. 'Darling, we bought the house for

quality family time together. And I spent fifteen years on photo shoots. They're irritating and boring. Do you really want to bring them here?'

Max waved a hand. 'We'll see how it goes. Anyway, turns out Willem has a house in Ménerbes. Bunged him a couple of K to come down for the day.'

The young man looked up and waved, then turned back to his equipment.

Amy peered into another of the boxes piled next to the pool: kaftans, she guessed, or perhaps headscarves. It was the sort of casual leisurewear Max's company sold by the truckload. 'I didn't know you had this planned.'

'I didn't, not until I saw Josie in the pool yesterday.'

Amy's eyes opened wide. 'Josie?'

Max nodded enthusiastically. 'She was looking so glorious splashing about with the girls, the sun was all hazy, dragonflies and whatnot, and I thought – pow! – too good an opportunity to miss. Got the entire beach range Fedexed overnight.'

'But Josie?' stuttered Amy. 'I mean, she's not a model.'

Max waved a hand. 'All the better. Models are a pain in the arse, eating lettuce and needing Evian twenty-four/seven. Anyway, our punters like to see the clothes in a natural light; they prefer the girl-next-door type. Models make them feel fat.'

Amy looked at the pool with her professional eye. Max did have a point. It looked perfect with the sun slanting off the water and the golden brick of the house in the background. But Josie? She couldn't put her finger on it, but the idea of the girl being in a fashion shoot made her feel uncomfortable.

'Josie is supposed to be looking after Tilly and the twins, remember?'

'Not a problem,' said Max, snapping his fingers. 'Peter's

doing a show with them in the pool house while she's in hair and make-up.'

As if on cue, Josie walked out of the house wearing one of the kaftans Amy had seen in the cardboard box. Wow, she thought. Josie's hair was sleek and bouncy, her skin tanned and shiny. She was pretty, but not beautiful. And sexy too, in a wholesome kind of way.

'Isn't she magnificent?' said Max, a pleased grin on his face, but Amy thought Josie looked awkward and nervous, standing with her arms folded defensively across her chest. She walked over to her.

'Are you okay to do this?' she said softly. 'You don't have to if you're uncomfortable.'

The girl looked stricken. 'I'm sorry, Amy, I didn't think to ask. I mean, Max was so flattering, and Peter said he'd watch the girls . . .'

'No, no, it's fine with me,' said Amy. 'That's why I asked: I know that Max can be very persuasive when he gets an idea in his head. I just wanted to check you wanted to do it.'

Josie straightened her back and smoothed her hands down her thighs, as if she were gaining control of herself. 'I'll do it. I don't want to let Max down, he's been so nice.'

'Josie, it's not about Max—'

'Mummy!' Amy was cut off as Tilly ran across and wrapped herself around her legs. 'Where have you been? Me 'n' Hettie and Alex are doing a play. I'm being Red Riding Hood.'

Peter was trailing behind Tilly looking exhausted. 'Does someone else want to take over?' he asked with a good-natured grimace.

'I'll be there in a minute, okay, Tilly?' said Amy, but when she turned back, Josie was being led away by the photographer. Amy watched as she laughed at something Willem had said, her eyes lighting up, her smile wide, genuine. And suddenly she saw Josie for what she was: not their new nanny, not Karen's daughter, just a young girl on an adventure, trying new things, having fun. Wasn't that why Amy had offered to help her in the first place? To get her out of Potts Field, to show her another side of life, opportunities beyond the high walls of the estate? But still, she couldn't shake her uneasy feeling.

She felt responsible for Josie, that was for sure. But she wasn't entirely convinced that the stiffening of her back was a protective maternal instinct kicking in. No, she didn't like watching the way Josie's presence made Willem behave. She didn't like to see her effect on men.

'Mummy?' said Tilly, her little neck craned back to see her face. 'Do you want to come and watch our play?'

Amy smiled. 'Of course I do.'

She looked over at Josie again. You've got to stop trying to be her mother, she told herself. You've got an actual daughter who needs you.

'All right, Peter,' she said. 'I'll take it from here.'

'Thanks,' he breathed, striding off towards the house without a backwards glance.

'Looks like Mummy's in charge now,' said Amy, ruffling Tilly's hair. 'Why don't we do the play outside on the lawn? It's much too nice out here to be stuck inside the pool house.'

'Yes! Yes!' said Tilly, jumping up and down. Amy smiled to herself, remembering how primary school teachers had pulled the same trick down the years, making sitting on the grass seem like a real treat.

'Let's go and get Hettie and the props,' said Amy. 'So if you're Red Riding Hood, can I be the Big Bad Wolf?'

'Oh no,' said Tilly, suddenly serious. 'Daddy is the Big Bad Wolf.'

* * *

136

It was a long play. Both Tilly and Hettie wanted to play the lead role, leading to a protracted negotiation that was only resolved when Amy suggested there should be *two* Red Riding Hoods, twin sisters who both needed to visit Grandma's house on urgent business. There was another hitch when David's turn as the Big Bad Wolf was cut short by Max calling him out to the pool, but it was the big finale involving all the girls' stuffed toys singing a rousing chorus of 'Somewhere Over the Rainbow' that took up most of the time. The song had to be rerun four or five times so that various teddies didn't miss their chance in the limelight. It was, however, a lot of fun lolling about there on the sunny lawn, and after the first ten minutes, Amy had allowed herself to relax into her role as stagehand and chief cheerleader. It was wonderful to watch the kids interacting with each other. Once they'd settled on a pecking order, they played nicely, laughing, teasing, making up crazy jokes that only made sense if you were under ten. Why couldn't adults get along so easily?

Amy left the children to get a snack while she walked back to the pool, stretching after too long bent-backed on the ground. Max was leaning back in his chair, see-sawing back and forth on two legs in the manner that universally drove teachers mad.

'How's the shoot going?' she asked.

'Great, great. Josie's a natural.'

Amy looked across to where Josie was emerging from the water wearing a green bikini, the sun glimmering on the droplets on her skin. Willem the photographer was peering into his camera and calling out encouragement. 'Yes! Yes! More of that! Now look over your shoulder and wave. Higher arm! Higher!'

'Isn't she gorgeous?' said Max. 'And don't they make a lovely couple?'

'Couple?'

Amy looked beyond Josie and for the first time noticed David, who was wearing ludicrous red Bermuda shorts and waving at Josie.

'Hang on, *David*'s in the shoot now?'

'Just background shots,' said Max, shrugging. 'The punters like to see a family set-up.'

Willem looked up from his camera. 'Day-vid, can you *please* look as if you're happy to see her? Look, she's wearing her new bikini.'

Amy watched as David gave a wider smile. He was usually uncomfortable having his photo taken, but he seemed to be enjoying this.

'Josie, smooth your hair back and walk towards David,' called Willem, the camera motor whirring. 'That's it, more slinky, more sex. Now touch his shoulder, like he's teasing you.'

Mesmerised, Amy watched the scene, this tableau of the fake couple at play around the swanky pool. Only it didn't look fake. It looked real, David and Josie, the handsome older man and his sexy cellulite-free trophy wife.

'All right,' shouted Max, clapping his hands. 'That'll do. We'll bring the kids in for the next one.'

'The kids?' said Amy. 'I hope you don't mean Tilly.'

'Don't worry, they won't be in shot – well, not really. Just cavorting about blurred in the background.'

'No, Max,' said Amy firmly, not sure she wanted her daughter all over Max's company's promo material. 'It's enough that you've co-opted my husband.'

'Don't you want to help my business, Amy?' said Max, in a ridiculous sing-song voice.

She shook her head in disbelief. 'Max, we both know that I have done a great deal to help Quinn, as has Juliet, as have all your friends.'

He couldn't deny it. The brand had received a huge amount of free editorial space from both *Verve* and *Living Style* down the years, not to mention the two women putting in a good word with other journalists and editor friends. But it was typical of Max to demand more and more, a sulky little boy with a quivering lip who stamped his foot whenever anyone said no.

'David was keen!' he said. 'He wanted to do it!'

'And I suppose you twisting his arm had nothing to do with it?'

'I may have twisted a little, but he's an adult. He can make his own decisions.'

'Not when it comes to Tilly. Not without my say-so. That's how it works when you're married.'

'Mummy?' Tilly was pulling at her sleeve, but Amy was intent on venting her anger on Max.

'Not now, Tills, I'm telling off Uncle Max.'

'I don't feel well, Mummy.'

That got her attention. She looked down at her daughter and gasped in sudden horror. Tilly's face was bright red.

'What's happened?' she said, kneeling down in front of her. 'Are you hot?'

'Really hot,' nodded Tilly. 'It's like my skin's made of lava.'

Amy gently put a hand on Tilly's face, and they both flinched, Tilly from the pain and Amy from the heat. The little girl was burning up.

'I think she's caught the sun,' said Max, looking at her warily.

Amy's stomach turned over. Oh God. In her rush to get the girls out onto the lawn, she hadn't made them put on any sunscreen – and they'd been in the pool all morning, washing off any protection they might have had. No wonder Tilly looked like a lobster.

Claire rushed across holding her daughter by the hand. Mercifully Hettie and Alex looked relatively unscathed. 'We should of been wearing hats,' she said piously, then looked up at her mother for approval. 'We do that at school.'

'Oh darling, does it hurt?' Claire looked at Tilly in horror.

'Yes, and I feel a bit sicky too. Can I have some ice cream?'

'Maybe later,' said Amy as David strode over. 'First we need to cool you down and put on some suncream.'

'It's a little late for that, isn't it?' snapped David, taking Tilly by the shoulders and leading her away. Amy noted that he didn't look in her direction. He didn't need to.

'Is Tilly going to get cancer?' asked Hettie. 'That's what Miss Baker at school said. She said if you don't wear hats and cream you die of cancer.'

'No, Hettie,' said Claire. 'Tilly's just a bit burnt. She'll be fine.'

Amy mouthed 'sorry' to Claire, then turned towards the house, walking quickly so no one could see the tears running down her face.

Chapter 13

Tilly was finally asleep, breathing gently in and out, one arm thrown around Mr Lion, today's favourite toy. Cool towels draped over her face and forearms had lowered her temperature, and the cream from Max and Claire's huge medicine cabinet had taken most of the sting from the burns. Alain, Max's driver, had been in the medical corps in the French military, and his gentle bedside manner – plus his prognosis that Tilly would peel a little but would otherwise be fine in a few days – had calmed both the little girl and her parents. Well, Amy at least. David was fuming, and this time, Amy couldn't really blame him.

She reached across and pulled the sheet a little higher. Without the pink skin, Tilly would have been perfect, and this moment – mother and daughter at the end of a long, warm day – would have been perfect too. It was Amy's favourite time of day, no question. Working mums got precious little time with their kids, and what they did get was concentrated at either end of the day, compressed like a handful of multicoloured Plasticine. Each moment with Tilly was a bubble of intense joy although it was often accompanied by a sense of exhaustion or the nagging feeling that she had to shoot off to do something

Today was no different, so there was both relief and

sadness when Tilly had finally flaked out. Amy sat there on the edge of the bed, stroking her daughter's perfect head, trying to hold the image in her head like an overexposed photograph. She was painfully aware that her time with Tilly was slipping through her fingers. Where had that tiny baby gone, the toddler with the golden hair and the single tooth? Disappeared already, passed into memory while she was fretting about cover lines and captions. She bent her head, listening. Air in, air out. Right now, it was all she asked.

She tugged the sheet over Tilly's shoulder and dropped a kiss on her forehead, then got up and went back to her own room. As she closed the door behind her, she heard a splash from outside, the slap and ripple as someone entered the water. She walked to the window and looked out. There were lights strung between the trees and underwater lighting in the pool, and she could see Josie diving beneath the surface, her body distorted, stretched by refraction, the green water churning as she surfaced and stroked effortlessly one end to the other – a tumble turn, then back again.

Where had she learned that? wondered Amy. Not at the Mermaid, surely, the crappy municipal leisure centre on the outskirts of Westmead, all cracked tiles and veruccas. You couldn't move for kids bombing and dunking each other most weekends; certainly no room to perfect a decent crawl. But then Amy hadn't been back to the estate in years; the sporting facilities in the area could have come on in leaps and bounds for all she knew. She stood watching Josie's sleek body cutting through the water – swish, swish, duck, swish, swish – and felt unsettled. There was no sense to it, no reason to suspect anything about her. But still there was that nagging sensation.

There was a click and David stepped into the room.

'She's so lovely, isn't she?' he said.

Amy's brow clouded. 'Josie?'

'Josie?' said David with surprise. 'I'm talking about Tilly. I've just been in to check on her.'

'Oh,' said Amy, looking down at the pool.

He walked across, glancing over her shoulder. Just a peek and a grunt: no interest. But then he would do that, wouldn't he?

'All right,' he said finally. 'Out with it. What's wrong?'

Amy shrugged. 'Nothing,' she said.

'Come on, you haven't spoken to me all evening.'

'You embarrassed me. At the shoot. Implying I was a bloody bad mother in front of everyone. About the cream.'

'I didn't mean it like that. But come on, Amy. She was burnt to a crisp.'

'I put suncream . . .' She stopped. There was no point trying to convince him. And anyway, it would have been a lie. She'd simply forgotten. People did.

'Look, I'm sorry, okay?' she said. 'I didn't mean any harm; we were all just having such a good time and . . .'

David took her gently by the arms. 'I know, honey,' he said. 'It's just that the stakes are so much higher when it's Tilly, aren't they?'

She moved to pull away, but he kept hold of her.

'Amy, everyone knows you're a great mother,' he said firmly. 'Beautiful and brilliant. If Tilly grows up to be half the woman her mum is, then I'd say we've raised a pretty sensational human being.'

Amy looked at him and nodded. She wasn't sure if the situation had been reversed that she would have been so understanding. 'Thanks,' she said. 'You're pretty good too.' She turned back to the window.

'So what else is bothering you?'

She looked down at the water, blue black in the moonlight, ripples spreading slowly to the edge. Should she mention it? From this distance, it all seemed so stupid.

'Look, I'm sorry, but I just didn't like the way you seemed so cosy by the pool this afternoon.'

'Cosy? Who?'

'You and Josie.'

'What?'

Amy didn't say anything.

'I was acting! Playing some stupid role for the camera.' He stepped towards her, but she wriggled away. 'Come on Amy,' he said, staring at her. 'What's going on here? You're jealous of the nanny now?'

She shook her head, struggling to put her feelings into words. 'There's just something . . . not quite right about her. I feel on edge having her here.'

She stopped herself, not quite sure why she'd said it. Yes she'd felt jealous by the pool, but that sounded . . . well, neurotic. Crazy, even. She looked up at him expecting accusations, but he just smiled and put his hands on her shoulders, gently massaging the knots.

'I know it's weird when we're so used to Claudia, but Josie's helping us out, remember? We asked her to come, not the other way around.'

'I know all that,' said Amy, arching her back, enjoying his touch. 'It's just it looked . . . like she was flirting with you. She was flirting with the photographer, too.'

David laughed. 'Honey, she's just a child. I think I can manage to control myself. And anyway, Tills loves her.' He turned Amy around to face him, his hands still working on her neck. 'And do you seriously want to spend the whole holiday staging Red Riding Hood?'

She gave a soft laugh. 'No, not really. I mean, I loved it while it lasted, but it's so *exhausting*.'

'Exactly,' said David. 'And as you have other things to be doing . . .' He nodded towards the notebooks and papers strewn over her side of the bed.

'David, you know why I'm doing this,' she began defensively, but he held up a hand.

'Not a criticism, don't be so sensitive. My point was that the application is important to you, and without Josie's help, it won't get done. You can't have it both ways.'

Amy pulled a face. She hated it when he was right.

'Look, I'd rather it was just us too,' said David. 'But it is what it is. We have to make the best of what we have, right?' He bent to kiss her nose. 'And don't forget that you gave her this opportunity out of a desire to help her pull herself up out of the same place you came from, which was – and is – a nice thing to do.'

'I suppose. But—'

'No buts,' said David, crossing to the bathroom and closing the door.

Amy looked out of the window, then instinctively ducked back. Sitting on the edge of the pool, long legs trailing in the water, was Josie. And she was staring straight up at their room.

Chapter 14

Today, the village was almost unrecognisable. Sleepy and off the beaten track, Lourmarin was not usually a draw for day trippers beyond the chateau on the outskirts. But then came market day, and it was as bees descending on a hive. The lanes were crammed with stalls piled high with everything from olives and wine to hand-fired ceramics and rustic furniture, each one besieged by eager punters buzzing and shouting and waving wads of cash. Getting from the little playground to the square – usually a two-minute stroll – had taken Amy and Juliet fifteen minutes, elbowing the basket-wielding Frenchwomen out of the way. And that was another curious aspect of the village: even the tourists were French. None of the usual mix of Germans, Spanish and Brits; Amy could have sworn she had heard nothing but the local rolling dialect in the week they had been here.

'I think the kids deserve an ice cream, don't you?' said Juliet, tugging Hettie and Alex through the crowd and out into a narrow space next to a deli.

'Ooh, yes, yes! Can we?' sang the children almost as one.

'Of course,' smiled Amy, nodding to Josie, who dutifully took the drooling children into the shop, where they pressed their eager faces against the counter, shouting out the names of flavours they wanted.

It had been two days since the photo shoot, and perhaps sensing Amy's unease with her, Josie had wisely kept herself in the background. Amy took a minute to study her now. Her beaten-up tennis shoes, thin ankle chain and pretty sundress, ever so slightly sheer in the fierce midday sun, was hardly the look of an overt temptress. It wasn't her fault that she looked fresh and sexy in the simplest of clothes, and it was not as if the girl had actually done anything wrong. Amy found herself feeling bad.

'Look at these,' said Juliet, wandering over to the shop next door, inspecting a case of silver and jade jewellery. There was a gorgeous green gemstone hanging from a gold chain that immediately caught Amy's eye, but her first thought was how it would look photographed on a velvet cushion across a double-page spread. She knew that David's dire predictions about getting over-stressed about the *Mode* application had come true. She couldn't think about anything else and had spent the past two days obsessively scribbling in a series of notebooks.

'It's a yes from me,' she said, pointing at the green stone.

'Yes to what?' boomed a voice, and Max put his arms around Amy and Juliet's shoulders. 'To a Maxie sandwich? I know you've both been dying to ask all these years.'

Juliet picked up Max's hand with her finger and thumb, her face pinched as if it were a dead rat. 'The jewellery, Max. Mind out of the gutter, please.'

'See anything you like?' asked David, joining them. Amy pointed out the green pendant. 'Hmm, that'd go with your eyes.'

'But my eyes are blue.'

'It's wotsit,' he said. 'Complementary, isn't it? Like a feature wall.'

'Thanks,' said Amy, smiling to herself.

'That's lovely,' said Josie, slowly licking an ice cream. 'Is it real gold?'

David bent closer to the cabinet, then took a sharp intake of breath. 'At that price, you'd hope so, wouldn't you? I thought little village markets were supposed to be full of bargains.'

'Not on market days,' said Max. 'I'm sure they double the price for the day trippers.'

'Are we day trippers, Uncle Max?' asked Tilly, holding out her dripping cone for him to lick.

'No, darling, we're practically natives.'

'What does natives mean?'

'It means people who live here.'

Tilly frowned up at Amy. 'Are we living in French now?' she asked.

Amy laughed. 'No, darling, just on holiday.'

'Can't we stay? I like it here.'

'No, precious, Mummy and Daddy have work in London . . .' She stopped, her head suddenly spinning. It was as if all her blood had drained out of her, and she reached over to a stone wall to steady herself. The others had already walked on ahead, and the noise of the market seemed to press around her, locking her in a muffled bubble of sound: alien accents, shouts and cries.

She tried to focus; wanted to shout out for someone to give her a glass of water or a chair to sit down on, but no one seemed to pay any attention to the stylish English lady who was struggling just to stand. Snapping her eyes shut, she began to breathe deeply, forcing her lungs to fill with air. It was a hot day and she could feel the sun burning on the nape of her neck. A touch of sunstroke, that was all it was. She just needed to rehydrate and have a lie-down.

She could see David up ahead, holding Tilly's hand at a stall selling a selection of paper kites. Tilly was smiling, happy at her father's side with her ice cream and her friends to play with. Amy made her way over.

'I'm going back to the villa,' she said quietly, rubbing her tight chest.

David spun around. 'Already?'

'I don't feel great.'

'What's wrong?'

'I feel a bit sick and dizzy.'

'I'll come back with you.'

She squeezed his shoulder and forced a smile. 'Don't be silly. Stay with the others. I'll just go for a little lie-down.'

'Are you sure?'

She nodded. 'I'll just slip off, otherwise Max will make a fuss.'

'I'll cover for you.' David winked.

It was just an ordinary washbag. Stripy, with a gold zip, stylish enough, but not the sort of thing that would make anyone uncomfortable. Yet Amy stared at it sitting on the bathroom sink, butterflies blooming in her stomach.

'This is silly,' she whispered, reaching for the bag and unzipping it, quickly emptying the contents. Miniature soap and body wash, travel toothbrush. And half a dozen BlissVit vials and a box of syringes. She had been worried about putting Dr Al Saraf's vitamin boost kit into her hold baggage, but clearly no one had bothered to X-ray it, or perhaps vitamin shots were a common item in French women's luggage, along with flimsy lingerie and Gauloises.

Remembering Dr Al Saraf's instructions, she pulled up her skirt and exposed the side of her right buttock. Not very dignified, but then medication rarely was. Opening a vial, she used a syringe to draw up the liquid, then, tapping the barrel, squirted a stream of the fluid into the air like the fountain in the courtyard. Pressing her lips into a grim line, she jabbed the needle into her buttock and pressed down.

She had always been dubious about the various procedures her friends and colleagues seemed to use with abandon – Botox, fillers and vampire facials – and had so far steered away from them, preferring expensive creams and a constant bottle of Evian water on her desk. Six months ago, she doubted she would ever have used anything like BlissVit, but when everyone else seemed to be doing it, when she just needed something to help manage the stress and keep her energy levels up, it seemed like a quick-fix solution to her needs.

She wrapped the used syringe in tissue paper and pushed it to the bottom of the chrome bin. Wouldn't want Max and Claire's cleaner to jump to the wrong conclusion, although Amy was sure that working in this household, an important attribute was being unshockable. Then she sat back and closed her eyes, but although she tried to imagine the goodness pumping around her bloodstream, she didn't feel any different. Actually a little more nauseous, if anything. Disappointed, she grabbed the vials and needles and stuffed them back into the bag, zipping it up and shoving it into the back of the bathroom drawer.

She wasn't sure if it had been sunstroke back at the market, but she wasn't entirely surprised that she had almost passed out. Exhaustion had been creeping up on her for weeks. Juliet had been right that she hadn't had a holiday for a year; she had even worked over Christmas. The office had been officially shut, but Amy had spent the time reading the competition and planning future issues, wanting to start the new year with six months of future issues planned.

Clarity of mind – that was what kept her sane. The key to being in control was being organised.

Sighing, she took in the bomb site that was their room.

Trousers draped over a chair, a shirt hanging from a cupboard door, two – no, three – damp towels just dropped on the floor; another on the desk near her *Mode* application.

'Why are men so incapable of picking stuff up?' she groaned, bending to grab a flip-flop poking out from under the bed.

Admittedly this was her room too, but she had barely spent any time here in the past few days; it was so hot in here, and there was more space to spread out her notes and magazines on the terrace or in the garden under the dappled shade of one of the trees.

She almost tripped over a pair of shoes David had evidently kicked off in a hurry, then scooped up a pair of shorts and a jumper, along with a pair of pants, which she dropped into a carrier bag. Seeing something peeking out from the rumpled bedclothes, she bent – and stopped.

Her heart was immediately in her mouth. Just touching the edge, she knew instantly what it was – *a bra, it was a bra* – and she knew it wasn't hers. Gingerly she lifted the edge of the sheet to look. It was lacy. Pink. Definitely not hers, then. Amy never wore pink; it just didn't suit her.

She sat down heavily on the edge of the mattress, her mind whirring through the possibilities. Another guest had left it behind? No, they had been there a week, and Max and Claire's maid service had changed the sheets twice already. A joke? Maybe David had put it there as a prank. She shook her head. He wasn't that kind of man. He had a dry sense of humour, not the juvenile sort required for practical jokes. Which of course led her to Max. But not even Max . . . He *was* an idiot, but this was far too subtle for him. He might put a live tiger in their bed, but nothing as straightforward as underwear.

'So what then?' she whispered, her head pounding. For a split second, she let the suspicion leak in: had David cheated?

She felt her stomach flip, then drop like the first loop on a roller coaster.

She forced herself to look at the bra again, feeling it in her hand. It wasn't expensive, its scratchy nylon a giveaway that it was from the sort of cheap fashion store where teenagers and students liked to shop.

Josie.

It couldn't be; he wouldn't, would he? After seven years of marriage, this was the first time Amy had ever seriously faced up to the possibility that David might actually cheat. But then why not? Means, motive and opportunity: she had seen enough TV cop shows to know that was the detective's trinity. Means? He was handsome, charming and rich. What else did you need? Opportunity? He worked long hours, went to conferences, hung out entertaining clients in hotel bars; Christ, he could be at it all day for all she knew. And motive? That was the killer, the one where the dark oozed in under the door. Why would he cheat? Because he'd fallen out of love with her? Because she wasn't putting out enough – or worse, she was actually crap in the sack? How would she know? The sex had certainly trailed off in the past few years, but wasn't that normal?

Breathe, Amy, breathe. She reminded herself that the chemistry she had seen between Josie and David at the photo shoot was just acting for the camera. Taking a ragged breath, she crossed to the dresser and stuffed the bra in the back of a drawer. Before she closed it, she took one last look at the offending article, at the lacy edges, imagining David kissing her there, his lips against her skin, his hands feeling for the clasp . . .

'Stop it,' she hissed, slamming the drawer shut.

She had to think logically. The question wasn't whether David *could* cheat – of course he could; any man could cheat – it was whether he *would*. And Amy had no reason to think that. Beyond a few arguments about work on both sides, they never rowed; in fact they seemed to enjoy each other's company a lot more than other couples they knew, who seemed to take every opportunity to get away from each other. So why *was* the bra there?

'Amy?'

David's voice from downstairs made her freeze, air half-way to her lungs. She could hear the sound of his footsteps coming up the stairs.

She rubbed her hands over her face, then, with a final glance at the dresser drawer, she made for the door. It was time to play detective.

Chapter 15

'Are you sure you don't want to come?' Claire said.

'What do I need more cheese for?' smiled Amy, scooping her hair up into a ponytail as she stood at the front door of the villa.

'There's always room for more cheese,' shouted Max from the window of the blue Range Rover. 'What about you, Josie? Camembert?'

Josie shook her head. 'I'm going to hang out by the pool for a bit,' she said.

Amy stood and waved as the Range Rover disappeared through the gates and Josie put on her panama hat and disappeared towards the pool. 'Finally,' she whispered. After an hour of fussing and goodbyes and running back into the house for a wallet and sunglasses and God knows what else, Max, Claire, Hettie and Alex had departed for a wine and cheese run into the village. She'd thought they would never leave.

But now she was alone. Juliet and Peter had gone for a walk, and David had pulled on his Lycra and headed off for a run. Most importantly, as it was Sunday, Josie's day off, she was doing what any young girl would do surrounded by the glorious French countryside: sunbathing by the pool, plugged into her phone.

'Are you okay, darling?' Amy asked, standing at the door of the media room, where her daughter was curled up on the huge cream sofa watching a cartoon.

Tilly nodded, her thumb in her mouth, too engrossed in the action to even reply.

Amy moved fast, running up the stairs, ducking down as she passed the landing window, her heart bumping, her breath coming fast, glad of the opportunity but knowing she only had a small window of time.

Josie's room was right at the top of the house, under the eaves, but with a tiny Juliet balcony and a view of the pool. Staying back in the shadows, Amy peeked out: the girl was still lying motionless on her sunlounger. *Good.*

She scanned the room, but there were few possessions on show. Then again, Josie hadn't arrived in London with much, just enough for a week of work experience. A watch, a hairbrush. There was a packet of cigarettes on the nightstand, which surprised her. She had never seen Josie smoke, never even smelled it on her clothes or her breath. Good at hiding things, perhaps.

She crossed to the dresser and opened the top drawer. It was full of knickers, high-street-branded thongs in an assorted rainbow of fake lace. On the surface they seemed pretty standard stuff for a twenty-one-year-old, but a voice in her head reminded her that they were garments designed to be seen and taken off. Not just sexy underwear, but underwear for sex. Josie had never mentioned a boyfriend, even though Amy had teased her, out of curiosity more than anything. So if these weren't for a boyfriend, who were they for? She dismissed the thought as quickly as it had come to her, reminding herself that she was practically middle-aged, and that even though she had a discount card for Agent Provocateur, she still preferred Marks and Spencer's midi pants.

In the second drawer, she found what she had come for – Josie's meagre selection of bras. Aware that her heart was beating faster, she checked the labels: 32D, the same size as the garment she had found at the bottom of her bed.

Her head swam. She needed air, couldn't breathe. Without thinking, she crossed to the window, forgetting she might be seen, and looked down at the pool. Josie was nowhere to be seen.

'Where've you gone?' she muttered, casting her gaze from left to right, past the line of cypress trees by the orchard to the outbuildings beyond the pergola.

She thought of David, running somewhere around the village, and felt cold. He'd mentioned casually a few days earlier that he liked to do a few warm-up exercises in the shade of the orange grove beyond the pool, and wondered if Josie had overheard him say that too. She turned and ran for the door.

It wasn't until she was tiptoeing down the narrow corridor towards the stairs that she realised how little she had thought this plan through. If Josie had returned to the villa and chose to pop back to her room for any reason, Amy had nowhere to go. She was trapped.

Taking the stairs three at a time, she banged painfully into the wall and bounced off, turning and speed-walking through the library and out onto the terrace, where she forced herself to stop, feigning nonchalance. She felt a flood of relief that she hadn't seen Josie – or rather, that Josie hadn't seen her – but relief immediately turned to suspicion. If she wasn't by the pool and she wasn't in her room, where was she?

As she turned, she caught movement in her peripheral vision: a figure moving through the trees on the far side of the pool house. She followed, keeping her distance, as Josie disappeared into gardens that grew wilder the further away from the house you went.

'Where are you going?' she hissed under her breath, the thought flitting through her head that perhaps David hadn't been for a run after all. Perhaps they had arranged a rendez-vous, a tryst. Out here was the perfect place, she thought.

She came to a fence; beyond, she could see the orchards that flanked the house to the south. She pushed her way through a rusty iron gate, taking care not to make it squeak. The fruit trees were not long off harvest, their branches heavy with lemons, oranges and pears. And now she could see where Josie had been heading: a small group of green wooden loungers set in a semicircle where the trees gave way to gently sloping fields and a luscious view of the valley in the distance.

Crouching behind a trunk, she watched as Josie settled on one of the loungers and opened her tote bag to pull out her headphones. She was just about to put them on when she seemed to have a change of mind and, crossing her arms, pulled her skimpy top over her head, quickly followed by her red bikini: one from the shoot, Amy noted. Fascinated, she stared at Josie's topless form. Even from this distance, she could see the tight mounds of her breasts and her small, perfectly round nipples.

An image came into her head. Was this what David wanted? Was this what he saw as Josie lay back on their bed, naked and covered in a light sheen of sweat? She imagined her husband's head lowering to the girl's nipples, sucking at them like warm cherries; hungry hands parting Josie's thighs, easing himself into her as she moaned his name over and over. Telling him that this was what she had wanted from the first moment she had seen him. *Yes, David, yes.*

Amy would have had to be blind not to notice the chemistry between them at the pool that day. It had always been there, she just hadn't wanted to see it.

She stopped, turning her head. Had she imagined it, or had she just heard her name being called? No, there it was again. She swivelled around. It was coming from the house.

She glanced over at Josie, but the girl was now lying back, headphones over her ears, oblivious to everything but the sun kissing her naked skin.

'Amy!'

She backed away, out of the orchard, through the gate. The shouts were more insistent now – and she recognised the voice. David. So he hadn't gone for a run, she thought, feeling suddenly filled with righteousness. She could see him standing by the pool, facing the house, and quickened her pace, ready to tell him exactly . . . but then she saw Tilly standing at his side.

'There's Mummy!' the little girl cried, pointing. David whirled around, and Amy saw the anger creasing his face.

'Amy, where the hell have you been?'

'Nowhere, I was just . . .' She gestured vaguely behind her.

'I came back from my run and found Tilly sitting on the edge of the pool!'

Amy's eyes widened, looking to her daughter with alarm. Tilly pouted up at David. 'But I didn't go in, Daddy.' She looked at Amy and beamed. 'I'm not allowed without an adult,' she said, proud to be able to recite the rules. Then she frowned. 'Why's Daddy angry?'

'He's not angry with you, darling,' said Amy, looking up at David. 'I think he's angry with me.'

'Damn right I am,' he hissed, then thought better of it and bent to look at Tilly. 'Why don't you go back and watch the farm thing on the TV, Tills? I'll be up in two minutes.'

Tilly nodded. 'Are you going to tell Mummy off?'

David shook his head slowly. 'We're just going to have an adult talk.'

'Okay,' said Tilly, running off up the terrace steps.

Once she was gone, David turned back to Amy. 'So where the hell were you?'

'I only left her for a minute. She was happy watching her programme.'

'What if she'd slipped? What if she had slipped and fallen into the water without her armbands?'

'You're being melodramatic, David.'

'Am I? She's five years old, Amy. She can't swim. You can't just piss off and leave her when the mood takes you.'

'I didn't—'

'You didn't what? Didn't leave her?'

'God, David, you can be such a sanctimonious prick sometimes,' she snapped, all the anger and frustration she had built up imagining David and Josie together spilling out. 'You're the one who wanted to go off running; you could have stayed and watched Tilly, you know.'

'You really can be unbelievably self-centred at times, d'you know that?' David shook his head in disgust and turned towards the house.

'Me? Selfish?' shouted Amy, following him. 'You're the one insisting that I do exactly what *you* want.'

He stopped and looked at her. 'Is this about the pact? Amy, we had an agreement and it wasn't just for my benefit. You're overworked and stressed out, and it's not healthy for anyone, least of all Tilly – as I think we've just seen.'

She glared at him. 'And now I'm a bad mother too?'

David rubbed a hand across his brow. 'You're putting words in my mouth,' he said. 'You're a wonderful mother, but you've got to look after yourself too. And this bloody job application is exactly the opposite of what we're supposed to be doing here.'

Deep down Amy knew that what he was saying had some truth, but she was too wound up, too irritated by his controlling manner.

'I knew you hated me going for the *Mode* job,' she spat, jabbing a finger at him. 'If you have a problem with it, why don't you just tell me?'

'I'd rather you didn't spend half your holiday doing job applications, true. But I do understand that you can't control when the jobs come up. What I do have a problem with is that you seem to have become obsessed with it. Obsessed to the point that you've neglected our daughter.' It was his turn to point at Amy. 'And I don't just mean today either. How often have you been swimming with her or read her a story since we've been here? You couldn't even spare five minutes to sit and watch her cartoon this morning because you had something more important to do.'

He looked at her, eyes narrowing, then glanced over her shoulder, only just seeming to register that she had come from the direction of the grounds, not the terrace, which was her usual place to work.

'What *were* you doing anyway?'

'Nothing! I was . . . I was walking around the garden. Is it so bad that I need five minutes to myself sometimes?' She felt herself grimace. Was that really the best she could come up with?

'Amy, it's not that—'

'All right, David, I get it,' she said, cutting him off. 'I'm the world's worst parent and I almost killed our daughter.'

Anger flared in his eyes, then his expression softened.

'I know you're under pressure,' he said, taking a step forward, arms reaching for her.

'I don't need your bloody sympathy, David,' she growled, dodging his approach.

'Amy, I was only trying to—'

'I know what you were trying to do,' she snapped, stalking back up the steps towards the terrace. 'I'm going to check on Tilly.'

'Amy, please,' said David to her back. But she just kept on walking.

Chapter 16

Amy wasn't sure what she'd been expecting, but the lavender festival was astonishingly lavender-heavy: stalls selling lavender soap, lavender scent, lavender pillows; even the baguettes on the bakery stall were lavender-infused. There was a parade of local farmers in traditional dress: berets, waistcoats and knotted kerchiefs for him, full skirts and bonnets for her, all driving tractors or horse-drawn wagons, each decorated with huge armfuls of lavender or sculptures of stags and horses twisted from the stalks. Tilly and the twins loved the spectacle, running around in circles, whooping and laughing. The only thing they didn't like was the ice cream, which tasted of flowers.

Josie trailed in their wake and Amy stole glances at her, then at David, when she knew she would be unobserved. She had been stewing on the bra, on their argument, for days. If they were having an affair, then they were damned blasé about it: the only time Amy saw David look at Josie was when he asked her if Tilly was wearing sunscreen. Still, what did that actually mean? One kind of deception was the same as any other, right? If you were capable of shagging in the wife's bed when she was a few dozen steps away, then pretending you had an entirely professional relationship the rest of the time would be a breeze.

Amy clenched her teeth and tried to put it out of her mind. There was nothing she could do about it now. She followed the rest of the straggling group through the stalls and up towards the lavender fields, where, according to the brochure handed out at the entrance, the highlight of the festival – the harvesting contest – would take place. A circular section of field to one side of the festival grounds had apparently been left unshorn, so that the most burly sons of the soil could wield the traditional scythe against the clock; there was even a grandstand positioned to ensure no one would miss the action.

Tilly had run on ahead and came back reporting in a disappointed voice that 'the flowers are all gone'. Another glance at the leaflet – exclusively in French, of course – revealed that the contest was over, having been sensibly run earlier in the day before the sun was too high.

'Ah well,' said Juliet. 'At least we get free lavender.'

A side benefit was that the rest of the field was open for visitors to wander up and down the long rows of lavender and pick as much as they wanted. Max and Peter took one look at the flowers and agreed that they would find a stall that sold wine: 'not lavender wine'. David, Claire, Josie and the children followed, leaving Amy and Juliet alone.

'This is amazing,' said Juliet, taking a deep inhalation. 'It's good to get out of the villa, out of town.'

'Hmm,' said Amy, still distracted.

'How are you feeling?' said Juliet intuitively. 'You've been quiet all week. David said you weren't well the other day.'

'I'm just stressed,' Amy said with a wave of her hand.

'Have you been taking the BlissVit?'

'I have, actually, though maybe I need Dr Al Saraf to up the dose.'

'Are you sure everything is okay?' Juliet persisted. 'I mean with you and David? There seems to have been a bit of an atmosphere the last few days.'

'It's fine. He just thinks I'm obsessed with work.'

'Well he's right about that, isn't he?' Juliet smiled.

Amy paused, then looked at her friend. She *had* to talk about it with someone, had to let it out or it was going to eat a hole in her brain.

'What do you think of Josie?' she said finally.

Juliet immediately looked up, her shrewd eyes searching Amy's. 'Why? What's happened?'

Amy gave a wry smile. That was the downside of knowing someone for twenty years: they could key into every nuance of your expression and voice.

'I found a bra in our bed.'

Juliet laughed, perhaps expecting a punchline, then fell silent when it didn't come.

'Hers?'

Amy shrugged. 'Don't know.' Her voice cracked, and warm tears began to trickle down her face. 'Wasn't mine, that's for sure.'

'Maybe it was Claire's?'

'Why on earth would one of Claire's bras be in the guest bedroom? Besides, Claire's a little bit more enhanced than that – this was 32D.'

'It's a pretty common size,' said Juliet reassuringly. 'They had guests staying before we came. One of Claire's friends, perhaps. 32D wouldn't be so unusual.'

'Perhaps,' said Amy. 'But what if it *is* Josie's? It's her size. I went into her room and checked her underwear drawer.'

'Oh Amy,' said Juliet, stepping over and rubbing Amy's arm. It wasn't consolation, more like disappointment, and Amy pulled away.

'Seriously, Jules, what if they're having an affair under my nose?'

'What's started all this? The bra?'

Amy shook her head. 'No, before that,' she said, trying to think about the question before she spoke. 'The photo shoot maybe. Maybe before that even. Nothing specific,' she admitted. 'It's just a feeling. But have you not seen the way men are around her? Max, the driver, the photographer, the gardener who tends the pool . . .'

'Max pants around anything female with a pulse. Besides, she's pretty, sexy, and men . . . well, men are men.'

Neither of them said anything for a few moments.

'So when is this bra incident supposed to have happened?' Juliet asked.

Amy didn't have the answer to that, but she had spent hours thinking about it.

'Maybe on Monday. Remember we took the kids into the village. Josie stayed behind and Max and David were supposedly playing tennis. But Max is always on the phone, isn't he? What if David crept away and shagged Josie in our bed, what if . . .'

Juliet conjured a tissue and handed it to her, giving her time to compose herself. Amy was glad they were at least five rows away from the nearest lavender pickers.

'You do know this is all pure speculation, don't you, darling? I mean, has there been anything else? Has David been acting differently recently?'

'Like how?' asked Amy, blowing her nose. 'I'm new to all this.'

'The classics: has he been working late? Taking more showers? Buying new clothes or aftershave, hiding his mobile phone? Things like that.'

Amy shook her head. 'Not that I can remember. He always works late, but the other stuff . . . I've been so busy at work, a circus could have rolled into our back garden and I wouldn't have noticed.'

'And do you have any reason to suspect Josie?'

'Nothing beyond a feeling that she's trouble.'

Juliet raised an eyebrow. 'Women's intuition?'

Amy managed an ironic laugh. 'Or just paranoia.'

Juliet walked on, pondering it.

'You do know there's a much more likely explanation, don't you? Max.'

'Max?' said Amy. 'You don't think . . .'

'Rich man with huge house, young girl's head gets turned: it's not exactly an original story, is it? Plus if we add Max's serpentine morals . . .'

'But why do it in our bed?'

Juliet shrugged. 'Better than his own with Claire on the property. And Max is exactly the sort to get a thrill from doing the mother–daughter double.'

Amy looked up sharply. 'Max and Karen?'

'That's what he told me.'

'Really?' Amy frowned, her mind flying back to that long-ago night. 'I'm pretty sure Karen told me that Max tried it on at the ball but she told him to get lost. Then Lee turned up so I'm fairly certain nothing else happened.'

'Who's Lee?'

'Karen's old boyfriend from home.'

Juliet looked sceptical. 'Why would Max lie?"'

'He had his stud reputation to protect. He was never going to admit that Karen knocked him back.'

'Either way,' added Juliet, 'it could have been Max and Josie in your bed. Frankly, Max and anyone. Or it could even have been Alain the driver, or the gardener. Don't jump to conclusions.'

Juliet was right. Amy had seen Josie talking to the gardener just a few days earlier. He was a handsome young man, who often worked with his top off. It wasn't a stretch of the imagination to think something had happened between them, and perhaps, for some twisted psychological reason, Josie had wanted to do it in Amy and David's bed.

Juliet tilted her head to one side. 'Darling, I've known David longer than most – longer than you, even. He has his faults, but he's loyal. I can't think of a single time he cheated on a girlfriend, even the dreadful Annabel, and that's saying something over twenty years. Besides, he adores you.'

Amy pulled a face, then nodded. 'I know. And I feel awful even thinking it, but what other conclusion am I expected to come to?'

Juliet took her arm and began leading her along the rows of fragrant purple flowers.

'Look, if you're uncomfortable about Josie, why don't you just get rid of her? Say you want to spend more time with Tilly, buy her a ticket home.'

'I can't, Jules,' said Amy.

'Why not? I thought you'd finished the application.'

'It's a favour to Karen.'

'Oh for goodness' sake.'

'She's my friend, Juliet.'

'*Was* your friend. You did them both a favour and now you're regretting it. Your loyalties should be to your family – to Tilly, to David, actually – not to someone you haven't seen for twenty years.'

'But I don't know Josie has done anything wrong.'

Juliet stopped, open-mouthed. 'Excuse me, a minute ago, you thought she was banging your husband.'

Amy looked back at her. 'But it's just intuition. You said it yourself: I have zero evidence.'

'Then get some. If I was in your position, I'd trust Peter implicitly, I'd dismiss any doubts. Then I'd wait until he went out and go through his emails.'

Amy laughed, but Juliet didn't join in. 'Seriously?'

'I have every faith that David's entirely innocent. But a girl's entitled to make sure, isn't she?'

Chapter 17

It was too hot to be eating outside, even under the pergola. Amy watched as the listless breeze gently moved the linen drapes, the drooping leaves of the sunflowers barely twitching. She wanted to pick up her gilt-edged bone-china plate and fan her face, or plunge her head into the engraved ice bucket. Even wafting one of the tasteful plum-coloured napkins might bring some relief. Claire had made a big effort – after all, this was Peter and Juliet's last night and Amy and David's penultimate one – but even the most controlling *Homes and Gardens* reader couldn't wrangle the Provence weather.

'Isn't it supposed to get cooler at night?' said Amy, wrapping both hands around her beading glass. 'It must still be thirty-five degrees and it's, what? Nine o'clock?'

David laughed. 'It's not that warm. I think you're just a bit drunk.'

'Maybe,' she said, although it was true that she'd had at least two more glasses of wine than usual, partly due to thirst, partly in an attempt to calm her clanking nerves. Despite Juliet's calm reassurance about David, she was on edge. Even though she had failed to catch him in the act, everything David did made her paranoid, running each innocuous comment or gesture over and over in her head, looking for meaning. She had already picked apart the conversation they'd had about the photo shoot. What had he said? Something about how helping Josie was a good thing, how she'd promised Karen. And he'd said he *liked* her, hadn't he? Or was that Tilly, that Tilly liked her? It was all so jumbled up in her head. If only she'd taped it, she could have played it back, checked for clues.

'It gets hotter than this, let me tell you,' said Max, his words running together. If Amy was tipsy, Max was definitely drunk; no real surprise there, since he'd started about lunchtime with his patented cocktail on the way to the festival. 'I have to sleep bollock naked with a gigantic fan pointed straight at my knob.'

'Max, please!' cried Juliet, placing the palms of both hands over her eyes. 'I'm never going to sleep tonight with that image in my mind.'

'You haven't been sleeping well as it is,' laughed Peter.

'It's too bloody sultry. It's not just the heat; it's so close, like the air's as thick as butter.'

David looked over at Amy and grinned. 'I actually find it quite sexy, all this heat.'

Amy flashed him a look, but he didn't seem to notice.

'David, not you too!' complained Juliet.

'There's got to be a reason people tend to get more frisky on holiday, hasn't there?'

'Pheromones,' said Max. 'More sweat equals more pheromones, stands to reason. And when you've got world-class pheromones like mine, who can say no, eh, Claire?'

Claire gave him a sarcastic smile. 'Not when you're passed out naked with the fan on full blast, no.'

'Looks like we're in for a party tonight!' shouted Max, banging the table.

David stood and raised his glass in toast. 'Here's to Max for the house, to Claire for this wonderful spread, and to

Max's fan for dealing with his naked horridness without complaint.'

They all clinked glasses and David was just sitting down again when he raised a hand in greeting.

'Hey, Josie, everything all right?'

Everyone turned. Josie was standing awkwardly at the edge of the light cast by the pergola.

Amy felt her hand clench into a fist at the sight of her. She was wearing a black kaftan with a thin sequinned collar, one that Amy instantly recognised from the Quinn collection. In the daytime, by the pool, it was a pretty cover-up, the sort of thing that thousands of women packed in their holiday suitcase to throw on at the beach. But tonight, backlit against the soft outdoor lights, the garment was completely transparent, showing off Josie's black bra and pants underneath, the curve of her breasts, the dark hollow of her belly button. It made her look seductive and dangerous.

Amy glanced over at David and saw that he had noticed the kaftan's sheerness too. She wasn't sure, but she thought she could see his cheeks colour in the low light, the slight nervous tremble of his hand as he raised his wine glass to his lips.

'The twins and Tilly are all sound asleep and I have this.' Josie held up the baby monitor.

'In which case, pull up a chair and come and join us,' said Max, getting to his feet. 'Seems mad you being stuck upstairs when we're all down here.'

He grabbed a glass and handed it to her as Josie sat down, perching nervously on the edge of a chair as if she expected to be sent away at any moment. Amy looked at her, wishing she could do exactly that, but they were all fussing around the girl, trying their best to make her feel included. Claire admired her earrings, Peter brought her some strawberries, and even Juliet asked her about her time at Vervo.

'So, Josie,' said Max expansively. 'How have you enjoyed Provence? Good job you were at David's when that poor nanny had her accident. Does anyone know how she is, by the way?'

'Claudia's fine, since you were asking,' said David, heavy with irony. 'The arm's mending nicely. The ankle too. She's up and around with a walking stick.'

'How come you were staying with David and Amy in the first place?' It was typical of Max to wait until Josie's final few days to ask her even the most basic of questions.

'Josie is my friend's daughter, Max. I've already told you. I helped her out with some work experience.'

'Friend? Which friend? Anyone I know?' he said with a slight raise of the brow.

'My friend Karen from Bristol. She came to the house once . . .'

'*Karen* Karen. Fuck. I thought there was something familiar about you. *Ball* Karen.'

'Yes, Max, that Karen,' said Amy. 'Josie did brilliantly well as an intern—'

Max burst into delighted laughter as his brain finally caught up.

'You're Karen's daughter!' he hooted, throwing both hands in the air. 'Fuck! I knew I recognised you. Karen. I took her to the Commem Ball in our final year.' His face broke into a lecherous grin and his hands described an egg timer figure. 'She was . . . Well, I can see where you get it from.'

'Max,' said Peter. 'Button it up, old man. You're embarrassing the girl.'

'Embarrassing? She should be proud! Karen was sexy in a . . . Well, she was sexy anyway. Isn't that a compliment?'

'Leave it, Max,' said David, lowering his voice. 'I'm sure Josie doesn't want to hear that about her *mother*.'

Amy glanced across at David, annoyed that he was defending Josie all of a sudden. Yes, Max was being an arse, but did he have to step in? Couldn't the girl look after herself?

Juliet defused the situation by telling Josie the story about how Max had been woken from his drunken stupor in the bath and press-ganged into asking Karen to the ball, then skilfully segued into asking about Josie's time at university and starting a discussion about the importance or otherwise of education in the internet age. Max sat glassy-eyed, seemingly having drunk himself to a standstill, and David said pointedly that he thought everyone could do with some coffee. As he stood up to go to the kitchen, his phone fell out of his pocket without him noticing. Juliet bent down, picked it up and handed it to Amy.

'You should probably look after that,' she said.

Amy knew what she meant. 'I think I'll just check on the children,' she said, and got up from the table. Making sure that David was still in the kitchen, she practically ran up the stairs, closing the bedroom door behind her before fumbling the phone out and turning it on. For a banker, David was surprisingly security-averse. He used the same password and PIN for everything, including the TV package, so Amy found herself using his codes more often than her own. She clicked on his messages and began scrolling through them.

'Work, work, me,' she whispered absently. 'Work, Max, me, his boss . . . Wow, they never leave him alone . . .' Fingers moving fast, opening anything vaguely promising, she quickly worked her way through the past few weeks, but there was nothing. Nothing at all. Sighing, she clicked onto his email account, flipping down the inbox column, her hope fading. If you discounted Amy herself, and David's secretary Dawn – late fifties, as sexy as a broom – he barely got emails from any women at all, let alone an illicit lover. She supposed she should be outraged or depressed that the world of banking was so very male-dominated – and she also supposed that she should be pleased that she had found no evidence of her husband's imagined affair. He *did* love her, he *was* faithful; wasn't that what she wanted? But whether it was the wine or the heat or the neurotic paranoia she'd managed to stir up within herself, she just felt let down, disappointed. She'd almost *wanted* to find something, wanted to be right, so that all this pain and confusion wouldn't just have been a pointless delusion.

Looking around the room, her eyes fell on David's wallet, squatting like a fat frog on the bedside cabinet. She snatched it up, emptying the contents out onto the bed. Credit cards, a cute photo of the three of them, driving licence, an Oyster card – when did David ever travel by Tube? – a coffee shop loyalty card, one stamp. She opened the money slot: fifty quid in tens, about a hundred euros and a load of crumpled receipts. She smoothed them out: drinks in the village square, ice creams, a slip for a cash withdrawal. And there: a receipt for something from 'Le Visage', 255 euros. She frowned. Le Visage, why did that seem familiar?

Nausea collected at the base of her throat when she realised where she remembered the name from. The boutique next to the ice cream shop. The one she and Juliet had been looking at, the one where Josie had glanced over her shoulder and said she liked the pendant. With David standing right there.

Amy's heart leapt. This was it: she knew it! David had heard Josie admire the necklace and had bought it for her. She looked at the receipt again. No description, just a number. Evidence, Juliet had said she needed evidence. Wasn't this good enough?

'Mummy? What are you doing?'

Amy gasped, clutching a hand to her breast. 'Tilly, God. You scared me. What are you doing out of bed?'

'I had a bad dream.' Tilly rubbed her eyes sleepily. 'Isn't that Daddy's phone? Can I play Happy Mrs Chicken?'

Amy had no idea what Happy Mrs Chicken was. 'No sweetie,' she said, slipping the phone back into her pocket. 'It's bedtime. Come on, I'll tuck you in.'

'Josie likes playing Happy Mrs Chicken with me.'

'I don't give a shit what Josie likes doing,' Amy said, feeling her teeth bare.

Tilly stepped back in surprise. 'Why are you always angry now, Mummy?' she said, her voice wobbling.

'I'm not angry, sweetheart,' Amy said, pulling her daughter into a hug. 'I'm just a bit tired. That's why we came on holiday, to have a rest.'

Tilly yawned, seemingly placated. 'Okay,' she said, her eyelids dipping. 'I'm sleepy too.'

Amy took her back to her room and sat there for a while, stroking her hair away from her face. She was beautiful, perfect, but even here, Amy couldn't stop her mind from straying to dark thoughts. Imagining Josie putting the children to bed. David coming to check on them, pushing her up against the wardrobe, his hands urgently seeking . . . Just because she hadn't found anything in his phone, that didn't mean he wasn't screwing the bitch, did it? He didn't have to be sending her sweet nothings; he could just be grabbing her on the stairs as she came out of Tilly's room, waiting until Amy was deep into her stupid note-making then slipping into the pool house, even behind a bloody tree.

Amy could feel her anger rising, her pressure on Tilly's head increasing. Stop, she told herself, standing up. Just stop. But she couldn't, wouldn't. She was going to find *evidence*, and screw anyone who got in her way.

She left Tilly and crossed back into her own bedroom.

She yanked the dresser drawer open, scrabbling in the back until she found the crumpled bra. 'Exhibit A,' she smiled, holding it up in triumph. Part of her brain was telling her it was a crazy idea as she swayed up the stairs towards Josie's room, but the rest of her wasn't listening. Even so, she pushed on the door gently. 'Hello?' she said. 'Josie?' No answer, just a darkened room, the sounds of conversation and laughter from the garden drifting in through the open window.

She stepped inside, aware that she was walking on tip-toes. I'm allowed to be here, she thought angrily. This is my friend's house, not hers. Why should I be creeping around? The pendant must be in here somewhere. Surely the little madam wouldn't be so brazen as to wear it.

'Amy?'

The light clicked on and she froze, her hands curled around Josie's things.

'What . . . what are you doing?'

She stood up, trying to be dignified. 'I could ask you the same thing.'

Josie frowned. 'But this is my room. Why are you going through my stuff?'

'As if you don't know.'

'I don't, Amy. What are you looking for?' She looked at her hands. 'And why have you got my *bra*?'

Amy held it up like a trophy. 'The bra I found in my bed, you mean?'

Josie looked utterly bewildered. 'Your bed?'

There was another click, and the light in the corridor went on.

'Josie?' called a voice. David's voice. 'Are you up there? Have you seen Amy?'

'She's in here,' shouted Josie, as if the two of them were suddenly complicit.

At once Amy was hit with the terrible knowledge of how this would look to David. She stepped forward, still holding Josie's bra in front of her, but the girl stepped back. 'Look, Josie, I know what's been going on.'

Before Josie could answer, David appeared in the doorway.

'Amy? What's happening? Why are you in Josie's room?' He turned to the girl. 'Josie?'

'Sorry, Mr Parker,' she said. 'I . . . I came up to get something and I found her here in the dark. She was, well, going through my things.'

'Amy?'

'I was looking for the pendant.'

'The pendant?'

'The one you bought for her. She left her bra in our bed, David. Don't try and deny it.'

'What bra? What are you talking about?'

'This!' she shouted, holding it up. 'It was hanging out the side of the bed.'

'And you didn't think to ask me about it first?'

'Oh, so you're admitting to it?'

'No! For God's sake, Amy!' He strode over and pulled the clothes from her grip, then turned back to Josie. 'Listen, I'm really sorry. Amy's had a lot to drink, she's been under a lot of pressure—'

'NO! Don't you dare try and wriggle out of it.'

'Amy!' he said sharply. 'Not here. Come on, we'll leave Josie alone and sort this out in the morning.' He took her arm and began to lead her towards the door. She tried to pull away, but his grip was firm. 'Sorry, Josie, we'll see you tomorrow.'

Amy had expected him to drag her back to their room, but instead he took her out of the side door and across the terrace to the pool house. as far away from the pergola and the diners as possible. He closed the door behind them, the anger coming off him like heat.

'Now do you want to tell me what the *fuck* that was all about?'

'David . . .' began Amy. She was aware that she was slurring even that one word, but he was far too furious to notice.

'You think I'm having an affair with the nanny? Are you *insane*?'

'That slut's underwear was in our room!' she hissed.

'And instead of confronting me about it, you go sneaking about in the dark, looking through her knicker drawer? What kind of fucked-up logic is that?'

'I was looking for the pendant.'

'What pendant?'

'The one you bought . . .' She turned away. 'Oh forget it.'

'No, Amy, I won't forget it. Can't you see how this looks? You've accused your best friend's daughter – half my bloody age, I might add – of sleeping with me, and based on what? A random bra and some imagined jewellery.'

'I found the receipt for the fucking pendant, David!'

'Yeah? So where is this pendant?'

Amy suddenly realised she had no idea.

'If you don't believe me, there's no point talking.'

'I don't need to believe you, Amy, because I happen to know that none of this is true. I'm not having an affair, I've never cheated on you with Josie or anyone else, and I never bought any jewellery. None of that happened.'

Amy couldn't help the tears coming. She wanted to stay angry, but it had turned to despair. 'It did,' she moaned. 'It did happen. I know it did.'

'No, Amy, it didn't.' He held her arms, his expression softening. 'Look, I know you've been struggling with work, and now you've put yourself under even more pressure with this application, but you have to see that it's all in your head.'

'NO!' she screamed, wrenching herself from his grip, and then she was running, running through the gardens, running, running across stones, bare feet running. She ran into the darkness and didn't look back.

Chapter 18

It was cold. Amy would never have believed after that sweltering evening under the pergola that the temperature could drop so dramatically. She pulled the towel tighter around her shoulders and tried not to shiver. Vaguely she remembered reading that alcohol made you colder – or was it dehydrated? She didn't know. She squeezed her eyes shut. She didn't know anything any more.

'I won't cry,' she whispered to herself. 'I won't bloody cry.'

She'd done far too much of that already. After tearing herself away from David, Amy had run and run into the darkness, blindly stumbling over potholes, whipped by tree branches, finally turning her ankle and falling to the ground. She had just lain there on the cold grass, listening to David and the others call her name and quietly weeping in frustration and shame. When they had all given up and gone back into the house, she had hobbled over to the pool house, closing the doors and sinking back into the darkest corner, pulling her knees up so her feet were off the cool tiles. And there she had sat, turning everything over and over in her head until it felt like a furnace, pulsing and ready to melt.

What *had* she seen? What did she really know? What was real and what was imagined? Here in the icy dark, nothing had any substance; everything seemed possible. The world itself seemed intangible and out of reach, as if Amy, in her pool-house ship, were floating away from the lights of the harbour, far out to sea.

She stopped and held her breath as she heard a noise. Footsteps? She frowned, listening. Was someone, or something, outside by the pool? A rat? A fox? A wild boar? She knew they were out here in the countryside, tusks and yellow eyes gleaming.

She gasped and shrank back as the door opened.

'Amy?'

She kept silent, hoping that the dark figure would shrug and leave, but instead there was the blinding flash of a torch lighting up the interior.

'There you are,' said Peter, stepping inside and closing the door. 'I was worried.'

Amy blinked and rubbed, trying to scrub the dazzling orbs of white from her eyes.

'Peter, I—' she began, but he clucked his tongue.

'I know, I know, you want to be left alone. Fair enough. Just wanted to check you were still alive.'

Amy snorted. 'I thought you were a wild boar.'

'First time anyone has called me wild before.' He smiled and took a seat beside her, leaving his torch pointing at the wall so she could see him.

'Want to talk about it?' he said after a moment. 'Or I can just leave . . .'

'No, no, stay,' said Amy. She'd had enough of being alone. 'I've just been sitting here trying to sort things out in my head, but none of it seems to go together.'

'Ah, the old jigsaw puzzle,' said Peter. 'You'll laugh at this, but I've had a few dark nights of the soul myself.' He held up a hand before she could reply. 'I know, silly old Peter, born with a silver spoon and an allowance, what can he have to worry about?' He shook his head sadly. 'I won't bother you with it, of course, but believe me, I've been where you are from time to time and I recognise the look.'

'The look?'

'Oh, despair, misery, my-world-is-at-an-end, all that rot. And it is all rot, Amy. May not feel like it now, but whatever's bothering you, it will sort itself out in the end. You never see a skeleton in a tree, do you?'

Amy shook her head. 'I'm sorry, what?'

'Oh, it's the old thing about how the fire brigade used to roll out to calls about cats being stuck in trees, sirens and bells, winding out the ladder and so on. But they stopped coming once they'd worked out you never see a dead cat up there in the branches. Cats – and people, for that matter – always find a way of getting back to safety.'

Amy laughed feebly. 'You're right. I do feel like I'm stuck right now. But I can't see a way down.'

He chuckled and then looked more serious. 'If you're honest with yourself – really honest – you generally know what's going on and who's telling the truth.'

'But Peter, I don't,' said Amy.

He gave a sad smile. 'Then think about what you *want*.'

'What I want?'

He stood up. 'The big things are never easy, old stick. That's why you're sitting in an outhouse in the dark trying to work it out.'

He picked up the torch and held out a hand.

'Come on, let's go where it's warm at least, hmm?'

Amy uncurled herself, her legs shaking in protest, and Peter gently took her arm.

'Thanks, Peter. For coming.'

'All part of the service,' he said. 'And don't worry about Josie. Juliet and I are going home tomorrow anyway, so we'll pack her up and take her along. I'll sort out the tickets and so on: one less thing to worry about.'

'Peter, I . . .' said Amy, her voice thick.

'No, no, we'll have no more of that,' he said, producing a handkerchief. 'The dark night is over; it's time to look at things properly in the cold light of day. Are we agreed?'

She dabbed her eyes and nodded.

'And Amy? Do me one favour, because I haven't always been able to do it myself. Be brave,' he said simply.

Amy gave a thin smile. 'I'll do my best.'

'Good enough,' said Peter, and they set off back towards the house, his thin torch beam lighting the way.

Chapter 19

Oxford, 1995

David looked in the mirror and decided he hated white tie. He hated black tie too, hated any kind of suit. Too stuffy, too restrictive, especially with those stupid stick-up collars that left a red ring of chafing around your neck. Thank Christ he hadn't gone to Eton, where they had to wear this ridiculous get-up every day.

'Stand up straight,' said Juliet, adjusting the white bow tie. 'If you slouch, you'll lose the effect.' She stood back with a satisfied look. 'There. Shoulders back and you look almost dashing.'

David snorted. 'I feel like I'm being squeezed into my funeral suit by the undertaker.'

Juliet wrinkled her button nose. 'Certainly smells that way. But if you will hire a suit instead of buying one like a real human, you're going to have to put up with years of sweat and wine spills.'

'I can't afford a bespoke three-piece from Gieves like Pog.'

'Not for long, sweetie. Soon you'll be ruling the universe with all those other thrusting young investment execs.'

David shrugged. 'Maybe.'

Juliet looked at him with surprise. 'Maybe? I thought you'd sewn up a grad position with Annabel's father?'

'Yes, well that's the problem, isn't it? The job's one thing, but it comes with . . . strings.'

Juliet raised her eyebrows over her wine glass. 'Everything not so rosy in the Garden of Eden? Do tell. I did notice you didn't stay at Annabel's last night.'

David turned away to look in the mirror again. That suit, clinging to him like . . . He closed his eyes, but all he could see was Annabel with her arms around him, pulling him down, down, like he was drowning.

'I just wanted a night in my own bed,' he said, not making eye contact. 'You know, tonight's going to be a big one, isn't it? We'll probably be up until dawn, so I wanted to get some beauty sleep.'

'Take more than that,' said Juliet, shoving him out of the way and adjusting her own dress in the mirror.

David looked at her with appreciation, glad that she wasn't pushing the point. That was why Juliet was such a good friend: she knew what he needed, respected it. Annabel would never have let it go, niggling, whining, wheedling it out of him. David sighed. She was a decent enough girl, he supposed. Most people would consider her a catch. She was pretty, connected, rich, the 'right sort': all the boxes were ticked. And yes, she had even provided him with his first opportunity in the City, via her father, for which he supposed he should be grateful. But the truth was, she was starting to get on his nerves.

They had started dating in the second year. Annabel was his first real girlfriend after the frenzy of partying and shagging that was a common pattern for public schoolboys suddenly freed from the constraints of a red-brick adolescent prison: he'd been like a greyhound let out of the trap, chasing any rabbit that caught his eye. Not that it hadn't been fun, but he had been glad to settle down with Annabel, or at least do couply things like dinner parties and little mini breaks; all that running around with a new girl every weekend was beginning to wear him out.

'Another drink?' asked Juliet, waving the champagne bottle.

'Don't see why not,' said David, holding out his glass. 'Plan to get completely ratted tonight. Last hurrah and all that.'

Juliet gave him a sideways look. 'Don't tell me you're getting all nostalgic already. You've spent the last three years slagging off Oxford.'

David laughed. 'Very true, but it's not Oxford I dislike; it's the people. All those red-faced twats with their stupid dining clubs and their ancient little cliques.'

'I think you're describing Max there,' smiled Juliet.

'Yes, I think I am. But there are worse specimens than Maximilian Quinn out there. At least Max has the decency to admit that he's an overprivileged nob and to revel in the role. And at least he's funny. I'm talking about the ones who live in their shiny Oxford bubble, the ones who treat everyone outside it as a servant or a plaything.'

'Well, get used to that, honey pie,' said Juliet. 'Those are the exact people you're going to be working with at Annabel's daddy's firm. And don't delude yourself that you're not in the bubble too, because you are.'

She was right, of course; she always was. David could rely on Juliet to give it to him straight, however uncomfortable it was. And he knew that part of his dissatisfaction with Annabel was that she belonged to that world, and that staying with her was funnelling him into it too. Sometimes he wondered if that was what he really wanted. Although he loved the down-to-earth easiness of their housemate Amy Shepherd, he still adored hanging out with Max. He couldn't actually remember when he'd first become friends with Max; it had been somewhere in that blurry first couple of terms of boarding school. Max, like David, was not a typical Harrovian, from money and privilege. Their parents were successful for sure, but they were first-generation successful, not families who had made their fortunes from land and industry in centuries gone by.

The two ambitious boys had stuck together, and had both got into Oxford, where Max had helped David move into the grandest college circles, getting invited to the best parties, attracting the prettiest girls, and somehow getting someone else to foot the bill for the lot. He'd even introduced David to Annabel, who had subsequently secured him an extremely plum job at her father's bank, a job that paid almost twice as much as the other offers he'd managed to land on the milk round.

'Well I for one am going to miss all this,' said Juliet, gesturing towards the stained ceiling and the curling wall-paper. 'They say school is supposed to be the best years of your life, but as you know, they were pretty shitty for me, while uni has been a blast, much of the time anyway. And you know what? I think we're all going to look back on this and remember it as pretty special.'

'You soppy old romantic,' said David, snatching up the bottle. 'Here, have another drink before you get all teary.'

'Not likely,' chuckled Juliet. 'Weeping's just a waste of good mascara.'

David nodded thoughtfully. Actually he couldn't remember a time when Juliet had ever been emotional, not even in the bad old days of boarding school – her alma mater Beddington specialising in cold showers, hockey before dawn and a strict 'no boys' policy. He'd first met her on the smart public school circuit that revolved around London and the Home Counties: house parties, teen balls and point-to-point racing. Juliet had been vivacious and self-assured even then, and David didn't mind admitting she had been his first crush. Beddington and Harrow were fifty miles apart, but the two of them had kept in touch via a series of letters, monthly reams of banter and confidences, so it had been no coincidence that they had ended up living together at Oxford.

'Earth to David,' said Juliet, clapping her hands, snapping him out of his reverie. 'I asked you if we were going to be stuck with her.'

'Stuck with who?'

'It's *whom*, numbskull. Didn't they teach you anything at school?'

'How to wank without making a sound.'

'Gross,' she said, rolling her eyes. 'The very last thing I want to picture.'

David didn't like to point out that she hardly needed to imagine. After attending so many school dances and birthday parties together over the years, there had, inevitably, been a drunken fumble during a particularly hot and heavy week-end in the Scottish Highlands in the summer before Oxford. But then came the many temptations of Freshers' Week and beyond, and somehow over that first year they had slipped into a much more solid relationship. Juliet was his cheerleader, confidante and, well, best friend – and he tried to be the same for her. It made more sense, especially now they were both poised to step out into the big wide world.

'I was talking about Karen, actually,' continued Juliet, lighting up a Silk Cut and blowing the blue smoke at the ceiling. 'You know, Amy's friend.'

'Obviously I know who Karen is,' said David, reaching forward and taking Juliet's cigarette for a drag, then handing it back. 'What do you mean about being stuck with her?'

'She's gone to the ball as Max's date.'

'What's wrong with that? I mean, apart from having a lot of sympathy for the poor girl.'

'Men,' she said, shaking her head. 'You walk through life with your eyes closed.'

'Huh?'

'Oh come on, think a few steps ahead. Max is either going to try and grope her or he's going to spot some other air-headed filly and disappear. Then she'll be wandering around lost, and seeing as Amy's insisting on playing the working-class martyr, we'll be expected to entertain her all bloody night.'

'I don't get why that's such a problem. Karen's nice enough, isn't she?'

Juliet sighed theatrically. 'It's not who she is. She's fine on a night out to the Bear or wherever, but this is the night, David. Our last night in Oxford, the big send-off. Don't you want it to be perfect?'

David pulled a face. The truth was, he was torn about the ball. Juliet had been right earlier about being in the bubble. Yes, they were friends with people like Amy and Karen, but almost everyone else they spent time with was from exactly the same background as them: private school, skiing holidays, dogs and horses. University was supposed to expand your horizons, but Oxford had a funny way of narrowing them, underlining that sense of privilege and expectation. And while David wanted desperately to escape from that trap, to leave Oxford, to get to London, spread his wings and find his own path, at the same time he was scared to leave the bubble. It was all he'd ever known.

'It's going to be like all the other balls, Jules,' he said. 'A load of nobs in loud waistcoats getting pissed and boasting about how their daddy's house is a tiny bit bigger than your daddy's house.'

'No,' said Juliet firmly. 'It's going to be the best night

ever. It's the end of an era; let's see it out in style, okay?'

David smiled and leaned across to kiss her. 'You're right,' he said. He slipped a throwaway camera into his pocket, deciding that he would try and take some snaps for posterity. This was his last big night at Oxford, and he should try and make it count.

Chapter 20

David looked at his watch, carefully concealing the gesture below the table. Ten thirty: *God*. The night was passing them by. For all his ambivalence about the ball, now that he was here, David was itching to get out there and have fun. Instead he was stuck here eating poached salmon and drinking warm white wine in some terrible parody of a restaurant. 'Dining' they called it, selling it as a VIP ticket for the ball, but despite the floral centrepiece and the candelabra, there was no disguising the low-rent wedding vibe. Or the dull conversation.

'You with us, darling?'

David looked up at Annabel and gave her a weak smile. 'Sorry, miles away.'

Annabel raised an eyebrow. 'I can see that, David,' she said under her breath, then, more loudly: 'Bruce was just asking about your father's yacht.'

'Hardly a yacht,' said David. 'One of those wooden things, a Devon yawl, two little sails, or is it three? Very big on the purity of being one with the winds and the tides, my father. He's always banging on about how boats should be sailed, not moored.'

'Quite right,' said Bruce, fiddling with his cufflinks. 'Will you be at Cowes this year?'

David could already feel himself drifting off, but forced himself to concentrate. He and Annabel had already had one hissed argument by the bar, and he didn't think he could muster the energy for another, not tonight.

'Doubt it,' he said. 'In fact, I rather hope not. I'm starting at Harvey and Keyne next month, so I'm hoping to be in the thick of it by then.'

'H and K, huh?' said Bruce appreciatively. 'Well, don't blame you. Imagine you'll be up with the Tokyo markets and whatnot, hmm?'

'Yes, that's the plan.'

David looked over at Annabel and was rewarded with a wide smile. Clearly the correct answer. Daddy would approve. He stole a glance past her shoulder towards the door of the marquee. In the early dark, illuminated by the red and green stage lights, he could see people weaving about, laughing, shouting, shuffling side to side in awkward dance moves.

'Office is off Cheapside, isn't it?' said Camilla, Bruce's slightly frumpy girlfriend. 'I'm starting at PNH across the road in September. We should meet for lunch. Have you got somewhere to live in London yet? I hear it's frightfully expensive in the centre now.'

David was about to reply when Annabel leaned in and squeezed his hand.

'We have a flat on Cadogan Square. My brother has the ground floor, but he's in Hong Kong most of the time.'

David looked at her in surprise. This was the first he'd heard of a flat. Or rather, he was aware that Annabel's father owned half a dozen desirable places dotted about Mayfair, Chelsea and St John's Wood, but they had never even discussed moving in together, let alone pinpointed a specific place.

'Lovely,' said Camilla with undisguised envy. 'I'd die to be in Chelsea. Bruce and I have been looking at Fulham, haven't we, darling? Until he gets all that pupillage stuff out of the way.'

Bruce had the decency to look as uncomfortable as David felt. 'Yes,' he muttered. 'That's the plan anyway.'

'Going to try and find another bottle of red,' said David suddenly, standing up. Annabel looked meaningfully at his almost full glass, then gave a tight shake of the head. 'Bruce? Millie? No? Won't be a tick.'

He strode across the hall, swerving around the identical long tables of young couples in ball gowns and white tie, all discussing the same things, all heading in the same proscribed arcs. He felt crushed, as if the gravity in the room had doubled.

Out in the quad, he headed to the bar.

'Vodka,' he said to the barman, pulling a tenner from his pocket. 'Make it a double, yeah?'

He flinched as he felt a hand on his shoulder, and turned. Annabel, a look of concern on her face. 'Everything all right, darling?'

'No, not really. I don't appreciate being ambushed like that.'

'Ambushed? Whatever do you mean?'

'Don't play the innocent. All that stuff about your brother's flat in Chelsea?'

'What's the matter with that? I thought you'd appreciate a decent place after living in that fleapit with Max.'

'It's not the place, Bel. It's the fact that you're making decisions about my life without even consulting me.'

She pouted. 'So you don't want to live with me now?'

'Don't try and turn this around. It's not about us, it's about blindsiding me in front of your stupid friends before we've even talked about it.'

'And now you don't like Bruce and Millie?'

David glanced back towards the dining hall. 'They're fine,' he said without much enthusiasm.

'Fine? These are my friends.'

'Come on, Bella. You only tolerate Bruce because his father is in the same club as your father.'

'Well I'm sorry if he's not as exotic as some of *your* new friends.'

Her tone needled him.

'Exotic?'

Annabel didn't respond.

'I hope you don't mean Amy.'

'Well I did hear she might be serving us wine later.'

The smug look on Annabel's face confirmed everything he'd suspected about her attitude to 'other people', her term for anyone who didn't come from exactly the same background as her.

'And Amy being a waitress is wrong how exactly? Because she's working rather than getting pissed? Or because work is inherently distasteful?'

'Oh don't be so silly,' said Annabel, flapping a hand. 'Work is fine in the right context.'

'Working for Daddy's firm is fine, I suppose. Whereas working in a factory or an office is not.'

'Are you calling me a snob, David?'

Yes, I am calling you a snob, he thought. You've always been a snob and so have all your friends. I can't believe it's taken me this long to work it out. She was, however, also the adored daughter of the chairman of the bank he was about to join. He took a deep breath.

'Of course you're not a snob,' he said, downing the vodka in two gulps.

'So why are you so angry about the flat?' she said, reaching up to adjust his bow tie.

'I'm not angry,' he lied. 'Just surprised. Especially as you've spent the last six months planning your trip to Thailand. Aren't you and Sophie leaving in two weeks?'

Annabel shook her head. 'Sophie's mother's taken a turn for the worse, and anyway, Thailand's much too hot. I'd rather be with you in London.' She gave him a suggestive smile. 'Just the two of us, in our own flat, no one to disturb us.'

David turned back to the barman and gestured for a refill.

'But Bel, I won't be there,' he said. 'That was why it was such a good plan you going away. I'm going to be working stupid hours from day one. Hopefully by the autumn it will have settled down a little, but I have to make a good impression from the start.'

She gave a little giggle. 'My businessman,' she smiled. 'Don't worry, I'll have a word with Daddy.'

'NO!'

She flinched as if he had slapped her.

'No, Annabel, you will not have a word with Daddy,' said David. 'I don't want any favours. I want to make my own way on my own merit. Is that too hard to understand?'

She jutted her chin out like a chastened child. 'Excuse *me* for helping you get started in one of the top banks in the City.'

'I appreciate it, Bel, of course I do, but I won't have you telling me where to live and how to run my life.'

'Is that what you think I'm doing?'

David just snorted.

Annabel's eyes narrowed. 'Well if *you* don't want my help, you know there are plenty of men who would be glad to date me.' She turned and stalked back to the dining hall, her shiny dark hair flashing in the light.

David took a half-step forward. His instinct – no, his conditioning – was to follow her, to apologise, his first thought for her feelings and not wanting Bruce and Camilla to think badly of him.

He coughed out a laugh. *Seriously?* Did he really care

what those brain-dead stiffs thought of him? He watched Annabel disappear through the doorway, her back ramrod straight, head held defiantly high.

Yeah? Screw you too, thought David, and headed into the party.

By midnight, David was drunk. After his bust-up with Annabel, he'd headed over to the crowded fug of the main bar, where he'd bumped into Dorian, a prep school friend. Dorian was going out to Stanford to begin a postgrad in something innovative and exciting – information technology, whatever that was – which had done nothing to lighten David's mood. Instead he sought out Max, who he found snogging a ginger girl with braces and a gigantic pink meringue of a dress. Seeing David's face, Max immediately dismissed the girl and ordered a round of tequilas, then led David in an arms-around-the-shoulders chorus of that song about living for ever, followed by the one about being common people, which obviously he found hilarious. David had then made the mistake of going on the waltzer with a couple of blondes from Wadham, feeling both dizzy and vaguely unclean as he stumbled back towards the bar. He stopped in a doorway, feeling the heat of bodies and the pulse of bass in his chest. Perhaps more booze wasn't the answer, he thought. Not right now, anyway. It was a long time until dawn, and he was determined to make it to the traditional survivors' photo at sunrise.

Pulling his cigarettes from his jacket pocket, he turned away from the beer tent, skirting around the side until he found the college cloisters. He lit up and took a grateful drag, the red tip dancing in front of him. Just another of the things Annabel disapproved of. Smoking, drinking anything but champagne, work, poor people, cars with four seats, and using the word 'toilet'. For all her eyelash-batting, she wasn't exactly keen on sex either. But David knew he had painted himself into a corner with his placement at the bank. Harvey and Keyne was as good as it got if you wanted to be in investments – and David did, badly. That was where the glamour was in banking, the high-risk, high-reward engine that powered the finance industry. It was where the real money was made. Not that David wanted to splash the cash on yachts and Rolexes and Lamborghinis; what he wanted was what money could give you: independence, the ability to make your own choices, run your own life. Since the age of four, on his first day at pre-prep, he had been told what to wear, who to talk to, what to say. He'd been through the class machine and come out the other side, shiny and fully formed, ready for a life of luxury and leadership. Ready to make money.

He gave a gentle snort and blew smoke at the sky. The irony was that while a job at H&K might give him financial independence, it came with golden handcuffs: the expectation that he would follow the rest of the script and marry Annabel. The flat in Chelsea would be followed by the house in Gloucester, then two angelic children named Ollie and Lottie. Couple of dogs, a horse or two. A social life that revolved around the local hunt. Did he want that? It wasn't the worst thing in the world, obviously. It was just so predictable. Regimented. *Expected*. And that was what had turned him off the whole gilded Oxford existence: you had to do what was expected.

He looked up as he heard soft footsteps on the grass, saw a dark figure silhouetted against the sky. 'Got a light for a lady?'

He smiled, recognising Amy's voice and feeling his mood lift immediately. She moved into the light and he could see she had changed out of her waitress uniform and into a ball gown, a slinky black number that clung to her curves.

'Wow,' he said.

'Yeah, shut up,' said Amy, sitting next to him and using his cigarette to light her own. 'The best I could do in the Portaloos.'

David stole a sideways glance. Her hair was pinned up, exposing her neck, and he was seized with the crazy impulse to kiss it. It unsettled him. He knew Amy was fit, of course; he wasn't an idiot. You only had to see the reactions of other men when they walked into a bar; but David had never really thought of her like that. They had always been too close as friends, as equals. God, what did *that* say about him?

'Seriously,' he stammered. 'You look amazing.'

Amy laughed and nudged his shoulder with hers.

'God, you are drunk, aren't you?'

'Yeah, maybe that's it.'

They sat in silence for a while, smoking and watching couples stumble about on the grass.

'So why are you sitting here on your lonesome? You lost Annabel?'

David blew smoke through tight lips. 'Kind of on purpose, actually. We had an argument.'

Amy turned to look at him. 'Bad?'

'Dunno. Maybe. I sort of told her I hated Camilla and Bruce.'

Amy hooted with laughter. 'Really? Well it's about time. Whenever those two walk into the room, it's like the end of *The Wizard of Oz*: like all the colour has been sucked from the world.'

'And what about Annabel?'

'What about her?'

'Do you like her?'

'Oh no,' said Amy. 'You're not dragging me into your relationship problems. I side with you and say you're well shot of her, then five minutes later you're back together and

I'm a disloyal bitch. You two sort this out between you.'

'No, but seriously, Amy, I need to know. Do you think we fit well together?'

She looked at him for a moment. 'Not for me to say, is it?'

'Perhaps not, but I respect your opinion, you know that.'

It was true. Amy was one of his social circle, just like Max or Juliet, but it was her opinion he always sought out. What did she think of the film? Did she like the hot new band? Did she think he looked good in this jacket? He asked other people too, of course, but he only really cared what Amy thought. In fact, now that he thought about it, the fact that his entire wardrobe was blue came down to the fact that Amy had once said he suited navy.

'Seriously, David, I can't tell you what to do.' She paused.

'But?'

'But I will say that out of all the people I know, you're the bravest.'

He laughed, anticipating a punchline, but her face remained impassive.

'Brave? I'd say I was the least brave person you've met.'

'Well that's crap,' said Amy. 'Take all this.' She gestured towards the college grounds with her cigarette. 'Oxford. It's the playground of the rich and privileged, right? And you're right at the centre of it, like the dictionary definition of a posh boy.'

He gave a twisted smile. 'Well thanks. Is this supposed to be making me feel better?'

'It should, because you're not like them, David, that's your saving grace. You don't kowtow to those chinless dicks and you don't play their silly little games. Do you really think I'd be friends with you if you did?'

'I was rather hoping that you found my clichéd posh-boy act sexy.'

'Not my thing,' she grinned. 'Still, I'm trying to com

pliment you here. It takes a lot to stand up to your friends and to walk your own line – that's why you're different.'

'But that's just it, Amy,' he said, sitting forward. 'I don't feel I am. I mean, what have I ever done other than what's expected of me? I went to a posh school, I played in the first eleven, I got into Oxford and I walked around wearing a bloody cape for three years. What's so special about that?'

'It's not what you did, it's the way you felt about it. You felt uncomfortable – you feel uncomfortable about it now, don't you? That's why you're sitting here on these steps instead of doing shots with Max. And that's why you're going to leave here and do something special.'

'What, like discover a cure for cancer?'

Amy stubbed her cigarette out, shaking her head. 'Uh-uh. You're too selfish. And not actually bright enough.'

'Hey!' laughed David, pushing her.

'No, I should think you'll still be a banker and you'll still make piles of cash, but you won't be like all the nobs in that marquee.' She turned to look at him, her eyes fierce. 'I walked around this ball for eight hours handing out drinks. D'you know how many times anyone made eye contact with me?' She held up her thumb and forefinger in an O. 'And I think I got three thank yous the whole night.'

David nodded. 'They expect everything to be handed to them because it always has been.'

'Exactly. And is that how you feel?'

'No, I expect to have to work for it. But . . .'

'But you feel bad because you're getting a leg up?'

'I suppose. I mean, I do appreciate the fact that I'm being given an opportunity – everyone needs a break to get their foot in the door. It's just I hate all the baggage.'

'Annabel, you mean?'

He paused, thinking.

'You know what? Bel said something to me earlier tonight; she said, "Plenty of men would be glad to date me", and she was right. She's pretty, she's smart enough in her own way, and she can be good fun.'

Amy raised a sceptical eyebrow and David chuckled. 'Seriously. She makes me laugh. Sometimes.'

'Oi!' laughed Amy, reaching out and yanking his bow tie. David grabbed her wrists and they fell sideways onto the grass, giggling. He felt the warmth of Amy's bare shoulders against him, smelled her skin, looked into her eyes. She stared back, the blue of her irises shining.

'What the *hell* is going on here?'

Their heads whipped around simultaneously. Annabel was standing over them, two tiny fists on her slim hips.

'Annabel,' said David, clambering to his feet. 'It's not . . . We just fell over is all.'

'Yes, it looks like it,' she snapped.

'I'll, um, see you later,' said Amy, smoothing down her dress and walking away.

David turned back to Annabel and found that she was already walking off. 'Bel!' he shouted, running after her. 'Bel, wait!'

He grabbed her arm to spin her around, and as he did, Annabel used the momentum to bring her hand up hard, slapping him across the cheek.

'Fuck you, David. Fuck you and fuck your townie slut!'

David pressed a hand to his face, actually more stung by her words. He had never heard Annabel swear before.

'She's not a slut.'

'Really? Trying to screw someone else's boyfriend? What do you call that?'

'She wasn't trying anything of the sort! And this isn't about her, it's about us.'

Annabel turned to face him, eyes blazing. 'Don't you

dare try and make this my fault!'

There were tears sparkling on her cheeks, and David immediately felt terrible. Annabel was a snob, she was entitled and condescending, but she wasn't a terrible person. She was a cross little princess bred for a life in society; a show pony. She didn't deserve to be hurt like this.

'Annabel, I'm so sorry, truly,' he said. He reached for her, but she pushed him away, turning so he couldn't see her face. 'I didn't mean to hurt you, I just . . . Maybe I'm not the right guy for you.'

'I know *that*!' she hissed. Her face had twisted, her anger erasing her beauty. 'Do you really think I'd let you finish with me?' She barked out a cruel laugh. 'I didn't come here to kiss and make up, you arrogant shit. I came here to tell you that I have phoned my father and told him exactly the kind of man you are. There will be no job at the bank, and I doubt anyone else in the City will touch you now either.'

'Bel, I—'

'Don't you ever speak to me again, David Parker. You have made a horrible mistake – no, *I* made a horrible mistake. You're welcome to that slag. Actually, she's about your level.'

David opened his mouth to defend Amy, but closed it again. It was pointless. Annabel had always regarded anyone not in her own narrow little set as somehow low, dirty, untouchable. Nothing he could say would change that.

'I am sorry, Annabel,' he said sadly. 'I really didn't mean it to end this way.'

She glared at him. 'Goodbye, David,' she said.

She turned and walked into the darkness. For a moment, David stared after her, then a chuckle began to build in his throat. By the time she had turned the corner, he was doubled up with laughter.

* * *

'Obviously you need to get laid,' said Max, splashing more champagne into David's glass. 'It's like the hair of the dog, isn't it? Shagging some other tart – especially one who looks just like her – is the best cure for getting dumped.'

'I'd rather stick pins through my knob,' said David, taking an angry glug of the bubbly. They were sitting hunched over a table in the main bar, by now a bacchanal of half-dressed students dancing on the tables and spurting drinks into the air like dolphins.

'Oof, don't even talk about that,' said Max with a theatrical shudder. 'Tried it once during my grunge phase. Hurts a lot more than getting your ear pierced.'

David managed a half-smile, but his brief euphoria at being released from his crumbling relationship with Annabel had quickly plunged into depression. Aided by the alcohol in his system, his mood was black: no job, no girl, no future.

'Come on, old man, it's not that bad,' said Max.

'Isn't it?'

'No, in fact it's good news. One, you get to shag every girl in Chelsea, two, you won't have to spend valuable week-ends choosing wallpaper, and three, you get to shack up with me.'

'You?'

'Of course!' said Max, clearly delighted with his idea. 'Look, you know I've deferred my start at McKinsey until January, but maybe I can spend just three months in Goa rather than six. I'll be bored by then anyway, seeing as you're only coming out for two poxy weeks. Anyway you know I've already got some digs lined up near the barracks. Very mod – all glass and marble, none of that period rubbish – and plenty of room for you, old boy. I get the en suite, obviously.' He grasped David's shoulder and stared into his eyes meaningfully. 'It's going to be fucking mental. Just you, me and half of Elite.'

'Elite?' asked David, his head beginning to hum. 'What's that?'

'The modelling agency, you sweet moron. All the hottest leggy numbskulls sign up when they're about sixteen. Was thinking of setting myself up as a photographer, get them in for castings, ply them with booze. Pretty foolproof, don't you think?'

Not for the first time, David wondered why he and Max were friends.

'But Max, I don't have a bloody job any more. I can't afford to live anywhere, let alone the middle of London.'

'Not a problem,' said Max, knocking back a shot and grimacing. 'My father's paying the rent at least until those juicy cheques start flowing through. Reckon I can persuade him to cough up for at least twelve months.' He belched and pointed at David. 'And don't worry about the job, either. I'll introduce you to Rory.'

David shook his head.

'You remember Rory. Drinks brandy, head like a bullet. Went out with that girl with the red Aston.' Max was, despite his venal personality, one of those people who collected acquaintances like rare stamps. He was 'close mates' with thousands of people. If they were even vaguely rich or influential, he would contrive to bump into them at a bar or social, carefully maintaining the connection, slapping backs, buying drinks, generally being the life and soul. Then, when circumstance made them useful – family had an empty chalet, say – he would pounce. 'Some people have actual talents,' he had once confided. 'I just happen to have brass balls.' His approach had certainly paid off at Oxford: along with endless party invitations and ins to the most exclusive scenes, he'd even managed to scam his way into a lucrative management consultancy job, even though he was likely to flunk his degree.

'Maxie, I can't keep track of all your so-called mates. What did Rory do again? Was he on your course?'

'Nah, he's a proper brain, graduated in '93,' said Max blithely. 'Went straight over to Lehman's on Wall Street, did six months, then jumped ship to Hong Kong. But his brother heads up recruitment for Nicholson James.'

'The investment bank?'

'More of a boutique outfit than a big multinational. But they're good. I reckon he'd take a chance on a loser like you, assuming you cheer up a bit.'

'Max, I've just split up with my girlfriend.'

Max gripped his shoulder. 'And it's a tragedy, I feel your pain. But life is not a rehearsal, Dave my boy, and we won't get another crack at our last ball in Oxford.' He pressed a glass into David's hand and pulled him up from the table.

'I appreciate what you're trying to do, Max, but I'm just not in the mood. I'd rather go home.'

Max grabbed his lapels and pulled David's face close to his. 'Are you a man or some girlie shirt-lifting ponce?'

'A man, but—'

Max held up a finger to silence him.

'Right then, here's what we're going to do,' he said, raising his voice as he steered David out of the tent and onto the now-packed dance floor in front of the stage. 'We're going to find ourselves some pissed-up fillies with big tits and we're going to dance like randy baboons. Here we go!'

He grasped David's sleeve and thrust him towards a pink-faced girl with frizzy hair. 'David, Helena, Helena, David,' he shouted. 'Now let's dance!'

David looked at the girl and shrugged. For the first song, he gritted his teeth, going through the motions; by the second, he had loosened up enough to clap along. By the middle of the third, when Max appeared with a tray of tequila slammers, he was actually enjoying himself, dipping the frizzy-haired girl and linking hands with one of her friends, a willowy brunette. After that, it all became a blur: a blonde with a drooping flower in her hair, a dark-skinned girl who snogged him then instantly disappeared into the crowd, and a gorgeous ex of Max's who led them all in a crazed conga line to some Euro-disco classic. After a while, he found himself dancing next to someone he recognised.

'Karen!' he cried, pulling her in for a hug. 'Where have you been hiding?'

'Just around,' she shouted above the music. David was aware through his own haze that she was flushed and tottering – hell, who wasn't at this time of night? – but he was glad to see a familiar face. Cheering as a cheesy singalong belted out of the speakers, he grabbed her and whirled her around, laughing, loving the way she laughed back. Annabel had never laughed. Annabel had never shaken her hair or her ass like that. Annabel had never been any fun. The cheesy pop faded to a slower-paced smoochy number, and David pulled Karen closer, staring into her eyes and striking an ironic flamenco pose. She wrapped herself around him, cheek to sweaty cheek, two drunken tango dancers locked in a deathless embrace. He felt her hips grinding against his, the curve of her breasts hard against his chest. One hand stroked her long neck, the other was on her full arse. She smiled, a lazy, sexy smile, and David could feel the desire rise in him, could feel the heat of hers. They moved together as one, two people with a single purpose, hearts beating together.

'Let's go somewhere,' she shouted in his ear, and David felt himself nodding, taking her hand, leading her through the crowds, out past the bar tent, further into the college, feeling the cold on his skin, hearing the music fade. He turned a corner, ducked into a stone archway, and immediately they were on each other, kissing, their bodies locked together. He ran his lips down that neck, tasting the salt, smelling her. Karen moaned and slid a hand under his jacket, pulled out his shirt, fingers on his back, into his waistband, gripping his arse. Annabel had never done that either. He cupped her breasts, pushed his face into her cleavage. She was so sexy. Why hadn't he seen it before? He didn't know, couldn't think straight; he was so hard he thought he might burst.

'Here,' she whispered, her voice hoarse, reaching for his belt, undoing it. 'Fuck me against the wall.'

Why hadn't he seen it before? Because he had always been looking at Amy, because Amy was the one he wanted. In that moment it all seemed so clear, like a white light flicking on. He wanted Amy.

'That's it,' Karen gasped, slipping her hand inside his boxers, gripping his hard cock. David groaned, tried to step back, but somehow he was pushing against her instead, thrusting against her hand. Christ, he wanted her. Yes, he wanted Amy, but at that moment, right now, Karen *was* Amy; they were blurred, like two superimposed images moving in and out of focus.

Karen was wriggling against the wall, pulling her long skirt up and guiding his cock down. 'Do it, do it now, David.'

David. It was that one word that broke the spell. That wasn't how Amy said it. When Amy said his name, it was a good thing, like she was happy to see him, to talk to him. Like she was proud of him.

'No, no,' he said, trying to pull away.

Karen laughed, her hand still on his cock. 'I think you mean yes.'

'No,' he said, stepping backwards and immediately tripping, his feet catching in the rented trousers tangled around his calves. He came down hard on his bum, pulling

Karen down on top of him, her knee catching him in the stomach, knocking the wind out of him.

'Shit!' she cried. 'What the fuck, David?'

'I'm sorry, I'm sorry,' he gasped, pushing himself backwards, trying to get away. 'I just can't, Karen. I'm sorry.'

'What's the bloody problem?' she said. 'I thought you were into me.'

'I was . . . I *am*,' said David, pushing himself up against the opposite wall and struggling to refasten his trousers. 'It's just . . . Amy.'

Her eyes flashed at him. 'What? What's Amy got to do with it?'

'Just don't tell her about this, okay?'

'Are you ashamed of me, is that it?'

'No, no, not at all.' He shook his head. 'I just think it's best if we don't tell her this happened. It'd hurt her.'

'Hurt her?' snapped Karen, clearly annoyed. 'And what do you care about that?'

David pressed his lips together, took a breath. 'Of course I care about Amy, Karen. We both do.'

She looked at him for a long moment, then let out a sigh.

'Sure, whatever you say. Maybe it wasn't the best idea.'

She awkwardly rearranged her clothes, shuffling to smooth her dress back down, then stepped over and kissed him lightly on the lips. 'You are sexy, though,' she smiled.

'You too. But—'

'Yeah, yeah, I know. Amy.' She pulled a face. 'Maybe we should agree not to tell anyone where we were.'

David held out a hand. 'Like a pact.'

She shook it. 'Our secret, yeah? Something to remember the night by.'

He nodded. 'Oh I think I'm going to remember this night for a long, long time.'

Chapter 21

Present day

David put his bag down in the hallway and didn't look at Amy as he took off his coat.

Amy was glad. She didn't want to talk to him either. It had been awkward enough on the plane journey home – both of them directing all conversation at Tilly, who had loved the attention and hadn't felt the atmosphere prickle between her parents, even though Amy and David had been acutely aware of it.

But now, away from the check-in queues and the squashed aeroplane seats, where it was easy to put your nose in the in-flight magazine, Amy was going to have to face up to the fact that she didn't want to be with him in the same room. Didn't want him to touch her, or come near her. If it wasn't for Tilly, she'd have checked into a local hotel, but there was no way of getting round this – she would have to go through it.

'Tills, it's time for you to go to bed,' she said, scooping her daughter up in her arms and breathing in her soft smell for just one moment.

'But I don't want the holiday to be over,' said Tilly, wriggling to get free.

Amy almost laughed at the irony of her daughter's remark. She could feel David looking at her but kept her own gaze fixed away from him.

'It's late, honey. Give Daddy a kiss goodnight and I'll come upstairs and read you a story.'

They were all hot and sticky but Amy couldn't be bothered putting Tilly in the bath. Instead she took her *Frozen* pyjamas out of her drawer and told her to brush her teeth. She sat on the edge of her daughter's bed, feeling momentarily soothed by the surroundings of Tilly's room: the soft moon-shaped night light over the headboard, the rainbow-coloured pile of soft toys, all of whom had a name and, according to Tilly, a personality, the framed drawings on the walls, the glittery princess costume and pink fleece dressing gown on the back of the door. They were heartbreaking in their innocence, a reminder of the reassuringly happy home they'd had before Josie had come into their lives.

Tilly ran back into the room, a white ring of toothpaste still around her mouth, and climbed under the duvet.

'Is Josie going to be our nanny now?' she said, looking at Amy wide-eyed in the low light.

'No, sweetheart. Claudia is coming back soon.'

'I like Claudia, but I like Josie too.'

'Josie was just helping out.'

'I'm tired,' said Tilly suddenly.

'No story?' said Amy, stroking her forehead.

'Tomorrow,' Tilly said, her eyes already wilting.

Amy closed the door and paused at the top of the stairs. For a moment she felt dizzy. It was a long way down and she didn't want to go. She could hear the gurgling sound of the coffee machine, which meant David wanted to talk. She put one foot in front of the other, knowing that she had to confront him sometime.

He was sitting at the breakfast bar pretending to read a copy of *The Economist*.

'That was quick.'

'She was exhausted.' Amy took the mug of coffee that was on the worktop.

'Have you spoken to Claudia yet?' he said after an awkward pause.

'A couple of days ago,' she said, hearing the crispness in her voice. 'She's signed off work for another two weeks. I don't suppose the situation has changed since then, but I can ask.'

David closed his magazine. 'What are we going to do? I've got to go to Hong Kong on Tuesday, and you've got the shows.'

'Hong Kong?'

She didn't know why she sounded so surprised. David was always flying around the world, meeting overseas teams and investors. Every month at least one of them was away for at least three or four days at a time. On the odd occasions that their work trips overlapped, David's parents, who lived in Esher, stepped into the breach.

'I go on Tuesday.'

Amy couldn't help but feel relieved. 'How long are you away for?'

'Five days.'

She nodded. 'Good. You'll be back before I go to the States.'

'So you're still going? Even with Claudia off.'

'It's New York Fashion Week, David. I've got to put in an appearance.'

'Of course you do.'

She wasn't going to let him get away with it. 'Do you have to go to Hong Kong?'

'We're pitching for a hundred-million-dollar piece of business.'

'So that's all right then. In the meantime, it doesn't matter if I don't show my face in front of the advertisers who spend hundreds of thousands of pounds with *Verve* every year.'

'You've been happy to let Janice go in the past.'

'Janice goes for the full week, but I've always shown my face and that's never more important than now.'

'Because of the *Mode* application.'

'That's right. Why don't you just admit it?' she challenged him.

'Admit what?'

'That you don't really want me to get the biggest job in my industry.'

'What are you suggesting? That I'm somehow emasculated by your success?'

'You said it.'

'Amy, I've supported you every step of the way. No one is more proud of what you've achieved than me. But look at where we are. Shipping our daughter off to my parents, reliant on nannies—'

'Don't bring nannies into this.'

'Something has to give, Amy.'

'And you think it's my job.'

'Unless you want to move house, downsize, take Tilly out of private school . . .'

She knew what he was saying. Her job was glamorous but not hugely well paid. Yes, there were perks aplenty, but perks didn't pay the bills, or the mortgage on a smart house in Notting Hill.

'This isn't the time to talk about it,' she muttered.

'When is?'

'I don't know, but right now it feels like you're shifting the blame, and conveniently avoiding what happened in Provence.'

'Nothing happened, Amy.'

'Just leave it.'

Silence vibrated between them. Amy could see the car keys in a copper pot on the mantelpiece and was tempted to leave the house and go for a drive.

'If I'm away on Tuesday and you're away the following week, we're going to need childcare help,' he said coolly. 'Should I ask my mum?'

Amy didn't look at him, but she was glad he was at least thinking of practical solutions for the situation they found themselves in.

'It's not ideal, but at least Tilly's off school for another week so she can go to their house if it's easier.'

'They were talking about taking her to Disneyland Paris. Maybe we can sort that out. Pay for it.'

'She'd like that,' said Amy, knowing how much her daughter would love to go to the famous theme park but still feeling like a bad mother. Without childcare, their world just didn't function.

But childcare has almost destroyed your marriage, a voice in her head reminded her.

It was beginning to get dark outside. Amy didn't need to look at the clock to know it was after eight o'clock. They had been travelling since lunchtime, avoiding the early-morning start that Juliet, Peter and Josie had made, but still coming back to London as quickly as possible.

Claire had pleaded with Amy to reconsider; Max had tried to persuade them to stay until the Sunday, when they had been originally planning to come home. But Amy had been too embarrassed to remain in Lourmarin, too aware what everyone was thinking and whispering behind her back. And when she'd managed to change her flight and Tilly's, David had agreed to come home too.

She curled her fingers around the mug and went to sit in the living room. Going upstairs was too confrontational;

besides, part of her wanted to hear what David had to say. She willed herself to remain calm, in case Tilly was still awake. So far, they'd managed to avoid arguing in front of her; Amy wanted to keep it that way.

'We should talk . . .'

'About what?'

'Provence.'

'David, there's nothing to talk about.'

'I want to know why you don't believe me.'

'Why I don't believe you? Josie is a beautiful young woman. I found her bra in our bed. Thousands of people have affairs and flings every day. What am I supposed to think?'

'I was hoping you might trust me. That you'd believe that I love you and wouldn't do anything to hurt our relationship or what we have as a family.'

Amy pressed her lips together to stop herself from crying. 'Do you think she's attractive?' she said.

'Objectively, yes,' he said simply.

Amy snorted.

'What do you want me to say?' said David, his voice rising a tone. 'Lie to you and say she's not good-looking, or be honest and admit that she is?'

She paused.

'Is it because we don't have as much sex any more?' She could feel her heart beating faster. 'This is how it happens, isn't it? We both work hard, we don't make time for one another, someone comes along . . . someone beautiful, who's good at flattery . . .'

She was thinking out loud, trying to make sense of it in her own head. Part of her did believe that David still loved her; she had to believe that, because the alternative was too painful to even consider. But she also knew that she had taken her eye off the ball, neglected him in the name of work, and now she was paying the price.

'Amy, stop it. How many times do I have to tell you, nothing happened between us.' David stepped towards her.

She wondered what Josie was doing now, where she was. Juliet had already texted David and said they'd put her on a train to Bristol after their flight had landed at Heathrow, and Amy pictured her arriving at Temple Meads and telling Karen everything. Nearly everything. Everything except her intimacy with David. She would tell Karen the story she wanted her to hear, and her old friend would hate her for ever.

'Don't come near me,' she whispered.

'I didn't have sex with her,' David repeated.

It occurred to her that it didn't even matter. The damage was done because she no longer trusted him.

'I'm tired,' she said, feeling totally drained. 'I think it's best if you sleep in the guest bedroom tonight.'

'Amy, don't—'

'Please. I want to be on my own.'

Neither of them said anything for a few seconds.

'Tomorrow . . . do you want me to go to my parents'? Settle Tilly in?'

Amy imagined what he would say to them. Stuart and Rosemary Parker were good people; decent, respectful. Both retired, they helped out as much as they could with Tilly; if they had ever noticed that she was being brought up by a nanny, they had never said so, and had always treated Amy like a daughter, stepping up their role when her own parents had passed away in quick succession. But Stuart and Rosemary weren't just kind; they were smart too. Amy knew that they would wonder why David wanted to stay over at their house with Tilly. She knew how upset they would be if they suspected their son's marriage was in trouble. But right now, it felt as if there was no alternative.

'I'll call them now,' said David. 'I think they've been in Dorset, but they should be back.'

A Greek chorus in her head told her to stop being so stubborn, but it was as if a thread had been picked and she was helpless to stop it unravelling.

'Fine,' she said quickly, blinking back tears. She wanted him to say something that would finally convince her that nothing had happened between him and Josie, do something to turn back the clock and make everything okay again. But it was as if the space between them was getting bigger and bigger, as if they were in space. She couldn't even breathe, could barely see him through the cloud of emotion in front of her eyes.

Chapter 22

'Daddy says we're going to Disneyland,' said Tilly, flying down the stairs, almost bumping down the bottom two steps in her haste.

'You're going to Grandma and Grandad's, and maybe, if you're very lucky, you can go to Disneyland at the end of the week.'

'I really want to go,' she said, her eyes wide. 'Sophie Jones has been and she said you can dress up as a princess and have breakfast with Elsa.'

'It's sorted,' said David, putting on his jacket. 'They're going Wednesday, coming back Friday night.'

'Really?' squealed Tilly, jumping in the air and skidding on her socks as she landed.

'Only if you're really good for Grandma, okay?'

Tilly looked up at Amy with a puzzled expression, her brows knitting together in a frown. 'Why aren't you coming, Mummy?'

'I'm going to be at work.'

'As usual,' said Tilly, rolling her eyes.

'Tilly . . .'

'Are you coming to Grandma's later?'

'Maybe, but I think Daddy wants to hang out with you there for a bit.'

'Just us?'

'Grandma and Grandad are his mummy and daddy, remember. Sometimes it's nice to just hang out together and have fun.'

'Good idea,' said Tilly, as if she was thinking it through. 'But what about when Daddy goes to Hong Kong?'

'Then I'll pick you up from Grandma's after work and maybe we can go to Biscuiteers and decorate some cookies, or perhaps Pizza Express for dough balls.'

'I love dough balls.'

'I know. And now they do chocolate-filled ones that I bet are absolutely yummy,' Amy said, tickling her daughter on the tummy.

She looked at David's neat silver case in the hall next to Tilly's rabbit-shaped Trunki and felt a wave of emotion. She turned to him, trying to pull herself together.

'I spoke to Claudia last night. She's got a hospital appointment on Thursday. If everything's healing well, she might be back by the time I go to New York.'

'That's something,' he muttered under his breath.

They'd managed to keep the tension turned down since they'd got back from Provence. It had only been one full day, and they had managed to avoid each other by taking it in turns to spend time with Tilly. Amy had gone to the Westfield Centre with her in the morning, losing hours in KidZania, whilst David had watched a film in the den with her when they had come home. But it was still there, the simmering discord that meant they couldn't even look each other in the eye.

'Tils, come and give me a big hug,' Amy said.

'I love you, Mummy.' Tilly wrapped her arms around Amy's waist.

'I love you too,' she said, stroking her daughter's hair.

David reached for Tilly's hand and looked back at Amy.

'Safe travels,' she said finally.

She didn't follow them to the door. Instead she just listened to the sound of it closing and Tilly's footsteps on the cold stone steps running away from the house. They were in the car with the engine running before she started to cry.

'So how was your holiday?' Tracey followed Amy as she walked through into her office sipping her bottle of breakfast smoothie.

'Good, good,' muttered Amy, clocking the teetering pile of post that had been deposited on her desk. She had never taken such a long break before, and she looked at her in-tray with dread.

'Only good?' laughed Tracey, watching Amy take off her coat.

'It was great. And now I'm back.' She didn't even look at her deputy as she fired up her computer.

'A little bird told me that Josie came with you,' said Tracey, sitting down at the sofa.

'Where did you hear that?' asked Amy with more interest.

'One of the PAs saw some pictures on Instagram and messaged her.'

Amy smiled thinly and made a mental note to check out Josie's social media accounts.

'Our nanny broke her ankle. Josie stepped into the breach.'

'You should have asked me. I'm not your trusty deputy for nothing.'

'That might not have been such a bad idea,' Amy muttered, picking up a padded envelope, which sent the entire pile tumbling to the floor. 'Bugger,' she said, crouching to pick it up.

'Let me,' said Tracey. If she had noticed Amy's hands shaking, she didn't say anything.

Chrissie came through with a coffee and Amy asked her to close the door behind her.

'So how's everything been?'

'The September issue sold like hot cakes. Did you get the sales figures I sent you?'

'Yes, thank you. How's everything going with the gala?'

Tracey sat forward on the sofa. 'The train was a very good idea. We got fifty replies within the hour.'

'What about the E-Squared dinner?'

'Get this, I've just got off the phone with their UK communications director, who was terribly sorry for the diary clash and is going to lay on cars to transport guests from their dinner to the gala. And when I suggested their event be moved forward an hour, she said she'd see what she could do. If you give her a ring to press the point home, I bet she makes it happen.'

'That's fantastic,' said Amy, feeling sparkier.

'There are a few other glitches,' said Tracey, looking more serious. 'The champagne sponsor has pulled out. Something to do with a change of management and a review of corporate partnerships.'

'They can't do that with two weeks to go.'

'Well they have, although before you ask, we've started ringing around the other drinks companies.'

Amy was sceptical. 'Someone else might agree in principle to giving us fifty thousand pounds' worth of alcohol, but it's still not a lot of time to get things signed off, especially when the invites have been printed.'

'We can do a contra deal another way . . . maybe give them a few pages of advertising.'

'That will have to be signed off by Douglas, and I'd rather not involve him at this stage.'

'We *can* do this, you know,' said Tracey reassuringly.

Right now, Amy didn't feel her deputy's confidence. With

the *Mode* job interview due any day, she had to push all her chips into the middle, go for the big win. Douglas had been suspicious of the Fashion 500 gala from the start. The company were sinking a lot of money into it, and it had to be a big success. It wasn't just the magazine's reputation riding on it; it was Amy's too.

'We start every month with empty pages and out of nothing we create three, four hundred pages of brilliance,' said Tracey, as if she had sensed Amy's stress. 'We do that twelve times a year. So there's no reason to think we can't put together some crappy party.'

'The world's greatest ever party, you mean.'

'Yes, that.'

Amy smiled warmly. Her team were the best. Loyal, resourceful, happy to get their hands dirty. It wasn't the norm in the media world, where back-stabbing and office politics were almost an art form. Given the car crash of her personal life right now, it was good to know that there was something she could rely upon.

Chapter 23

'Are you sure you've got everything?' Chrissie looked at her as if she were a trainer about to give her prized athlete a pre-race pep talk. Amy was half expecting her to stretch over and Swedish-massage her shoulders.

'What do I need? I've got my laptop for the PowerPoint, the mock-up covers, and my mood board. Tell me if I've forgotten anything or forever hold your peace.'

'Just go and kick ass,' grinned Chrissie.

Amy was glad she had confided in her assistant that she was going for the job. She'd been a huge help pulling every-thing together, scanning photos and working Excel. It was just as well that Tilly was with her grandparents, because Amy hadn't been home until nine every night, preparing for the interview that Douglas had sprung on her on her first day back in the office. She'd wanted to throw everything into it, because the *Mode* job traditionally only came up every ten or twenty years. But it wasn't just that: work had kept her from focusing on the looming loneliness at home. Her dream house, which she had loved from the moment she had set foot in it, felt cold and hollow.

She grabbed her tote bag and headed out towards the lifts. She had spent almost a month absorbing every scrap of information she could find about *Mode*, its history and current performance. She knew who its advertisers were and how much they were paying – one of the advantages of sharing an in-house ad team. She had analysed which covers had done well and which had failed. She knew the strengths and weaknesses of the editorial team. Above all, she had thought about what she would do with the magazine if by some miracle they decided to give her the job. No, that wasn't the attitude, was it? she told herself, checking her hair in the lift mirror. She deserved this job; she was more qualified than any other potential candidate and she would do it better than anyone else.

She exhaled slowly. This was it. The thing she had been working towards for almost twenty years. She didn't want to let herself down.

The lift doors opened and she strode out, trying to centre that sense of purpose. Yet still she felt as if she hadn't got sufficient armour; only Chrissie knew about the interview, and although her PA had wished her luck, it didn't seem quite enough.

It didn't feel that long ago since she had gone for the *Verve* editor's job, which at the time had been a big step up from the features director position she held. She was newly married at that point, and for the first time in a long time, not completely focused on her career. David had encouraged her to go for it, even though Amy knew she was woefully underqualified. He'd sent her a huge bouquet of peonies the morning of the interview, saying it didn't matter whether she aced it or not, but his quiet belief that she was good enough had helped Amy to wow William Bentley and win the job.

This time round, David didn't even know she was having the interview. They'd barely communicated since he'd left with Tilly the previous Monday morning: just the odd text to say that he'd arrived in Hong Kong, and to check how

Tilly was doing with her grandparents.

Breathe, breathe, Amy told herself. You can do this.

She gripped the handle of her tote bag tightly as she moved down the photograph-lined corridor towards Douglas's office. She was momentarily thrown when she saw an unfamiliar blond woman sitting at the PA's desk, before remembering that Douglas's assistant Grace had been fired after William's party.

'Oh, hi,' she said. 'I'm Amy Shepherd. I have an appointment with Douglas.'

'Yes, of course,' said the blonde. 'He's actually with someone at the moment, but if you'd like to take a seat, he'll be with you shortly.'

Amy was just turning towards the nearby sofa when the office door opened and she felt the floor drop away. For a moment, she thought she was seeing things. But no, it was her. It was Josie, coming out of Douglas's office, wearing a tight white blouse just like Amy's, a smile on her face.

Amy stood rooted to the spot as Douglas followed the girl out. He was saying something to her and they were laughing together. Amy's mind spun.

'Amy,' said Douglas, catching sight of her. 'Look who's here.'

Josie raised her eyebrows at Amy and gave a half-smile.

'Josie,' said Amy, barely able to catch her breath.

'As you might know, Grace has left the company, so this young lady is starting on Monday while I look for someone permanent. Tanya's been great, of course,' he said, nodding politely at the blond temp, 'but she's found a permanent position elsewhere, so I need someone flexible but reliable.'

Amy watched with a fixed smile as Josie shook hands with Douglas, who beamed at her warmly.

'Douglas, you have a call,' said Tanya.

'Of course. Amy, I'll just be a minute.'

As Tanya put the call through to Douglas's office, Amy stayed rooted to the spot. When Josie also didn't move to leave, she knew she had to say something.

'Congratulations,' she managed through thin lips. 'This is a great opportunity for you.'

Josie broke into a big smile. Amy noticed she had thicker make-up on than usual. She was used to seeing the girl tanned and natural, but now she had a full face on that made her look older than twenty-one.

'I've always wanted to work in magazines, so it's a dream come true. You hear stories about people having to do work experience for ever, but this way I should be able to get a deposit together for a flat in London.'

'I thought you'd gone back to Bristol.'

'I did, but I came back as soon as I got this offer,' she replied.

'Look, Josie, about what happened in Provence . . .' An apology hovered on Amy's lips before she stopped herself. She was an inveterate apologiser: when people bumped into her in the supermarket; when people elbowed her out of the way to get on the Tube during rush hour. David used to laugh at her and say it was a British thing, but Amy didn't know anyone else who said sorry quite as much as she did, and in her quieter moments she wondered if it was because she was so grateful for the life she had, a life she wasn't entirely sure she was worthy of.

'I'm just glad you're all right,' Josie said. 'Peter and Juliet were very worried about you. We all were.'

There was a smugness to her words that put Amy on edge. *We all were.* Who was the 'we'? Was David involved in that collective? She desperately wanted to ask Josie if she'd spoken to him since Provence, but she didn't dare. Instead she shook her head. 'Let's just put it behind us, shall we?'

'Good idea,' shrugged Josie. 'Seeing as we're going to be

working together.' She gave Amy a ghost of a smile. It was knowing, triumphant, a punch in the stomach.

More and more questions were on the tip of Amy's tongue now. She wanted to know how the Genesis job had come about; what exactly Josie's relationship with Douglas was. It seemed strange that she would be offered a role like this so readily, but as she had found out, Josie would stop at nothing to get what she wanted. She didn't suppose Douglas would be any more immune to her sultry charms than David had been.

But of course, she couldn't ask those things. Instead she gave Josie an awkward smile as Tanya called her name.

'Amy? Do you want to come through?'

'Well done again. On the job.'

Josie shrugged, like she was used to walking into top-level secretarial roles. 'It's only for a few weeks,' she said, but Amy was damn sure that wasn't her plan. Josie played the grateful ingénue well, but she was ambitious. She'd get her feet under the table, parlay the temporary into permanent, use her position to keep on top of openings in the company – and when you had the MD in your corner, who needed a CV?

'Good luck.' She winked, and Amy bristled.

As she walked into Douglas's office, her head was still whirling. Josie had manoeuvred herself into a top position in the company. Did that make her lucky, pushy or manipulative? And what did it mean regarding David? He was still protesting his innocence, and of course Amy hoped with all her heart that he was telling the truth, but if Josie was the player she was beginning to appear, then perhaps he had been used. But why? What was in it for Josie?

'Are you not going to sit down?' said Douglas, motioning towards the chair in front of his desk.

She told herself to get a grip. 'Sorry. I was just thinking

how great it is you're giving Josie this opportunity.'

'It should work out. The way she sorted out that whole cock-up at William's leaving party was quite impressive, didn't you think?'

Amy smiled weakly.

'But right now, I want to concentrate on you.'

He sat back behind his desk and put his hands behind his head.

'So I've read your proposals for *Mode* with interest.'

She could see that a tiny section of his shirt had popped open, exposing a flash of white flesh.

'Do you want me to go through it point by point? I've got a PowerPoint presentation with me . . .'

'There's no time for that today. This is just a preliminary chat. Short-listed candidates will have to make a formal presentation in the next week. The final three will be asked to meet Marv Schultz when he comes over to London for Fashion Week.'

Amy pressed her lips together to mask her disappointment. It was obvious what Douglas was saying.

There was a knock at the door and Josie came through with two cups of coffee.

Douglas flashed her a smile. 'Thank you, Josie.'

Amy looked straight ahead as Josie put the white china in front of her. She was determined not to look at her directly, even when she felt Josie's sleeve brush against her own.

'Doesn't even start until Monday and she's already part of the team,' said Douglas with something approaching affection as she left the room.

What special power did Josie have? Amy found herself wondering. It couldn't just be her looks. Douglas had many faults but he was not a senior management sleaze; Genesis was full of attractive, highly groomed women, but he always seemed more focused on his spreadsheets. Could it be something as simple as a suntan? Amy had never noticed David give Josie any particular attention until they got to Provence and her skin had toasted golden brown.

'So what do magazines have to do to get ahead in the digital age?' asked Douglas, cutting through the noise in her head. 'Now that everyone's on their phone. Email, text, social media, movies, even books have gone digital; how do magazines compete?'

'The website needed to be improved, for a start,' said Amy, trying to pull herself together. 'At the moment, we're not good enough. Companies like BuzzFeed are expert at SEO, data, clickbait. We need to recruit staff who are really, really good at those skills.'

Douglas nodded thoughtfully. 'You're right. I was just talking to Josie about how we pull young people in, and she said the same. They want the instant fix, the hottest news. She suggested videos, selfies, messaging forums. We have to make mobile the priority.'

Amy tried to stop a small frown forming between her brows. Why was he spouting the opinion of Josie as if it was gospel?

'How do we do that, Amy?'

She hadn't expected such a general chat. She had a bag full of slides, notes and images about her vision for *Mode*, but Douglas was provoking her into a discussion about media platforms.

'Invest in the website and increase our reach on other social media platforms,' she said, realising that was what he wanted to hear. 'It's not good enough having a five-page news section at the front of the print magazine any more, because it's not news. Face creams, shoes, celebrity news, it-bags. Anyone who has even a passing interest in fashion has already seen it all before the magazine even hits the newsstands.'

'So you think there's merit in the argument that we should be a digital-first product? Josie says she hasn't read a magazine in five years. Why are we bothering with the expense of print when everyone wants short and snappy on their phones? Josie says she just follows bloggers and influencers.'

Josie says, Josie says. Why did men listen to her? What had she said to David to lure him into bed? Their bed. How had she got him to buy her the necklace? What had she been doing staring into their bedroom the night Tilly had had sunburn? *Josie, Josie, Josie.*

'What do you think, Amy?' asked Douglas, but she could hardly hear him, as if she were swimming underwater, drowning.

She was tempted to say that Josie did read magazines. That she had confessed to being a fan of *Verve* and *Living Style*, but she didn't want to sound petty.

'Well, we have to compete with them. Beat them. Give the consumer more than the blogger can offer. A slick e-commerce division, glamorous events, corporate tie-ins and digital TV.'

'The last time I looked, the most successful bloggers are selling their own products, quite successfully I might add. As for events, I've just had to sign off the budget for a deluxe train. Are influencers hiring the Orient Express to get followers? I'm not sure they are.'

'Then why don't we just recruit an army of bloggers?' said Amy, finally snapping.

Douglas shuffled some papers on his desk. If the hard copy of her presentation was amongst them, she couldn't see it.

'I'm sorry,' she said, feeling suddenly panicky.

'Don't worry,' said Douglas. It was clear that their preliminary chat was over. The look on his face told her she'd blown it.

Her breath started to stutter. 'I go to New York on Tuesday, so if you want me to make my presentation before then . . .'

'I'm aware of the problems of Fashion Week when we have such a short time frame to make the appointment. Nothing that we haven't done before, though.'

He glanced at his watch and stood up, stretching his hand over the desk.

'I'm sure you've got a busy week. Keep me in the loop about the gala.'

'But Douglas . . .'

He was already at the door and holding it open for her to leave.

Amy's head was swimming, her heart pulsing hard. She was so angry with herself. Angry with Josie, angry with David, even with Claire and Max for inviting them to Provence. Josie had destabilised her, but she had allowed herself to be distracted.

She had once interviewed Liv Boeree, an English high-stakes poker player with model looks and a posh accent, who had explained the notion of going 'on tilt' when playing in Las Vegas. It meant getting out of control, losing concentration and making stupid mistakes, one leading to another. 'On tilt' was a phrase that had kept going around in Amy's head as she'd talked magazines with Douglas. She'd stuttered, mumbled, said dumb things. It was like having an out-of-body experience, like she was looking down on herself, flunking the interview.

It was particularly upsetting because she knew how good she could be, how good she *should* be. She had prepared, she knew the market and the magazine world inside out, and her ideas for *Mode* were good, she knew they were. But she'd blown it. Tears welled in her eyes and she just wanted to speak to David, despite everything that had happened between them. But it was mid-afternoon, and from the itinerary his PA had emailed over earlier that week, she knew he would be on the flight home from Hong Kong.

Loneliness consumed her. She pulled her phone out of her bag and scrolled to Juliet's number, but the call went straight through to message. Using the main switchboard number and extension number, she tried her office, but only got connected to Abigail, Juliet's assistant.

'It's Amy Shepherd. I'm trying to get hold of Juliet. Do you know where she is?'

'I'm sorry, Juliet's already gone for the afternoon,' said Abigail.

'Has she gone to the house in Hampshire?' Juliet had mentioned earlier in the week that she was looking forward to a weekend at the cottage: the calm before the storm that was the whirlwind of fashion shows.

'She didn't say, but that's where she usually goes on Friday afternoon. You could try the landline there,' said Abigail. 'I can text the number to you.'

'Don't worry, I've got it,' Amy said, and headed for the door.

Chapter 24

At least she had the car. Tilly was due back from Disneyland Paris at nine that evening, and Amy's original plan had been to work late and then pick her daughter up from Esher. But now her little Fiat in the basement car park seemed like the perfect getaway vehicle. She couldn't stay at Genesis a second longer. The walls felt as if they were closing in around her, and with Josie working on the top floor, the place that had once felt like her second home was now hostile territory that she had to escape from.

Her keys, phone and purse were in her tote, so there was no need to go back to her office. She called her PA.

'I have to leave the office early. If anyone needs me, I'm on the mobile.'

'Cool,' said Chrissie. 'About time you left before the cleaners. So how did it go?'

'We'll see,' Amy said quickly, and rang off.

As she drove out of the underground car park, she could feel her cheeks burning pink and her leg tapping against the car seat with nervous energy. For the first time in a long time, she didn't know what to do, and it was a feeling she hated. She had always prided herself on being decisive. In moments of introspection, when she had wondered how she, a girl from Westmead, had ended up in one of the most glamorous jobs in London, she realised that it was because when she made up her mind to do something, she just worked her hardest to make it happen. No dithering, no regrets, just forward motion to take her where she wanted to go. But now she felt amateur, inept. She had allowed herself to be completely destabilised. Sent off kilter by Douglas and Josie.

Juliet liked to boast that the journey to Walnut Cottage took a little over an hour, but in the rush-hour traffic, it took Amy almost two, not helped by a horse on the road, standing still and square and staring straight at her, as she turned into the village. She beeped the Fiat's horn, but the little brown horse just looked up at her through a fringe of hair, like a surly teenager.

'Come on, horsey,' she muttered, leaning on the horn again. 'I feel tired too, but you can't go to sleep in the road.'

She rolled the car slowly forward and was relieved to see the horse finally stroll away in a leisurely manner until it found a juicy-looking patch of grass, where it bowed its head and began munching.

Still, it added to the idyllic scene: rolling grasslands, dappled trees, sudden tiny hamlets or grey stone churches, their lychgates covered in moss. Every time she came down this way, Amy could see why Juliet found the countryside so soothing. She and David had often discussed getting their own place nearby, but something had always got in the way: jobs, projects, cash flow. Maybe they hadn't wanted it enough, or maybe they'd just realised that given the tiny amount of time they ever had free, their cute cottage would be standing empty fifty-one weeks of the year.

In any case, Juliet and Peter were very generous with their place, having friends down whether they were in residence or not. Amy briefly crossed her fingers that Peter was elsewhere this weekend; she wanted Juliet to herself, at least for tonight. She needed a full and frank debrief on the interview, and while Peter was achingly polite, there was a limit to how open she could be with him there, especially after her meltdown in Provence.

She thought back to the times she and Juliet had sat together in their shared house in Oxford, poring over magazines, discussing them, dissecting them, their likes and dislikes, what they'd do to improve them. She wasn't sure when the idea of actually considering journalism as a career had begun, but she knew the seed had been sown on those long nights of tea, magazines and Garibaldis. She had Juliet to thank for that, and right now she hoped Juliet's head-girl pragmatism would help get her back on track.

She was so deep in thought that she nearly missed the village sign, almost covered by the leaves of a hawthorn. She took the next right, passing the King's Arms, then slowed as she reached the turning to Dawes Lane, invisible unless you were looking for it. Juliet's cottage was actually down a one-lane track, which was a nightmare to reverse out of, so Amy had long ago taken to driving past and parking in a turn-off next to an overgrown wood.

Locking the car, she pulled out her phone – one bar, about all you could expect out here. No messages from Juliet, but she could easily be suffering from the same patchy coverage. Walking towards the cottage, she called David's mum, and was surprised when she picked up immediately.

'Amy, how are you? We're just buying toffee apples.'

Amy couldn't help but smile: at least Tilly and her grandparents were having a good time.

'Can you put Tilly—' she began, but her daughter was already on the phone.

'Mummy, is that you? I love it here. It's so cool, and I've seen Elsa, and Tiana and Olaf waved at me from the parade.'

'Well you be a good girl, okay?' She was desperate to see her, and feel her comforting softness in her arms.

'Okay,' said Tilly breathlessly. 'Love you.'

'I just wanted to check you were still back at nine p.m.,' Amy said when Rosemary came back on the line.

'It might be a little later. Stuart's talking about moving into Cinderella's castle, but I'll tear him away for the early-evening Eurostar.'

'I'm glad you've had a great time.'

'We really have. David said you'd had a very big week at work. Is everything okay?'

She felt a dart of envy for David's parents, happily retired and happily married, pottering around Disneyland with nothing more to worry about than what to have for lunch.

'Fine, Rosemary, fine. Just glad it's Friday,' she said.

Rosemary said goodbye, and Amy slid the phone back into her bag and continued down the lane. As she turned the corner, she saw the little red sports car parked under the shade of a tree and smiled. Her guess had been correct; it would have been annoying if Juliet hadn't been here after all when she had driven all this way.

The cottage was to the right, a high hedge shielding it from the road, a wrought-iron gate opening onto a little stone path. Amy swung it open and walked up, trying the latch to the front door. Locked. Curious: Juliet never locked the house when she was in.

She went back to the lane and followed the hedge down to where the sports car was parked. Its bonnet was making that 'tick-tick' noise suggesting it had been driven recently. She knew there was a side gate leading into the back garden. Juliet often sat out there in good weather, her work spread across a gnarled wooden table, Radio 3 turned up full blast. Amy cocked an ear: no music, but the sound of a door opening. She put her hand on the handle to the side gate, then stopped.

Something wasn't quite right.

The gate was slatted, with gaps between the wood. Craning her neck, Amy peered through and saw a man walk across the back patio. He was tall and tanned, perhaps late twenties, with a floppy blonde fringe. And he was muscular too: she could see that because he was only wearing boxer shorts. Careful not to make a sound, she stepped back, her thoughts in a whirl. Was this why Juliet hadn't told her PA where she was going, and why she hadn't answered her phone? Was she having an affair?

She held her breath as another figure came out of the house. Not Juliet; Peter. Wearing an unbuttoned shirt and not much else. Amy watched with rising horror as he smiled, crossed to the tanned guy and kissed him full on the mouth.

She closed her eyes, stifling the scream she knew was building. She had to get out, had to get away. She stepped carefully on the path, using all her concentration to avoid snapping twigs or scuffing stones, anything that might alert Peter and his friend to her presence. *Peter and his lover.*

As she turned the corner of the house, she stumbled into a patch of brambles, snagging her tights. She stopped again, freezing as she heard laughter. Distant, still in the garden. No doubt preoccupied with other things. Oh Christ, she thought. Juliet. What was she going to say to Juliet?

She ran up the lane to her car, checking over her shoulder every now and again to make sure she hadn't been seen, then jumped in and fired up the engine, only concerned with putting distance between her and that scene in the garden.

She stopped after just a few hundred yards, when she was far enough away, and sat frozen, listening to her own breath, gripping the steering wheel as if it were a life raft. As she stared at her hands, she could see the gold band of her wedding ring glinting on her finger. She had to close her eyes to stop looking at it.

Was there anybody you could trust any more?

She'd always thought of Peter as steady and reliable. Too steady if the truth be told, but his presence was comforting and reassuring. She thought back to Provence, where his kind calmness had got her through that last night at the villa.

This would destroy Juliet, rip her whole life apart. Peter had never been Amy's idea of a perfect match for her friend, but Juliet loved him – and this was how he repaid her.

For a moment, Amy considered the alternative. Let sleeping dogs lie? Wasn't that the phrase? How appropriate. She shook her head. She couldn't, not now she knew the truth. Juliet deserved to know. Some women might be able to live with it, but not Jules. She was straight-down-the-line, uncompromising; she wouldn't stand for it.

So that meant Amy had to tell her.

Swearing, she pressed the ignition and turned the car back onto the road. New York, she thought; she would tell her in New York.

Chapter 25

Crossing the bridge into Manhattan was one of Amy's favourite things. It was breathtaking at any time of day, but at sunset it was nothing short of spectacular. The dark outline of the concrete ramparts, the random fairy-chain lights of the skyscrapers, the Vegas wattage of the lit-up Empire State: it always gave her shivers of anticipation. *Almost* always. Because this time, there was a dark cloud hanging over Manhattan. A trip to the New York shows was the last thing she needed. The gala was a little over a week away, she'd had no word about the job application from Douglas – not that seeing her around the Genesis office would prompt him into putting her on the shortlist, but she could still hope – and she had hardly seen Tilly.

It was a weekend spent with her daughter that had saved Amy from sinking further into depression. Listening to Tilly's gleeful stories from Disneyland had cheered her up no end, even when David had returned from Hong Kong on the Saturday morning.

Her phone beeped and she read the incoming text.

At the Whitby. Call when you get in. Drinks? Jx

She looked at it again, then clicked off the phone, concentrating on the city skyline, urging the magical city to work a miracle.

'Straight to the hotel, ma'am?' asked her driver from the front seat of the town car that had picked her up from JFK.

'Thanks, Jimmy.' She grinned. The old Irishman was her regular driver for the shows. You had to have a dedicated and experienced driver for Fashion Week if you wanted to get anywhere on time. And Jimmy was the best: he could find a way through traffic and seemed to know every cop in New York. If he double-parked, they wandered over to chew the fat.

The town car was moving through the deep shadows of Manhattan now: twenty, thirty floors towering above them, like a forest of vast concrete trees so tall you couldn't see the sky, however much you craned. But at street level, the avenues were awash with backlit neon signs and flashing headlights; all bustle, energy and excitement. Despite her mood, Amy couldn't help but smile. It was all so alien yet so familiar: the corner delis, the pizza joints, the yellow cabs, the distilled essence of a million Hollywood film sets and eighties cop shows. Just being here made you feel like you were a part of it all, dropped into your own little adventure in the city where anything was possible. At the same time, she suddenly felt old. Manhattan was a young person's town, all hot eateries and underground clubs, and here she was crossing Seventh Avenue weighed down with work and marriage problems.

'Your hotel, ma'am.'

'Thank you, Jimmy,' said Amy, climbing out of the car.

'Always a pleasure, Mizz Shepherd,' replied Jimmy. Always? That made her feel old too. This had to be the tenth – twelfth? – time they'd worked together. Maybe it *was* a young person's town.

'You ready for another week of this madness, Jimmy?'

'I was born ready,' he grinned. 'And fashion ain't nuthin'. You want crazy, you come on over for the dentists' convention.' He whistled through his teeth. 'Those guys *really* let loose.'

Manhattan hotel rooms – even suites – were notoriously poky at the best of times, but Amy's room was particularly crowded. A huge pile of invitations and VIP passes for the shows sat on the desk, with various parcels and gifts from the fashion houses on the floor next to it. And right by the window, a large bouquet of flowers that made her heart jump. From David? she wondered, snatching up the accompanying card. No, from the hotel manager, welcoming Amy and her 'team'.

She had a quick shower and changed into a Valentino jumpsuit even though she was tempted to climb into her pyjamas. She was here to press the flesh, make a good impression with advertisers and the industry, and she had to look forward-facing at all times. During Fashion Week you never knew who you were going to bump into, and she knew she had to make an effort.

Juliet was staying around the corner at a new hotel called the Whitby, which described itself as 'the hottest new destination in Midtown'. The unimaginatively named Sky Bar was on the twenty-ninth floor, with a view of the park, glorious in the day of course, but a strangely ominous blank space at night, like someone had forgotten to finish the city.

'That was quick,' she said as Amy arrived.

'I can't stay long.'

'Make that call after you've tasted their amazing gingertinis.'

'Great place,' said Amy, looking around her.

'Great people-watching. I've seen two world-class strops already and I've only been here ten minutes.'

They both laughed.

'How was the flight?'

'The usual,' said Amy. 'Matt Damon movie, two G and Ts and about half an hour of sleep. When did you get here?'

'Sunday. I spent all day yesterday and today shooting the CEO of the hotel group in the penthouse suite. But at least I get to sleep in it.'

'Lucky thing. Genesis keep downgrading the hotels I'm allowed to stay in. Once upon a time it was the St Regis. Now I have to beg for the YWCA.'

'It's not that bad,' smiled Juliet.

'No, it's not,' said Amy, enjoying their moment of banter. The waiter brought over two drinks in elegant long-stemmed glasses.

'I've hardly seen you since Provence,' said Juliet. 'How've you been?'

'Okay. At least Claudia's back on her feet. Literally. She came back yesterday.'

'That's good news.'

'You know Josie has landed a job at Genesis?' Amy asked.

'Where?' Juliet said with surprise.

'She's Douglas's new PA.'

'You're kidding.'

'Nope. Grace has been fired and Josie is the temporary replacement. Apparently she impressed him at William's party.'

Juliet puffed out her cheeks. 'She certainly lands on her feet.'

'By chance or design?'

'You think she hustled for the job?'

'It wouldn't surprise me if she slept with him.'

Juliet didn't laugh. 'It was quick work if she did. We only got back from Provence on Saturday.'

'Josie is the sort of determined young woman who can accomplish a lot in a short space of time.'

Amy took a sip of her drink before she spoke again,

impatient for the heady kick that came with drinking spirits, bracing herself to bare her inner thoughts.

'I think she's got it in for me,' she said finally. 'I went to Douglas's office for my *Mode* interview and she was there. And the look on her face – it was as if she knew she was unsettling me and was enjoying it. I lost my step in the interview, I couldn't think straight—'

'You've had the interview?' Juliet said. 'How did it go?'

'It was awful, Jules. I totally blew my opportunity and it's all because of Josie.'

Juliet reached over and put her hand on Amy's.

'Are you going to let some stupid twenty-one-year-old get the better of you?'

'She's not stupid, Jules. That's what scares me. She's tough, determined. She knows what she wants and the only thing standing in her way is me.'

Juliet gave a sympathetic smile. 'She's a kid, a little ambitious perhaps, stars in her eyes, but I very much doubt she's out to get you.'

Amy didn't respond.

'Call Douglas, ask to see him again,' said Juliet briskly. 'Make your pitch.'

'I tried that yesterday. He didn't even reply to my email.'

'He will. How are things with David?'

'He's still in the spare room.'

'Awkward.'

'I'll say.'

They'd moved on from the silent treatment over the weekend, but they were still using the sort of clipped, over-polite demeanour usually reserved for tradesmen they suspected of ripping them off. Amy knew she was getting a glimpse of some terrible future where they were forced to tolerate each other for Tilly's sake, but she couldn't seem to back down, and the longer things went on, the more David seemed to harden from apologetic to obstinate.

'How was she? On the flight home?' Amy had dreaded asking.

'Josie? She fell asleep on the way to the airport and we weren't sitting together on the plane. She expressed some concern about your levels of stress, but other than that she seemed pretty unbothered by everything that had happened.'

'Unrepentant,' said Amy through tight lips.

'Or maybe she felt she had nothing to be repentant about.'

'The bra, Jules. The invoice for the necklace.'

'It's hardly a smoking gun.'

Amy finished off her gingertini and summoned the waiter for another one; not because they were so good – although on any other occasion she would have found them deliciously smooth and spicy – but because she wanted to blot everything out and forget.

'Can I ask you a question?' Juliet asked. Amy nodded. 'Is it Josie you don't trust, or David? Is it her you feel threatened by, or is it David?'

'I hope you're not making excuses for her, Jules.'

'All I'm saying is that sometimes, when we worry about something, we project it onto the wrong thing.'

'She wants my life, Jules. My husband, my job, my house.'

'Maybe. And do you blame her? David's rich and handsome. You're a magazine editor with an amazing home in Notting Hill. She's hungry and ambitious – you were too, but she might just have fewer morals about what she has to do to get what she wants.'

Amy didn't want to admit that her friend might be right. Increasingly these days, she was feeling old. Old when she came to New York, old when she talked about social media with Douglas, old when her hairdresser at the Charles Worthington salon suggested a colour, not as a playful change but to cover up the silvery grey at her temples. Her forty-second birthday was just a few weeks away, but sometimes she felt a decade older.

Her husband, on the other hand, looked in his prime. Success, maturity suited him. She'd been ready to believe that he was having an affair with a woman half his age because in her heart she'd been expecting someone like Josie Price to come along and seduce him, and for him to let it happen.

'I thought you said David loved me,' she said quietly.

'He does. But plenty of marriages wobble because you don't pay them enough attention. Forget Josie for one minute, and think about David. Why you've banished him to the spare room on a hunch. Why you were quick to think a bra in the bed meant he was having an affair.'

Amy looked at her friend incredulously. She had expected sympathy; instead she was getting tough love.

'I can't believe you somehow think this is my fault. I came all the way out to your cottage on Friday because I was so upset, upset because that girl is trying to wreck my life. And it's working, too. My marriage, my job . . . it's as if she's there, everywhere, putting the boot in. And you think it's just me being complacent . . .'

Her head was spinning now. That second gingertini had been a mistake.

'Amy. I'm just saying you need to be more honest about why you're upset. Why you're so suspicious of David.'

'Don't lecture me about honesty and relationships, Juliet.'

Juliet flinched. 'It sounds as if there's a point in there.'

Amy bit her lip. 'It's nothing,' she said quickly. 'I'm just jet-lagged and drunk.'

'What are you not telling me? At least we can be honest with each other after all these years.'

Amy took a deep breath. The thing that had been gnawing away at her for days was her need to know the truth. A confession from David that he had slept with Josie would crucify her, but at least she would know. She would know and she could move forward. It was the not knowing that was driving her mad; the constant sense of feeling so stupid that was grinding her into the ground. Would Juliet want the truth too?

'Like I said, I went to the cottage on Friday. I needed to talk to you about my car-crash interview with Douglas and you weren't answering your phone.'

'I was at the Four Seasons spa.'

'I didn't know that. I just took a chance and drove down. I saw Peter. He was with a friend.'

'A friend?' said Juliet, the penny beginning to drop.

'I didn't recognise him.'

'Him? What are you suggesting here, Amy? Just tell me.'

'I saw them kiss.'

'So what? You know what Peter's like. He's so fey with some of his school pals. They like to think they're still twenty-three and in a college production of *Brideshead Revisited*.'

Amy knew this was the point at which she could pull back, but Juliet was no fool.

'It wasn't a school friend. And it looked intimate. You need to have an honest conversation with Peter about where he was on Friday afternoon and who he spent it with.'

'She's poisoned your mind, you know that.' It was Juliet's turn to let rip. 'You neglect your marriage, and instead of working out how you can improve it, you just lash out at other people. If you have to be miserable, then so does everybody else,' she mocked harshly. 'You need to grow up.'

She slid out of the booth and summoned the waitress.

'Put that bar bill on my room,' she said, and walked out without looking back.

Chapter 26

Amy pushed her hands into her pockets and stepped out onto the street, unable even to raise a smile for the bellboy who held open the door as she left.

In a city of ten million people she had never felt more alone. She was barely speaking to her husband, and now her best friend had every right to cut her out of her life completely.

Josie. It all came back to that girl. Her influence was creeping everywhere, like poison ivy taking over a country garden, twisting its roots around flowers and trees, choking, suffocating, infecting.

Juliet had had a point when she said that Amy wanted to lash out. True, she didn't want her friend to feel foolish if it came out about Peter's affair; after all, she would hate to think that Claire, Max or Juliet knew something about David's private life and were whispering sympathetically behind her back but not telling her about it. But there was also a little part of Amy that didn't want to be alone in her marital suffering. Telling Juliet about Peter had been a way of offloading her own troubles, as if sharing them with her friend might make it a little less painful.

She quickened her pace, wanting to get back to her own hotel, where the minibar was waiting. She hated drinking alone, but she needed to block out her pain and frustration somehow.

It was a few moments before she recognised the man coming out of the St Regis, the smart hotel on the corner of Park Avenue.

Marvin Schultz was a legend in magazine publishing, rarely seen but much whispered about in the corridors of Genesis. The son of the original founder, and the current CEO, he'd launched half of the glossies you saw pinned to the outside of Manhattan street-corner newsagents, and acquired half a dozen more ailing vintage titles that he'd brought back to life with hand-picked editors and millions of dollars' worth of investment.

Amy had met him only once, at the company's fiftieth anniversary party, shortly after she had got the *Verve* editorship. Marv, as he was affectionately known, didn't do social lunches, certainly not with editors from the satellite territories, although she'd received the odd missive from New York: handwritten notes that commended particularly good covers or features that garnered buzz.

The root of an idea began to take hold, and she quickened her pace without thinking to stop and wonder if what she was about to do was wise. Marv was on his phone, but it was clearly his driver waiting for him on the busy street. He was only feet away now, and Amy knew she had just seconds to strike, seconds to try and claw back her dream job.

Her heart was pounding. She was not naturally very assertive. When she had first arrived in London and realised she would need more push and polish to get on in the glamorous and judgemental world of magazine publishing, she had hung a framed picture in her flat that said 'Feel the fear and do it anyway'. It was schmaltzy and American, but those words had served her well, helped chip away at her insecurities and boost her self-worth.

When he ended his call, she made her move. 'Mr Schultz? Amy Shepherd. I'm the editor of *Verve* magazine in London.'

He looked momentarily surprised, but then extended his hand. 'Of course. Amy, how are you?' She wasn't sure if he recognised her, but he had the good grace to be the epitome of charm.

'I'm fine, thank you. I'm in New York for the shows.'

'Have fun. I hear Ralph Lauren's is going to be on the High Line.'

His driver opened the car door.

'So, *à bientôt*.'

'Actually, I was wondering if we could have a word. About *Mode*.'

'What about it?' He gave a small smile, toying with her. He was old, but he wasn't stupid. Far from it. 'I'm going as far as 75th Street. If you're heading to that part of town, how about I give you a lift and you can tell me what's on your mind.'

Amy hopped in, grateful.

'Where to?' asked the driver, starting the engine.

She couldn't face telling him that her own hotel was less than fifty yards away. Besides, that wouldn't be long enough to say what she had to say.

'I'll get out where you're going,' she said.

'We met once before, am I right?' said Marv, taking a seat beside her. 'Genesis dinner at the Savoy, maybe three years ago?'

Amy nodded gratefully. 'I didn't think you'd remember.'

'We spoke about how the internet was killing journalism, right?'

Amy found herself blushing. 'Yes, it's a bugbear of mine.'

Marv nodded. 'I thought at the time, she's smart. Wrong, but smart.'

'Wrong?'

'Oh, I agree with you that we need some way of funding long-term investigative journalism, if only to hold government or wrinkly old media moguls like me to account. But I disagree that the internet is killing magazines.'

Amy raised her eyebrows. 'You mean we're killing ourselves?'

Marv smiled. 'See? I was right, you're smart.'

'Mr Schultz, this is exactly what I wanted to talk about. I'm applying for the *Mode* editor's job in London and I had a preliminary chat with Douglas Proctor. But I wasn't honest with him about what I thought the magazine needed. I talked about SEO and e-retailing, Snapchat and corporate partnerships. What I didn't talk about was the magazine itself. *Mode* hasn't just lost its way. It's stuck in its ways. It's dull and predictable. There are no surprises any more, the interviews are bland, and PR-regulated fashion shoots are there to please the advertisers not the readers. Everything feels like a curated advertorial. Where's the wit and the wonder, the fun and the fabulousness? We need to go back to the beginning and remember why people got excited and passionate about magazines in the first place, not spend all our time thinking about the method of distribution. We've all become too distracted by that. Too distracted by the future of digital, rather than thinking about legacy.'

'So what are you saying? That *Mode*, our flagship title, stinks?'

It was time to throw her chips in.

'I'm saying if you make a shitty product, don't be surprised when no one wants it.'

She turned to face him more directly, glad that the back seat was expansive so she had some room to move.

'If magazines were giving people what they wanted, people would still buy them. As it is, what is the point of throwing resources at digital and events when our core brand, our magazine, is the weakest thing about us?'

'Old-fashioned thinking, Amy.'

She wasn't going to back down. 'Old-fashioned maybe, but I believe it's the future. Right now, one magazine does a party page, everyone has to have a party page. Some website has a million hits from pictures of celebrities falling over in the street, suddenly every magazine copies it. Nothing's new, nothing's original or confident or bold. It's no wonder people are going to the internet instead. They will carry on doing so until we make our magazines amazing again. And when we do, people will want to buy into the brand in every form. We can sell them clothes off the page, turn features into TV or web shows, get them to come to our events. Not to mention ads and sponsorship.' She held up a finger. 'But that only works if you get the core product – the magazine – right.'

'And I happen to agree with you.'

'You do?' she said, eyes wide.

He nodded. The car had stopped and he opened the door. 'Daniel will give you a lift to wherever you want to go.'

'I can put a world-class magazine together, Mr Schultz. Let me show you my vision.' She tried to hide the desperation in her voice, but she knew it was the only way of getting her application back on track.

'The only thing I want to see right now is my coffee machine,' he said with a good-natured smile.

Amy felt her heart sink.

'But I am in Europe next week. Let me get my secretary to contact you and see what we can do.'

Chapter 27

In forty-eight hours in Manhattan, Amy had seen six shows, been to four parties, had lunch with Michael Kors and lost track of time in American Girl buying a doll for Tilly.

She'd got hardly any sleep on the red-eye flight, but as the plane touched down at Heathrow, she realised how glad she was to be back, even if she was going straight into the office. Her conversation with Marv Schultz had made her feel as if she was back in control, even if it was at the wheel of a car with its brakes cut.

She glanced at her watch as she dashed through customs, eyes peeled for the car that was going to take her into work. Waving at the driver holding a hand-written sign marked 'Shepherd', she pulled her mobile out of her pocket and called home, aware that it was 8.30 and Tilly would soon be off to school.

Her heart jumped when her daughter answered the landline.

'Tilly, honey. How are you?' she said, a broad smile spreading across her face.

'I can't wait to see you, Mummy.'

Amy laughed. 'I've got you something nice from New York.'

'What is it?'

'You'll find out tonight.'

'What time are you coming home?'

'I'll get out of work early. Have you had fun with Daddy and Claudia?'

'Yes. And with Josie too.'

Amy's hand clutched the handle of her wheelie case tighter.

'Josie?' she said more slowly.

'She came to the house last night. She told me some jokes and brought me chocolate.'

'Did she?' She could barely get the words out.

'Should I take that, miss?' asked the driver, trying to pick up her case.

'Tilly, what was Josie doing at the house?'

'I don't know. Claudia went home. Josie was talking to Daddy.'

Amy's head started to spin, and it wasn't through jet lag or tiredness. She didn't know how she got into the car, but she found herself sitting silently in the back seat, replaying Tilly's words over and over again.

She thought about calling David, but stopped herself. There would only be more lies. At least when she saw him face to face she would be able to read him better. Only then would she get a sense of why Josie had come round.

'Can you drop me off outside the coffee shop,' she said when they got to the South Bank.

She ordered a black Americano and stood by the counter for a minute taking a few fortifying sips before she went into the Genesis offices. As she rode up in the lift, she stared at her own reflection in the mirrored walls, and for a moment she felt calm as if life was on pause for just one fleeting second.

Focus on the job, she told herself as the lift pinged open. She hadn't been able to keep a watchful eye on her husband when she had been in New York, but at least she had managed to salvage her career.

As she stepped into the office, she could hear the low, industrious buzz of a team already deep into their week's work. At least she had that to be thankful for: colleagues she trusted and who didn't need the boss to be there to get the job done.

'New issue,' beamed Gemma, her art director, as she walked past the desk.

Amy took a moment to admire it. The way her luck had been going recently, she wouldn't have been surprised if the cover had come out blank, but it hadn't; it was glossy and beautiful, Miranda Pilley's face staring back at her with her direct grey-eyed gaze, the primrose-yellow gown she had worn on the day of the shoot softened so that she looked as though she was draped in an ivory cloud: every inch the blushing bride-to-be.

'This is stunning,' Amy said. 'It's going to be our biggest seller of the year.'

'Try the past five years. I went to Smith's at Waterloo this morning and they'd already sold out.'

Amy felt a flutter of excitement, the shock of Josie having been round to her house the night before fleetingly forgotten. She couldn't remember the last time she had felt like this, giddy and energised. The past two years, spent fire-fighting one thing after another – poor sales, irate celebrities, budget cuts – had been enough to make her file for early retirement.

'I'll just take this through to my office,' she said. 'Chrissie, I would love a coffee.'

She went into her room and closed the door behind her, leaving her wheelie case in the corner. Sitting at the desk, she began to flick through the pages. It was a good issue. *Such* a good issue, she thought with a sense of relief. And so well timed, after Miranda had officially announcd her engagement on Instagram two weeks earlier. Douglas Proctor, Denton Scoles, Marv Schultz – no one could deny it didn't tick all the boxes. The Love Issue had been a last-minute idea but it was as if they had planned it from the get-go. The fashion was breezy and romantic; a hard-news story about an initiative in the Sudan to distribute microloans was topical but heartfelt. But most of all, everyone would be intrigued by what Miranda had to say about bad boy fiancé Leif Tappen. That was the only downside – she hadn't actually said anything, although Liz Stewart's piece had referenced their cloak-and-dagger relationship.

Amy took a moment to wonder if her readers would feel short-changed, but then dismissed it. The pictures of Miranda on three double-page spreads were better than any indiscreet interview. It was inconceivable that a publicity-shy couple like Miranda and Leif would do a *Hello!*-style wedding shoot, but reading the October issue of *Verve* was like peeking behind a curtain, allowing people to imagine what the wedding would be like.

There was a knock at her door and Amy looked up, expecting to see Chrissie with a mug of coffee. Instead, it was Tracey, her deputy.

'I know you've just got in,' she said, 'but do you have a minute?'

'Of course,' said Amy, gesturing to the sofa.

'Have you been on Twitter this morning?'

'No,' said Amy, laughing. 'You know me and social media.'

'You should,' said Tracey seriously. 'The Miranda Pilley interview is trending.'

'That's great. I was just about to come out and congratulate everyone on a terrific issue.'

'I think you'd better take a look.'

It was the top headline on Growler, one of the most popular internet gossip sites: 'Miranda Hates Gays? Gay pride group slams model for "anti-gay propaganda", while top feminists criticise her "prehistoric" views on marriage.'

'What the hell? When did this happen?'

'About an hour ago, as far as I can tell. It looks like some gay pressure group has got hold of an early copy of the interview and has chosen to take it out of context.'

'Which bit?'

Tracey read out the passage: '"I'm kind of a romantic when it comes to marriage. I love all that boy-meets-girl, love-at-first-sight stuff, one man and one woman together for the rest of their lives. It's a nice idea."'

Amy frowned, confusion fighting with her rising panic. 'I don't understand, what's anti-gay about that?'

'This pressure group, the Pink Panthers, are taking the "one man and one woman" quote entirely out of context and saying that Miranda's against gay relationships. They're seizing on it to make a point about gay marriage still not being recognised in dozens of countries.'

'But she wasn't saying anything even close to that!'

'I know that, you know that, but that's not how the internet works. All anyone is going to see is the headline "Miranda Hates Gays".'

Amy felt her head begin to pound. 'Can't we do something? Put out a statement or something? Isn't this what the lawyers are for?'

'It's already too late for that. Hundreds of other sites – even some of the newspapers – have jumped on it, so now it's going viral. And the way it's spinning, it looks like we're complicit.'

'What? What's it got to do with us?'

'Well, we're running the story, not questioning the gay line, going on about how great marriage is.'

'*Her* marriage, we're happy for *Miranda*!' cried Amy. 'That's all!'

Tracey nodded. 'I totally agree. But you know how social media can twist everything out of context.'

Once Tracey had left, Amy picked up her phone and called Miranda's manager, Karrie. Within the hour, Miranda had made a statement on Twitter clarifying her position, saying that she had championed same-sex marriage from the start, and apologising for any confusion. Verve.com posted a feature about the magazine's favourite same-sex couples, whilst Amy took to her own barely used Twitter account to write a heartfelt and passionate post: 'Let's celebrate love, not use it to divide humanity. Let's celebrate freedom of speech, not abuse it in the name of clickbait.'

Never had 140 characters created such a storm in one afternoon.

Radio 4, LBC, even CNN all got in touch to ask her views on whether journalism was in crisis, sacrificing the truthfulness of news to bolster web traffic and ad revenues.

Amy gave one short interview warning media companies not to jettison trust and truth because of digital panic, and within fifteen minutes, her opinions were trending even higher than the original controversy.

Whether it would be enough to stop Douglas Proctor coming on the war-path only time would tell.

Chapter 28

The Twitter storm died down as quickly as it had started. So much so that by mid-afternoon, the story had been relegated to a minor corner of the *Daily Mail* homepage and the anti-Miranda tweets had slowed to just a trickle. At the same time, WHSmith, McColl's and supermarkets around the country were reporting that they had sold out of *Verve*'s October issue in less than a day.

Tracey suggested nipping out to Tesco Express to get some champagne to celebrate, but the jet lag was setting in and Amy felt exhausted. She took a long swig of lukewarm coffee and reached for the Pret salad that had been waiting for her since lunchtime. She ripped open the box and picked at some avocado and crayfish, hoping it would revive her.

The events of the day had distracted her from thinking about David. She had tried not to dwell on Josie going round to their house whilst she was in New York, consoling herself with the fact that surely they were not so brazen as to have sex in the house with Tilly there. But you never knew.

'Amy, have you got a minute to come and look at some clothes?' Renee was a junior fashion editor being allowed to do her first shoot, thanks to the rest of the fashion team being at the shows.

Amy smiled and stood up, following her to the fashion department at the far end of the office. She could tell that Renee was anxious and made a mental note to be as encouraging as possible. She knew she was lucky to have such a talented and down-to-earth fashion team, having heard horror stories from around the industry about the diva antics and demands of some fashion editors. That said, she still had to keep a close eye on the *Verve* team, reining them back from selecting £5,000 boots and the to-order gowns that were fashionista favourites but well out of the reach of the average reader.

'As you know, red is a really big story for autumn/ winter,' said Renee, showing Amy the rail of clothes she had selected for the next day's shoot. The colours looked delicious even at first glance. Sour-cherry cashmere knits and crimson floor-length coats made Amy long for the weather to turn cold so that she could start wearing them.

Her eye caught a scarlet dress on another rack and she took a sharp intake of breath.

'Do you like that?' asked Renee, noticing her boss's reaction. 'It didn't make the final cut, but I can put it back in if you want . . .'

But Amy was lost in her memories, remembering that day over seven years ago when she had gone to Threadneedle Street to see a show. As a member of the features team, she rarely went to fashion shows, but when an invite had landed on her desk, she had dressed up specially, borrowing a designer dress from Juliet to look the part.

She had felt invincible that day. A photographer from the *Evening Standard* had asked to take her picture for a street-style segment, and for the first time ever she had felt glamorous and stylish and ready to conquer the world. It was also the day that she met David again. Their college friendship had dwindled to almost nothing throughout her late twenties and early thirties – reunion drinks missed through hectic work schedules. But when he had seen her coming out of the show, and they had gleefully reconnected on the street, it was as if they had never been apart.

She touched the fine red crêpe of the dress on the rail. It was just like the dress she had fallen in love in, she thought. The dress that had got her noticed. Her heart felt heavy when she thought about going home, the tense atmosphere and the clipped conversations. Only a month ago, she'd thought she had the perfect marriage – as good as it got, anyway – but now it hurt just to think about David.

'If you really like it, do you want me to call up the designer and ask if you can have it?' said Renee, cutting through her painful thoughts. 'They do seventy per cent press discounts and I know the PR really well, so I'm sure I can sort it out.'

Amy looked at her, an idea forming. 'Do you think you could do that for me?'

Renee nodded. 'Why don't you just take it now? I'm sure it's your size.'

Amy took the dress off the rail and went into the ladies'. In the cubicle, she changed out of her skirt and blouse, slipping on the red crêpe de chine and smoothing it down over her hips. Then she opened the loo door and looked at her reflection.

She had never been truly obsessed with clothes, not like some of the fashion girls, who would go without lunch for six months so that they could buy an Erdem dress on sale, or comb eBay looking for vintage finds. But now she understood their transformative power.

Gone was the cuckolded wife who would let a twenty-one-year-old get the better of her. Instead, she looked like the kick-ass editor everyone thought she was; the woman who had spontaneously pitched the company CEO for one of the biggest jobs in the industry.

She returned to her office to collect her suitcase. It was almost five, and already people were beginning to drift off.

'You look great,' said Chrissie, putting a bunch of Post-it note messages on her desk.

'I have to go,' Amy said, picking up her bag.

'I don't know how you do it,' grinned Chrissie.

'Let's see if I can,' she mumbled as she pulled her jacket off its hanger.

A taxi took her straight into the City and dropped her off outside David's office.

The nights were still long, but the height of the buildings surrounding her seemed to block out the light and made her shiver. She looked up at the rows of windows above her, the shadows of workers sitting at computers, and pulled her phone out of her pocket.

Her text was simple.

Come to reception.

She stood on the pavement, watching his world through the floor-to-ceiling sheets of glass. She was nervous and unsettled at the thought of seeing him, more nervous than her first day at the house in Oxford, when she'd turned up with her two suitcases of possessions, wondering whether she was making the biggest mistake of her life moving in with a group of people she didn't really know and who were certainly not from her world. Back then, she had found her steel, reminding herself that Pog's offer was a remarkable opportunity and she couldn't let her fear and insecurity stop her from grabbing it.

She felt that same fear and uncertainty now. What if she and David didn't come to some sort of truce? What was the next step? Selling the house, splitting the assets and sharing custody of Tilly; meeting David only to hand over their daughter in some polite exchange every other weekend.

She didn't want to stop and dwell on it.

Instead, she watched as the commuters began to leave in their droves: post boys and secretaries, the lower-paid employees, who had smaller pay cheques but no doubt bigger lives outside the office.

For the first time in her marriage, she wondered if David's late nights were just an excuse to stay away from home. After all, not everyone leaving the bank was a junior. She'd always assumed that he genuinely had been working till eight, nine o'clock every night, but maybe she'd been played like a fool then too.

She was about to leave when she saw him exit the big glass lift in the middle of the foyer. She could feel her heart starting to beat harder, but she steadied herself enough to take off her jacket. She was surprised at how cold it was out of the evening sun, but perhaps her mind was playing tricks; perhaps it was because she felt so naked and exposed that she was shivering. She watched the quiet deference with which David was treated by the people around him, and felt pride first, and then longing.

He glanced around reception, looking puzzled and – dare she hope it – disappointed. She was just about to wave at him when he saw her and moved towards the revolving doors. She wanted to put her jacket back on, but she wanted him to see her in her red dress even more.

In a few seconds he was out on the street beside her, keeping a cautious, awkward distance. He had definitely noticed what she was wearing, but she couldn't work out what he was thinking.

'What are you doing out here?' he said finally.

She was glad he had spoken first, because everything she had planned had suddenly escaped her.

'Waiting for you,' she said as he took a step closer.

He reached out an unsure hand and she took it, and then she was in his arms, her head against the soft wool of his suit jacket, and she could feel his hands settling into the small of her back.

'I've missed you,' he said into the top of her hair.

She drew away from him. She knew she hadn't come all the way to the City not to discuss Josie Price.

'Why was Josie at the house last night?' she said.

'She said she'd forgotten some things. She didn't stay long.'

Amy nodded.

'It's the truth,' said David quietly. 'She can't have been there more than twenty minutes. I think she realised I wanted her to leave.'

'Can we just forget she ever came into our lives? Forget she ever existed?'

'Only if you believe that nothing happened between us. Nothing at all.'

'I believe you,' she said, for the first time almost accepting it as the truth. 'I'll believe you if it means we can just get back to where we were.'

'Believe me because you understand how much I love you,' he said, holding her hand. 'I've always loved you, even before the moment I saw you on Threadneedle Street in that other red dress.'

She didn't say anything, wanting to let him just talk. It was true that before Josie they'd had a good marriage and often told each other that they loved one another. But it was *why* people loved that was perhaps not vocalised enough. Everyone wanted to hear why they were special, why they had been picked, and Amy was desperate to hear his reasons now.

'I knew I loved you the night of the Commem Ball,' he

said finally. 'Maybe even before then. You were always the one I wanted to sit with at the kitchen table, the one I wanted to talk to when I got home from the pub. If you ever wondered why Annabel didn't come round to the house much, it was because I didn't want you to see me with anyone else.'

Amy remembered those days too. Remembered going out to buy a Christmas tree with him from Oxford's covered market and decorating it over mugfuls of home-made eggnog. Suddenly she just wanted to do all those simple things again. She pulled her jacket back on and raised her arm for a cab.

'Let's go home,' she said, her face breaking into a smile. 'Let's go and see our daughter and make some hot chocolate.'

Chapter 29

The platform was packed. Steam rose from the polished black engine and a buzz of voices filled the air. Dozens of partygoers were dressed to the nines, the women in gowns and faux-fur coats, the men in DJs or wide-shouldered suits, some even sporting capes and rakish hats. The scene was like a particularly glamorous Agatha Christie adaptation, while the atmosphere was light-hearted, excitable, like the start of a school trip to the zoo.

'You'd have thought none of them had been on a train before,' said Amy.

David smiled. 'I shouldn't think they have,' he said, raising his voice as the engine gave a screeching lurch, sending up a delighted flutter of squeals from the crowd. 'I mean, imagine you're Jack Nicholson. I wouldn't think he's been on public transport since the sixties.'

Amy grinned. Jack Nicholson wasn't on the guest list, but a smattering of Hollywood A-listers were, along with TV stars, singers, artists and at least half of fashionable London. A handful of invitees had pulled out after the short-lived Miranda scandal, citing prior commitments, children's birthday parties or sudden illnesses, and Miranda herself had declined to come, which was disappointing if understandable.

Amy knew she would have worried about it more if she hadn't spent the last week in a state of constant panic, dealing with every last detail of the party from the light bulbs to the forks. Everything that could go wrong did on a daily basis. A shipment of gin went missing, the temp agency providing waiters went bankrupt, and a shrimp shortage in the North Sea meant they had to rethink the nibbles. Some days it felt as though they were cursed. But little by little it had all come together.

'You look at home in that suit,' she said, touching David's arm with one finger. It was true. He had always looked good in pinstripes, but in this navy Savile Row three-piece, he looked like a 1940s heart-throb; Cary Grant in his prime. He didn't often attend *Verve* events, not because she didn't want him there, but because it was invariably 'just work', but today, it seemed important that he was by her side.

David tugged at his cuffs modestly. 'You don't look too bad yourself.'

Amy glanced down at her peacock-blue Dior gown. It was vintage, one of a kind, and accessorised with pearl earrings and a midnight-blue overcoat draped off her shoulders. She knew she looked better than she had in years. Perhaps it was because she felt good too. Going to David's office last week to resolve their problems had been the best thing she could have done. They had gone home to a delighted Tilly, who was thrilled to see her parents back so early, and made hot chocolate and cuddled up on the sofa, the sub-zero atmosphere slowly rising click by click until it actually felt as if they were back to normal. Almost.

And now here he was, standing at her side, supporting her on her big night. On the outside they were the very picture of a glamorous power couple, but inside? Only time would tell.

'You'd better not have put me next to that idiot MD of

yours at dinner,' said David, looking around.

'You've got Suzie Grazer the film director and one of the advertisers, I think.' Amy had made sure she'd seated him between two happily married sixty-something intellectuals who wouldn't have the slightest interest in flirting over petit fours.

A guard in a peaked cap blew his whistle and half a dozen conductors opened the dark-green-and-gold doors of the carriages, helping the eager guests inside.

'Showtime,' said Amy, moving forward.

Stepping through the doorway, she almost gasped. She turned to watch David's reaction and saw that he was equally impressed: the interior designers deserved their reputation as wizards. It was wonderful, like stepping into a classic 1940s black-and-white movie, only here, everything was in gleaming Technicolor: deep-purple velvet upholstery, white linen tablecloths, polished walnut wall panels. And the guests were as glamorous as the surroundings: ball gowns in peacock shades of blue, green and gold, furs and pearls, tie pins and spats.

'Wow, is that who I think it is?' muttered David from the side of his mouth. Amy just laughed and shrugged as they threaded their way along the corridor from one carriage to the next. He could have been referring to any of the guests crowding the train. A film star here, a model there, a racing car driver laughing with them both. Clearly everyone had forgotten the faux-pas of Miranda Pilley. Never let a little thing like fake outrage get in the way of a good party, thought Amy. And this was a *great* party – and they hadn't even set off yet. She smiled. Even if she didn't get the *Mode* job, she knew this would impress the top brass.

'Whoa!' A cry of delight rang up and down the train as it jerked into motion. Wavering on her high heels, Amy fell sideways only to feel David's strong arms around her. She leaned against him gratefully, catching the grin on his face before they bounced apart again.

The journey to Oxford would take less than an hour, and Amy was determined to enjoy every minute, knowing that it would pass almost as quickly as she could click her fingers. She passed Janice deep in conversation with her old flame, rock musician Cody Cole, surrounded by a huddle of edgy pop stars she could barely name. She grinned as she saw Juliet approaching from the other direction.

'Amy, this is just fabulous,' Juliet said, air-kissing. '*You're* fabulous.'

She had clearly pulled out all the stops herself, slinky in a sequin-covered silver sheath, her hair a cascade of curls.

'I'm glad you're here,' said Amy honestly. The two friends hadn't spoken since their heart-to-heart in New York, and Amy hadn't been sure if she would come. 'Maybe we can talk later on.'

Juliet gave a small shake of the head. 'Not tonight,' she said. 'Tonight is your night. Everything else can wait.' She glanced away, a chink in her confident, unflappable aura, and Amy wondered what had gone on in the week since she had told her about Peter.

'You look like a hot mermaid,' said David, taking a glass of champagne. Juliet slapped him on the arm, but Amy could see she was pleased.

'It seems funny to be going back to Oxford.'

'I've never really thought of it like that,' Amy admitted.

'Seriously, though, this is a master stroke,' said Juliet. 'Everyone is on this train. How have you pulled it off? There can't be anybody at the E-Squared dinner.'

'Hard bloody work,' said Amy with a rueful smile. 'It helped that we invited the E-Squared CEO as well. Apparently he's coming by helicopter later.'

'Look at him go,' smiled Juliet, watching David moving

easily around the carriage, shaking hands, making jokes, the handsome, cheeky life and soul of the party.

'He's always good in these situations,' smiled Amy, watching him. 'Hard to be impressed by the world's most successful designer or supermodel when you've never heard their name before.'

'So you've patched things up?'

Amy nodded. 'It's been horrible living in such a toxic atmosphere, avoiding each other.'

'You've forgiven him?'

Amy looked at her friend, not wanting to get emotional. 'What's the alternative? Divorce?'

And that was when the train stopped abruptly with a screech of brakes, metal on metal.

With a crunch, the entire carriage lurched forward, then back, people flying in every direction. Amy crashed against a window, her fall mercifully cushioned by the heavy drapes. She held onto the back of a booth, just missing hitting her head. There was a pause of perhaps a second, then uproar. Squeals turned to screams, a cacophony of pleading voices, cries and wails.

'Attention, ladies and gentlemen, please!' A commanding baritone voice drew everyone's attention. Even Amy looked up in surprise as she recognised her husband's voice. 'Please don't panic, we have everything under control. The train has simply had to make an emergency stop because the driver had a report of an obstruction on the line. It will just be a few minutes and then we'll be on our way again.'

He paused, and immediately there were calls for more information, cries about injuries, pleas for help.

'I know a few of you have had a bump, so if you could look around at the people immediately next to you and see how you can help them, I will be back in two minutes and we'll get you sorted.'

There was more shouting, questions, general hubbub, but Amy could tell the panic had subsided. Clearly the VIPs had bought David's bluff, and as she helped Jasmine Craig, the supermodel, to her feet, she could hear him already moving through the next carriage spreading his message of authority and calm.

'Bloody hell,' said Jasmine, her big eyes wide. 'That was pretty intense, wasn't it?' The girl next to her, a celebrity chef, echoed the sentiment, and nervous laughter began to bubble up as people suddenly began discussing what had happened. It was quickly apparent that no one had suffered any lasting injuries, and relief turned to amusement, then a sort of jovial Blitz spirit of shared adventure. It was almost as if they were treating the accident as part of the entertainment.

Amy was just reassuring Gerard Harper, star of the West End, that the train would still arrive on time when she saw David in the doorway beckoning to her.

His face was set and serious. 'Look, I've just spoken to the driver – for real, this time. There was an abandoned car on a level crossing; he only just spotted it in time.'

'You're kidding?'

David shook his head. 'Can you imagine if we'd hit it? The whole train would have derailed for sure.'

Amy shivered just thinking about the tragedy that had been narrowly averted.

'So can we get moving now?'

David shook his head. 'Procedures. Apparently they have to wait for the police to make an assessment as to whether it's safe to proceed.'

'How long?'

'How long's a piece of string?'

Amy ducked down to peer out of the window. It was dark, no houses or buildings anywhere near – certainly no stations close enough to unload their precious cargo.

'Is anyone hurt?'

'I think everyone's okay,' said David. 'Shaken up, but nothing beyond a few bruises – apart from one woman who was in the bathroom at the time and hit her head pretty hard. I think you'd better come and see.'

She followed him down through two carriages, stopping briefly to check on guests with the odd word of sympathy and encouragement, to where a uniformed guard was sitting with an elderly lady she immediately recognised as Louisa Bourne, grande dame of the fashion world.

'I seem to have had a bump,' she said, holding a wet towel to her head. 'Sorry to be such a bore.'

'No, no, I just want to make sure you're all right.'

'I've already asked someone to bring me a glass of bubbly, if it hasn't all been too shaken up.' She gave a whisper of a smile and then lolled back on her seat, her eyes rolling back into her head.

'Louisa?' said Amy urgently.

The woman didn't respond, and Amy touched her cheek to try and get a reaction. She had no medical training but she could tell that Louisa's head wound was serious, blood already beginning to congeal around a wide gash in her scalp.

'David,' she shouted, knowing that she needed help.

Her husband came running.

'I think she's fainted.'

They both knew it was more serious than that.

'We need a doctor,' Amy said. 'We need to get her to hospital.'

'But we're in the middle of nowhere.'

'A level crossing means a road.' Amy was trying to think. 'Which means an ambulance can get to us.'

David came round behind Louisa to prop her up while Amy felt her pulse. It throbbed underneath her fingertips but the old lady's eyes were still closed.

As David pulled his mobile out of his pocket to call for help, Amy moved back through the train. Everyone seemed to be talking at once, laughter and jabbering voices coming from all directions: a holiday atmosphere was prevailing for now at least. That was something.

She found Janice and Juliet deep in conversation.

'Ladies, thank God I've got you both.' She filled them in on the situation and the need to get Louisa to hospital.

'You must go with her,' said Juliet immediately. 'We're more than capable of keeping people happy until the train's moving again.'

Janice nodded. 'We have about fifty cases of champagne in the guard's van. That'll keep them going. And I'll speak to Cody about bringing the entertainment forward.'

Their can-do spirit was exactly what Amy needed, and she felt a little of the weight lift from her.

The guard came and introduced himself. 'I've checked all the carriages, ma'am.'

'No one else is hurt, are they?'

'Young lady in the bar. I think it's only whiplash, but better safe than sorry.'

Amy's mind was full of imaginary headlines: 'Fashion Sweetheart Dies in Rail Smash, Magazine Editor to Blame for Everything'. 'Why is this happening to me?' she whispered under her breath. Her rational mind was trying to tell her that it was all just bad luck and could have happened to anyone, but Amy wasn't really listening.

It was another twenty minutes before the ambulance arrived. The blue lights and the siren sent another wave of panic through the guests, with some of them asking if they could get off the train. The guard made several announcements keeping everyone up to date with what was happening; the police had also arrived and were attempting to remove the vehicle from the crossing, but no one knew how long it would be before they were allowed to continue their journey.

'I've contacted the coach firm who were supposed to be picking us up in Oxford,' he told Amy. 'They reckon they can be here within an hour.'

'That's something,' said Amy, glancing at her watch. The event was due to start at any moment. There were a few dozen guests who had chosen to go straight to the venue, and who would now be rattling around in the grandeur of Blenheim with nothing but a plateful of canapés for company. Douglas Proctor was one of those going by car, thanks to the proximity of his weekend retreat to Blenheim; she could only imagine his face when nobody showed up.

Ahead of her, Louisa was being stretchered into the ambulance. Amy could see the front of the train, its buffers barely feet away from a Volvo estate, still diagonal across the tracks.

'God, that was close,' she whispered, and David nodded, his eyebrows raised, clearly imagining his own headlines.

Amy approached the ambulance and peered inside. Louisa's eyes were open, and she managed a weak smile.

'You gave us a fright,' said Amy, touching her hand.

'Are you coming to the hospital, miss?' asked the paramedic.

She glanced towards the train and the guests inside, then back to Louisa, frail and alone. She had no choice.

'I'll come with you,' said David.

Chapter 30

Louisa needed stitches and a night in hospital for observation. By the time Amy and David got back to Notting Hill, grey light was creeping into the sky and the birds were beginning to sing. David dropped his jacket on the banister and zombied his way into the bedroom, where Amy heard the *whoomph* as he fell onto the mattress.

She herself knew she couldn't sleep. She kept running the night over and over in her head, wondering if she had done the right thing abandoning the party to take care of Louisa. She knew the older woman was grateful for everything she and David had done, keeping her company in A&E until her daughter, who lived in Devon, had been able to get to the hospital. Morally it had been the right decision; she only hoped Douglas Proctor would see it that way. Louisa was one of the most powerful women in the fashion industry, a former president of the Fashion Council and founder of the Exmoor chain of boutiques, which had started in the sixties with a single shop on Bond Street but was now one of the biggest fashion e-retailer powerhouses in the world. That alone should have been enough to excuse Amy from the party, but you never could tell with the MD of Genesis Media.

She walked through to the kitchen, flicking on the lights

and firing up the coffee machine. There was little point sleeping now anyway: she'd have to go straight into the office and begin the mop-up operation. Flowers to be sent, sponsors to be reassured, bills to pay.

'Hell to pay, more like,' she muttered, picking up her phone as it buzzed.

'Amy Shepherd?' asked a male voice, unbearably perky at this time of the morning. 'Derek Morgan at the *Chronicle*.'

Amy's heart fell. She had been expecting Juliet or Janice with sisterly words of support. She fought the urge to just hang up. She knew she'd have to face up to it sooner or later.

'Derek, how can I help?' she said, not even questioning how he had her number.

'We're running a piece on the biggest party that never was,' he replied.

Amy considered a terse 'no comment', or even better, 'bugger off', but knew she needed to do her best to spin the story in her favour.

'I'm not sure that's quite accurate, Derek. It was just smaller than we expected. Getting Louisa Bourne, one of Britain's most important exporters, to hospital was more than worth compromising the scale of the event for. She's fine, by the way, if you're asking.'

'Great, great. And any comment on the rumour that it cost the company five million pounds?'

Amy gave a polite laugh. 'I think you've been misinformed. We didn't take over Blenheim Palace in its entirety.'

'Ah, that's not what it looks like from here. I don't think it will look like that to the readers either.'

She held her breath and the hack filled the silence.

'Do you want me to send you the footage? One of our reporters went along last night . . . Hang on, I'm sending it now . . .'

Amy closed her eyes and silently swore. How many times had she spoken to the event's security team about keeping the press away? Obviously her concern had been for different reasons: keeping their own shots of the party exclusive and protecting the privacy of the VIPs, allowing them to let their hair down without worrying about embarrassing drunken antics appearing in the *Chronicle* the next day. But the principle was the same, and she made a mental note to speak to the man in charge of manning the cordon.

Her phone beeped and she thumbed open the email, clicking on the attachment, an MPG movie. Oh crap, she thought as it rolled. It was obvious the angle the piece was going to take. The reporter had clearly just walked straight into the party, his camera recording everything. The grand entrance of the palace, the flaming torches either side of the doors, the vast flower arrangements, the trays and trays of untouched champagne and expensive canapés, the brightly lit stage crammed with instruments and nothing else. The camera panned around. It wasn't just the stage that was empty; it was the whole party. It looked like the first reel of a zombie movie where the hero wakes to find everyone dead. The biggest party that never was: that was exactly what it looked like. A five-million-pound folly. It didn't matter that after sponsorship, the party had cost Genesis almost nothing; recent experience told Amy that the truth never got in the way of a good headline.

'Any comment?' said Derek.

The newspapers all went big on the empty party story. Amy couldn't really blame them. She was shuffling through the papers strewn across the kitchen table as David came downstairs, looking bleary-eyed. As he headed for the coffee machine, he caught sight of the headlines over her shoulder.

'Oh shit,' he said. He picked up the *Daily News* and

scanned the story. 'At least the *News* have run the human interest angle on Louisa,' he said. '"Glamorous *Verve* editor Amy Shepherd, 43, personally took the fashion legend to the hospital",' he read out.

'They've got my age wrong, but it's something,' she said.

'Let's hope Douglas Proctor is a *News* reader, hey?'

Amy gave a soft snort. Even if the party had actually cost the magazine – and the company – less than William Bentley's leaving party, the headlines were going to stick, she knew. In an economic downturn, people liked a bit of escapism; they loved to see pictures of celebrities in fancy dresses, but they certainly didn't like to hear about money being poured down the drain, money they could have used for food or rent or a holiday to Spain. No one liked to hear about overprivileged idiots making fools of themselves.

'It doesn't matter, you know,' said David, sitting down opposite her. 'I know you're panicking that this is going to lose you the *Mode* job, but if they judge you on this, if they mark you down because you did the decent thing and stayed with Louisa, then they're not worth it.'

She mulled over her husband's words on the way into the office. There were certainly some people who would be happy to hear about her misfortune: any of the other candidates for the *Mode* job, for starters. Because Amy knew that the chances of her landing the post were now somewhere between 'bugger all' and 'none'. The fact that Marv Schultz was due to fly into London any day was little consolation. Once he'd had Douglas whispering in his ear, her off-piste meeting with him was as good as dead.

As she approached the front of the Genesis building, Amy half expected to see reporters waiting there, barking questions, looking for a follow-up from the woman who'd single-handedly screwed up the party of the decade, but there was no one, just a girl she recognised from *Verve*'s fashion department puffing on a cigarette. Seeing Amy climb out of the car, she looked panicked and quickly threw her butt away.

'Sorry, Amy,' she said. 'Been trying to quit, I'm down to one in the morning and one at night, honestly.'

Amy gave a weak smile. 'Good for you . . .' she tilted her head to the side, 'Jo, isn't it? Sorry, terrible with names.'

'Oh no, that's fine,' said the girl, falling into step with Amy as they pushed through the doors and across the foyer to the lifts. 'I've only been here six weeks. Janice brought me in straight from college, pretty much. I'm loving it.'

They stepped into the lift and Amy pressed the button.

'Were you at the venue last night?' she asked. The most senior members of the team had been on the train to look after the VIP guests, but the rest of the staff had gone straight to Blenheim.

Jo nodded sympathetically. 'I was supposed to be on hand for any fashion emergencies: you know, ripped gowns, pinching shoes, false-eyelash slip . . . Wish I'd been on the train, though. It looked like brilliant fun. People are going to be talking about it for years.'

Amy frowned. 'I think the sooner we all forget about it, the better, don't you?'

'Really?' said Jo, puzzled. 'It looked a right laugh.'

Amy shook her head, utterly confused now. 'Look, Jo, I have to confess I haven't the slightest idea what you're talking about. What do you mean about the train?'

'You mean you haven't seen it?' Jo scrabbled in her shoulder bag and brought out her phone, thumbing through the apps with a speed only a digital native could achieve before holding it out to Amy. 'Look, it's all over the net.'

Baffled, Amy clicked the play button on the phone's screen, expecting to see more tumbleweed footage of the empty corridors in Blenheim. Instead she was greeted with the interior of a train carriage. Warm orange light shone out from the wall lamps as a group of beautiful people in shimmering gowns leaned over a table covered in crisp white linen. 'Now put the card face down on the table,' said a male voice, strangely familiar, off camera. There was a hushed pause as a tattooed hand slid forward and flipped a playing card over: the ace of diamonds. Amy flinched as a roar came from the phone, delighted laughter and hoots of 'No way!' and 'How did you do that?' The camera pulled back to reveal that the conjuror was none other than Evan Ridley, the drop-dead-gorgeous American actor currently breaking box office records as the star of the latest superhero franchise.

Amy looked up at Jo and the girl nodded happily. 'There's loads of them on there,' she said. 'I think there must have been a camera crew on the train.'

Amy nodded dumbly as Jo cued up another clip, this time of two soap actors in fits of hysterics as Ginny Hough, the famously dour BBC arts presenter, took her turn at charades, eventually giving up in frustration and protesting to further hilarity that she had been doing Jay-Z's '99 Problems'.

The lift had arrived at the office floor, but Amy held the door as Jo showed her another clip, of Cody Cole leading the entire carriage in a chorus of 'Live Forever': actors, singers, models, everyone singing their hearts out. It did indeed look like it had been the party of the year after all.

'And this is all over the net?' asked Amy, stepping out of the lift and handing the phone back.

Jo nodded. 'It's the big news this morning. Everyone's talking about it.' She pointed at the papers wedged under Amy's arm. 'Everyone except them. They missed it – they always do.'

Amy nodded her thanks and walked into her office, her head in a whirl. Sitting down at her desk, she fired up her computer and clicked onto her browser. Before she'd even typed in the address of a gossip site, she saw that Jo was right. In the 'Trending Now' sidebar, there were at least half a dozen references to it. 'Party on wheels', 'Steam-powered fun on *Verve* train', 'See *that* Cody Cole singalong here'.

She rubbed a hand over her mouth. Could it really have turned around so quickly? Hope flared in her heart until her gaze fell on the newspapers she'd tossed onto her desk and it blinked out again. Jo from the fashion department might have seen the 'party on wheels' clips, as might millions of others hooked up to the web via their phones. But Douglas, Denton Scoles and Marv Schultz would be reading the *Mail* and the *Sun* and the *Chronicle*. That was their reality, whatever lip service they paid to the onward march of the new digital order.

She began scrolling through her emails, but didn't get very far. The first one her eye fell on was marked with a red exclamation mark: urgent. And it was from josie.price @ genesis.inc, subject title: Douglas Meeting Today. She barely needed to open it to know what it would say.

Amy: urgent. Douglas would like to see you as soon as you get in today. Please come straight up. J.

'What, no kiss-kiss at the end?' muttered Amy, clicking off and reaching for her bag.

As the lift doors opened, Josie's face was the first thing Amy saw. She was expecting a sly smirk, but instead Josie gave her a warm smile.

'Thanks for coming, wasn't sure if you'd got the message.' She tilted her head sympathetically. 'Sorry to hear about last night.'

Amy tried to remain calm and professional.

'I believe the party on the train has gone viral, so you can't call it a complete disaster.'

'You can go in,' said Josie, ignoring her comment and motioning towards Douglas's office.

Amy hated that she had to get permission from Josie for anything, and didn't look back as she rapped twice on the door and went inside. Immediately she knew it was going to be a bad morning. Douglas's face was stony. The overall atmosphere of the room was sub-zero.

'Take a seat, Amy,' he said. Whichever version of events he had absorbed, it clearly hadn't pleased him. He looked at her for a moment, as if he was deciding how to start. 'Not the result we were hoping for, was it?' he said finally.

Amy couldn't help smiling, though clearly Douglas hadn't been aiming for irony or gallows humour.

'No,' she said. 'It wasn't exactly a triumph. But not a total train wreck either. If you'll excuse the pun.'

Douglas, however, didn't crack his totem-pole face.

'Yes, I have seen the digital coverage, but I think we can all agree that is down to chance rather than planning. Certainly not what you and your team have spent the last six months preparing for.'

'Douglas, the most important thing was getting Louisa to hospital. Everyone accepts that. The car on the crossing was a freak incident we couldn't plan for. Given the circumstances, I think we've got decent PR out of it. Money can't buy publicity, actually.'

'None of this would have happened if you hadn't insisted on transporting most of the guest list by luxury train. What was wrong with "make your own way there"?'

'Douglas, we needed to tempt people to the party.'

'Tempt? If the idea of a *Verve* party was good enough in the first place, surely people wouldn't have to be tempted.' He tapped one stubby finger on the desk in front of him. 'Look, you should know that in the light of this and other recent developments, we've decided we just can't take your

Mode application any further. It's a big job, attracting the very best candidates . . .'

Amy was determined not to let this slip through her fingers. 'Douglas, I can do incredible things with that magazine. If you've read my vision, you'll know I can. Don't let what happened on the train last night detract from the fact that I am the best person for *Mode*.'

'It's not just the party,' he said flatly.

Amy felt as if she had been punched in the stomach. They had simply gone for another candidate.

'Have you spoken to Marv Schultz? I saw him in New York. He wants me to present my strategy for *Mode*—'

'Amy, please. Just leave it.'

Amy nodded, struggling to stop the hot tears from flowing. 'Well thank you, Douglas, for considering me,' she said. 'I would have relished the opportunity, but I'm sure you'll find the right candidate for the position.'

She glanced up, expecting him to stutter out a few platitudes: 'your application was strong', 'a fine candidate', 'moving in another direction', all the usual flannel. Instead, he looked at her unflinchingly.

'We think you should take some time off, Amy,' he said. 'It's clear you're overworked and that fatigue is having a negative impact on the magazine and your staff.'

Now Amy felt the breath catch in her throat. *What?*

'I can't, it's Milan,' she said. 'I'm flying out on Tuesday.'

'I've already had Josie cancel the flights. Janice will still go to represent the magazine, of course.'

'Janice? You can't send her alone. The editor has to go to Milan. The advertisers will think—'

'You should probably keep a low profile with the advertisers right now.'

'Is this about the Miranda thing, then? That was a storm in a teacup and the ad team assures me—'

'It's you, Amy,' said Douglas suddenly. 'Not the magazine, not the brand. You, you're the problem.'

She gaped at him. 'Me?'

Douglas nodded, looking as awkward as she'd ever seen him. 'It's been brought to my attention that you have a problem.'

She was speechless for a second.

'What kind of problem?'

'The drugs, Amy. We know.'

Amy actually laughed. 'I've never touched drugs in my life!'

Douglas pressed his lips together in what she presumed was supposed to resemble a pained look.

'Last night, a cleaner found some paraphernalia in your office. Needles, Amy.'

She dropped her head back, letting out a groan of relief.

'Oh *that*,' she said. 'It's not drugs, it's a booster shot. Amino acids.'

Douglas was shaking his head sadly. 'The first step to getting well is admitting you have a problem. We'll give you all the support we can; we've already been in touch with a clinic . . .'

'It's not drugs!' she snapped, pulling up her sleeve to show him her inner arm. 'Do I look like a junkie? It's vitamin shots! It's like Botox or fillers.'

'Amy, this isn't a suggestion.'

'You're firing me?'

'Asking you to step back. There will be a cash incentive. Plus we will pay for a stay in a facility for you. Never let it be said that Genesis doesn't support its employees.'

'Douglas, I don't want to step back and I don't want to go to a facility, whether you pay for it or otherwise.'

He was leaning forward, making a patting motion with his hand, as if he was trying to calm a snapping Dobermann.

'There's no shame, Amy, honestly. We're here to help in any way we can. And obviously no one outside this room will hear a hint of it until you're better. Tracey can step up in the short term.'

'Douglas, this is total rubbish, you have to believe me.'

His stony face had returned. 'You're suspended pending investigation and/or treatment,' he said. 'HR will send you the paperwork.'

'I'm not a drug addict!'

'Frankly, Amy, it doesn't matter. The rumour is out there, and the one thing the industry won't tolerate is drugs. You know that. It's a multi-billion-dollar industry; we can't have even a whiff of it attached to us. Advertisers are fickle and advertising is our lifeblood. Apparently Dolce & Gabbana have already got wind of it.'

Amy stood up so suddenly that Douglas shrank back in his seat. Perhaps he didn't like drama after all.

'It's always about money, isn't it?' she said, her voice low, tight. 'It's never about people. *That's* why this company is going under.'

'I think it's time to leave, Amy.'

'But I haven't done anything wrong,' she said, her voice trembling.

'We don't want to have to call security.'

'Security? Douglas, listen to yourself. I am not a drug addict. I have never touched drugs.'

An image flashed into her mind. That afternoon she had come back from Dr Al Saraf's. Josie sitting in Chrissie's chair, a phone call, a flurry, a knocked bag spilling its contents on the floor. She'd let Josie pick it up and the girl had obviously seen a stray syringe.

'It's Josie, isn't it?' she said, pointing towards the door. 'Josie told you I was on drugs. She saw a syringe and made up a story to discredit me.'

Douglas raised a hand. 'Amy, listen to yourself. I know you're upset, but there's no need to start throwing accusations around.'

'That little tramp seduced my husband. Did you know that?' She was pointing at Douglas himself now. Her heart was hammering hard and she could feel sweat beading at her temples.

Douglas had got up from his desk and had walked round to her side. Now he put a hand on her shoulder to direct her out of the room. She spun away.

'Get off me,' she hissed.

As he opened the door, she could see Josie standing there holding a mug of tea. She couldn't hold her anger and frustration in any longer.

'Are you happy now?' she screamed. 'I have only ever tried to help you, and you do this to me. You want my life, is that it? And if you can't have it, you want to destroy me.'

Douglas was now openly restraining her. Denton Scoles had appeared out of his office eating a biscuit.

'Watch her, just watch her,' Amy said, trying to wriggle out of Douglas's grasp.

'Amy, are you all right?' said Josie in a smooth, calm voice. 'Do you want me to call David?'

'I don't want you going anywhere near my husband,' she screamed.

She watched Josie and Douglas exchange glances.

'I've called security,' said Denton, not looking Amy in the eye.

'Don't worry,' she spat. 'I'm leaving. This business, Douglas. It isn't about magazines. It's about people.' She flashed a look at Josie. 'And the moment you make the wrong pick is the moment you find it all unravelling.'

Chapter 31

Max's Holland Park house was big. No real surprise there; everything about Max was big, overblown. Maybe he's overcompensating for something, thought Amy, then immediately regretted it, not wanting to think about Max's endowment, large or otherwise.

She stood outside the shiny black door, psyching herself for a minute before she went in.

Max Quinn wasn't the ideal shoulder to cry on, but David was locked in a key meeting with Japanese investors all morning and she didn't want to disturb him, not when she felt so hysterical. Besides, when it came to fighting back against Douglas Proctor, who better to call than the ruthless snake himself.

Rehab. It was just more corporate arse-covering of the worst kind. Even if she really had been hooked on heroin, did anyone seriously believe that Douglas was committed to getting her off the black tar and into recovery? And once she was whole again, was he really going to let her back in charge of Genesis Media's number one cash cow? Was he hell. All they had to do was make the right noises, pretend to be sympathetic to her 'issues', then scoot her off with whatever token redundancy payment would keep her quiet. No, Amy knew her career was over – at Genesis certainly;

possibly in the media as a whole, depending on how much of the story the gossips swallowed.

She took a deep breath and pressed the bell.

It might be over for Amy, but that didn't mean she was going to let this go. Not in a million years. Because someone had created that story, fabricated it and spread it. She had seen through it immediately.

According to Douglas, a cleaner had found the needles the previous night, yet in the next breath he was telling her that Dolce & Gabbana already knew about the rumours. Yeah, right. Either the cleaner had immediately rung Milan, or someone was lying. More than that: someone had decided to use the lie to bring her down. And Amy was going to find out who.

'Amy!' said Claire, opening the door. 'Such a surprise. What on earth are you doing on a social call at this time?'

'It was actually Max I wanted to speak to. I called his office. His PA said he was straight off a flight from New York but was stopping off at home first.'

'He's just in the shower freshening up. He's gutted to have missed the Blenheim party.'

'I assume you've read the papers today.'

Claire nodded and looked down. 'It was unlucky.'

'You could say that. They've fired me.'

Claire wrapped her friend in a hug. 'Oh honey,' she said, pulling away. 'I'll make tea.'

Amy followed her through the spotless house into the kitchen. It was like a spread from *Vogue Living* magazine: endless white marble with sparkling copper pans hanging from the central island. There was a neatly squared-off pile of letters on the counter, and a single coffee mug stood on the gleaming stainless-steel sink.

'Max!' shouted Claire. 'Amy's here!'

She rolled her eyes at Amy as she directed her to a sun-trap conservatory off the kitchen. 'He announced he's work-ing from home today, but it's no coincidence that Pog is in town. Apparently they've made plans for dinner and drinks. I assume they're starting early.'

'Not too early, I hope,' said Amy, flipping through her phone to look at her schedule. 'I'm supposed to be seeing him for lunch.'

She perched on the edge of a cream sofa as Claire fussed around arranging coasters for their tea, smiling inwardly and wondering as she always did whether this was what Claire had imagined when she had set her sights on Max Quinn, millionaire. Was it satisfying staying at home all day making sure the cleaners kept the taps polished, or popping out to get a blow-dry? Amy had never even considered this way of life; to her, forging her own career, earning her own money was the only possible route, but as she'd got older, marriage and children had made her wonder. What was so wrong with a life of leisure and luxury, especially if you got to spend time with your child and husband instead of stuck in meetings or fighting through traffic every day?

Though of course, if your husband was Max, she thought as he entered the room, maybe you'd be making excuses to stay longer at the office.

'Darling!' he cried, throwing his arms wide and scooping Amy into a bear hug. 'My day – no, my week is complete! Fuck *Call of Duty*,' he added, vaulting over the back of a sofa and landing fully prone, arms behind head. 'This is more important. Tell me everything: how can we help?'

Amy blinked at him, then glanced across at Claire, who gave a shrug.

'Well, I assume something's gone pretty badly wrong if you're coming out here in the middle of the day. In fact it must be totally fucked up if you're turning to Maxie for help.'

Amy couldn't help but smile at that.

'What's happened? David finally run off with that wotsit – Josie?'

She closed her eyes, in no mood for his flippancy.

'Oh come on,' said Max. 'I may be stupid, but I'm not deaf. It was hard to miss you and David having a screaming match at the villa. Then you bugger off to London and Juliet's herding the poppet in the bikini into the back of a cab. I've seen enough episodes of *Falcon Crest* to work out the rest.'

Amy snapped her eyes back open.

'No, Max, David hasn't run off with anyone. Not that I'm aware of, anyway. And yes, we've been having . . . a few problems, but this is something different.'

Max waited patiently. He clearly wasn't going to take the hint.

'If you must know, I've been fired. Well, as good as. Suspended pending investigation.' Sighing, she related the events of the morning. To her irritation, Max started laughing.

'Sorry, sorry,' he said. 'Just the idea of you as a drug addict is hilarious. A Notting Hill Lou Reed you are not.'

'I'm glad it's so amusing to you that my career is over.'

'Bollocks it is,' he said dismissively, fishing a phone from his pocket. 'These tinpot media outfits only bully you because they know you'll roll over and take it.'

He held up a hand to stifle Amy's protests and put the phone to his ear.

'Seriously, Amy, there's no way anyone would try to pull this shit in banking.'

He began barking instructions into the phone. 'Yeah, it's me, put him on. I'm not paying you to dick me about. Here's what we've got . . .' The conversation then descended into legalese: phrases like 'constructive dismissal', 'outrageous hearsay' and 'a load of libellous cockwash'. He finished with 'Just get it sorted, I want these fuckers to pay.'

He clicked off, then looked at Amy.

'Right, I've got James Callen all over this like leprosy.'

'James Callen?'

'Top employment lawyer on the planet,' he said. 'Guy makes Wolverine look restrained. I know for a fact he's got enough dirt on Marvin Schultz to bury that weasel six feet under.'

'Max,' said Amy nervously, 'it's good of you, but it's not going to change anything. And to be fair, Marv Schultz hasn't really done anything . . .'

'Maybe not, but it'll scare the Christ out of those buggers. No one screws with my friends and comes away with all their fingers.'

Amy softened. She'd always thought of Max as a slightly irritating buffoon, just one of the gang who was always there making a mess at parties, but she supposed to the outside world he was a force to be reckoned with – and it was heart-warming to see him outraged on her behalf.

'I'm going to make some more calls, lob over a few more grenades. You may be right, maybe it won't change anything, but I'm going to find out who's been fucking with you. Leave it to me.'

He kissed her on the cheek and was gone. Claire just stood there awkwardly, fiddling with the strainer. While Max obviously enjoyed a crisis, she was reduced to pouring tea.

'I totally embarrassed myself today,' said Amy after a moment.

'How?'

'You know Josie is Douglas's PA now?'

'No way.'

Amy nodded. 'She impressed him before Provence. There was a job opening, she got it.'

'Sounds a bit convenient.'

Claire had a point. It was Josie who had found William's humidor and saved the day. Grace had been fired for her ineptitude, but what if Josie had planned it that way? The more she thought about the young woman, the more her stomach seemed to twist inside.

'I was called in to see Douglas. But when he told me he was suspending me, I should have kept my dignity. Instead, I saw Josie looking smug outside his office door and I just lost it.'

Amy leaned forward, resting her elbows on her knees, clasping her fingers together to stop them from shaking.

'She's trying to destroy me, Claire. She goes after my husband, my job . . .'

'They're hardly going to give her the editorship of *Mode*.'

'No, but it's enough for her to see me *not* get the job. Which is why she set out to discredit me. The drugs accusations . . . even the Fashion 500 party was constantly beset by problems.'

'Sweetheart, you can't seriously think that Josie was behind that. I remember planning Max's fortieth at that castle in Scotland. Everything that could have gone wrong did. It's what happens with large-scale events.'

Amy was disappointed that Claire hadn't sided with her completely, but a voice in her head told that she was beginning to sound paranoid. She picked up her cup of tea and it rattled against the saucer.

'Look,' Claire said, 'Josie may have flirted with David on holiday. It might even have gone further, although honestly, I don't believe it did. Perhaps she hustled her way into the job with Douglas Proctor, and good luck to him if he chooses to recruit someone like that. But any glitches with the gala were down to bloody bad luck, and if someone has been spreading rumours about drug use, about syringes, it's more likely to be someone who wants you out of the running for the *Mode* job so that they can have a clear run.'

Amy had to admit that what Claire was saying made sense.

'Whoever started the drugs rumour had to have known about the vitamin shots. Who else knows about BlissVit?'

Amy shrugged. 'Only you and Juliet. But I think Josie saw the syringes in my bag.'

'Anyone in your office?'

'Probably Chrissie, my PA. I kept the vials in the office fridge, so she could very well have seen them. But putting aside the fact that I'd trust Chrissie with my life, why would she do anything to hurt me?'

'What about your deputy? The fashion director?'

'I'm not sure either of them would be in contention for the *Mode* job.'

'But they might get the *Verve* job if that became available.'

Amy refused to believe that Tracey or Janice would be so duplicitous. She forced herself to think hard. That day she came out of Dr Al Saraf's with her syringes and vials.

'Suzanne Black,' she said, with sinking realisation.

'The editor of *Silk* magazine?' asked Claire.

Suzanne was certainly poisonous enough to do something this underhand, and it would make sense in a professional sense. She was in pole position for the *Mode* job; getting Amy fired from the parent company would have her doing backflips.

'I bumped into her when I was coming out of the clinic.'

'Then you should talk to her,' said Claire.

Chapter 32

Amy was nervous and she didn't know why. If Denton Scoles were to draw her paranoia on one of his graphs, her jumpiness would be a jagged red line shooting upwards like a rocket. She should have been excited; overjoyed, in fact. She hadn't seen Pog for two years and this was one of his rare flying visits to the capital. But although she had been looking forward to their lunch for weeks, suddenly it did not feel like the day for a casual catch-up. She was hardly going to be good company. She hadn't even told David yet what had happened. She wanted to do that face to face, but first she needed to calm down and try to wash Josie Price out of her thoughts before the conversation about her suspension from Genesis turned back to what had happened in Provence.

She settled down in the booth and tried deep breathing. The choice of venue didn't help either. Simpkins was an establishment institution. It was perfect for Pog, with his old-school accent and stripy ties. The fact that he had spent his life as an explorer was even more fitting; she'd always felt he should have been born 150 years earlier. But what was perfect for Pog made Amy jittery. She felt like an impostor here; she *was* an impostor, just a girl from a council estate whose idea of fine dining for the first twenty years of her life was the all you can eat buffet at Pizza Hut.

She looked around, checking her watch. Typical of Pog to be late; he'd always marched to the beat of his own drum. Even back in Oxford, he'd always been late for work in the Bear. She supposed living most of your adult life in places where no one had even seen a clock would only make your timekeeping worse.

She was so deep in thought, she didn't hear her name called until the second time. When she looked up, there he was: tall and suntanned, his lopsided smile the same and his hug still as big as a bear's.

'Oh gosh, Pog,' she said into his shoulder, 'it's so good to see you.'

'You too, old girl,' he laughed. 'Now if you'll just let me go, maybe I can actually have a proper look . . . Yes – still in one piece,' he said with a smile.

'So Max told you.'

Pog nodded. 'He wanted to come and join us, but I managed to hold him off.'

'Actually he's been a great help,' said Amy, inspecting a bottle of red wine from the sommelier.

'How things have changed,' grinned Pog.

They each took a sip of claret and Amy felt her shoulders relax.

'Do you want to talk about it,' Pog said, 'or do you want to hear about my time in Papua New Guinea?'

'I want to hear all about life in the jungle, of course,' she smiled.

Pog returned a knowing look. They'd been friends for too long for her to pull the wool over his eyes.

'Why don't you go first,' he said, so Amy told him everything, from the plan to have a work-free holiday at Max's villa to the ensuing and inevitable blow-up. 'Hey,

hey,' said Pog, passing his napkin across. 'It's not that bad.'

'Isn't it?' she snapped, feeling bad but unable to stop herself. She used the napkin to wipe at her face, then looked up, eyes sparkling.

'You seem to have got things back on track with David. You take him on a hot date on the Orient Express and he ends up in A and E.'

'I know how to show a guy a good time.' She laughed despite her emotion.

He tried to top up her wine glass, but she shook her head. Claret was not the answer, no matter what the vintage.

'Go on,' smiled Pog. 'It's not like you've got work in the morning.'

Amy laughed. Pog always knew the right thing to say, even back when they had spent their evenings serving up cider and black to the students of Oxford. Whenever Amy had a problem with a truculent boyfriend, a rude customer at the Bear or an unbending tutor, Pog could always lift her spirits. And come to think of it, drinking had often been the medicine he'd prescribed back then too.

He took a thoughtful sip of his own drink. 'You know, I find myself in the unusual situation of agreeing with Max for the first time in my life,' he said just as the waiter brought their starters: potted shrimp for Pog, salad for Amy. 'Get his Rottweiler lawyer friends onto them and twist a year's salary out of them. But you're talented, experienced, you'll find something else. The most important thing is that your marriage is still intact.'

'But how can I let her get away with this, Pog?'

'Let it go, Amy. She's not worth it. And if you keep banging the drum, blaming it all on her, you're in danger of looking like you're having a childish fit of pique. What do you want? Revenge? How is that going to help? There's no way this Douglas Proctor is going to backtrack and reinstate you: too much loss of face. And I suspect there's some office politics going on that you don't know about. Otherwise why resort to such questionable methods?'

Amy allowed herself a smile. 'Like you know about office politics.'

Pog grinned back. 'It's been a while since I had a boss, but you'd be surprised what goes on behind the grass huts in the jungle: people wanting to be in charge, people wanting more than the next guy, whether it's status or wives or chickens.'

He speared a prawn and waved it at Amy.

'You always have to ask yourself in these situations: who profits? What's the motivation for someone to push you out of the nest? Usually it comes down to someone wanting what you have.'

'Josie,' whispered Amy. It all came back to her.

'Who is she?' said Pog after a moment.

'She's the daughter of my friend Karen from Bristol. You remember Karen: she stayed at the house and went to the Commem Ball with Max. I don't think Josie had it easy growing up. Her father Lee was a violent bully. He and Karen never married and I don't think he was part of Josie's life when she was growing up. It must have been tough for Karen, a single parent on a low income, but she's a good, decent person. It's hard to believe she'd have such a psycho for a daughter.'

Pog had gone quiet.

'What is it?' asked Amy, but he just grimaced and shook his head. He looked troubled, like he'd had a piece of bad news. 'What aren't you telling me?'

'It's about that night,' he said finally. His face had lost some of its usual ruddiness. 'Look, it's only a theory, let me emphasise that. But something happened that night, the night of the ball, that I never told anyone about.'

He took a deep breath, but didn't seem to want to meet Amy's eye.

'I was dancing with Jules, out on the floor, you know.'

'Shaking your stuff, huh?' She didn't know why, but Amy wanted to make light of the conversation. Pog, though, didn't smile.

'We were quite near the middle, right in the thick of it, and we saw, well, David and Karen. They were dancing, but, you know, getting pretty frisky.'

Amy could see why Pog didn't want to tell her. Your husband and your best friend? No one wants to hear that.

'Go on,' she said.

'They pushed past us, don't think they actually saw us, and went out into the grounds. I wondered what the hell David was doing. He'd told me once how he felt about you, and so I thought it was madness behaving like that with your best friend.'

'You followed him?'

Pog nodded.

Amy felt the air around her grow hot. 'What did you see?'

He shrugged, embarrassed.

'Pog, I have to know.'

His eyes flicked up to hers, then down again. 'I didn't see anything else. They were kissing, I can say that much. And they were oblivious to us . . . they were pretty into it. I felt like a perv watching, so I left them to it.'

'So they had sex?'

Pog didn't reply.

'Pog, you have to tell me.'

'It looked like that, yeah,' he finally conceded. 'You said Josie is twenty-one?'

'That's right.'

She didn't need him to ask her to do the maths. She was

finding it hard to swallow, hard to breathe as the full horrific implication sank in.

'Oh God,' she whispered, a shaking hand covering her mouth. 'So you're saying that David . . .' She looked at Pog, and he nodded.

'Maybe David is Josie's father.'

Chapter 33

The station looked the same as it ever did; it smelled the same too. As she stepped down onto Platform B, Amy felt the same feelings wash over her. Dread. Disappointment. That deflated feeling when you realised the party was over. The other platform always carried the opposite sentiments. Standing there, only a few yards across the tracks, she'd always felt happy, upbeat, excited. Because being on Platform A meant she was on her way east, heading out of town towards Bristol or London, heading to possibility and adventure.

She looked down at the chewing-gum-pocked asphalt under her £400 shoes. Even now, decades later, with a career and a husband and a house in the capital – for now, at least – she still felt herself cloaked in a feeling of dread that there was nothing to look forward to except chip fat and dirt and shops that seemed to close half an hour before you got there.

Sighing, she left the station, tearing her ticket in half, and walked along Sunderland Street, a ragged retail backwater of kebabs, phone shops and the lone bright beacon of Luv Me Do, Westmead's one and only wedding outfitter. She flipped up her coat collar as she felt a spatter of rain. One thing you could say about the old neighbourhood: you never needed to look at a weather forecast. It was always shitty.

She didn't need to look at a map either, that was another plus. She knew exactly where the florists was. Past the bakery where Jenny from school had worked, across into Church Street, then past McDonald's – they'd been so proud when that had finally opened – and the Red Lion on the left. She wasn't at all surprised that the florists was still going after all these years: it was perfectly placed near the pub, the funeral home and the little Tesco car park. Guilt, grief and convenience. What did surprise her was the fact that Karen still worked there; that her best friend hadn't moved far away.

Amy paused on the other side of the road, letting the wind ripple her skirt. It had been a rash decision to head to Paddington after her lunch with Pog; rasher still to jump on a train to Bristol. But after leaving Pog, she hadn't wanted to go home, unable to face seeing David, not after they had clawed their marriage back from the brink once already that week. It had taken over two hours to get to the florists at Westmead, and now, at a little after five o'clock, she wasn't even sure if Karen would still be at work.

But as she looked into the window, past the display of cut flowers, she could see her, standing at the counter, a telephone clamped between ear and shoulder, presumably taking an order or arranging a delivery, just normal everyday things, what people did to get through the day. This was Karen's life now: she lived here, worked here; did it really matter what had happened twenty years ago? Some drunken fumble in a doorway, just a bit of fun to pass the time. Why bring all that up now?

Because sometimes sleeping dogs wake up, thought Amy. And sometimes they turn around and bite you.

She crossed the road, hearing the tinkle as she pushed through the door, watching Karen look up, for a moment still lost in her conversation, not recognising her. When she did, there was surprise, yes, but no delight; no 'Wow, my old friend is here, how nice!' No, Karen looked scared, and that was all Amy needed to know.

'Amy,' she said, hanging up the phone. 'What are you doing here?'

It was cold in the shop and Amy pulled her jacket a little tighter around her to stop of sliver of icy freeze slip down her back.

'I've come to talk,' she said simply.

Micro-expressions. She had seen something on the TV about it once. How the emotions work faster than the rational brain and how, caught off guard, people can't help showing their true feelings. Fear, disgust, anger. And sadness. Amy saw them all pass across Karen's face.

'Talk? What about?'

She inclined her head towards the door. 'Shall we go to the Lion?'

There was a tiny pause, then Karen nodded, her expression resigned now. 'Just give me five minutes to close up. It's time anyway.'

Amy was surprised to find the pub so quiet. Just one old guy hunched over the fruit machine and a couple with shopping bags pooled around their feet. Only the barman, barely old enough to drink himself, looked up as she walked in. She resisted the urge to order a pint of cider and black – the great-grandmother of the alcopop, she supposed – and took two glasses of warm white wine to a table at the back.

So many memories rushed in. The New Year's piss-ups, when it was standing room only and it took a good five minutes to thread your way to the bar. Bryn's birthday, when Mad Kev had let off a fire extinguisher, covering everyone in foam, like some low-rent Ibiza rave. The endless powwows with Karen about who fancied who and who was shagging who and what to wear to which party. Carefree times, but it had never felt that way at the time; it was all so life-and-death.

Maybe everything feels important at the time, thought Amy. It certainly did right now.

She looked up and gave a half-wave as Karen walked in. Her old friend looked grave; no, she looked old. As though all those worries, all those struggles had been etched into her face. Do I look like that? wondered Amy as Karen sat down.

'So what's this all about?' she said, taking a sip of her wine. 'Josie, I guess.'

Amy's surprise must have shown, because Karen snorted.

'I knew she'd do something stupid in the end. You're going to fire her, right?'

Amy frowned. 'Why would you think that?'

'Why else would you come all the way out here?'

'Karen, *I'm* the one who's been fired.'

Karen looked at her wide-eyed. No micro-expressions, no evasion; it was all there to see. She wasn't surprised to hear that Amy had been kicked out; in fact she had been *expecting* it.

'She did it,' she said, her voice almost a whisper.

'Did what?'

Karen gave her a look of disdain, one Amy recognised from all those years ago. She had always been the streetwise one, the cynic, and she reserved her most withering look for Amy: so easy to fool, always sucked in, innocent and trusting. 'No one's going to give you anything, Ames,' she would say. 'You have to take it for yourself.' It was one of the things – along with French kissing and rolling fags – that Amy had learned from Karen, and the one thing she had packed in her suitcase when she had shipped out to Oxford. And *of course* Karen would have taught the very same lesson to her daughter, wouldn't she? If nothing else, that would be the one thing Karen would pass on. *Take it for yourself, Josie.*

'She got what she wanted.'

Amy nodded to herself. She had been right all along, no matter what Pog or Claire or David or Max had said.

'Karen, I saw Pog last night,' she said.

'Pog? That posh bloke from the Oxford house? What's he doing these days?'

Amy didn't want to be diverted. 'He told me about that night at the ball.'

Karen didn't react. Not even a flinch. Amy sat forward, determined to get it all out.

'He said he saw you and David . . .' She trailed off. *Say it, say it.* 'He said he saw you two making out.'

Karen blinked at her, then burst out laughing. '*That's* what this is about? You've just lost your job and yet you're worried your precious David might have shagged some other girl twenty years ago? Christ, Amy. Haven't you got anything better to worry about? Is there really that much money in the bank?'

Anger rose in Amy. It was funny how with old friends you slipped so easily into ancient roles so long left behind. She had forgotten how Karen used to put her down, belittle her. But not now, not any more.

'I'm not asking you if you shagged my husband twenty years ago. I'm asking if he's Josie's father.'

Karen's jaw dropped. 'Josie's father?' She shook her head slowly, then gave a bitter laugh. 'I don't know what Pog thinks he saw, but if he thinks he saw *that*, he got it wrong. David and I . . . We were pissed, we fancied each other, yeah. We even snogged for a bit, but . . .' She closed her eyes, as if she was reluctant to say it. 'We didn't do it, Amy. In fact, David stopped because of you.'

'Me?'

Her mouth twisted into a sneer. 'The old story: he was kissing me, but thinking of you. It was you he wanted all along.'

Amy sat there, stunned, not knowing what to say, relief flooding every cell. David wasn't Josie's dad: he'd turned Karen down for her, he'd wanted her even then. And then another emotion replaced the relief and she wanted to bang her stupid head on the table. She'd been such an idiot. Maybe she simply didn't deserve David.

'So if David isn't her father, why would Josie want to hurt me?'

'Why not?' Karen swept an arm around the run-down pub. 'Look at this bloody place, Amy. Does it look any better to you now than it did when you left? No, it's still a shithole, it will always be a shithole.'

'But what's that got to do with me?'

Karen pointed a calloused finger at her. '*You* got out. You've lived a charmed bloody life, haven't you?'

'But Josie got out too; she went to uni.'

Karen laughed. 'Did she hell.'

'But you said . . .'

'Typical Amy. Always looking at the big picture, never checking the details. Josie left school at sixteen – was asked to leave, truth be told. She worked at the leisure centre for a bit, until they closed that down. Then bar work where she could get it, but mostly she brooded. About you.'

'Me? What did I ever do to her?'

Karen sat forward, her eyes blazing. 'What did you ever do?' she spat. 'What *did* you do, Amy? Did you ever come to see us, ever send her a birthday card, even take the time to friend either of us on bloody Facebook? Did you? The times she used to ask me when Auntie Amy was going to come and see us, and I got tired of making excuses. I told her the truth. That you'd outgrown the little people like me and her.'

Amy pressed back into her chair, genuinely stunned.

'I . . . I know I should have done more, I know that, Karen, but it never seemed to be the right time.'

Karen pursed her lips and waved a hand, as if she was bored with the subject. Or perhaps just bored with Amy's excuses. Amy could relate to that: she was bored herself.

'It doesn't matter, Ames,' she said. 'None of it matters.'

She reached for her glass and drained it in one gulp. She looked tired, all the fire gone from her eyes.

'I know I should never have put all those ideas in Josie's head,' she sighed. 'Truth is, I was jealous of you. You had this perfect life in London with a nice flat and fancy friends, going out to parties and clubs, while I was stuck here knee-deep in shitty nappies. And it grew. As the years went on, the whole thing grew. It started as jealousy, but I suppose after a while it was like everything was your fault.'

'And you passed that on to Josie.'

Karen nodded, her expression bleak. 'It's been tough, Amy. Never having tuppence at the end of the week no matter what I gave up, and kids? Christ, kids just keep needing stuff. Shoes and books and a bleedin' scooter at Christmas.' She shrugged helplessly. 'And then there's you, pictures of you in the newsagent every month, flying to LA or meeting some film star, a new dress in every photo.'

Amy squirmed, suddenly seeing it from Karen's point of view – and understanding.

'Karen, I'm so sorry.'

'Yeah, me too. But life's like that, isn't it? Fucks you up.'

'Didn't Lee help you?'

Karen barked with laughter. 'That deadweight? Ha! You know he came to Oxford the night of the ball? Scared the crap out of me, threatened me – not that that was anything new. Beat me black and blue when he was drinking, which was most of the time. And this is how screwed up I was: he'd practically strangled me, but he'd come all the way to Oxford, so I took it as a sign that he cared, God help me. We got back together just long enough for him to get me up the spout.'

'What happened then?'

Amy had come here to confront Karen, to get the truth about her own drama, but now she found herself fascinated, desperate to fill in the blanks on an old story she could barely remember.

'Remember Lee was a mechanic? Well, his brother got him a job on the North Sea oil rigs and he moved up to Aberdeen. So up I went to Scotland with the happy news.' Karen looked at her. 'You know what? He couldn't have been less interested. Thought I should get an abortion, but wasn't prepared to do anything to help.'

She held up her hands. 'So that was that. Along came Josie, and from then on, it was me and her. She was *everything* to me, Ames; she was all I had. And I'm not proud of how I turned her against you, but you know what? It felt good having something in common, something to share.'

'I invited her into my home, Karen, and she tried to ruin my life.'

Karen paused as if to take it in.

'Josie was always wilful. She could always twist people around her little finger. Bat her eyes at the ladies in the supermarket and get a lolly, that sort of thing, sweet-talk her teacher when she hadn't done her homework. But when she got older, it went toxic. Bullying, I suppose, mean-girl stuff.'

Amy started shaking her head.

'She really began to focus on you,' said Karen in a softer

voice. 'Buying all your magazines, looking you up on the internet. It was like an obsession. If I resented you for having everything I never did, Josie came to see you as the devil incarnate.' She gave Amy a bleak smile. 'She persuaded me to get in touch. I didn't like it at first, but then I thought, why not? What I said to you in London was true. I wanted to give her a start, because, well, Josie's capable when she puts her mind to it. But I was worried, too. I wasn't sure how far she was prepared to go to get what she wanted. That was why I freaked out when you walked in just now. I thought something terrible had happened.'

'Depends how you look at it. My husband almost moved out and I've lost my job. It hasn't been great for me, Karen.'

Karen's blank expression said it all. She didn't think it was all that terrible. Why would she?

'So that's why you came?' she said. 'You think Josie might have been involved? In you being fired, I mean.'

'Do you?'

Karen shrugged, then nodded. 'Could have been.'

'Could have been, or was?' said Amy. 'I need your help here, Karen.'

'You need my help? Oh that's rich. For twenty fucking years you gave me nothing – nothing, Amy. And now you come asking me for help.'

'Just tell me if Josie got me fired, please.'

Karen stood up and grabbed her bag. 'You were always the clever one, Amy. I'm sure you'll work it out.'

She walked towards the door, then turned.

'You can have this one for free: maybe you should start by asking Josie herself.'

Chapter 34

It was almost eleven o'clock by the time she got home, and drizzling with rain. As the taxi dropped her at the house, she took a moment to take in its prettiness; golden windows winked back at her like amber eyes behind the thin sheen of rain so it looked like a snow globe.

She thought of her daughter, tucked up safely in her cosy bedroom, and tried to push Josie Price out of her mind. She understood her now, but just needed to accept that it was all over.

She slid her key into the lock, but David was already standing at the door as it swung open.

'I was worried sick about you,' he said as the warm air seemed to suck her in.

'Did you not get my texts?' she asked, wiping her shoes on the mat.

'Yes, but Max and Pog both called me to say what had happened. When you texted to say you'd be late, I started to think all sorts.'

As he put his arms around her, she felt conflicted. She couldn't get the image of David and Karen in some remote corner of the ball out of her head, and yet she was glad to be back home, glad she could just move on.

They went into the living room. David had lit the fire,

and the newspapers and a tumbler of Scotch were on the ottoman.

'I've been to Bristol,' she said finally.

'What for?' he asked, in the tone of someone who already knew.

'I went to see Karen.'

'You've just lost your job, and instead of telling your husband, you go chasing off after your old friend. I can only imagine why.'

'And what *do* you imagine, David?' she said, challenging him. Perhaps he had just realised that he had been caught out. 'Josie has been out to get me from the minute she turned up in this house,' she added, trying to keep her voice low. 'I knew it, and Karen basically confirmed it.'

'So she's a damaged young woman, but she's not part of our lives any more.'

'Really?'

'What's that supposed to mean?'

She took a deep breath. She wanted to let it go, but she couldn't.

'Why did you never tell me about you and Karen? That something happened between you? You were my friend, David. My best friend. You never told me then. Never mentioned it once in all the time we've been together.'

'I didn't lie to you, Amy. It just never came up.'

'What's the difference?'

'It was pointless to tell you. It would have hurt you.'

'Well guess how I feel right now. Really, really stupid, thinking my husband might have had sex with my oldest school friend.'

'We didn't have sex.'

'That's what Karen said,' she admitted.

'We didn't.'

'It's just as well.'

'What's that supposed to mean?'

'Christ, David, after everything that happened in Provence, imagine if she was your daughter.'

The light in the room was dim, but there was enough of it for Amy to see her husband go pale.

'Karen got pregnant straight after the ball. With that idiot Lee.'

'I didn't have sex with Karen, Amy, and I didn't sleep with Josie. I guess that's enough for us to try and put this whole thing behind us.'

She felt her breath start to stutter, the emotion of the day rising into her throat.

David came towards her and put his arms around her waist. This time she coiled her own around his back, resting her head on his shoulder like a pillow.

'I want to talk to her,' she said after a moment.

'Let it go, Amy.'

She shook her head. 'No, it's important. She hates me because she thinks I abandoned her.'

'Really? Or does she hate you because Karen has been jealous of you for twenty years?'

'Either way, I've got to do the right thing,' she said, taking his hand and leading him upstairs to bed, trying not to think about the conversation she would need to have with Josie tomorrow.

Chapter 35

'Chrissie, it's Amy.'

Her PA almost hyperventilated at the other end of the phone. 'Amy, where the hell have you been? There have been all sorts of rumours floating about the place. Tracey keeps getting called to Douglas Proctor's office, and Janine said you might not be coming in for a few days.'

'It's true, I'm having a bit of time off,' said Amy, imagining the state of panic in the office.

'This is about the Blenheim party, isn't it?'

'It's complicated,' she replied.

'Because I don't believe the other stuff. I sent Douglas an email myself to say that I'd seen vials in your fridge but they were vitamins and everyone took them.'

Amy felt a wave of affection for the younger woman.

'Chrissie, I need you to do me a favour. I've been trying to get hold of Josie Price, but apparently she's not in work today. I need you to try and find me her home address.'

'Josie? What do you want to talk to her for?'

So Chrissie had heard about the showdown outside Douglas's office.

'Please, just try,' said Amy.

'Okay,' agreed her PA, not sounding terribly convinced. 'I'll see what I can do.'

* * *

It took Chrissie all day to come through. Eventually she got the address from one of the post boys, who lived near Josie and had shared an Uber home with her on a couple of occasions.

'Sorry, miss. Traffic's shocking today,' said the taxi driver taking Amy from Notting Hill to Islington. 'The road ahead is closed as well. Honestly, it might be better if you hop out here.'

Amy craned her neck to look at the line of stationary cars ahead. 'Just pull over wherever you can.'

It had been a long time since she had been to this pocket of north London, but somehow it still felt like home. Years ago, she had rented a tiny basement flat in a grand white-washed Georgian terrace with a postcode that meant she could tell people she lived in Barnsbury, although in truth it was actually closer to the sticky pavements of Caledonian Road – and, come to that, Holloway women's prison.

She walked past the chichi restaurants and chic interior shops on Upper Street, past the bars full of young people relaxing after a busy day at work. Turning off, she headed into the quieter residential area, away from the lights and the laughter. Normally she would have been nervous walking alone on such deserted streets, but tonight it felt right, like this was her territory. God, she thought, a wistful smile on her lips, I must have been twenty-four, twenty-five when I lived here. Where has that girl gone?

Where were any of them? All those hopeful, energetic people who'd jumped on a train into Euston or Paddington or London Bridge, the bright-eyed ones who'd grown up different, who didn't fit into the small towns in Dorset or Gloucestershire, who felt hemmed in by Nottingham or Leeds. Because this was where they all came, wasn't it? Even the privileged ones like David and Jules. They were all modern-day Dick Whittingtons come to see if the streets really were paved with gold.

Even Josie.

She crossed the wide thoroughfare of Liverpool Road, always strangely empty compared to its glitzy neighbour, thinking about Karen trapped in her home town, struggling to keep her head above water, no support network, alone. Well, she had Josie, at least. Someone to tuck in at night, someone to tell stories to. Stories about evil Aunt Amy, the black-hearted fairy-tale queen in the golden palace. It sounded crazy, because it was, and yet it made perfect sense too.

But had Josie really been behind her fall? Sure, Karen had given her daughter the motivation, but that wasn't a smoking gun, was it?

Amy turned the corner, stopping outside a small, scruffy block of flats. For a moment, she didn't understand what she was seeing. Blue lights bouncing off the white walls, an ambulance and a police car blocking the road, a small crowd gathered, their faces grim. Increasing her pace, she walked up to a woman in a cardigan at the back.

'What's happened? Has there been an accident?'

'Some young girl in one of those flats,' said the woman. 'Taken an overdose, looks like.'

'Overdose?' Amy felt a shiver of panic but tried to convince herself that plenty of young women lived in that block of flats. 'Is she . . .'

'Dead? Nah,' said the woman. 'Flatmate came home and found her, apparently. Called 999. They brought her out on a stretcher and loaded her in the ambulance a few minutes ago. Such a shame; pretty thing too.'

Amy crossed to the opposite pavement, but her way was blocked by a young policeman, who gave a weary sigh and gestured back the other way. 'Nothing to see, madam, please keep moving.'

'But I need to get past. I'm going to number twelve.'

The policeman looked at her properly for the first time. 'Number twelve? Who were you coming to see?'

'Josie Price,' said Amy, her heart starting to speed up. 'Why? Is there something wrong?'

The policeman shook his head and waved a gloved hand. 'I think you'd better talk to my colleague.'

An older WPC walked over, her face set. 'You know the lady at number twelve? May I ask your relationship?'

Amy paused for a beat and looked across at the ambulance.

'I'm her old friend Amy.'

In the bright fluorescent light of the hospital room, Josie looked so young. Seventeen, eighteen at most. Lying there so peacefully, eyes closed, no make-up, she was a dead ringer for the girl Amy had so often shared a bed with, sleeping off the night before, wrapped up in their shared adventures. Where had it all gone so wrong? She and Karen had been as close as two girls could be, sharing everything. Yet had it all been so perfect? Nostalgia always took the edges off things, didn't it? You remembered the belly laughs, but never the screaming rows. The funny thing was, Amy had always thought of Karen as the leader of their little clique; she'd been the bossy one, the one with all the ideas. And many of the dreams Amy had had as a girl had been Karen's too. Karen hadn't loved Westmead either; she had yearned to leave, to 'climb the barbed wire', as she'd put it, to go to Europe or Thailand or Australia – anywhere but where they were. And yet Amy was the one who had gone. Was that what had made her friend so bitter, so angry that she'd poisoned her daughter's mind from the crib?

She reached out to touch Josie's hand, lying motionless on the white sheet, the ugly lump of the drip taped to the back. Whatever she'd done, she was still just a screwed-up little girl, as lost as her mother ever was. But what had made her so miserable that she'd taken an overdose? At least half a bottle of Valium, according to the doctor who'd pumped her stomach. Was it guilt? No, that didn't fit the profile. Someone driven to revenge didn't suddenly turn around and have an attack of conscience at the eleventh hour. Fear of exposure? Amy shook her head. Who would care even if they *did* know? Spreading rumours wasn't exactly a capital offence, was it?

She was so wrapped up in her thoughts, she hadn't noticed that Josie had opened her eyes and was looking at her.

'Josie! God, you startled me,' she said, pulling her hand back as if she'd been caught doing something wrong. 'I didn't know you were awake.'

Josie gave a wan smile. 'Not sure I am really,' she croaked. 'What did they give me?'

'I think it's the stuff still left in your system, though the doctor said you'd probably have slept most of it off by now.'

'Bit of a headache,' she said, shuffling backwards to sit up. 'Can I have something to drink?'

Amy handed her a cup of water and Josie took it gratefully.

'This is where you say, "You've got some explaining to do, young lady",' she said bleakly.

Amy shook her head. 'No one's angry at you, Josie, we're all just glad you pulled through.'

'Do you really mean that?'

She had a point. There were times during the past two weeks when Amy had almost wished her dead, had blamed her for everything that had gone wrong in her life, but right now, she would give anything to make sure she was all right.

She leaned over and put her arms around the girl, holding

313

her as she sobbed, her body jerking with the effort. Finally her breathing evened out and she lay back.

'I'm sorry,' she said finally.

The doctor had warned Amy that she should avoid stirring up any painful memories or emotions in the first few days: 'Just let her work it through in her own time.'

'Forget it,' she said quietly.

'No, I mean it. I'm sorry. Sorry for telling him.'

Amy felt her stomach drop. 'What do you mean, Josie?'

'Douglas Proctor wanted to know about your personal life. So I told him. I really wanted the job full time and I thought it might get me some brownie points.'

'What did you tell him?'

She didn't speak for several seconds.

'Douglas told me that there were rumours about you taking drugs. That you had a serious addiction. He wanted to know if I had ever seen any evidence of it. Whether I had seen you high, or with any drugs paraphernalia.'

'So what did you tell him?' Amy knew that she should just tell her to forget it, but she was desperate to know.

'I said that you were acting strangely in Provence. I told them that I had seen syringes.'

'I don't take drugs, Josie. I never have.'

'Then what were the syringes for?'

'They're for vitamin shots.'

Josie looked away from her.

'Why did you take the overdose, Josie? You could have talked to me, to David.'

'No, I couldn't.' Josie's gaze was trailing out of the window. The rims of her eyes were pink, her eyeballs glistening. 'I know about David,' she whispered.

'What about him?' asked Amy, feeling her heart speed up again at the whiff of treachery.

'He's my dad, isn't he?' A tear leaked down her cheek.

Amy closed her eyes. It was all making sense. That was why she'd taken the Valium. Guilt, shame, disgust. The bra in her bed *was* Josie's. She had slept with David in Provence, and when she'd found out that he was her father, she couldn't stand what she had done.

'No. No, he's not. Your mum came to Oxford when I was in my final term. Something happened between her and David, but they didn't have sex. Karen did fall pregnant that month, but David couldn't have been the father. It was Lee. I went to Bristol yesterday. She told me so herself.'

'You're not lying?'

'No.'

'Not even to protect me?'

'Amy, I think it's about time we started telling each other the truth.'

Tears were spilling down the girl's cheeks. 'I've always wished I had a different dad, but now . . . now I'm glad,' she whispered.

'Josie, who told you?' said Amy, trying to collect her thoughts. 'Who told you David was your dad?'

Josie looked away again. 'It doesn't matter.'

It had to be Max. It was the only explanation Amy could think of. She reached forward and took the younger woman's hand. Josie rewarded her with a weak smile.

'You didn't deserve any of this,' she whispered.

Amy took a sharp breath.

'I never slept with David,' Josie continued. 'Nothing happened in Provence. The bra? I have no idea how it got in your bed. Believe me.'

'We should just forget about it.'

'No, I need to tell you. I might not have slept with him, but I wanted to. I tried really hard to make him want me. He's great-looking and rich and kind. It's hard not to fall a little bit in love with him.'

315

Josie's voice and gaze trailed off simultaneously.

'I knew he liked going to exercise in the orchard. I used to go down there too, take my top off, hoping I'd see him, waiting. I told him a few times where I was going, but he never came. I'm not even sure he knew I was coming on to him.'

'Oh Josie,' said Amy, but the girl didn't seem to be listening, tears rolling down her face as she continued in a hushed voice.

'Nothing happened, but I wanted it to. So when I found out that he was my dad, I thought about all the times I'd dreamed of having him; the time I shagged the gardener but wished it was David. I thought about all those times and I felt horrible. I just kept thinking, what if he had gone for it, what if I'd actually shagged my dad?'

'But you didn't have sex with him and he isn't your dad.'

'It doesn't even matter,' Josie said bleakly. 'When I thought about the fact that he'd rejected me, I realised that everyone has rejected me. My father – Lee – he didn't know me from a hole in the road. Never held me, never came to a birthday party, barely acknowledged my existence. I couldn't bear it any more.'

'Who told you?' Amy asked again.

'Don't be angry,' Josie whispered.

'I won't,' promised Amy.

'It was Juliet.'

At first Amy wasn't sure that she had heard correctly.

'You wanted to know who told me about David. It was your friend Juliet. She said if I did everything she asked, she'd tell me the truth, tell me the secret my mum had been keeping from me all these years.'

'And you believed her?'

'Why wouldn't I?' said Josie, her cheeks pinking. 'Juliet's known Mum, you, David, all of you for twenty years. And she said she had seen something back in Oxford that would change everything.'

She looked down at her hand, picking at the tape holding the drip.

'I've wondered, fantasised about it all my life. Imagining my dad wasn't Lee Bishop but someone smart and rich and handsome. But when Juliet told me it was David, I felt sick to my stomach.'

'Juliet's lying,' Amy assured her. 'She didn't see anything in Oxford.'

Josie slumped back on her pillows, the relief obvious. 'I've been feeling so guilty, and so dirty. I mean, I could have slept with my dad.'

'What else did Juliet say to you, Josie?'

'She said you were a lucky bitch. Said you were too grand for everyone back home, but that you never really fitted in at Oxford either. She was the one that got me the job with Douglas. Said I had to keep my eyes and ears open. When Douglas asked me if you took drugs, I told him you did. I was jealous as hell about your job, your husband, your life. If I couldn't have any of what you had, I didn't want you to have it either. So I told him about the syringes. I'm so sorry, Amy. I'm sorry about everything. You deserve everything good and I deserve nothing.'

Chapter 36

She sent Juliet a text.

Have you heard what's happened? I need a drink.

She felt it struck the right note: not accusatory, or finger-pointing, but not quite an SOS, a plea for support from one friend to another.

Juliet's reply came back immediately. Peter was out and she had the house to herself. Dinner was in the oven and if Amy could get there within the next thirty minutes, she was welcome to share it.

It only took minutes in a cab to get from the Whittington Hospital to Hampstead, to Juliet and Peter's tall, dark-brick Georgian house a stone's throw from the Heath. Amy had always admired Juliet's eclectic home, a riot of souvenirs and trinkets from the couple's travels – rugs from India, tapestries from Peru, books in a dozen languages – but found it a little spooky. Tonight, it was particularly sinister. As she approached, all the leaded windows were dark except for one square of light where she could see Juliet pouring some wine.

On any other occasion, she would have arrived with a bottle of good red herself, sometimes with David, sometimes alone. She thought about Peter and wondered where he was tonight. With his lover? Or was this one part of the puzzle where Amy had been mistaken?

When Juliet answered the door, she was holding a wine goblet and wearing jeans and a cashmere sweater rather than her usual work outfit of a severe trouser suit. Amy almost felt guilty that she wasn't here for a social call, and wondered if Juliet had any idea of what had happened to Josie.

She followed her through into the kitchen and let Juliet pour her a glass of wine, although she had made up her mind she wasn't going to drink it.

'I can't believe it,' Juliet said, shaking her head. 'Max called me trying to find out what I knew. Turns out he knows more than I did.' She flashed Amy a little look. 'At least he has the lawyers all over it. It's obviously a transparent case of unlawful dismissal.'

'You know it's complete rubbish, don't you?'

Juliet rolled her eyes. 'I think I'd know if my best friend had a heroin addiction.'

Amy tried to collect her thoughts.

'Is that what I am to you, Juliet? Your best friend?'

She saw a little vein start pulsing underneath the pale skin below Juliet's eye.

'I called you at least half a dozen times yesterday. I'd have come round but I had no idea where you were. Eventually I spoke to Claudia and she said you weren't due back until late. David and I were both worried sick.'

'You got Josie the job at Genesis, didn't you, Juliet?'

Her friend looked stunned, but Amy couldn't put up with the pretence any longer.

'Don't deny it,' she said before Juliet had the chance to even open her mouth.

Juliet tossed back a slug of wine, leaving a red rim around her lips, and levelled Amy with a formidable stare.

'Yes, I did,' she said after a few moments. 'Why? Because

I felt bloody sorry for her.'

'Why did you feel sorry for her?' said Amy, unable to believe that Juliet felt so little remorse.

'It was after Provence. Peter gave her three handkerchiefs on the flight, she was crying so much. Her eyes had disappeared into slits by the time we got to Heathrow. The least I could do was make a call to Douglas and HR to see how we could help out. I only imagined it would be some temp work, but Douglas apparently liked her.'

'You're my friend, Juliet. You know what Josie did to me in Provence.'

'What *did* she do in Provence, Amy? Tell me. You found a bra and a receipt for a necklace – or so you say. You were stressed out, paranoid, and you took it as an excuse to crush her.'

'She tried to seduce David. She admitted it herself.'

'So she didn't actually sleep with him?' Her eyes were bright and challenging.

Amy didn't reply.

'Amy, I'm worried about you,' said Juliet, her voice softer. 'We all are. You're behaving as if you're having some kind of breakdown. You're irrational, jealous, crazy. Perhaps you really do need some time in rehab.'

'Do you know where Josie is tonight?' said Amy after a pause.

That rattled Juliet.

'She's in hospital. The Whittington. She took an overdose this afternoon.'

Juliet reached out to the table to steady herself. 'An overdose.'

'She's fine, but it was a close call. Karen should be arriving in London any time now.'

Juliet sat down on a chair. Amy could see that her hand was shaking.

'Why did you tell her that David was her father?'

'I didn't say that outright. I told her that Karen had had intercourse with David. She must have done the maths.'

Her voice was quiet now, and Amy let her speak.

'She deserved to know the truth, Amy. Don't you think we all saw the way she was flaunting herself around him in Provence? It was embarrassing. And when you told me you had found the bra, I felt sick. I mean, this is beyond *Daily Mail* headlines territory. So I told her to stay away from him, and I told her why. It obviously hurt her. That was another reason why I helped get her the job.'

'But David isn't Josie's father.'

Juliet paused, her lips pressed into a thin, frozen line.

'How do you know?'

'Because Karen told me. As did David.'

'And you believe them?'

'Actually, I do.'

Amy turned to leave. She hadn't even taken her coat off. She paused in the doorway.

'I thought you were my friend,' she said.

'I am your friend.'

'Goodbye, Juliet.'

Juliet gave a soft, unrepentant snort. 'I know you're looking for someone to blame, Amy. Truth is, you've brought all this on yourself. You let yourself drift away from your husband, you messed up your interview for *Mode*, you let a complete stranger into your life without knowing who she was or what she thought of you. You flew too high and you just got burnt.'

But Amy wasn't listening. She stepped out onto the street and slammed the front door behind her.

Chapter 37

'Should you not be going to work?' Amy was jamming a piece of toast in her mouth as she pulled on her hoodie.

'Nope,' David replied. 'Thought I'd go in late this morning and accompany my wife and daughter to the school gate.'

'Tilly will think it's Christmas,' laughed Amy, secretly thrilled. 'Not just her mum, but her dad too doing the school run.'

'I've booked dinner for us as well. Me and you, somewhere nice, and don't even ask because it's a surprise.'

'Tonight? But what about a babysitter? Claudia has to leave at five thirty today to get to a physio appointment.'

David held up a reassuring hand. 'Don't worry. It's covered. Mum is going to be here at six. Tilly has already planned that they're going to watch *Mulan* together.'

Amy threw an admiring glance at her husband. 'Is this a taste of things to come?' she said, cocking her head playfully.

'If you play your cards right,' said her husband, and kissed her.

The day passed quickly. A walk with David in Holland Park and a Pilates class and it was almost two o'clock. Her mind occasionally drifted to the *Verve* office, and there were emails from Tracey, Janine and Chrissie asking how she was. But for now she didn't give anything away to anyone; just perfunctory replies at the recommendation of Max's lawyers, though that seemed overly cautious to her.

Despite the nagging worry at the back of her mind, she found herself enjoying the day. Collecting Tilly from school and hearing her enthusiastically recount her day – a change from the usual 'good' when she asked at bedtime – was a particular treat.

When the doorbell rang at six, she welcomed Rosemary Parker with a hug.

'What are you doing home at this time?' smiled the older woman. Amy realised that David hadn't told her about her suspension.

'I'm having a few days off. How was the drive?'

'The A3 was busy, as usual.'

'Thank you for coming. We should have some back-up babysitters, but Claudia has always been so reliable. Until the accident anyway.'

'I'm glad you two are having a night out,' Rosemary said. 'Did you clear everything up between you?'

For a moment Amy didn't know how to respond. She had a good relationship with her mother-in-law, but the woman was as sharp as a tack and it was only to be expected that she would ask questions.

'Work has been stressful and we took it out on each other,' she said eventually.

'It happens,' said Rosemary more softly. 'Now, why don't you go and get ready? I want to spend some quality time with my granddaughter.'

Smiling, Amy slipped away and ran a bath. As she wallowed in the bubbles, she reflected on the fact that although she had mocked this life before – the empty days of the trophy wife – right now she could totally see its appeal.

It was another hour before David arrived, his face slightly flushed. Amy felt like Cinderella as the car gunned away into the night, bursting into a fit of giggles when it stopped just a few minutes away on Westbourne Grove.

'We could have walked that,' she laughed as he manoeuvred into a parking space.

'Not in your heels,' grinned David, coming round to the passenger seat to take her hand.

'So where are we going?' asked Amy.

'Suko,' said David, looking pleased with himself.

Amy gawped at him in gleeful surprise. The pop-up Japanese restaurant was so mythical, she hadn't even been sure it existed. Rotating around various venues in London, it had fewer than a dozen covers and was said to serve the best sashimi this side of Tokyo.

'How the hell did you manage to pull that off?' she said, squeezing his hand in appreciation. Japanese food was one of Amy's great loves and David knew it.

'A gentleman never tells,' he said bashfully.

When they reached the restaurant, they were led to a corner table, where they made small talk, keeping the conversation light and frivolous. Amy couldn't help but think it was like a first date and, on the one hand, that seemed appropriate. After everything that had happened over the past few weeks, it felt like a time of new beginnings, a time to put everything behind them – the arguments and jealousies – and just reboot.

But she swerved around any reference to Josie and Juliet as the whole situation felt too raw. She'd told David about Josie's overdose and her visit to see her at the Whittington the night before, but she didn't want to dwell on it, as it was painful to discuss.

'How's Josie, do you know?'

'I called the hospital today. She was discharged this

afternoon. Karen is in London looking after her.'

'That's good news,' he said as tiny plates of food started being delivered to their table.

Amy nodded.

'So you'll never guess who got in touch with me today,' he said, detecting that his wife wanted to change the subject.

'Tell me,' she said nervously. The last thing she wanted was more surprises.

'Louisa Bourne from the train,' he said, biting into a square of yellowfin tuna. 'Apparently she's been trying to get hold of you all day. Did Chrissie not let you know?'

Amy frowned. 'She left me some texts and messages asking me to get in touch, but Max said I shouldn't communicate with anyone at work.'

'Max Quinn. Caution personified. Who'd have thought it?' David put down his chopsticks for a moment. 'So it seems Louisa is fully recovered and wants to take us both out for lunch. By the way, she's appalled by what has happened to you. Wants to discuss everything when we meet.'

'We should set that up then,' said Amy, feeling curious about Louisa's offer, but wondering if it was still too soon to think about work. She'd had the stuffing knocked out of her, and all she really wanted to do for the next few weeks was take Tilly to and from school and listen to Radio 4 whilst she pottered about the house pruning the cupboards.

David took a sip of green tea and folded his arms on the table.

'I spoke to someone else,' he said after another moment.

Amy frowned. His tone of voice had become more serious. 'Who?' she asked, raising an eyebrow.

'An officer with Thames Valley Police. He says they're looking further into the abandoned vehicle on the train tracks.'

Amy waved a finger at him. 'You know, I was just having

a nice night back then. Let's not talk about this any more. I want to forget about it all. For now, anyway.'

But David wasn't going to let it drop.

'They think it's strange that an old banger would be left like that on such a desolate stretch. They want to find out why.'

'Why?' said Amy, sitting straighter in her seat. 'How can you rationalise anything that punks, joyriders or criminals do? They do it because they think it's a laugh. They probably stole it, were drunk or high and just left it there for a laugh, without thinking of the consequences of what might happen.'

'Apparently there's a CCTV camera right by that crossing. The night of the party, it wasn't working, but it had been fine the day before.'

'So what are you saying? That it was vandalised the day of the party?'

David nodded. 'Sounds a bit convenient to me.'

Amy sipped her own sake thoughtfully. 'People have been calling me paranoid for weeks,' she said, lowering her voice to barely a whisper. 'Now you're suggesting this was some sort of sabotage? This is serious stuff. If that train had derailed, dozens of people could have been killed.'

'It's not a stretch of the imagination that Josie might have known some lowlife who could arrange for a car to be put on the track,' David persisted.

'She wouldn't do that,' Amy said, thinking of the girl lying in the hospital bed.

David looked at her, confused. She didn't entirely blame him.

'I'm not saying she had thought through the consequences; simply that it's possible. She wanted to bring you down so badly, she might have gone to any lengths to do it.'

'I don't want to discuss this any more,' Amy said, looking

down at the table and then back up. 'It's gone, over. I have my life back. I have *you* back. That's all I care about now.'

He stretched his hand across the tiny table. 'I don't think you know how much I love you.'

Amy let her shoulders relax.

'Why didn't we just get together in Oxford?' he continued. 'Just think, Tilly would be twenty-one herself now. We'd be empty-nesters. We could do this every night.'

'Would we, though? Or would we be working till nine, ten every evening, reading proofs or closing a deal? Don't you think we have enough money, enough status? You've said it before, David. We can't keep chasing it, because we'll never be happy.'

Her husband smiled affectionately at her. 'One afternoon with Pog and already you're ready to drop out of the rat race.' He lifted her hand and kissed it. 'Let's go home.'

They'd barely been in the restaurant an hour, and although she was grateful that David had planned this delicious dinner, right then she wanted nothing more than to curl up in front of the TV with him in her cosiest pyjamas.

They paid the bill, and she tucked her arm though his as they walked towards the car. As she climbed into the passenger seat, her phone beeped to indicate an incoming message. She was tempted to leave it, but old habits died hard.

It was a text from Janice.

Juliet? Unbelievable: call ASAP!!!!

Amy sat in silence for a moment.

'Is everything all right?' said David, sliding into the seat beside her.

She wanted to put her phone back in her bag and just forget about it, but she had an unmistakable sense of foreboding. Her finger hovered over the screen, then she brought up Janice's number.

'Amy!' The fashion director's voice was excitable over a background of music and chatter.

'Where are you?' said Amy, simultaneously working out that she must be in Milan, at the shows.

'Some party at the Bulgari. God, what on earth's going on, Amy?' said Janice without further preamble. 'It's like the world's turned upside down. First you, now Juliet. I mean, what the hell?'

Amy flicked her eyes nervously over to David.

'Slow down, Janice,' she said. 'I don't know what you're talking about. Tell me what's happened.'

There was a pause.

'You don't know?'

'Obviously I know I've been suspended. But what's this about Juliet?'

'Amy . . .' said Janice, her voice uncertain. 'Rumours are going round the party like wildfire that the new editor of *Mode* is going to be announced tomorrow. Word on the street is that the person who's bagged the job is Juliet James.'

Chapter 38

Amy sat frozen in her seat.

'What's wrong?' said David after a moment.

She stared in front of her, not even able to focus.

'Juliet. She's the new editor of *Mode* . . .' she said, her voice fading away. She could feel her phone trembling in her hands.

'How do you know?'

She could feel thick bile rising in her throat.

'That was Janice. She's heard the gossip at the shows.'

Her eyes were welling up with tears; her stomach was tight and knotted as if all the air had been squeezed out of her body.

'How could she do this to me?' she croaked. 'All the time we were in Provence, she never said anything. Even yesterday, when I saw her . . .'

David took the phone away from her and held her hands, turning in the confined space of the car to face her.

'Amy, just stop. It's gossip, nothing more. Guess-the-new-editor is just the latest parlour game. Until there's an official announcement, no one knows.'

'She sounded sure . . .'

'Jules might have said she wasn't interested, but it's the

biggest job in the industry. If she did apply, we can't exactly blame her.'

She shot him a look. All she wanted now was complete loyalty from her husband, not excuses and deflections.

'She's not exactly played fair, has she?'

David didn't reply, and she used his silence to let her thoughts take hold.

'It all makes sense now,' she said, her mind mulling over everything that had happened in the past few weeks. It had begun to slot together like a very elaborate jigsaw. 'Juliet knew I was taking BlissVit and started the heroin rumours, because she knew it would be believable if anyone had seen any vials or syringes around the office. She knows better than anyone how the industry thrives on gossip, and also that Genesis would never hire anyone for the *Mode* job who had any scandal around them.'

'Juliet is your best friend, Amy. Listen to yourself.'

'I am listening, David. Josie told me that Juliet got her the job at Genesis. Hell, Juliet even admitted that much herself. She said it was because she felt guilty about what had happened in Provence, but Josie gave me a different version of events. Juliet told her to spy on me.'

'Spy? Or keep an eye on you? Big difference, especially as we've all been worried about you.'

She knew that David's allegiance to Juliet ran deep, but it was time for him to pick a side.

'I'm your wife,' she whispered with a quaver of fury.

'I know,' he said, squeezing her hand. 'I guess I don't want to believe that Juliet could do this to you.'

'And you think I do?' Her voice was barely a whisper.

'You should speak to her.'

The prospect made her feel sick, but she knew that her husband was right. She had to hear it from Juliet's own lips that she had stabbed her in the back. She was aware how painful that would be, but she had to know the truth.

'She'll be at the Design Week party. She mentioned it in Provence.'

'You don't have to speak to her tonight.'

'Don't I?' she whispered. 'David, I can't even think straight. I have to hear her try and justify this, otherwise I don't think I'll be able to sleep.'

'Just call her then.'

Her hands were still trembling as she dialled Juliet's number and held the phone to her ear. When it rang out, she wasn't entirely surprised, although she still left a message that they needed to talk.

David had put the key in the ignition, and as the engine purred to life, Amy placed her hand on the wheel.

'Will you drop me off at the party?'

'Amy, leave it. Just for tonight.'

'Please. If you're worried about your mum having to get back to Esher, just drop me off and I'll find my own way back. I have to talk to her.'

'In which case, I'm coming with you.'

The London Design Awards was one of the most prestigious events of its kind, showcasing the latest architectural projects and honouring the greatest names in the field; a splash of glamour and excitement once the fashion circus had rolled out of London and on to Milan.

Amy knew that Juliet would be there, not because *Living Style* was a particularly important magazine in the design world, but because Juliet was thick with that creative crowd. In Provence, she had told them all about the pre-Awards reception she had been invited to. At the time, Amy had smiled at her friend's less-than-subtle insinuation that she was important enough to have been invited; but looking back, she had always been genuinely excited about attending the event. There was no way she wouldn't be there that night.

'How are we going to get in?' asked David, slowing the car to a stop near Leighton House, the grand venue in Holland Park where the bash was being held.

'At Oxford you were the best blagger I knew.'

'I think you'll find that was Max. His motto for ball season was "no ticket no problem". I just went along for the ride.'

'Channel your inner Max Quinn then,' she muttered. 'If you don't, I will.'

She gripped her husband's hand as they walked through the park towards the venue. It was dark out here, with just the faint sound of music coming from the party.

Ahead of them she could make out a couple standing by a black chauffeur-driven car. She watched the woman touch the man's cheek before he got into the vehicle, leaving the woman behind. For a moment, Amy lost her breath – it had been a simple but touching gesture that made her grip her husband's hand a little tighter.

'Are you okay?' asked David.

Amy nodded, standing back for a moment to let the car drive past them. Her eyes drifted to the side window, and she frowned as she peered inside.

'I don't believe it,' she whispered.

'What?'

'That was Marv Schultz.'

David buttoned up his jacket. 'No real surprise that he's here. I think *World of Architecture* magazine is one of the sponsors.'

'Then who was that woman?' she said, quickening her pace. She hadn't been able to make out the woman's identity in the low light, but she had been wearing a distinctive feathered cape that Amy knew would be easy to spot.

Juliet. It had to be. That was how she had got the job.

Otherwise it was too much of a leap – an interiors magazine editor becoming the editor of *Mode*. Okay, so Anna Wintour had gone from *House & Garden* to British *Vogue*, but for Juliet it was too much of a stretch.

Amy was almost running now in her spindly black heels. There were two bouncers on the door, and she knew she had to get past them first. David caught up with her and touched her shoulder.

'Goldman's are also a sponsor,' he said, looking up at the huge banner over the door. 'Think I might have a little piece of magic in my pocket to sort that out.'

He pulled out a business card, then drew himself up to his full height and addressed one of the bouncers with all the dazzling public school polish he could muster.

'Jonathan Reade, Goldman Sachs. Sorry I'm late. I've been caught up in a deal.'

The bouncer looked at his colleague for the guest list. The other man shrugged.

'Bit late in the day for that. Someone took it. People are leaving, not arriving.'

David pressed the card into his hand. 'We're one of the headline sponsors for this evening.'

The bouncer nodded officiously and waved them through.

'Slick,' smiled Amy.

'Business card I picked up yesterday. Fraudently used. Sure he'll forgive me given the circumstances.'

Amy stopped when she saw the feathered cape disappearing into the ladies'.

'Wait there,' she said.

She inhaled deeply and stepped inside. The loos were empty except for one cubicle. She could see pointed feet under the door, expensive shoes with a diamanté buckle. It wasn't the ideal spot to confront Juliet, but at least it was quiet. But when the door opened, she gasped.

'Suzanne?'

'Amy, what are you doing here?'

Amy took a moment to think. Perhaps David was right after all that Juliet's appointment was just a rumour. And that look between Suzanne and Marv suggested an intimacy that went beyond mere colleagues.

'I was sorry to hear what happened,' said Suzanne. 'I do know a very good clinic if you need it.' There was a genuine concern in her voice that surprised Amy. It just didn't make sense.

'Should you not be in Milan?' she said quietly. 'Or do you have to be in London for something else?' Her mind was joining the dots now. If Suzanne was still in London, that meant she was going to be presented to the *Mode* team the next day.

'It's my mother's eightieth birthday so I took her to lunch. I'm flying out to Milan tomorrow.'

'I saw you outside with Marv, Suzanne.'

She watched the woman colour.

'Don't worry. I won't tell,' said Amy honestly. 'I won't tell anyone if you'll just give me the heads-up on the *Mode* job. It's you, isn't it?'

Suzanne looked suddenly relieved. 'No, Amy. It's not me.'

Amy frowned. She'd been so sure.

'The announcement. It's tomorrow. Isn't that why you're here?'

She saw a trace of a smile on Suzanne's polished scarlet lips.

'I never even applied for the job. I'd be under too much scrutiny. People would ask questions.'

'About Marv?'

'About Marv.' She nodded, as if to confirm their affair, and her face softened. Amy had never seen her look anything other than inscrutable. 'Marv is a brilliant man, we all know that. He's built Genesis up into a titan, and I don't want rumours of nepotism or special favours to sully that. The *Mode* job isn't worth it.'

Amy couldn't resist finding out more gossip. 'You and Marv? When, how?'

'Please, Amy. Don't. He's very special to me and I would rather not discuss it.'

Amy's eyes clouded with emotion. She had always had Suzanne Black down as a kick-ass powerhouse. But she loved him. Suzanne Black was in love with Marv Schultz.

'You're right,' she said. 'No job is worth your relationship.'

'The new *Mode* editor,' Suzanne said after a moment. 'It's Juliet James. Marv was meeting her this afternoon for the final sign-off. It's being announced tomorrow morning.'

'So the rumours are true.'

'As is the chatter that she's sleeping with Douglas Proctor, although you didn't hear that from me.' Suzanne plumped up the feathers on her cape.

Amy was stunned. 'Juliet and Douglas?'

Suzanne looked amused. 'Don't tell me you've never had a little office dalliance. The heart generally doesn't want to look very far.'

She touched Amy on the shoulder as she left. Amy remained rooted to the spot for a moment, then she pulled the door open and followed Suzanne out. She found David waiting for her.

'So?'

'Janice was right. Juliet is the new editor of *Mode*. It's being announced tomorrow.'

He turned and pulled her into a hug. 'She's not worth it,' he said into her hair. 'The job isn't worth it. Is that really what you want? Another five, ten years of working for

335

snakes like Douglas Proctor, competing with people like Juliet who are so desperate to get what they want?'

She couldn't even look up at her husband but she knew he was right.

'I'm just so angry,' she whispered.

Over his shoulder she could see Lysanne Flowers, Juliet's deputy at *Living Style*, standing by the stage. She pulled herself away from David and went over, tapping the younger woman on the shoulder. Lysanne spun around, looking embarrassed when she saw her. Amy knew this was something she was going to have to get used to.

'Have you seen Juliet anywhere?' she asked.

'She left a few minutes ago,' said Lysanne.

Amy felt dazed, on autopilot, stuck between a desire to confront her former friend head on and wanting to leave all this behind her. Parties, people, the judgement of others. For years she hadn't minded being so exposed, but now she didn't care if she was hot or not. She had allowed herself to be taken in, seduced by it all. What a fool she was.

They were silent on the way home.

Amy let her gaze trail out onto the dark streets of London. It had begun to rain, dappling the grey pavements like droplets of oil.

David was half right. It didn't matter any more. But she couldn't get over the betrayal by such a close friend. She had known that Juliet could be brusque and insensitive, but this was something else.

A voice in her head told her that she should just sleep on it. Tomorrow, she felt sure, it would hurt less. She would plan a family holiday for half-term. Sooner than that: a weekend in the Cotswolds would be good for the soul. She thought of Tilly running along the banks of a river or through a meadow. She just wanted to scoop her daughter up in her arms. That always made her feel better.

David stopped the car outside the house. She thought about a nice bottle of claret in the rack in the kitchen, and wondered if there were any cookies left from a batch that Claudia had made the day before.

She pushed the key into the lock and the door swung open. The first thing that struck her was the smell coming from the huge vase of lilies in the hall. The second was the unnatural quiet and calm inside the house.

'We're back,' called David, slipping off his suit jacket and hanging it over the walnut curve of the banister.

'Rosemary?' Amy went into the living room, but it was empty. 'Where is she?' She glanced at her husband, but he didn't look concerned.

'They've probably fallen asleep upstairs watching *Mulan*.' Tilly wasn't allowed a TV in her room, but there was a big set in the master bedroom, where the three of them would sometimes watch the latest movie that had caught the little girl's imagination.

'I'll go and check,' Amy said.

She took the stairs carefully, quietly, not wanting to wake her daughter. The main bathroom was ahead of her, but the door was open, suggesting that no one was inside. The guest bedroom next to it was also empty. She popped her head around the door of the master suite. The duvet was smooth, cushions and pillows still neatly stacked against the head board.

Tilly's room was on the next floor up. Amy expected to hear Rosemary creeping downstairs as she approached, but there was still not a sound. She quickened her step. Tilly's bedroom door was ajar, the soft glow from the night light seeping onto the landing.

As she crept inside, her heart seemed to stop beating. Tilly's bed was empty. The covers were crumpled, the soft imprint of her head still on the pillow, as if she had been there only recently.

'Tilly?' she said out loud.

She felt her hand come up to her chest as she forced herself to breathe.

'David! She's not here!' she called, backing out onto the landing. She could hear the panic in her own voice.

David came running upstairs, taking two steps at a time. 'They're not up there?'

Amy shook her head. An image flashed into her head: Rosemary's grey woollen coat had been on the banister when they had left to go to dinner. But it was no longer there when David had put his own jacket in the same spot.

'Where are they?' said David, looking at his watch. 'Surely she hasn't taken her out?'

Amy tried to hold onto that thought. That was what it must be. Rosemary was a soft touch when it came to her granddaughter. She imagined them watching a movie together, mischievous, laughing, snuggling up, Tilly demanding popcorn.

'Call her,' she said urgently.

David pulled out his phone and frowned as he looked at the screen.

'"Have a good night",' he muttered out loud.

'What? What's happened?' asked Amy.

'Mum sent me a message.'

'How could you not have noticed?' she said, suddenly feeling more anxious.

'We were driving, at the party, I don't know . . . She sent it at nine thirty.'

'Call her,' said Amy, louder, more desperate now.

David was stabbing at the keyboard. He put the phone to his ear.

'Where are you?' A pause. 'What do you mean, on your way back to Esher?'

Amy's heart was pulsing louder as she waited for him to tell her what was going on.

'Why? Why did you do that?'

He barely waited for Rosemary to answer before he ended the call and looked at Amy.

'Mum's gone home,' he said, his face pale and rigid.

'Has she got Tilly with her?'

David shook his head. 'Juliet came to the house. Said that we'd asked her to take over the babysitting so that Rosemary didn't have a late night with such a long drive home.'

'Juliet came to the house?' Every nerve ending turned cold.

David nodded. 'Mum set off half an hour ago and left Juliet and Tilly here.'

'Then where are they now?' said Amy. She knew without a doubt that her daughter was in danger.

Chapter 39

Amy ran down the stairs, slipping twice in her haste and banging her coccyx. Somewhere she registered pain reverberating around her body, but she could think about nothing but finding Tilly. She called her daughter's name over and over, but the silence that rang back made her blood run cold.

She rested her head against the wall for a moment, trying to recover her cool. This was no time for hysterics. She needed to think, plot her next move, try and climb into Juliet's head.

Why had she come here? Where had she gone? Where had she taken Tilly?

David was on his phone, dialling Juliet's number again and again, but she was not picking up.

'Keep trying,' pleaded Amy, knowing that Juliet was far more likely to speak to David than to her.

'I can't get through,' said David with undisguised panic.

'Bloody Rosemary. Why did she leave Tilly alone with her?'

She didn't need her husband to tell her the answer to that one. Juliet and Rosemary had known one another for over twenty years. On Tilly's birthday, when Amy always threw a tea party for close friends and family, the two women would huddle in a corner for almost the entire time. Amy had occasionally thought darkly that perhaps Rosemary would have preferred her son to marry Juliet.

Rosemary knew how close David and Amy were to their old Oxford friend, how they moved in the same circles and shared the same high-flying lifestyle; it wouldn't have seemed so unusual to her for Juliet to turn up to the house and offer to relieve her of her babysitting duties. That was what friends did.

'Try Peter,' she said, snapping out of her thoughts and grabbing the car keys.

'Where are you going?' David said.

'Hampstead.'

'To their house?'

Amy nodded. 'You wait here in case they come back.' But she didn't believe for a minute that they would.

Thank God she hadn't had a drink at the Design Week party, thought Amy as she drove up Elgin Avenue. She had driven this way hundreds of times before, and could almost have done the journey blindfolded, which was just as well, since she could hardly see through the clouds of emotion in her eyes.

She wiped the tears from her cheek with the back of her hand as she tried to concentrate on the road, cursing every red light and parked car that slowed her down. She had no idea why she was driving to Hampstead. She should just have called the police, even though they would have been unlikely to take her report seriously; so her best friend had taken over babysitting duties from her mother-in-law and they now weren't where they were supposed to be – it was hardly the stuff of *Crimewatch*.

But there had been something nagging at Amy ever since Janice had told her that Juliet was going to be the new editor of *Mode*; the pieces of the puzzle beginning to fit together. Josie working at Genesis, the car on the train tracks, even the small details of the fashion party that had not gone to plan: it all told her that Juliet would stop at nothing to get what she wanted.

But where did Tilly fit into this? Juliet and Peter had never had children. 'We can't,' was the only explanation that Juliet had ever given. Amy had always assumed that it hadn't bothered them too much; they'd never tried to adopt or look into surrogacy. But perhaps Juliet was desperate for a child in the same way she had clearly been desperate for the *Mode* job.

Tilly, oh Tilly. Where has she taken you?

Amy was in Hampstead now, the Heath to her right like a gaping black hole in the city. As she turned into Juliet's street, she looked around for her car and saw it parked just a few feet ahead under a street light. She glanced at the house. The living room shutters were closed, warm light shining through the slats.

She pulled her phone out of her pocket and called David.

'I think she might be home,' she said breathlessly. 'The car is here and the lights are on.'

She ran up the stone steps, pushing her phone back in her pocket, and knocked hard on the door.

'Juliet,' she cried, hearing the desperation in her own voice.

When there was no reply, she plunged her hand into her bag and produced the spare set of keys that Juliet had given her years ago – back in the days when they had trusted each other. Her fingers were trembling, but she managed to slot the metal into the lock and pushed the door open slowly. She could hear soft classical music coming from the living room. Someone *was* home.

'Juliet?' Her heart was hammering, but her voice was

steady and controlled as she called out.

The music was louder now: soaring violins and a melancholy cello that sounded half familiar: David, Max, Juliet – they would all know the piece, the composer, but now it felt like another way in which Juliet was shutting her out.

She stood at the door of the living room and took a moment before she stepped inside. She could feel the warmth of the fire, crackling in the semi-dark, before she saw Juliet sitting in the club chair in the corner, her face ghostly pale like the moon.

Amy gasped. Relief and fear combined to make her shiver.

'You're here.'

She noticed that Juliet had something on her lap – a photo album, as far as she could see. Shredded paper surrounded her chair like confetti She tiptoed closer, as if approaching a wild animal; Juliet sat motionless, her red-rimmed eyes and puffy cheeks betraying the fact that she had been crying.

'Where's Tilly, Juliet?' Amy asked evenly.

It was an agonising moment before she replied.

'She's upstairs, asleep,' she said, her voice cracking.

Amy exhaled deeply. *Thank God*. She turned and ran up the stairs, praying that Juliet was telling the truth.

The guest bedroom was at the end of the landing. She crept inside and could make out a child-sized hump under the duvet. She pulled back the cover and saw Tilly's golden hair. Her eyes were closed and there was the faint noise of breath escaping from her chest – up and down, up and down.

She took out her phone and called David.

'I'm on my way,' he said.

Amy ended the call and fell to her knees by the bed, stroking Tilly's forehead softly.

'Tilly, wake up, sweetheart. We have to go.'

The little girl's lashes fluttered as her eyes slowly opened.

'Mummy, I'm tired,' she said in a sleepy voice.

'I know, honey. I know.'

'Why did I have to come to Auntie Juliet's? Why did Grandma go home?'

'We'll talk about it tomorrow,' she whispered. But Tilly had already fallen asleep again.

Amy walked slowly back down the stairs, trying to steady herself with every step. Perhaps there was a rational explanation for it. Perhaps an emergency had meant that Juliet had to return home. Perhaps something had happened to Peter, she thought, suddenly feeling uncharitable. But why had she turned up at Amy and David's house in the first place?

When she walked into the living room, Juliet still hadn't moved from her chair.

'Are you going to tell me what happened tonight?' she asked finally.

'I suppose you want an explanation about the *Mode* job,' said Juliet, turning her head so that she didn't have to meet Amy's eyes.

'I want to know why you took Tilly from the house. We were worried sick.'

Juliet closed the shredded photo album and put it on the floor beside her, then picked up a remote control from the arm of the chair and turned off the stereo.

'I deserve the *Mode* job,' she said when the room fell silent. 'I was approached about it weeks ago, if you must know.'

'Where? In Douglas's bed?' said Amy, unable to resist the barb, even though she knew that nothing good ever came from poking the hornets' nest.

Juliet shot her a caustic look. 'Did you expect me to just roll over and let you have it?'

'I never expected anything,' Amy said evenly. 'I wanted it, yes, and gave it my best shot. But that wasn't enough. Not when I seemed to be sabotaged at every turn.' She tried to contain herself, aware that Juliet had an edge of unpredictability about her.

'Think how it feels to be me for a moment,' said Juliet through thin red lips. 'I made you, Amy Shepherd. You'd never have had the balls to go to London if it hadn't been for me getting you a start at Genesis, letting you stay in my flat. And yet you didn't even ask me if I was interested in the *Mode* job.'

'I did ask,' replied Amy.

Juliet scoffed. 'Not in any serious way. You thought I didn't have a chance, because how could I compete with the great Amy Shepherd.' She paused, her eyes wide and bright for a moment. 'Well guess what. I'm smarter than you think. Better than you know. You're not the only one who can charm and seduce and manipulate to get what they want.'

Amy thought about Juliet and Douglas, wondering how their affair had got started. She had never seen Juliet as a femme fatale, although it was impossible to ignore the fact that there was something formidable and dazzling about her. From the moment they had met, Amy had always wanted to be as witty and sophisticated as Juliet James. She had allowed herself to be in her shadow for their entire time in the Oxford house share, following her lead, letting herself be shaped and moulded. Karen was right that she had turned away from her old life because she had been seduced by a new one. And oh, how easy it had been to be seduced.

'It was you, wasn't it? The car on the train tracks. That wasn't coincidence. The rumours about heroin. Josie was like putty in your hands and you used her to do your bidding.'

'A simple girl,' Juliet said with a brittle laugh. 'Smarter

than you, though. More streetwise. More ambitious. I saw that steel in her eyes the moment I met her. It didn't surprise me when she made a play for David in Provence. The only surprise was that she wasn't his type.'

Amy let her words settle.

'She *was* telling the truth,' she whispered, fitting it all together. 'The bra in our bed. The receipt for the necklace. *You* did all that to make me suspect David of an affair he never had.'

Juliet narrowed her eyes. 'Don't blame me for the fact that you were neglecting your marriage. Everyone could see it was dying, but neither you nor David had the guts to put it out of its misery.'

Amy stayed rooted to the spot, shaking her head. 'You tried to ruin my life,' she said slowly. 'My relationship, my career . . . What was Josie? Collateral damage?'

'She was the one who chose to take the pills,' Juliet said tartly.

'This isn't about the *Mode* job, is it?' Amy said in a low, even voice. 'You can't stand to see me happy. You can't bear to think that the girl from Westmead has done well.'

Neither of them spoke for at least a minute. Finally Juliet rose from her chair and crossed the room to a drinks trolley. She took a crystal tumbler and filled it with whisky, not offering Amy one.

'You asked me why I took Tilly tonight,' she said, tossing back the drink. 'I wanted you to know what it feels like to have someone you love taken away from you, even if was only for a few hours. I wanted you to feel that pain.'

Amy took a step back, edging towards the door. She thought of Tilly upstairs in the bedroom. Suddenly it didn't feel safe being here. But still she was desperate to know everything.

'I did what I had to do, Amy. Just like you did. Tarting

around the Oxford house in those tiny nighties, trying to look seductive for David. Do you know how stupid you looked? I didn't think for one minute that he'd fall for it – the cheap tricks of the girl from the sticks – but you never can underestimate the propensity of men to think with their members. You blinded David – *my* David – with that little Eliza Doolittle act, and he fell for it.'

Amy frowned. 'Is that what this is all about? David?'

Juliet looked wounded now. 'We have known each other since we were thirteen,' she said, gripping her glass so tightly that Amy could see her knuckles turning white. 'I knew even then how right we were for each other. When we ended up at college together, I thought it would just be a matter of time before we settled down. But then you came along and ruined everything, and I ended up with the gay best friend, the marriage of convenience and the nice little interiors editorship. It's not quite David, is it? The glorious love affair. Or *Mode*, the biggest job in publishing.'

Amy heard footsteps behind her, and turned to see David standing in the doorway, open-mouthed with shock.

Chapter 40

Oxford, 1995

It was supposed to be the greatest night of her life, the Commemoration Ball, and yet Juliet felt sick with nerves.

She had to tell him. Tonight was the night. She had put everything else in place. The dress had cost her a fortune, made her without question look her very best. Her hair had been cut and blow-dried by Oxford's top stylist, nails painted with Hard Candy, body defuzzed and buffed with Body Shop, a cloud of Anaïs Anaïs finishing the whole look off.

She had waited so long for David Parker that part of her wondered if another few weeks or months would make all that much difference. They'd both been invited to Hugo Pearson's twenty-first in September – his father owned a stables in Wiltshire and there was to be a weekend of riding and fine dining. Juliet could hardly wait. But still, it was finally time to tell David how she really felt, and she felt sure he would reciprocate her feelings.

It didn't seem that long ago since that magical weekend in Scotland celebrating Angus McGregor's eighteenth. A-level grades were just out, and she and David had both aced them all. Grouse season was in full swing, and David and Juliet had arrived a day early to take advantage of the glorious late-summer weather.

They'd spent the afternoon before the party on the moors, with champagne and a picnic, planning their future at Oxford: the societies they would join, the countries they wanted to travel to in the holidays, the secrets of Oxford they had already gleaned from open days and research.

Waves of teenagers had started arriving by the time they got back to the castle. There were several worryingly pretty girls among them, but it didn't matter: Juliet felt as if she and David were already a couple, and was sure that something would happen that night to seal the deal.

At midnight, after a huge fireworks display that must have set the McGregors back thousands, they had wandered into the grounds together and watched another sort of light display: ribbons of acid green and purple that danced on the dark horizon. Juliet had never seen anything as beautiful as those Northern Lights before, but the moment became even more perfect when she felt David come up close behind her and plant a soft kiss on the back of her neck. She could remember, as if it were yesterday, time standing still as they kissed passionately and he murmured his longing.

The lights had brought half the party out into the grounds, and the spell had been broken, though Juliet was sure the magic could easily be reignited.

She hadn't slept that night. There was a tight little group that stayed up until dawn, drinking the dregs of the champagne. When she had finally gone to her room – a tiny space in the eaves that had once been used by the staff of the castle – she'd hoped that David would come and find her, that he would slip into her single bed beside her and make love to her under the covers. He never came.

'Juliet, can I get you a drink?'

She looked across to see Francis Harris, a postgrad

student from Keble she had zero interest in, holding up a bottle of champagne.

'Survivors' photo is another three hours away yet. Gotta keep drinking. Gotta keep drinking.'

She smiled thinly and shook her head, hoping he'd get the message.

'David, over here!' Juliet prided herself on being a cool customer. She had a policy that people should come to her, but found herself waving to her friend enthusiastically.

He stalked over, holding a flute of champagne.

'Fancy coming on the rides?' she asked.

'I think I'll probably vom if I go anywhere near those things.' He snorted.

'What have you been doing?'

'Avoiding Max. He's still trying to persuade me to spend six months in Goa with him. Two weeks isn't enough apparently, and he doesn't understand the concept that I have to start work.'

He looked drunk and irritable and Juliet wondered if he had been taking drugs. She'd heard that Mungo Descales was so off his head on coke, he'd already had to be carried home by three members of the rugby team.

He handed her the empty glass and looked back towards the dance floor. 'Back in a tick,' he said, and staggered off again.

Pog appeared by her side with a fresh glass of champagne. 'For you, my dear,' he said, loosening his white tie.

'What's wrong with David?' frowned Juliet, watching him latch onto a drunk-looking brunette.

Pog followed her gaze. 'Had a terrible row with Annabel, apparently. She's been putting all sorts of pressure on him to move in with her. Think he's finally seen sense and dumped her.'

'Thank God,' she said, feeling her heart race a little.

'Don't know what that means for his employment prospects, though. He was supposed to be starting at Annabel's dad's firm in a few weeks. Slightly stuffed with that now, I should imagine.'

'He'll find something else,' she said with absolute confidence. 'David is brilliant. Any bank in London will be lucky to have him. I know lots of people in the City. I'll start making some calls on Monday.'

'You don't have to sort out everyone's problems, Jules.'

'Don't I?' she said, feeling buoyed. 'Anyway, let's forget about real life for one night. Would you care to dance?'

She led Pog to a spot close enough to David that she could keep an eye on him but just far enough away that she could monitor the entire room. She liked to think of herself as a strong and independent woman; liked to think a couple of steps ahead and plan accordingly.

David was looking very red in the face now as he swayed to whatever track it was that the DJ was playing. But hell, he looked sexy. Cigarette hanging out of the corner of his mouth, his white shirt loose at the neck, he was easily the most handsome man at the party. Juliet knew she had to make her move. Annabel was lurking somewhere, and she'd seen Amy half an hour earlier too, behaving as if she belonged at the ball. She was looking pretty tonight, Juliet had to admit that. The warm weather had given her face some colour, the sun streaking her hair with highlights.

David's friendship with Amy had started to worry Juliet of late. It had been a novelty having her in the house at first. When Pog had suggested his friend from The Bear joining them as the fifth housemate, Juliet had been sceptical but practical. Amy was an outsider – she was from the poly, for goodness' sake – but no one else would want the attic room, which smelled overpoweringly of damp, so eventually she had agreed to the girl joining them.

At the beginning she had even quite enjoyed having her around. Juliet had a lazy streak when it came to domestic chores, and Amy kept the house spick and span. She would even do the washing-up, unasked, after it had piled up to mountainous proportions.

But lately, things had changed. On at least three occasions, Juliet had come back after lectures and found David and Amy sitting at the kitchen table, laughing, having fun, their conversation slowing on her arrival as if they had secrets they were unwilling to share.

At least David had a puritanical streak – a strong sense of decency that made Juliet fairly sure he would never two-time Annabel with his pretty housemate. But now that Annabel was out of the picture . . . well, she didn't want to think about it.

'What is he doing now?' said Pog, peering over the top of the crowd. 'He seems to have moved on to *Dirty Dancing*.'

Juliet squinted through the crowds. Was that Karen he was dancing with? Amy's trashy friend from Bristol?

The track changed to one she recognised. Pulp's 'Common People'. She almost laughed out loud, but then quickly sobered as David took Karen's hand and led her off the dance floor.

'He's having fun,' grinned Pog. 'Phwoar . . . look at them go.'

'Pog, this isn't funny.'

'Why not?'

Juliet gritted her teeth. She couldn't have anyone interfering with her plan. She had to tell David how she felt, tonight. Pick up from where they'd left off at the McGregor castle. This was no time for curveballs. She grabbed Pog's arm.

'You've got to stop him,' she said.

'I suppose you're right. I don't imagine Amy will be happy.'

It was a strange thing to say, but Juliet let it go.

'Hurry up, then.'

Pog looked at her. 'Are you coming?'

Juliet shook her head. It was not like her to remain passive in any situation, but she didn't want to follow David and Karen into the dark. She was afraid of what she might see. It was one thing snogging on the dance floor; another thing entirely to go somewhere quiet.

As Pog followed David and Karen, Juliet glanced towards the bar. Amy caught her eye and winked at her. Panic fired to every nerve ending. Suddenly she wanted to know exactly what David and Karen were up to. It would be just like Pog to get distracted en route, to bottle out and give them some privacy.

She took a flute of champagne from the waiter for Dutch courage. She wasn't a great drinker, and it went to her head almost immediately. As she moved away from the dance floor, the music grew fainter, until all she could make out was the *thud, thud* of a bass line. Or maybe it was her heart.

She didn't know New College well, had little reason to come here. She knew there were cloisters and stone corridors that were perfect for secret assignations, but Pog had followed the couple into the dark depths of the garden, past the fairground rides and the happy crowds and a makeshift railing designed to keep people from exploring further. She glanced back. The college looked glorious against the background of the night sky, its honey stone shining like bars of gold bullion.

She heard them before she could see them, and slid behind the trunk of a birch tree to avoid being seen herself. The moon appeared from behind a cloud and illuminated Karen's bottle-blonde hair and the back of David's head.

353

Her hands were all over him, helping him slip off his jacket, fingers burrowing under his shirt. David's own hands rolled down the top of her green stretch dress.

Juliet gasped as they pulled apart for a moment and one white breast was exposed in the darkness. Then David lowered his head, burying it in Karen's cleavage, settling his mouth on her nipple. Juliet closed her eyes. Why hadn't she lent the tramp a different gown?

They were hungry now, desperate. The top of Karen's dress was round her waist now, her long creamy legs exposed. Juliet could hear her moans even from this distance. David was making Karen feel so good, she felt her own desire stir, a tight, warm pulse of pleasure that it was impossible to ignore.

David's trousers were around his knees now, Karen's eager, experienced fingers rolling down the cotton of his boxer shorts.

There was something raw and unbridled about the scene. Juliet had never had a sexual experience like the one unfolding in front of her; even when she had imagined herself and David finally consummating their glorious friendship, it had never been like this.

The noises were louder now, the pair of them half naked. She couldn't bear to watch any more. Struggling for breath, she gathered up the folds of her chiffon skirt, then turned and fled back to the ball.

Dawn light was beginning to flicker in the sky, and she knew it was time to go home. She grabbed a flute of champagne and downed it in one, desperate to numb the pain. Would David bring Karen back to the Holywell Street house? Would he have sex with her there, under Juliet's nose? Was he that crass; was she that cheap? She had no idea.

She saw Amy still working at the bar; pouring one glass

of champagne then another. It was all Amy's fault. She had brought Karen into their lives. Into David's bed. She felt a hatred for her housemate so strong she thought it might knock her over.

She looked back at the moonlight shining on the castellations of the college, wondering if she should run back and break up the passionate tryst. But she knew it was too late for that. Too late to tell David about her feelings, too late to stop him spoiling her final night in Oxford. It was over.

Chapter 41

Present day

'Oh Jules. Why?' he asked so quietly they could hardly hear him.

Amy stepped back and grasped her husband's hand. She had no idea how he had made it across London so quickly – he must have broken every speed record to get here – but she was so glad to see him.

The sight of him had made Juliet waver, her pale, cool armour melting to the thinnest sheen.

'Why did she have to move into the house?' she asked, her voice wobbling. 'I found that house. I wanted to live with you and Pog and even Max if he came as part of the package. But not her. She came along and ruined everything.'

'Is this really what you want?' asked David simply. 'Our friendship destroyed, Amy crushed, Josie in hospital. What's it all for?'

Tears started to leak from Juliet's eyes. 'I wanted to fix things. I've always wanted to fix things. Ever since the night of the Commem Ball. But I never knew how until Josie came along.'

She was crying now, deep sobs from the depths of her

soul, but neither Amy nor David moved forward to comfort her.

'Claudia's mugging. That wasn't an accident, was it?' said David slowly.

They heard Juliet take a sharp inhalation of breath.

'Was it?' he said more fiercely.

She looked taken aback at the force of his emotion. She squeezed her eyes shut, then snapped them open before she spoke again.

'I'd been advising on a gallery renovation in the East End. I overheard a couple of the scaffolders saying they'd had someone roughed up for not paying a debt. I knew they could help me.'

'Poor Claudia,' whispered Amy, wondering at how little she really knew about the woman in front of her.

'Josie was beautiful, sexy, useful. I didn't want her to go back to Bristol or wherever it was she came from.'

'You wanted her to come to Provence and seduce my husband instead,' Amy said.

Juliet's voice hardened. 'She was another low-rent tart who saw what she wanted and would stop at nothing to get it.'

'Really? Admit it, you planted the bra, bought the necklace. Josie didn't do any of that,' said Amy, imagining Juliet scuttling to the village, buying the pendant that Josie had remarked on and planting the receipt in David's wallet. The number of times over the years they had all been out for dinner, gone on holiday, to the theatre or Sunday brunch . . . and all that time she was trying to ruin Amy's marriage.

'I did it for you,' Juliet said, clutching the glass to her chest as if she would never let it go, looking at David with absolute devotion. 'I did it all for you, David, because I love you.'

'If you cared about me at all, you'd want me to be happy.'

'We could have been happy. We would have been happy if it wasn't for her. Remember that night. The night in the Highlands. Our whole life could have been that magical. I thought we could recapture it at Oxford. But we didn't. I wanted to tell you how much I loved you at the ball that night, but it was never the right moment, and then it passed . . .'

'That was a long time ago, Juliet. We were only ever friends. I moved on, and so did you.'

A noise escaped from Juliet's throat; a sound of pain and longing. She put her glass on the mantelpiece and tried to compose herself.

'Go and get Tilly,' said Amy, squeezing her husband's hand. She didn't want to be here another minute. The longer she listened to Juliet, the more she admitted, the more she was convinced that the woman was mad, that envy and bitterness had twisted her core, her values and her mind.

David disappeared upstairs. When he had gone, Juliet took a step closer to Amy.

'I didn't get the man, but at least I got the job,' she said. 'Let's see how dynamic and interesting and sexy you are when you're just another stay-at-home mother killing time between yoga classes and school pick-up. Let's see how long it is before David finds himself a pretty, ambitious thirty-year-old he can mould into wife number two.'

'Don't get too comfortable at *Mode*,' said Amy, wanting to lash out in return. 'The police will find out about the car on the train tracks. They'll find out it was done deliberately. David spoke to them this afternoon and they're pulling together their evidence. They might even link it to Claudia's mugging.'

'I doubt it,' replied Juliet.

'You could have killed people with that stunt, Juliet. The police aren't going to ignore that.'

David came back downstairs holding Tilly in his arms. 'Let's go,' he said, touching Amy on the shoulder in a tender gesture.

They turned to leave the house and didn't look back as they descended the stone steps towards the car.

'Stop! Don't go. I'm sorry,' shouted Juliet behind them.

It was cold outside, a chilly wind seeping between the folds of Amy's coat. David fastened Tilly into her car seat in the Range Rover and got into the driver's seat. Amy was desperate to go home with them, but they had come to Hampstead separately and she didn't want to leave her own car here. After all, she had no desire to come back to Juliet's house ever again.

The engine of the Range Rover growled into life.

'Please, don't go!' screamed Juliet, running down the steps, her grey trapeze-line dress floating out to either side of her body. With her pale face and red lips, she looked like a banshee. 'I'm sorry. I'm so sorry. I'm sorry for everything.'

Amy got into the Fiat and put the key in the ignition, ready to follow her husband. She watched Juliet scrabble around in her pockets and run towards her own car. As she waited for David to pull out, she glanced in her rear-view mirror and saw Juliet behind the wheel of her little Triumph.

'Shit,' she muttered, following David towards the junction at the end of the road. The lights started to change and she put her foot on the accelerator. With a bit of luck, Juliet would get stuck on the red and she could shake her off. She was hardly going to chase her back to Notting Hill.

As she glanced behind her again, everything seemed to contract into slow motion. There was a huge bang and a flash of light, the screech of metal against metal. Amy slammed her brakes on and jumped out of the car, running as fast as her heels would take her.

A 4x4 had gone into the side of Juliet's tiny sports car as

she jumped the lights. The front of the car was crushed like a tin can trampled by a heavy boot, spirals of grey smoke rising from the bonnet.

'No!' screamed Amy, pulling out her phone and desperately dialling 999. 'Ambulance. We need an ambulance,' she barked.

The driver of the 4x4 was standing on the road, dazed and motionless as he looked at the car.

Amy punched another number into her mobile.

'David. Get back here. There's been an accident. Juliet . . . driving too fast. The car's trashed.'

Other cars were stopping at the scene. A cyclist rode onto the pavement and dismounted. A runner in a fluorescent bib slowed and pulled his headphones out of his ears.

At first, she was too frightened to look. Holding her breath, she crept forward and peered into the driver's seat. Red hair straggled across the dashboard. In the distance, she could hear the sound of sirens. The moon disappeared behind a cloud, and Amy felt her shoulders slump in sadness.

Epilogue

Juliet's appointment as editor-in-chief of *Mode* magazine was not announced during the Paris shows as had been Douglas Proctor's plan for his on-off girlfriend. At first, it seemed wholly inappropriate given that she was in an induced coma at the Royal Free Hospital. But even when her condition improved, Genesis Media held off from confirming that she had got the job, and the matter was left in the hands of the HR department and lawyers.

The rumours that Juliet might never walk again worried Douglas, even though he acknowledged that some diversity among the Genesis Media editors might be good for PR. But he was particularly bothered about how things would look for him, given that the police were sniffing around the events of the Fashion 500 party. He had no idea what an abandoned banger on the train tracks had to do with him, but they had been asking some very uncomfortable questions about how well he knew Juliet James, and he realised that he should keep his distance from her as much as possible.

Once Amy had given various statements to the police, she, David and Tilly took off to Lyme Regis, where they spent a long weekend combing the beach for fossils and going for bracing walks along the coast with flasks of tea. It felt indulgent taking a holiday so soon after Provence, but she needed to be out of London to get some head space, to think about the direction her life was now going to take.

Marv Schultz had been in touch within days of Juliet's accident about going back to her old job back at *Verve*. It was hers if she wanted it, he said, via a transatlantic phone call, acknowledging that there had been some crossed wires that were being investigated. He also made noises about exciting opportunities at Genesis Media in New York, which Amy politely deflected, much as she acknowledged the need for a fresh start. She had no idea why Marv had contacted her; she had never whispered a word about his affair with Suzanne Black, for which perhaps he was grateful. Nor had she gone public about her unfair dismissal, which she just wanted to put behind her.

With lines of communication open with Marv, Amy had been tempted to tell him about her toxic relationship with Juliet. How Juliet had sabotaged the Fashion 500 party, spread rumours about her drug addiction and seduced Douglas Proctor as destructive revenge for unrequited love. But however much she wanted to clear her own name, however much she knew the CEO deserved to hear about the backstage drama at Genesis, she also knew that she had no proof for the allegations, and that therefore the elegant response, the right response for her sanity, was simply to walk away and let the police deal with it.

Louisa Bourne, on the other hand, was more difficult to turn down.

Amy and Claire looked up at Amy's mood board, which she had pinned along one wall of her new office at Exmoor in Ladbroke Grove. 'I know I probably should have moved into the modern age and done a Pinterest board,' she smiled, touching one of the glossy pages cut out of a coffee-table book. 'But I'm still an old-fashioned print girl at heart, and

I thought this would be the best way to show people what sort of feel I want for the site.'

'Louisa loves you because you *are* an old-fashioned print girl,' said Claire, sipping her coffee. 'I've seen the average age in the office out there. They might understand SEO and user interface, but no one knows how to build desirable lifestyle worlds from words and pictures like you, honey.'

'What are you saying?' said Amy, tapping her friend playfully on the shoulder. 'That Amy Shepherd the old-timer might be able to bring value to the table after all?'

They both laughed, but it was how Amy had felt when she had first said yes to the offer of the role of chief creative officer at Exmoor. three months earlier. Seventy-six-year-old Louisa Bourne had been as convincing as a thirty-year-old tech titan as she explained why Amy should jump ship from magazines into e-retailing, but Amy still felt way out of her comfort zone.

Under the stewardship of Michel Gagner, Exmoor's impressive French CEO, brought in from Net-a-Porter two years earlier, profits had jumped over 200 per cent. But still Louisa felt that the site lacked great content. She bombarded Amy with statistics proving that the longer customers stayed on the site, the more they would buy, and told her that she felt sure she was the person to conjure up that editorial stardust, but Amy still wasn't sure whether she could pull it off, feeling like the girl from Westmead who had turned up at Genesis Media all those years ago.

'I know you only came in to talk about doing this one shoot, but there's as much work as you want on the new editorial team,' she said now, turning to Claire. 'A contributing fashion editor position is yours if you'd like it.'

Claire looked at her wide-eyed. 'Contributing fashion editor? Me?'

Amy nodded.

'But I haven't worked for ten years . . .'

'You are a great stylist, Claire. I'm not doing you a favour just because you're my friend.'

Claire gave a little squeal of glee, and for a moment, Amy remembered Juliet pulling strings with William Bentley to get her a job as a junior writer at Genesis. Claire was a fantastic stylist, but deep down, Amy was aware that she had ulterior motives for offering her a job. She knew Claire was fed up being simply Max Quinn's wife, and she wanted to help her get back into the professional marketplace without having to go to her husband for help. For her own part, Amy wanted people around her at Exmoor that she trusted. Was that why Juliet had smoothed her way into Genesis all those years ago? Had she wanted to help Amy out? Was it to have an ally at the company? Or to keep her friends close and her enemies closer? Amy would never know.

'Max saw Peter yesterday,' said Claire, as if she had read Amy's thoughts. 'Apparently the police investigation seems to have cooled off.'

Amy pressed her lips together.

'Without CCTV evidence, they can't prove who abandoned the car on the railway line. They know whose it is, but they can't join the dots.'

Amy nodded. For a long time, she had wanted Juliet to get her just deserts for trying to ruin her life, for putting people in danger. But deep down she knew that she had been punished enough. A punishment harsher than any jail sentence. David had cut off all communication with his former friend, sending back the reams of letters that had arrived at the house apologising for everything she had done, ignoring every call and text. He hated Juliet now, and his icy silence was the most effective way of showing it.

'We should go,' said Amy, looking at her watch. It was

past four o'clock. David had left work early and picked Tilly up, and she was meeting them back at the house, just fifteen minutes' walk away from the Exmoor offices.

The weather was crisp and cold as they stepped out onto the street. Amy flipped up the collar of her coat and said goodbye to Claire. In a week's time it would be Christmas. The blue skies of summer and those balmy August evenings seemed so long ago now. At least they had a trip planned over Easter: a three-week safari in Botswana. Tilly in particular couldn't wait and was spending hours poring over brochures and books. She could already spot the difference between a waterbuck, an impala and an eland antelope. It was safe to say they were all looking forward to it.

Where are you? texted David when she was almost home. She smiled, knowing how keen he was to set off and get out of London. At this time on a Friday evening it was a three-hour drive to Dorset, although they both knew it was worth every minute. It had been love at first sight when they'd viewed the cottage on that late September weekend in Lyme Regis. At first she'd wondered if it was an impulse buy, a reaction to everything that had gone on over the summer. Six months previously, a weekend cottage had seemed an indulgence. Not any more. Work to live, not live to work.

Popping to Tesco Express to get some snacks for the journey, she texted back. *Why don't you pick me up outside?*

She ran into the shop and gathered up an armful of crisps, fruit and drinks, then stood on the pavement to wait for her husband and daughter.

At first she didn't recognise the young woman coming down the street towards her, flanked by other girls around her age. She looked different. Her hair was shorter, her summer tan had faded, and she was dressed in the winter uniform popular in this part of town: coat, skinny jeans, sneakers, a beanie hat pulled low over her ears.

Their eyes met and Josie stopped. Her friends peeled away and disappeared into a popular bar.

'Josie.'

'Hello, Amy,' she said, clutching her handbag a little tighter.

Amy smiled to relax the mood. 'What are you doing in this neck of the woods?' She'd meant it as light-hearted conversation but regretted asking the question almost as soon as the words left her mouth. She didn't want Josie to think she was checking up on her.

Josie shrugged. 'It's my friend's birthday. Bunked off work early to get to the pub. It's Christmas, after all. Every night is a Friday night this week though I think I might have overdone it a bit.' She grinned.

'I remember what those days were like,' Amy said, remembering her twenties, when she and Juliet had marauded from party to party for pretty much the whole of December. She'd thought those days of fun and friendship would last for ever. 'So how is everything at Genesis Media?' she asked.

'You know Douglas is leaving?' Josie's tone was mischievous.

'I didn't know.'

'It was announced today. He's going to head up special projects at the company's German headquarters.'

'Germany?' said Amy with surprise.

'He likes to call it a promotion, although he's the only person who thinks it is.'

They both laughed.

'How are you, Josie?'

'Good. I'm working for Denton Scoles now, although I don't want an admin job for ever so I might start looking for something else in the new year. And the therapy is going well, thank you.'

Seeing Josie regularly had been too painful for Amy,

dislodged too many conflicting emotions, but she was glad that she was paying for a weekly session with a highly recommended counsellor who specialised in self-harm.

She put her hand in her bag and pulled out a business card.

'Send me an email tomorrow so I've got your up-to-date details. You'll find something, don't worry. I'll make sure of it.'

'Do you mean that?'

It was a loaded question, but Amy chose to deflect it light-heartedly.

'Of course I do. You must keep in touch.'

Neither of them spoke for a few seconds. A cold gust of wind reminded them that Provence was a long way away.

'How's Juliet?' Josie asked.

'She's walking again. With a stick, but apparently she's doing well. Peter's been incredible. Her rock. How's your mum?'

'Got a new man. He's really cool. One of the good ones.'

The door of the bar opened, and for a moment, music flooded the dark street, only to be swallowed up by the building again when the door swung shut.

'I wish we could start all over again. You and Mum. Me and you,' said Josie quietly.

'So do I,' replied Amy.

Another pause.

'Look, I should let you get back to your friends.'

Josie nodded.

'Happy Christmas, then.' Amy held out her hand and Josie took it. It felt formal at first, but then Josie stepped forward and Amy pulled her close.

In that moment, she remembered a fragment of a poem she had once read about friendship. That people came into your life for a reason, a season or a lifetime. She'd thought that Juliet James was a forever friend, but despite everything, some good had come out of what had happened. She now worked a four-day week, had a better work–life balance, and reminded herself daily that her marriage, her daughter were not to be neglected in the name of ambition.

She didn't know why Josie Price had come into her life. Perhaps it was to teach her that no one was perfect; that sometimes you just had to forgive. To remember where you came from, not just to think about where you were going.

'I'd better go,' said Josie. 'Say hi to Tilly from me. I miss her a lot.'

Amy squeezed her hand and let her go. Then she closed her eyes and breathed deeply, only opening them when she heard a car stop at the kerb in front of her. David, her handsome husband, was smiling at her through the Range Rover window.

'You getting in, then?' he said.

She hopped into the passenger seat, and he fired up the engine.

'Hope you didn't get cold while you were waiting,' he said as she gave him a quick, grateful kiss on the cheek.

'I was fine. I bumped into an old friend,' she said, and didn't look back.

Acknowledgements

Thanks to the wonderful team at Headline; Sherise Hobbs, Fran Gough, Mari Evans, Jo Liddiard, Yeti Lambregts, Vicky Palmer, Becky Hunter and copy-editor Jane Selley. And all the sales teams at home and overseas.

Thank you to my fantastic agent Eugenie Furniss, Liane-Louise Smith and all the team at Furniss Lawton.

I spent over a decade working in the magazine industry and the friends I made there have been incredibly supportive since I jumped ship and became an author – thank you to everyone who has read my books and championed them – it means a lot. Also Adele Parks for our Ivy brunches, Bella Andre for our girls' writing trips and the lovely lady authors who lunch.

Thank you to my family, especially John and Fin, who is always right when he tells me how I can improve my social media. I'm glad I have you on my side.

The Pool House

Someone lied. Someone died.

To Jem Chapman, it's the chance of a lifetime. An invitation to join a group in an exclusive Hamptons house-share, who could say no? But when she discovers what happened last summer, Jem can't help but feel a chill. A young woman was found drowned in the house's pool. The housemates said Alice was troubled. She'd been drinking. She couldn't swim . . .

As Jem gets to know her glamorous new housemates, she realises each has something to hide. What really happened last summer? And who would go to any lengths to keep a person quiet?

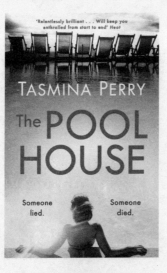

Available now from

The House on Sunset Lake

No one forgets a summer at Casa D'Or . . .

Casa D'Or, the mysterious plantation house on Sunset Lake,
has been in the Wyatt family for over fifty years. Jennifer Wyatt
returns there from university full of hope, as summer by the lake
stretches ahead of her. Yet by the time it is over her heart will be
broken, her family in tatters, her dreams long gone.

Twenty years later, Casa D'Or stands neglected, a victim of tragic
events. Jennifer has closed the door on her past. Then Jim, the man
she met and fell in love with that magical summer, comes back
into her life, with a plan to return Casa D'Or to its former glory.
Their reunion will stir up old ghosts for both of them, and reveal
the dark secrets the house still holds close . . .

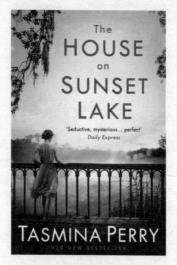

Available now from

The Last Kiss Goodbye

Everyone remembers their first kiss. But what about the last?

1961. Journalist Rosamund Bailey is ready to change the world. When she meets explorer and man about town Dominic Blake, she realises she has found the love of her life. Just as happiness is in their grasp, the worst happens, and their future is snatched away.

2014. Deep in the vaults of a museum, archivist Abby Gordon stumbles upon a breathtaking find. A faded photograph of a man saying goodbye to the woman he loves. Looking for a way to escape her own heartache, Abby becomes obsessed with the story, little realising that behind the image frozen in time lies a secret altogether more extraordinary.

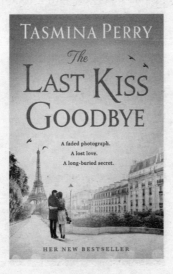

Available now from

The Proposal

1958. At eighteen, Georgia Hamilton is sent to London for the Debutante Season. Independent, and with secret dreams to be a writer, she has no wish to join the other debs competing for a husband. But when tragedy strikes, her fate appears to have been sealed.

2012. Hurrying to meet her lover, Amy Carrell hopes tonight will change her destiny. And it does – but not in the way she imagined. Desolate and desperate to get out of London, she accepts a position as companion to a mysterious stranger, bound for Manhattan – little knowing she is about to unlock a love story that has waited fifty years to be told. And a heart waiting to come back to life . . .

Available now from

H

REVIEW

Deep Blue Sea

Beneath the shimmering surface lies a dark secret . . .

Diana and Julian Denver have the world at their feet.
With a blissful marriage, a darling son and beautiful homes in
London and the country, Diana's life, to the outside world,
is perfect. But nothing is as it seems . . .

When Julian dies suddenly and tragically, Diana is convinced
there is more to it than meets the eye. She calls on the one person
she had never wanted to see again – her sister, Rachel.

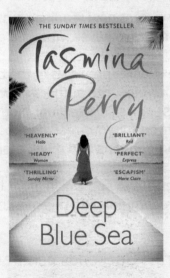

Available now from

REVIEW

Bookends

(logo)

When one book ends, another begins...

Bookends is a vibrant new reading community to help you ensure you're never without a good book.

You'll find exclusive previews of the brilliant new books from your favourite authors as well as exciting debuts and past classics. Read our blog, check out our recommendations for your reading group, enter great competitions and much more!

Visit our website to see which great books we're recommending this month.

Join the Bookends community:

www.welcometobookends.co.uk

 @Team Bookends   @WelcomeToBookends